LOUDER THAN BOMBS

"Alistair, you are a young and, at first glance, able-bodied man. You will draw attention because you are not in uniform. As a woman alone, I shan't attract a second glance. You endanger both of us by accompanying me."

Alistair snorted. "You underestimate yourself. You're stunning, and will always garner a second glance." He moved closer.

Stunning? He thought her stunning? Looking up into his eyes, she saw they were warm and inviting. He stepped closer again, and she could smell his sandalwood cologne mixed with a male muskiness.

She hadn't let herself feel attraction to a man for a very long time. There was a war on and men died. So did women. He lifted her chin and leaned nearer, giving her every chance to back away. But she didn't. Loneliness and the air raid had taken their toll.

Other books by Morag McKendrick Pippin:

BLOOD MOON OVER BENGAL

Blood Moon Over Britain

Morag McKendrick Pippin

LEISURE BOOKS NEW YORK CITY

This book is dedicated to my mother,
Cicely Tolhurst McKendrick.
You've always been there for me, Mom.
Thank you, you're the best!

A LEISURE BOOK®

December 2005

Published by

Dorchester Publishing Co., Inc.
200 Madison Avenue
New York, NY 10016

ISBN 0-8439-5582-1

Visit us on the web at www.dorchesterpub.com.

ACKNOWLEDGMENTS

A very big THANK YOU to my husband, Loren Pippin, for setting up my desk and computer through two moves. For spending hours debugging my computer and for his constant encouragement. And for putting up with Cheerio casseroles. Thank you, Sweetie!

Another big THANK YOU to my critique partner Danielle Bailey for being there, and for her wonderful insight and right-on critiques. Thanks, Dani!

Thank you to Dr. Craig Smith for explaining a few dandy drugs for me. Any mistakes are my own.

Thank you to Dr. John D. Howard of the Pierce County, Washington State, Medical Examiner's office for points in toxicology. Again, any mistakes are mine alone.

Blood Moon Over Britain

ONE

Some return from the fields of glory.
—traditional Scottish song

London
December 1942

"You don't want to go in there, guv. Bloody mess, it is."

Alistair Fielding snapped shut his Special Branch identification holder and returned it to the breast pocket of his tweed blazer. The rank odour of stale blood brought back memories with merciless clarity.

"Aye, well, Sergeant, we all must do things we find distasteful nowadays," he said and entered the bathroom. It was large, probably a redesigned dressing room, and bare. A cold radiator hugged the far wall, and beside it, a deep-bowled pedestal sink with an age-spotted mirror hanging above.

A claw-foot tub occupied the centre of the room. Fielding felt his jaw clench and forced himself to keep his eyes open. Enduring four days of butchery and slaughter on the beach at Dunkirk could not inure him to human suffering. At least it didn't look as if this poor sod had suffered long.

The tub was full to the rim with blood and water. A

foot dangled over the end and an arm hung over the side. A vertical gash ran from the man's wrist to nearly his elbow, and although the wound no longer dripped, the evidence on the floor clearly attested that it had done so for some time.

Fielding skirted the pool of congealed blood and stepped to the head of the bathtub. The dead man's glassy eyes stared sightlessly at the wall opposite, and his nose rested on the surface of the water. His skin was pallid, waxen. Rigour had come and gone. He'd been dead at least two days. Maybe more, as the flat was ruddy cold.

"It's a suicide, guv, plain as the nose on your face." The middle-aged sergeant still stood in the doorway, a dubious look etched on his plump features. "Don't see the need for Special Branch to muck about with some poor tosser cockin' up his own toes."

Fielding shot him a warning look. "It's not your concern why I'm here, Sergeant. Let it suffice that I am." He tugged the victim's head backward by the hair and thumbed the eyelids fully open, examining the pupils. The motion set the water in the bathtub gently lapping at the sides, revealing the well-healed stump of what remained of the man's right leg.

Shutting his eyes and steeling himself, Fielding bent close to sniff the mouth of the corpse. He stepped back hastily, fished for the handkerchief in his pocket, and took a deep breath through it. "Who found the body and when?"

"His cousin, about an hour ago. A Miss Winterbourne. She's in the sitting room now. A bit shaky, she is."

"Did she touch anything? Did you, Sergeant—?"

"Cummings, Sir. Shouldn't think she'd want to, and I certainly didn't."

2

Probably hadn't even entered the room, Fielding thought as he bent, peering under the tub. He picked up the carving knife by the handle using his handkerchief. It was black and crusted with dried blood. "Find a bag to secure this."

The sergeant made a choking sound and fled. He returned a moment later with a canvas shopping sack, hesitating at the threshold. Fielding dropped the knife into the sack and closed the loo door behind him as he left. "No one enters that room, is that clear, Sergeant? Now show me the cousin."

Cummings led him down a dark corridor and opened the door to the sitting room. Painted a cheery yellow in a bygone era, now the room appeared drab and colourless in the lengthening shadows of the late afternoon. A layer of dust clung to the utilitarian furniture, and no ornaments adorned the room save for a few old hunt scenes hanging on the wall. The fireplace was empty and cold.

At first he didn't see her, and then he wondered how he could have ever missed her. She sat straight and motionless in a ladder-back chair, staring out the window at the rain. The one spot of colour in the musty room, she turned the full power of her stunning beauty toward him.

Her hair, a vivid auburn, waved back from the translucent skin of her forehead in tall Victory rolls. She had high Nordic cheekbones, a sharply defined chin, delicate brows, and lips that looked as if they were still red and swollen from kissing a lover.

"Miss Winterbourne, I'm Inspector Alistair Fielding, Scotland Yard." Something murky in her dark blue eyes flickered, but was instantly gone. "I realise you've had a difficult day. I'll do my damnedest not to prolong it, but I have a question or two."

3

She placed the plain white cup and saucer she'd been cradling in her lap on the windowsill with a clatter, and turned her serene gaze to him.

Miss Winterbourne was either frightened or hiding something. He wondered which it was.

She turned toward the Metropolitan Police inspector with the gravelly voice. This Scotsman had missed his calling. He could have made a fortune as a matinee idol—or even a professional rugby player, for that matter. He stood several inches over six feet and weighed fifteen stone at least. His features were chiseled, proud, and aristocratic. Black hair quarrelled with the effort he had made to ruthlessly slick it down. A slight cleft marked his chin. He stared at her with fathomless dark brown eyes. A poet's eyes. But a soldier's bearing. He frowned slightly and reached into a pocket of his smartly tailored wool trousers for his cigarettes.

Her perusal complete, she replied with a twist of her lips. " 'Difficult,' Inspector Fielding, is discovering a ladder in one's last pair of pre-war silk stockings. 'Difficult' is queuing for hours at the butcher's and then being turned away empty-handed. 'Difficult' is a rather anaemic word to describe my day. 'Harrowing' is far more appropriate, Inspector."

Standing, Cicely Winterbourne turned her back to him and gazed out the rain-lashed window. The bitter December wind blew in through cracks in the casement and she shivered. Charcoal clouds massed on the horizon, threatening a thunder and lightning storm. Her hands gripped tightly at her waist. She nearly jumped when Fielding spoke.

"Cigarette?" he offered. She hadn't heard him approach, and now he towered over her so closely that she could smell his sandalwood cologne, feel his body heat, and see the individual whiskers of his late afternoon beard.

After she pulled a cigarette from the extended box, he clicked open a silver lighter. Over the flame, his eyes drew hers like a magnet. As soon as the tobacco caught, Cicely stepped toward the fireplace and stared into the empty grate, exhaling a cloud of smoke.

"When did you last see your cousin, Miss Winterbourne?" Fielding remained by the window.

"Five days ago—Friday. Graham and I took the train down from Buckinghamshire together. We work—in different departments, of course—in a supply directory in Bucks." Cicely flicked ash from her cigarette into the grate and swung around to face the police inspector. "We decide who receives what. Usually, although not always, we stay at the Directory during the week and come down to London on the weekends. He hadn't shown up for work this week, nor answered his phone, so I arranged for a bit of leave to check on him."

His gaze rested on her speculatively. "You and Graham were close? Maybe you are aware of his reason for taking his own life?"

Cicely threw her unfinished cigarette into the fireplace. "Just what is this bosh about, Inspector? My cousin committed suicide. What is Scotland Yard doing mucking about with some poor sod who split open his wrists? Have you nothing better to do? Able-bodied men are desperately needed; you might sign up for service!"

Fielding shot her a gimlet look and snapped, "Aye lass, you see there's this wee bit of annoying shrapnel lodged in my knee, left over from an exploding bomb on the beach at Dunkirk. HMG sent me back to my former profession and sees I generate enough bumf to justify my existence." He switched on a lamp and sat on the shabby plaid chesterfield, stretching out his left leg. "So why don't you do your patriotic duty and keep me busy tonight?"

She froze at the words she and every other young woman heard from the soldiers. Especially the oversexed, overpaid, and over here Americans at the Women's Voluntary Services dances, in the Underground, and at the shops. But Fielding wasn't even looking at her—he was rubbing his left knee.

She lifted her chin, gave her hair a quick pat and said, "My apologies, Inspector." Taking a deep breath, she went on. "You . . . you saw his . . . what remained of Graham's leg?" At his nod, she continued. "He lost it at Dunkirk. They discovered him on that bloody beach beneath a pile of dead bodies, Inspector Fielding. It was no longer an evacuation when they found him, but a recovery. For four days he lay in his own blood and that of his fellow soldiers. His entire company perished except for him. For two and half years he's found it . . . *difficult*,"— she threw Fielding's word back at him—"to live with."

Making her way to the opposite end of the room, Cicely opened Graham's drinks cabinet, extracted a nearly empty bottle of Hennessy VSOP and poured herself two fingers. The bottle hovered over a second glass. "Inspector?" He shook his head and she shrugged, taking a long sip. Fire slicked down to her stomach and expanded in her veins like lava, giving her courage. A fool's courage. She took another sip.

"No, we weren't particularly 'close,' Mr. Fielding. Graham didn't let anyone close to him. Always a bit of a loner, he was. No siblings, and his parents emigrated to Canada before the war. None of them shared a particular fondness for pen and paper. Besides my parents in Cornwall, he's the only family left to me." She shrugged again. "He needed to feel useful after Dunkirk, so I arranged a job at my place of employment." And if she hadn't, Cicely thought bitterly, he might still be alive. She drained her glass.

The door to the sitting room burst open, bringing in a draft of chilly air and a tall, thin brunette in an Air Raid Precaution uniform. She strode straight to Cicely and engulfed her in an embrace. "Cicely! You poor thing! How frightfully dreadful! I came as soon as I received your telephone call."

Monty's sympathy nearly threatened Cicely's hard-won composure, but she hugged her friend back, then broke free, blinking her eyes against gathering tears.

"And you are?" Fielding's voice cut across the room like a lancet. He rose from the chesterfield.

Monty started and whirled round. Lifting a hand to her hair, she eyed him boldly. Monty loved men. Especially tall, dark, handsome men in uniform. Cicely didn't think the lack of the latter really mattered in this case.

Cicely set her empty glass on the drinks cabinet. "This is Monetary Smith, my flatmate, Inspector. This is Inspector Fielding of Scotland Yard, Monty."

Monty extended her hand and approached Fielding with a sparkle in her eye. "So pleased to meet you, Inspector . . ." Her step faltered and her hand fell to her side when Fielding merely regarded her with a flat stare. She frowned and retraced her steps. "Why is Scotland Yard responding to a suicide?"

"Apparently we are to answer his questions, dear, not the other way. Well, Inspector," Cicely said, a cheeky tone to her voice now that the liquor was taking effect. "You

7

must be feeling quite useful now there's two of us to keep you busy. What may we do for you?"

Monty's brows lifted in disapproval, and Fielding frowned darkly. Cicely knew she was out of line and didn't care. She wanted out of Graham's flat. She needed someplace safe to gather her thoughts, to think what to do. But where was safe?

"You may go now, Miss Winterbourne," Fielding said slowly. "Our conversation can wait a day or two."

"An excellent idea." Monty took Cicely by the arm and threw Fielding an annoyed glare over her shoulder. "Come on, old girl, we have just enough time before my shift for a nice cup of tea."

Outside on the pavement, Cicely gathered the collar of her wool coat around her neck against an icy east wind. Thunder boomed in the distance. Nearly everybody looked apprehensively at the sky and scuttled for shelter. Except for two men across the street. Cicely spotted one, directly opposite, dressed as a labourer, leaning against the wall of a newsagent's and leisurely smoking a fag. Catching her eye, he glanced quickly away. The other chap, sporting a mac and a trilby, half a block behind, scrutinised a toy store window.

Monty started to run. "Come on, old girl, the Underground's just around the corner," she called. "If we hurry, we shan't be soaked."

They boarded the train at King's Cross, and ten minutes later disembarked at Russell Square, making their way south toward the British Museum. Normally in the late afternoon, light would be glowing between the enormous pillars and students, scholars, and tourists would be pouring in and out. But it was wartime, a repository had been bombed two years before, and the massive building stood empty, the

Empire's treasures evacuated. With blackout in effect the pillars were shrouded in shadow and surrounded by sandbags. Few people came and went. Only the dimmest possible illumination was allowed at dark. Otherwise, cities and towns made easy targets to German bombers, and enabled clear navigation by enemy pilots.

Across the street, the Museum Pub made up for the museum's lack of custom. Although it too was piled high with sandbags and its windows were painted black, the sounds of singing and tinkling glasses leaked out, following them two doors down, where they entered an arched doorway.

Just as Monty and Cicely ducked inside and mounted the wide concrete steps to their flat, thunder boomed, exploding like a Jerry bombing raid. The sky unleashed torrents of rain.

The second-floor landing was narrow, with a flat at either end and a blacked out window in the centre. Cicely slotted a key into the lock of the right flat. Inside was dark and draughty, and after hanging up their coats, the girls went straight to the kitchen.

"Brr, the Aga needs turning up." Cicely rubbed her upper arms and headed for the bright yellow stove.

Monty pulled a ladder-back chair away from their small dining table. "Sit. You've had a frightful shock. I'll feed you bikkies and tea before my shift, and you can fill me in on the details—that is, if you are up to it, old girl." She filled the kettle from the tap and set it on the burner. "That Inspector chap was a nice bit of alright." She shot Cicely a speculative look. "He didn't seem interested in me, worse luck, but I glimpsed a touch of curiosity about you."

Cicely rolled her eyes and settled herself into the chair. "Really, Monty! Don't your RAF chaps keep you busy?"

Monetary shrugged. "At this point I could likely teach

the green ones to fly a Spitfire or a Hurricane—and I haven't seen the cockpit of either one. I've decided to try Americans for a change of pace. Besides, they're such fun to listen to—'Hey, Princess, aren't you just a livin' doll.' And the chocolate!" She winked. "They couldn't possibly eat all those Hershey bars by themselves." She reached into the cupboard for the tea tin, measured out two tiny pinches, then turned around, leaning on the counter and folding her arms across her chest. "Now then, why did Graham do such an awful thing? Who did he think would find him if not you?"

Cicely propped her elbows on the table, resting her face in her hands. She kept seeing Graham as she had found him: naked, pale, and so still, in a bathtub full of blood. She wanted to block out the sight and the smell, but was afraid it would never go away, never leave her in peace. She must move past the shock and discover just what Graham had known.

Taking a deep breath, she said, "He must have reached his breaking point. I wasn't due back from Bletchley until the weekend—for three more days. Likely it occurred to him his cleaning lady might find—" Cicely started as the kettle screamed.

"Ballocks." Monty turned to pour the boiling water into the teapot. "He may not have nurtured any closeness between you, but he knew bloody well if he didn't turn up for work for several days, you'd come down to London to see why." She brought the tea and a plate of vanilla biscuits to the table. Pausing, she looked carefully at Cicely. "Might it have anything to do with . . . with your work? I'm aware . . ." She swallowed and started over. "Mum's the word, of course, but I know you don't ruddy well work in a supply distribution centre at Bletchley."

Cicely froze, then lowered her teacup. She searched her dearest friend's face. "Why would you not think I distribute supplies?" She gave a small laugh. "Goodness, you don't imagine I'm into the cloak and dagger stuff?" Monty stared at her. "Really, Monty! It's all these anti-spy propaganda posters. My job is quite innocent, I assure you. And dull. I'm a file clerk." That much was true, at least. But it wasn't dull and it wasn't innocent.

Monty continued to regard her with a speculative gleam over the rim of her teacup. "I'm no boffin, but I know when I hear a load of double Dutch. I realise you can't blow the gaff. We'll say no more about it." She swallowed the last of her tea and stood. "If any hypothetical situations arise and you need to talk, you have a sympathetic—and discreet—listener. Now I'm off for my shift, keeping an eye out for the Hun in the sky," she said, lifting her hand in a playful salute.

When the door slammed behind Monty, Cicely rose from her chair, flipped off the light switch, and made her way in the gloom to the window. Very carefully she lifted the tight-fitting blackout blind and peered outside.

Heavy clouds and pelting rain contributed to an early darkness. The streetlights were dimmed and the few vehicles out burning petrol wore shields over their lamps, allowing a mere pinprick of illumination.

Monty ran across the road, her neck hunched into her collar and her mac flying out behind her from the force of the wind. She dashed right by a man leaning against the iron spike fence surrounding the museum. He wore a trench coat and a trilby pulled low over his face.

Cicely's gaze darted in every direction. Not many ventured out in the blackout. The few who did hurried to find shelter, or had already found it in shop doorways.

11

She glanced back at the man in the trench coat. He'd pushed his trilby to the back of his head and was staring up at her. Rain poured down his face, but he didn't blink. Cicely felt those eyes burn through her like red-hot daggers. Finally, he righted his hat and strode away, enveloped in blackness and a torrent of rain.

She jumped when the loud banging on her door started.

Two

Alistair hung up the phone and went to answer the clamouring on Graham Mason's door.

"Bloody hell, man, what took you so long!" Dr. Percival Cardew, a tall, thin man, whisked himself inside, his thinning grey hair plastered wetly to his head and his trench coat dripping. "Corridors are damned draughty. My driver was called up, so I was forced to take the Underground. I'm not doing a damned bloody thing for you, m'lad, until I'm reasonably dry and warm." He shrugged out of his drenched garment and held it between finger and thumb at arm's length. "Is there a fire?"

Alistair took the doctor's coat and led the way into the sitting room. "I'll start the fire directly, Percy. In the meantime I believe there's a finger of cognac to warm you. Good enough?"

"How many times have I told you *not* to call me that God-awful name," Dr. Cardew said, taking the cognac. "Anyone would think I'm a pouf with a name like that." He swallowed the spirit in one gulp. "Much better. Now you may build a fire while you tell me why I had to come

13

here willy-nilly, braving the worst storm since thirty-six. Can't work with numb fingers, y'know."

Alistair crinkled newspaper, stuffed it under the grate and reached for kindling. "Chap slashed his wrists in the bathtub. Near as I can tell it happened two or three days ago." Cardew was silent while Alistair lit the fire and added coal from the scuttle. He straightened, shoved his hands in his pockets and stared into the burning glow. "He worked in a top-secret project north of London. Can't tell you anything more about that—even I don't know. The thing is, a coworker of this fellow shot his own brains out a month ago."

Cardew nodded. "You're not sure if this is suicide."

Alistair looked up from the fire. "Spot on, Percival. I want you to collect the usual tissue samples, but leave no records of the undertaking. Do the post mortem here. I'll see the body is taken care of."

"One can always count on you, old fellow, not to ask the impossible," Cardew said. "Tell me, do you possess a potion for invisibility? Something like the Hollywood films use? How am I supposed to use the needed equipment and storage in the laboratory with no one noticing?"

Alistair lifted his brows. Cardew closed his eyes and pinched the bridge of his nose. "Bloody hell, you want this done tonight, don't you? You and that pal of yours; Alex Walker—you're always asking me to go above and beyond. Lead on, then. If I make good time I *might* get some kip before sunrise."

Trembling, Cicely peered through the spy hole on her door. Sighing in relief she opened it to her elderly neighbour, Violet Lang.

"I'm so glad I caught you, dear. I wonder if you might

do me a favour?" Violet stepped in, followed by a monster of a long-haired white cat. Cicely wondered how anyone so slender could keep such a portly cat. Henry must weigh over a stone. He curled around her ankles, purring.

Cicely bent down to pick him up. "Are you hungry *again*, Henry?" The cat meowed loudly and presented her with a cold, wet nose. "Come on, I have a bit of leftover cod in the icebox."

Violet beamed. "Oh Cicely, dear, you really mustn't spoil him. We can't have him getting fat."

Cicely placed the plate with a bite of cod on the floor. Henry dived in. Cicely laughed. "There's no danger of that, Vi."

Violet handed her a changepurse and a ration book. "Would you mind terribly going to the market tomorrow morning, dear? Adele is doing so poorly, I hate to leave her alone for more than a few minutes. I don't think it will be long now."

Adele, Violet's flatmate of over thirty years, had been diagnosed with stomach cancer. Sometimes Cicely could hear her crying out in pain during the night.

Cicely squeezed Vi's hands. "Of course. I'll acquire anything available. Shall I stop by the chemist for more of Adele's powders?"

"Oh, please." Vi touched the back of her hand to her eyes. "I don't know what I'd do without you and Monetary. Come, Henry, that's all you're getting. You don't want to spoil your supper."

Henry gave them a blue-eyed stare, swishing his tail and making little gasping noises, which meant he wanted more to eat. Violet stared back and declared, "Men! You are impossible, the lot of you!" Picking up the cat she headed for the door. "I'll bake you a batch of my raisin scones, dear," she called over her shoulder before closing the door behind her.

Cicely was retrieving the dish from the floor when another knock rattled her door. Flinging it open, she said, "Goodness Violet, you could have just walked in—Oh!"

THREE

Weighty secrets . . .
—Sarah Chauncey Woolsey

The bit-of-alright Inspector Fielding stood on her doorstep. He removed his trilby, shook off the raindrops, and gestured behind him. "Does that great white beast hold his own ration book?"

Cicely couldn't help smiling. "Everyone in the building saves scraps for him." The smile slipped from her face. "What do you want, Inspector? Surely we said everything we needed to at Graham's flat? I must write to his parents."

Fielding stepped over the threshold, closing the door behind him.

"Your safety may be at risk, Miss Winterbourne. We're going to chat, so make yourself comfortable."

Suddenly Cicely was cold all over. Gooseflesh rippled on her skin. She raised a trembling hand to her throat. What did he think he knew? As she was incapable of physically throwing him out and a scene was out of the question, she took him to the kitchen. On the way, Fielding pulled off his coat and threw it and his trilby on the chesterfield.

In the kitchen Cicely sat huddled in a chair, pulling her

17

cardigan tighter around her. She had no idea what she was going to tell him, except of course, that it was not going to be the truth.

"I know whatever is going on at Bletchley is top secret. I'm aware it's more than a supply directory. It's some sort of code-breaking headquarters, but I don't expect you to tell me about the work done there," the police inspector said, pulling out a chair and turning it around to sit astride in it. "I have reason to believe your cousin didn't commit suicide, but was in fact, murdered."

Cicely gasped. If he knew, how many others did? "But . . . why?"

"Your project is the crux of it. This is the second Bletchley employee to die from suicide in a month. I can't believe your work is that stressful—"

"Of course not! I told you he was depressed about being the only survivor—"

"Might he also have been distressed because his lover thrust a Browning pistol in his mouth and pulled the trigger a month ago?"

Cicely stared at him in dismay.

"You weren't aware he was homosexual?"

"Not directly, no. He never mentioned it. But I guessed." Her trembling hand reached for her box of Du-Mauriers. A tremendous gust of wind hit the flat and the rain slammed against the window. The lights flickered twice and went out.

"Have you any candles?" Fielding's disembodied voice drifted across the table.

"Yes. It'll be a moment." The candles were in a drawer by the window. Feeling her way in the blackness, she passed him, found the drawer by touch and started back. Another gust shook the flat and she stumbled. Fielding caught her. He was standing, holding her securely from behind, not pressing against her, but she could feel the hard muscles in his chest. His warm breath fanned her neck.

"Steady on, then," he murmured.

"I'm fine, thank you." Nevertheless, he didn't sit down until she fitted the two candles into their holders and lit them. Back in her chair, she picked up her fallen cigarette and re-lit it from a candle.

The twin candleflames fluttered, sending shadows cavorting on the walls and ceiling. Fielding resembled a spectre—still, shrouded in gloom, only the spark in his almost-black eyes showing a sign of life. Slowly he reached into his breast pocket for his own cigarettes, lighting one without taking his gaze from her.

"You're a savvy girl, Miss Winterbourne." His quiet voice carried clearly despite the tempest raging outside. "Otherwise you'd not be working on some ultra top secret war venture. My job is protecting Britain. If some bludger is killing off our best, I want to know. You could be next."

God, didn't he think she'd already thought that very thing? But her best chance to stay alive—and of finding out just what was happening at Bletchley—was playing dumb. Oh lord, though; she wasn't entirely sure she wanted to find out. All she wanted at the moment was to take a holiday, to visit her parents in Cornwall. But the problem wouldn't simply disappear. In fact, it might follow her. Inhaling one last time, she crushed out her cigarette with deliberate strokes.

"The ATS declined to take me. Some nonsense about my, er, hearing not being adequate," Cicely prevaricated. "So Daddy, Sir Harold, you know, had a word with one of his acquaintances in the Home Office, and here I am doing my bit as file clerk."

"General Sir Harold Winterbourne is your father?" Fielding asked sharply.

"He's retired now, of course." Cicely wondered if she'd overplayed her hand. The policeman wouldn't trot off to Cornwall asking Daddy questions, would he?

He smiled. "Perhaps I'll pop down for a soldier-to-soldier chat."

"No!" Cicely stood abruptly, her hands fisting on the edge of the table. "This has gone quite far enough, Inspector! I'm still in shock from finding my cousin, for God's sake. I don't give a damn about your ludicrous suspicions. Leave me alone. In fact, leave this flat immediately!"

Fielding stood and headed toward the kitchen door. Cicely turned her back to him, sighing in relief.

"Cicely . . . ," he whispered from the doorway. Her head whipped about. "Hard of hearing my—"

His words were lost when she slammed the door in his face.

FOUR

For every inch that is not fool is rogue . . .
—John Dryden

At six A.M. the following Monday, Cicely locked her flat door, gripped the handle of her overnight case firmly, and briskly made her way down the staircase out into the drizzle. A man in a plaid cap and a worn wool overcoat promptly folded his newspaper, snapped it under his arm and started after her. He was a copper, she was sure of it; one of Fielding's. He had been her daytime tail since Thursday, and he hadn't bothered to hide it. The others stayed out of sight. Cicely wondered if the copper had spotted them yet.

Thankfully, Fielding had not made good on his threat about visiting her father. She'd spoken to her parents by telephone just the night before. So far, Fielding had stayed away from her, too. She'd wanted desperately to confess all to him—and nearly had. She was so weary of carrying this burden alone. But she didn't know Fielding, didn't know how he worked. The last thing she needed was Special Branch blundering about like a bull in a crystal shop. Who else might he call in? Would he keep her informed, or force her to work blind? No, it was best to do this herself. And if Graham proved to be a traitor, perhaps no one needed to find out.

Cicely caught the Underground at Russell Square, transferring to the rail at St. Pancras, heading north for the two-hour trip to Bucks. Fortunately, she quartered at Bletchley in a Nissen hut during the week, making a daily trip unnecessary.

Stepping smartly off the train at the village of Bletchley, Cicely walked briskly to the omnibus that ferried the workers to the park. She waited while it emptied of the weekend night crew who hurried to catch the London train, then got on.

The coach did not follow the winding drive to the entrance of the palatial mansion, but rather a side drive, pulling to a stop in front of an assortment of outbuildings. Most were old concrete structures called "huts," where the foremost mathematicians in the country decoded messages sent from the German Enigma machine. There were a few Nissen huts scattered about, but Cicely wasn't entirely sure what transpired inside. Nobody here knew everything.

Exiting the crowded coach, Cicely headed toward an outlying concrete building named Block C. Every scrap of ultra top secret information the Enigma surrendered passed through Cicely's fingers. She filed it on the small index cards in the scores of wooden library file cabinets lining the walls.

"There you are, luv." Ruby, her coworker, greeted her from the desk across the main room. She was short and plump with a penchant for clothing herself in red. In Ruby's opinion, it combined delightfully with her luxurious head of short, dark brown curls. "It looked like you were running late, so I pinched a vacuum flask of tea from the café." She pronounced it *kaf* in a London accent.

"You're a doll. Thank you," Cicely said, shrugging off her coat and hanging it on the tree beside the door. She walked over to her desk, which faced Ruby's and was adjacent to a small iron-grilled window high in the wall. It was the only window in the building. Pouring the tea into a mug, she sipped and sighed blissfully.

Ruby glanced up from a short stack of index cards, her eyes twinkling. "You're not supposed to sound like that after only tea, luv. Save it for something, er, more profound."

Cicely rolled her eyes and pulled a few of the cards closer. "Good lord, you are as potty about men as Monetary. War is not the time to become involved with one. They leave, they fight, they die. It's heartbreaking enough hearing about boys you *don't* know killed by the thousands."

"No guarantees in life, luv. Many of us celebrate life so enthusiastically for the very reason it could be snuffed out tomorrow—in the next hour even. Acquaint yourself with love now because who knows if you ever will again. Live for the moment. It may be all you have."

Spot on in spades, thought Cicely, lowering her eyes.

"What a moggins I am!" Ruby declared. "I forgot about Graham, and I'm giving you speeches. I am sorry, luv. I suppose no one would know better than you just now."

Cicely cleared her throat. "Forget it, Ruby." She waved her hand over the dearth of index cards. "It seems we receive fewer of these to file every day."

"Until our codebreakers untangle the new four-rotor Enigma used in the U-boats for the last ten months, this is our lot. It's horribly depressing. What if they can't break it? What if those damned Jerries start with a five-rotor Enigma?"

"We've got the best math people in the Empire, and now America, too, working on it. As well as those huge computing machines at the manor," Cicely assured her, referring to the Bombes. "Listen Ruby, I think we should start a log for the workers who come in searching the files for information. They sign their name and the time upon arrival and departure—and the subject they are researching."

Ruby lifted her brows, surprised. "Whatever for? Everyone working on this property is extensively investigated. Besides, I don't think the toffs at the manor will care for that."

"But they could only approve. Don't you see, we're increasing security. Haven't you noticed, in the last month or so, some of the researchers acting, well, furtive? And secretive?"

"Of course! This is ultra top secret. Your imagination's gone wild, luv. You need a date with a strapping big man. He would put things in perspective for you." Ruby grasped a handful of index cards and left for one of the file cabinets.

Immediately the image of Inspector Fielding popped into Cicely's mind. He was large and strapping. Really quite handsome, too. And annoyingly persistent, a quality that could get them both killed.

She opened a drawer, pulled out a legal pad, dated it and placed it on a small catch-all table that she moved to the doorway. "I've set out a signing paper anyway, Ruby. It can't do any harm."

Ruby glanced over her shoulder. "Suit yourself, luv."

* * *

All week Cicely watched the researchers coming in to access the information files. Some signed the log without question, while others made a fuss. In those cases, she made note of who it was, but gleaned no data on what they were after. Ruby developed a sudden interest in keeping the log, too. It was after an intelligence official had shouted and sworn at Cicely that he wasn't signing a bloody thing, and to get out of his goddamned way or else.

Ruby, dear girl, had grown up with eight loud brothers. As soon as she heard the raised male voice she was across the room in an instant and had stood face-to-face with the berk, red-cheeked and using language even he probably hadn't heard before. He left abruptly and returned a quarter hour later with his supervisor. Under that stern man's visage he blushed and apologised profusely. After he disappeared into one of the back rooms, Ruby dusted her hands and nodded wisely to Cicely.

"That, m'dear, is how one deals with a carny sod. You give better than you get. Sometimes they think you're barmy to stand so firmly up to them and make more noise than they can, but that's to your credit. Who do you know wants to argue with a barmy bloke?"

Word apparently traveled. Everyone was eager to sign. Now she had a respectable list of names. But none this week had appeared furtive or nervous, as Rupert had, or Graham, after Rupert had blown his brains out.

Both Rupert and Graham were codebreakers, so likely that's where the problem was. Cicely didn't dare speak to a supervisor or the department head. In the two years she'd worked in Block C she'd lost all naivety. She knew things she'd take to her grave untold. She knew things that sounded so improbable that no one would believe her if she did tell. And she knew her country enacted gruesome, appalling deeds in the name of winning the war. If Graham and Rupert had proved themselves traitors, it was quite feasible they were assassinated by MI-5, the security service dealing with in-country espionage. These were the darkest hours of the war. The populace didn't need to hear about British Judases; they craved news of victory. Make it look like suicide and Bob's your uncle, problem solved.

Or perhaps it was a shift supervisor or another code-breaker feeding secrets to the enemy. Maybe there were no traitors. One of the directors of the Bletchley Park operation was a blatant homosexual-hater. And he really hated it that Bletchley's star mathematician had a fondness for young men.

"Blazing hell, luv, don't look now, but it's that bloody wanker, Flynn Dooly," Ruby groaned.

"Well, well, two of Bletchley's prettiest birds in the nest all by themselves." Dooly stood just inside the door, tapping the registry pen against his mouth. Of medium height, slender with sparse sandy hair on both his head and face, Dooly considered himself a ladies' man—in spite of his wife and three children. He looked the girls over thoroughly, ogling them lustfully.

"Ruby, love, if you don't go out with me soon I'll begin to think you're playing hard to get—and I've heard otherwise. Can't have that lovely set of ta-tahs getting lonely." He smirked and stared at her breasts. "Come get a quick half with me and I'll give them a good squeeze."

Ruby's eyes shot daggers, then she smiled sweetly at him. "Your wife must be delighted to lose a ponce like you for five days at a time, Dooly. I'd say go visit the kerb-crawlers, but even they have standards. And I don't do anything by halves."

"Jesus, I don't know why I bother. You're worse than the blister and strife at home." He leered at Cicely. "What about you, love? I hear you don't get out enough. Too much work isn't good for you. I know this cozy jazz cellar in Soho. How about—"

Cicely's lip curled in disdain. "Clear off, Dooly."

"Miss High and Mighty Sir Harold's daughter too good for a bloke like me, is that it?" Dooly's face reddened and his hands fisted at his sides. "You one of those cows who go for women? Must be, because you don't seem interested in men except for that rear-ender cousin of yours."

Cicely glared at him. "I fancy men, Dooly, not barnyard animals."

"You b—"

"Speaking of barnyard animals," Ruby interjected in a smug tone, "we've heard the rumours about you." She paused, eyes sparkling maliciously. "Word is you've been caught in the pasture behind the manor with your knickers around your ankles buggering the sheep—or any other poor animal you can catch!"

Dooly's eyes bulged from their sockets and the veins in his neck stood up like livid ridges. He took a step toward Ruby, raising his hand.

Cicely whipped open her top desk drawer, snatched out the army-issue double-action Enfield revolver, pulled back the hammer, and aimed it at Dooly in a two-handed grip.

"Back off, Dooly! Now, or I'll plug you where you stand!"

Dooly stopped dead in his tracks when he heard the click of the safety switch. Slowly his hand lowered to his side and he swung to face Cicely, his eyes glued to the pistol in her unwavering grip.

"Steady on. No need for theatrics." He let loose an uncertain laugh. "That thing is dangerous and you probably don't even know how to use it. Don't know what the toffs are thinking, giving a gun to a woman. Put it down and let's all go back to work."

"I'm an excellent shot, so don't tempt me. I don't want to see you in here again. Either send someone for your information, or come when Ruby and I aren't on duty."

He gave her a contemptuous look. "You wouldn't shoot me. You'd be up on charges. I'll come here anytime I like and say anything I please. Nothing but slags, the both of you."

"You're so brave, Dooly, but apparently you lack the necessary reasoning power." Cicely grinned. "I wouldn't shoot to kill. My revolver would slip while I was cleaning it, and Bob's your uncle, Dooly's got a gaping hole between his legs."

Ruby giggled. "You'll earn Mrs. Dooly's neverending gratitude, Cicely."

Dooly's lips contorted grotesquely and his eyes blazed. He strode to the door. When he reached it he turned back to Cicely with a sneer.

"Scrubbers don't plug me—I plug them." His burning gaze dropped to the vee in her legs. "Hard enough so's they never forget."

Cicely lowered the Enfield when he'd gone, and slipped it into her handbag. It was supposed to stay on property, but she'd been taking hers home. She collapsed in her chair and took several deep breaths.

"Well done, luv!" Ruby clapped her hands in appreciation. "Wouldn't have missed that for a pre-war supper *or* a new winter coat!" She threw her head back laughing. "God, did you see the look on his face when you pulled out that gun? Damned blighter was about to strike me. This is going to give me a glow for the whole weekend."

"Watch out for yourself, Ruby. I wouldn't put an attack in a dark alley past him."

Ruby snorted. "I grew up with eight brothers, I know how to take care of myself."

"Good, you may need to." Cicely gathered her coat and handbag. "I'm catching the early train back to Town." She sighed and shook her head. "I promised Monty two weeks ago I'd go out dancing with her tonight. I'm sure she's right, that a little recreation will be good for me, but dancing only a week after Graham—"

"She is right, luv. There's a war on. Never know when you're going to buy it," Ruby advised her seriously. "Knowing what we do, it's unlikely you'll pop off in a bombing raid. Still, no accounting for an error in calculations. Nobody grieves for long now or that's all we'd be doing. Stiff upper lip is how to win this war. Ballocks to the Jerries—spite them by kicking up your heels. Besides, I hear you are one of the best when it comes to the Jitterbug. Don't lose your edge to another bird!"

Flynn Dooly leaned against the wall at the far end of Block C, watching the red-haired bint hurry across the lawn. His lip twisted and he lifted his hip flask to his mouth again. The whisky burned down his throat and fed his anger.

"Bad luck with the ladies?"

Startled by the voice, Dooly swung around. A yard or two away a tall, rangy man leaned against a bare apple tree, smoking. Dooly relaxed, pushed his flask inside his trouser pocket and shrugged. "What do you know about my luck, or lack of it, with the ladies?"

"Voices carry."

Dooly flushed. "I'm not interested in a pair of bush bumpers."

The other man laughed. "Whatever you say." He drew on his fag and studied Dooly, then slowly flicked his ash by rolling the cigarette between his fingers. "I certainly wouldn't let those cows get clean off, holding a gun on me and speaking so disrespectfully."

"They're bloody well *not* 'getting clean off.' Who are you, anyway?"

The man tapped the side of his nose. "Need to know only, old sport. Brilliant place, isn't it?" he said, glancing up at the manor. "Nobody knows what his neighbour is doing."

Dooly grunted and lit his cigarette.

"That kind of insolence needs a suitable reckoning. Have anything in mind?"

Dooly exhaled a cloud of smoke and gave the other man an irritated look. "Not yet."

The mystery man grinned. "I do."

FIVE

Nothing's so hard but search will find it out.
—Robert Herrick

Cicely exited the train and hurried through Russell Square station. It was dusk and she hated walking alone in the blackout, especially recently. Rain drizzled down the back of her neck but she didn't open her umbrella, fearing it would obscure her vision. Also, the pointed end made a handy weapon if she didn't have time to fish her Enfield out of her handbag.

A block past the station a small group of people huddled in what was left of the doorway of a bombed-out building. As she neared, she heard a woman say, "No, that's far too dear. Give me a better price and I'll consider."

It was an impromptu black market sale. Since the rationing had taken effect, one could buy anything on the sly if one possessed the lolly. Spivs or black marketeers were considered scum. Wealthy scum.

She was about to pass, but abruptly changed her mind and shouldered her way through the shoppers.

"'Ello, luv." The spiv grinned at her. His crooked teeth were at odds with his flash Henry appearance. He wore a double-breasted pin-striped suit, an excellent quality wool overcoat, spats, and his trilby was set at a rakish an-

31

gle to cover one eye. His portable table held an array of delicacies: strawberry jam, a bottle of Mumm's Champagne, lavender soap, fresh eggs, several colours of lip rouge. "How about this nice tin o' peaches then?"

"That's mine!" A short rotund woman seized the tin from the spiv's be-ringed fingers. "I'll give you ten shillings."

"Well now, luv." He pried the can from her hand. "The price is fourteen bob."

The woman glared at him. "Oh, very well," she said ungraciously. After counting out the necessary coins, she snatched her peaches, gathered her fur collar around her neck and huffed off into the gloom.

"I'll take these," Cicely said impulsively, pointing to a pair of silk stockings.

"I'll be wanting a pair, too," one of the other ladies spoke up.

"Excellent choice, luv," the spiv said, looking at Cicely, ignoring the older shopper. "Just what a pretty bird like you needs. At great personal loss, I'll let you 'ave them for only a quid."

The older woman gasped. "That's robbery, that is!" Taking one last longing glance at the stockings, she left.

Cicely, not in the mood to quibble, handed the black marketeer a well-used pound note and headed for home.

When she reached her flat door, she slotted her key in the lock and flicked her wrist to the left. The lock didn't click. Slipping the key into her pocket, Cicely grasped the doorknob. It turned easily so she pushed the door inward. Ice crawled down her spine. As fun-loving as she was, Monty never forgot to lock the door—even if she was home alone.

Cicely pulled out the Enfield, pulled back the hammer

so that with a mere touch of the triger it would fire, and pushed the door wide. "Monetary!" she called. Silence. Taking a deep breath, she stepped into the corridor of the flat, leaving the door open to provide herself an escape route. All the doors were shut to conserve heat.

She walked slowly to Monty's bedroom door. Forcing herself, she reached out to grasp the knob. It opened easily under her trembling hand. Nothing out of place. Happy-go-lucky Monetary's room was neat as a pin, nobody behind the door or in the wardrobe. Taking a deep breath, she flipped up the coverlet, and on hands and knees checked under the bed. Her heart pounded in the moment it took her eyes to adjust to darkness. Nothing but dust mice.

"Cicely!" Monty's sharp voice caused her to bang her head on the bed's baseboard. "Are you daft? What are doing with your head under my bed and your arse waving in the air? The flat door is wide open, as well!"

Cicely stood, rubbing the back of her head with her free hand.

"What the devil! Why are you holding a revolver?"

"The door was unlocked when I came home. I thought perhaps we might have an intruder." She held the weapon behind her back, not quite ready to release its safety and put it away, but not wanting to alarm Monty more.

Her friend frowned. "I locked the door when I left this morning. Why would someone with such sophisticated abilities pick the lock to *this* flat? Surely they'd choose a more prosperous area?"

Cicely regarded her with a wary expression. There was no point in lying to Monty; now her safety was threatened, too. But it didn't mean she'd tell all.

Realisation dawned, and Monty nodded. "I think I see.

You weren't expecting an ordinary burglar. It has something to do with your secret work." She stepped out of the doorway and moved toward Cicely. "Could he still be here?" She lowered her voice to a whisper.

"Yes. Stay here while I look."

"Not on your life. I'm coming with you." When Cicely hesitated, she added, "I'll stay out of your line of fire. Go."

It took several tense minutes, checking the flat room by room. Perspiration broke out on Cicely's upper lip and she could hear the roar of blood in her ears. Monty was as good as her word, staying out of the way, and proved useful by flinging open doors while Cicely pointed the Enfield inside. Finding nothing out of place, they finally sat down at the kitchen table and turned up the Aga.

"I don't know about you, old girl, but I could certainly use a large whisky," Monty remarked before retrieving a bottle of Lock Dubh from the sitting room.

"Monty," Cicely said slowly when her friend returned. "Did you open the box of Graham's belongings?" She pointed to a large cardboard box in the corner. The flaps stood open.

Puzzled, Monty looked up from pouring the whisky into two cut-crystal aperitif glasses. "Of course not. Why on earth would I ruddy well go rooting about in Graham's bits?"

"The flaps are open. I shut them."

Monty swung around, looked at the box, shrugged her shoulders and sat down. "I suppose that might explain the intruder. Nothing appears to be missing."

"Monty," Cicely said carefully. "I suggest you invent a sickly family member and leave for a week or ten days furlough."

Her friend gulped her whisky, then poured herself another. Regarding Cicely wryly over the rim of her glass, she said, "I don't suppose you are about to tell me why. You're into some kind of dangerous game, and if shadowy characters are riffling through Graham's effects, he was involved, too." She emptied her glass and set it down with a firm thud. "Now you're carting around a monster revolver and suggesting I hie myself north of Watford. I don't like this one bit!"

"We're all making sacrifices in this bloody war, Monty." Cicely tossed down her own whisky and welcomed the fiery trail it left. "Your mum and dad will be ecstatic to see you. They never did like you joining the Air Raid Precaution team."

Monty eyed the Lock Dubh bottle longingly and snorted. "Now they'll suggest—again—that I join the Women's Land Army so I may stagnate with them on their rural farm. After ten days with them I *am* returning. Even the threat you are suggesting is preferable to cows, chickens, and mud. Not to mention the bracing country air. Too bloody fresh for me." She stood. "If this is my last night in civilisation for the foreseeable future, then I'm tarting myself up right proper—so I'd best start."

Cicely stayed in her chair until she heard Monetary's bedroom door shut. Then she made her way to the box of Graham's belongings. Everything looked as she had left it, but she had left the box closed. She'd carefully searched Graham's flat and found nothing. No letters, no seemingly random numbers scrawled on a scrap of paper, no highlighted passages in newspapers or magazines. Had the searcher found anything? Might as well inspect the contents again.

First she lifted out a leather-framed photo of Graham's class at Cambridge. Taking out the picture, she opened the frame. Nothing. Next she pulled out a hardbound volume of the work of Kipling. It fell apart in her hands. The spine was split and the leaves gaped open. She gasped and dropped the remnants of the book.

How could she have been so stupid not to have done the same thing! There was no speculation now. In the back of her mind Cicely had hoped, prayed that she had an overactive imagination. This was proof. Graham's death was no suicide. And the mysterious "they" were watching her.

The Aga creaked as the heat inside expanded the metal, and she jumped. Suddenly her fingers were ice cold and trembling as she reached for Graham's best wool suit. It was neatly folded, but upon picking it up the seams hung open and ragged. His dress shoes were mutilated as well. Even his shirts, ties, and wool jumpers were ripped open. Either they'd found something in the last item they ripped open, or the search had proven unsuccessful.

Cicely sighed and reached for the mother-of-pearl shirt studs and cufflinks scattered at the bottom. As she retrieved them, she felt rather than saw a small lump in the folded box bottom. Reaching under it, she found Graham's silver cigarette holder. Tears welled in her eyes as her fingertips traced the etched initials, GRM. She'd given it to him on his twenty-first birthday.

Wiping her eyes, she took the jewelry and the silver case to her bedroom and placed them on her dresser. She'd post them at a later date.

If she were still alive.

Cicely was straightening the seam in her new silk stockings when Monty entered with her mac over her arm. She wore an aqua silk frock with a narrow belt and a jaunty pillbox perched on her loosely pinned brown curls.

"Well, well, I haven't seen you looking so posh in recent memory." Cicely noticed Monty's eyes were glassy, which meant she'd enjoyed a thimble or two more whisky. Monty always put on a good front, but this afternoon had clearly thrown her.

Cicely opened a shoebox, smoothed the tissue aside and pulled out her best pair of pre-war dancing shoes: gilt, gold leather sandals with three-inch heels. Not everyone could perform the jitterbug in heels, but she could. "Everyone seems to be telling me lately to live for the moment. I listened," she said, fastening the shoe straps.

"We'll knock 'em dead, old girl." Monty grinned and tugged on her gloves. "Or should I say Veronica?"

Cicely touched her loose hair self-consciously. When she'd taken the pins out of her hair after her bath, it had fallen in deep waves down to her shoulders, covering her left eye in the style of Veronica Lake. Her gold cap-sleeved silk dress cut low across her chest and gathered tightly in the middle down to her hips, where it swayed in gentle folds to her knees. Even to her own eyes she looked glamourous.

Cicely clicked off her dresser lamp. "Since we're going all out tonight, let's take a cab. I'm not ruining my best shoes in the rain. I suppose you're taking me to that rowdy place you meet all your fly-boys?"

"Plan on getting tiddly and jiving like billy-oh, old girl. It seems the war will start in earnest tomorrow," Monty informed her. She twirled her mac around her like a cape, and headed for the flat door.

SIX

Lassie, come and dance!
—Andy Stewart

Inside the Jive Palace the war didn't exist. Although nearly every man in attendance wore an Allied military uniform, the swing music, soft lighting, and the gaiety belied the blackout covers on the windows and the very real possibility of an air raid.

The glitterball hanging from the ceiling sparkled through the clouds of cigarette smoke. The twenty-piece band, all in white dinner jackets, played the latest Dorsey hit on a stage above the huge waxed dance floor. Although most of the tables were occupied, the action on the floor was modest. It was too early yet for the acrobatics of well-lubricated drinkers.

Monty led the way through the maze of merry-makers to an empty table bordering the dance floor. She popped the reserved sign into her handbag, and at Cicely's raised eyebrows, said, "When one doesn't act like a hermit, darling, one can make the most useful contacts." She fluffed her hair, sat, and scanned the room. "Nice pickings tonight. Lots of Yanks."

Cicely smiled and shook her head. Monty could be

quite direct when seeking male attention. "Don't you find them a bit forward?"

Monty's eyes sparkled. "Spot on, old girl."

"Hey, if it ain't my favourite swing-sister! How are ya, Duchess?" An American in an Army Corps Air uniform pulled out a chair and sat down. Monty's eyes gleamed at him.

"Can't believe all the management could get was a team of paper men tonight," he commented. "What say my pals and I pool our coins, buy 'em a bottle or two to loosen 'em up, have 'em improvisin' so we can cut a rug?" He glanced at Cicely, grinned and swept his short fair hair back. "So introduce me, sister—and don't tell me she's no ickie, 'cause I don't think my poor ol' heart could stand that!"

Monty laughed and Cicely sensed a particular alertness about her. "Hep, this is my flatmate, Cicely. She's no ickie, she's won several prizes at the jitterbug. You name a variation and she knows it."

"My ol' heart is flippin' and a-floppin'." Hep clasped a hand to his chest. "If you're as good as sis here says you are, you shoulda been competin' in San Fran or the Big Apple. Once these cats"—he jerked his head toward the musicians—"get good and liquored up so's they get into the groove and kick out, we'll cut the rug, see how good you are."

"Hey, got any gum, chum?" Two more Americans in similar uniforms approached, and Hep stood to greet them. After several slaps on the back the newcomers—introduced as Bland and Freddie—pulled up chairs.

Bland sported slicked-back red-blond hair, a spare and tall frame, and periwinkle-blue eyes. He fell instantly for

Monetary. Of the three, Freddie looked as if he'd seen the most action. He was tired, and a haunted expression tainted his craggy face. When he nodded at the introductions, a lock of his dark hair came loose from the thickly applied styling creme, but he didn't seem to notice.

Cicely watched as the men emptied their pockets, counting out money with which to buy the band a bottle of "good corn squeezins." Hep gathered the combination of paper and coins and manoeuvred through the crowd to find a barman. In the meantime, much to Freddie and Bland's relief, the band took a break.

Freddie reached out to light Cicely's cigarette. His hand shook, but he quickly shoved it back in his trouser pocket. "Don't think any band is going to please Hep unless it's Dorsey, Miller, or Ellington."

"They *do* need to loosen up a bit." Cicely turned to the waiter who had just arrived, and ordered a gin and tonic.

"They sounded okay to me," Bland spoke up. "But I'm a novice at this swing stuff. Afraid I don't even know how to jitterbug."

"Surprised you've even heard of it, living in the woods up in Oregon." Freddie shook his head in disgust. "Don't know what we're gonna do with a rube like you, Aloi."

Monty fluttered her eyelashes and patted Bland's hand. "Not to worry, Galahad, I'll show you the ropes. We can start with something a little slower than the jitterbug." She reached into her evening bag for her cigarettes and stopped abruptly, staring across the room.

"Well, well, well, if it isn't that bit of—that inspector. Hmm, he seems to prefer blondes."

Cicely followed her friend's gaze. Inspector Fielding escorted an elegant blonde through the jumble of tables. He looked quite smart in a dark suit with a dazzling white shirt and cufflinks. His companion, dressed in a russet brown velvet evening suit, walked with the superior air of the aristocracy.

A mischievous glint entered Monty's green eyes. Her hand shot up, waving. "Inspector! Over here. We have plenty of room."

"Monty!" hissed Cicely.

"Too late." Monty leaned back in her chair, a lazy smile curving her mouth. "The more the merrier. Especially men." Taking advantage of the moment while their American companions looked curiously at the newcomers, she added in an undertone, "It seems to me you can use all the protection you can find."

Cicely stiffened and waited for her "protection" to arrive.

"Please endeavour not to scowl so, Alistair," Helen commented dryly. "This is meant to cheer us both. Live a little, old boy. Nowadays one never knows when one's number is up."

"Touché, my dear." Alistair's countenance lightened with some effort. "But why here of all places? You're aware I'm not much good on the dance floor."

Helen lifted her perfectly groomed blonde eyebrow. "I can't very well attend by myself—or with my female friends. You know well-bred girls only come with an escort. And who better than you, old boy, who might as well be the brother I never had. You recognize just when to blend into the background and when to square those delightful shoulders of yours and do a bit of huffing and puffing."

"So glad to be of service. Please tell me when you plan to inform your father of my brotherly status. He's gagging for me as a son-in-law."

"Pish." Helen waved her hand in a dismissive manner. "I'll talk Daddy around. It's not very convenient just now for him to hunt alternate beaus. Not with all these lovely soldiers about. Besides," she said, sobering. "I don't wish to be married in wartime. All that worrying over a husband off fighting the Jerries or Japs. No, I don't fancy a telegram informing me my husband is missing or dead. You know I don't manage anxiety well, dear. Breaking out in hives is just not the thing, you know. Now, who is that person waving to us?"

Alistair brightened and, positioning his hand in the small of Helen's back, gave her a little push in the direction of Cicely's table. "Well, it may prove to be an interesting evening after all. I trust you recollect how to fade into the background as well, my dear."

Helen gave him a look, but her eye took on a twinkle when she caught sight of the sandy-haired, uniformed man standing by the table with a bottle in his hand.

Freddie and Bland rose as the gorgeous blonde led the tall man to the table. At that moment, Hep returned from delivering hooch to the band and froze, staring. The blonde was petite, gorgeous, and her hair was swept up in a French twist.

Monty stood, directing the moving of chairs.

Hep placed his remaining bottle of liquor on the table and pulled out a chair with a grin. "Hey, Princess, this throne was made for you."

Monty shot Hep a sharp glance as the attractive blonde took the seat. She next looked to Alistair, her face curiously expressionless. "Fancy seeing you here, Inspector. You seem far too serious to patronise a jive club."

"It was my idea," the blonde said brightly. "Who better to escort a lady than her brother, or"—she shot Hep a glance from under her darkened eyelashes—"the next thing to a brother."

Cicely watched Monty's eyes blaze at Hep and her knuckles turn white as she gripped her cigarette case. Perhaps Monetary wasn't as easy-going as she preferred everyone to think. Easing her grip, Monty withdrew a cigarette and held it for Freddie to light. "Do introduce us, Inspector." She nodded her thanks to Freddie and exhaled a cloud of smoke.

"This is Lady Helen Hawthorne. We grew up together. And the gentlemen are?"

Introductions were made and glasses were filled from Hep's bottle. The orchestra sounded the opening notes from Glen Miller's "Little Brown Jug."

Monty cleared her throat. "Hep, didn't you say you were determined to suss out Cicely's skill at the jive?"

Both Alistair's and Hep's heads shot in Cicely's direction. Alistair was curious, Hep chagrined. "Of course, Sis." He gave Helen a rueful look and stood holding out a hand for Cicely. "These guys haven't properly warmed up yet, but yeah, let's give it the ol' Army Air Corps try."

Cicely felt a wave of relief. She wasn't yet ready to face Fielding. She had a feeling her secrets wouldn't stay secrets for long in his company.

Reaching the dance floor, Hep began snapping his fingers, entering into the spirit of the dance. They started jig-walking, measuring one another's skill.

"Okay, sis, you ain't bad. Let's try a little shag." He took her in his arms and she kept perfect time with the slow-slow, quick-quick, slide-and-drag six-count rhythm.

Hep swung Cicely out and brought her back in. "How 'bout the West Coast swing?"

Cicely smiled. "We call it the jive here."

While Hep moved in place, Cicely danced around him in a set of complex foot moves that showed off her legs and wiggled her hips. Suddenly Hep swung her underneath him. Cicely slid perfectly between his legs, jumped up, twirled around him while gripping tightly onto his hands, and, her back to his front, glided backward on her heels until she sat on his feet, her legs stretched out in front and her dress slipping past her garters. Hep bent over her, gripping her forearms and lifting her to her feet. Facing each other they shimmied the length of the dance floor.

By this time, many of the dancing couples had retreated to the edge of the floor, tapping their feet in time to the music, watching Hep and Cicely.

"You do aerials, Sis?"

Cicely grinned. "How about the back flip, over head, and the snatch?"

Hep's eyes sparkled. "You got it, Sis!" He promptly lifted her and flung her over his head. She slithered down his back, sliding to the floor on her belly, where she threw herself onto her back and jumped to her feet. Jigging her feet in a twisting motion, she positioned herself in front of Hep. He grasped her waist and, as he lifted her toward his body, she parted her legs; her thighs grasped Hep's waist a moment before he swept her away and underneath him again. Just as she gained her feet, the last note echoed in the ballroom and a round of applause greeted them.

Hep swept his hair off his forehead and, grinning at their audience, escorted Cicely off the dance floor.

"You kick out real good, Swing Sister. Put all these ickies to shame."

"Perhaps we may do the rock-n-roll next time."

Hep whistled. "You can do those aerial somersaults?

44

Only met one other gal who can do those, and she's back home. Shoot, sis, you belong at the Savoy!"

Cicely returned to the table still out of breath from her exertions. Lady Helen raised her glass in a salute to Hep, which he took as encouragement to sit close to her. Monty wore a bright smile and flirted—almost desperately, to Cicely's ears—with Bland, who beamed head over tail at the attention.

Freddie gulped the last of his beer and stood. His face was greyish, and deep shadows had settled under his eyes and beneath his cheekbones. "I'm off. Making an early night of it." He grasped the edge of the table a moment, as if unsteady. "Enjoy yourselves."

Hep frowned as his friend swayed between the tables toward the exit. "Poor old chum. Apparently he's not completely recovered from pneumonia. The Jerries shot down his kite over the Channel. He managed to parachute without a scratch but ended up spending too long in the drink. Damn lucky he didn't die of exposure."

Lady Helen placed a comforting hand on Hep's sleeve. "We should all be proud to have had the opportunity to sit with a hero. But the brave chap certainly has no business out on such a damp evening." She lifted her gin and tonic. "To Freddie and all the heroes of this nasty war."

"Hear, hear!"

After toasting, Fielding reached for a cigarette in his jacket pocket and gave Cicely a sideways look as he lit it. "Quite jammy running into you tonight, Cicely. Surprising, though. I rather thought this might be the last place on Earth to find you."

"Now, why would you think so, Inspector? Everyone burns the candle at both ends these days. We work ruddy hard with this thrice-damned war on—so we play ruddy hard, too."

Fielding's brown eyes turned hard and he leaned toward her. "You know bloody well you're in danger, lass. I can protect you."

"From whom?" Cicely hissed. "*I* don't even know that. Nor from what, for that matter." She sipped her weak gin and tonic, aware she'd admitted too much. "You are barking up the wrong tree, Inspector Fielding. Take a closer look at Graham and his friend, and don't bother asking me about my job. The government has a way of taking care of people who know too much . . . or who tell too much. Maybe *that's* what happened to Graham." She was thoroughly out of temper now. Although she really hadn't felt like gaiety at the outset of the evening, she had managed to forget her imminent danger—until she caught sight of Fielding.

"Did I hear you call Alistair 'Inspector' old girl?" Monty stubbed out her cigarette with a ferocity it didn't merit, and glanced at Fielding. Her voice brittle, she continued, "We are all on first names here."

Hep and Helen rose from the table, making their way to the dance floor, heads close and whispering. Monty's gaze switched to Bland. "Bland was just asking me to dance. We can't leave you two at the table alone. Surely you wouldn't mind dancing with Cicely, Alistair."

The opening notes of the recently popular "Perfedia" echoed through the ballroom. One of Cicely's favourites.

"Come on then, you two," Monty said, standing and holding Bland's hand. "We're not allowing any—what do you Americans call them? Party poopers, that's it! No party-pooping tonight."

Alistair rose to help Cicely from her chair. "I'm not

such a cripple I can't manage a more civilised dance than the, er, jive. Come, Cicely." He took her hand in a firm grip on the way to the floor. "We'll tread a measure."

Alistair held her closer than strictly necessary. She could smell his sandalwood cologne and a whiff of lavender, as if he packed his clothing in it. He stepped smoothly to the haunting melody. His hand moved in a caress on her back and he bent low to whisper in her ear.

"What a coincidence the orchestra should play this tune. I don't think I've met anyone so . . . perfidious as you, Cicely."

"You will notice I still breathe, Inspector," she answered caustically.

"And you will continue to do so, if you tell me what you know about your cousin's death. If you continue wedging your head in the sand—or worse, attempting to solve the problem yourself—you will most decidedly cease to breathe. Someone out there is compromising Britain's security. I intend to find out who."

A prickling sensation traveled up her spine. "Are you threatening me, Inspector? Has it occurred to you that Graham's death was indeed a suicide or, if it was murder, it may have been personal?"

Fielding's hand lowered, resting on the curve of her spine just above her buttocks. Her blood tingled in her veins—until she looked up into his face. He smiled as if he were saying, *Two can play your game.*

"Please, call me Alistair. Even Monetary can do that and she doesn't particularly like me." His voice turned hard. "Don't insult me, Cicely. I know bloody well it's something to do with code-breaking."

Now her blood ran cold in her veins. She stumbled in surprise, but caught herself before stepping on his feet. It wouldn't do to let him become aware he'd put her out of countenance. Not that she wouldn't love to jab her stiletto heel into his toe. Could he be bluffing? If he did know about Bletchley, maybe, just maybe . . .

A test first.

"Those tails you set on me—have they noticed how many men are shadowing them?"

SEVEN

*I speak truth, not so much as I would,
but as much as I dare . . .*
—Michel, Seigneur de Montaigne

Cicely watched as Alistair's eyes widened in astonishment. She continued: "Your men are amateurs. How do I know you are any better?"

The police inspector's eyes smouldered, and his lip curled in disgust. "Bloody, flaming hell," he muttered. The music ended, so he led her to a private corner where the phones were situated. Annoyance covered his features. "You *know* you are being followed, and yet you blithely gad about London?" His voice was incredulous.

"And just what am I *supposed* do, Inspector?" Cicely gazed calmly back at him. "Lock myself in my flat? Likely whoever it is would become tired right quickly of waiting for me to sneak out, and then they'd break in, rough me up or even kill me. Should I confront them? I think not. That's rather similar to teasing a wild animal. No, I'll ruddy well go about my business. Eventually they'll realize they are wasting their time." Her eyes slid away.

Alistair grasped her shoulders, tempted to shake some sense into her. "You are *supposed* to inform me." He sighed. "You are correct, my men are second-string. The best are defending our nation. But when these berks are dragged in for interrogation, then we'll find out what's happening."

Cicely gasped. "You don't know what you're saying!" She tossed a glance over her shoulder and drew him deeper into the shadows. Taking a deep breath, she explained, "You must realize, Insp—Alistair, you are not dealing with your . . . typical criminals. I've been silent because to do otherwise will endanger your life."

He snorted. "And this is novel?"

She began fiddling with her gold bracelet. "For all I know, you're part of it."

Alistair rubbed his thigh and leaned on the wall. "Start talking. I'm losing patience."

"You are no doubt aware by now that I work at the ultra secret decoding headquarters at Bletchley Park. Graham and his . . . lover operated as interpreters. First the signals are intercepted at the Y Stations. After delivery by courier to Bletchley they are decoded into the original German. The messages are then translated into English. The appropriate people are notified of the intelligence. Then everything comes to C Block—that's me—for filing. It's rather simplified, but there it is. I read every piece of intelligence decoded at the most ultra secret government installation in the country."

Alistair used more pressure rubbing his leg and gazed down at his whitening knuckles. He'd known it was both delicate and dangerous, but this went far deeper than he'd imagined. "Go on."

"After Rupert died, Graham began acting strangely. Not so unexpected when one's lover commits suicide, but this was different. It was as if Graham were . . . frightened. He was always glancing over his shoulder." She paused as a drunk shambled past and out the side door. Looking at the inspector with frightened eyes, she whispered, "Alistair . . . I know things. Things about this country, this war, that would make your skin crawl." She looked into the shadows momentarily before continuing. "The head of Bletchley is a blatant homosexual-hater. Unfortunately for him, Bletchley's foremost mathematician, a genius really, is homosexual. He can't be touched. But that doesn't mean others can't."

"You don't seriously imagine someone in that position might indulge in such a venial vendetta? To kill your cousin and—"

Cicely shook her head. "You have no idea, Alistair. Oh yes, the head of Bletchley is a petty, mean-spirited individual. But he is only one possibility. As appalling as I find the idea, my cousin may have been functioning as a spy. And if indeed he acted as such, for whom did he do it? The Germans? The Russians? Another branch of the government? Or did he know something the government didn't want him knowing?"

Alistair quit rubbing his thigh and ran both hands through his hair. Pushing away from the wall, he paced several steps away, his leg aching, paused, and returned. What a bloody mess. He was beginning to wonder whether either of them would live to solve this puzzle. "You have no idea of the nationality of the men following you?"

Cicely shrugged. "They look just as British as you or I."

"Well, then. I can think of only one solution. It's only temporary, but—"

"There you are!" Monetary hurried down the dark hall toward them, carrying their coats over her arm. "We've been looking everywhere for you. Don't worry, I shan't ask what you've been doing." She smirked. "It's been decided to blow this joint for something quieter."

* * *

Outside, only the dim, shaded headlamps of the few passing motorists illuminated their way on the pavement. Cicely could feel the fog curling around her ankles and pushed her hands deeper into the pockets of her thick prewar winter coat.

Making one's way in the blackout was a favourite pastime among the young men and women of London, such a convenient excuse to lean on or to grasp one's partner for steadiness in the pitch darkness, and it sounded as if Lady Helen and Hep were already indulging. Cicely could almost hear Monetary grinding her teeth, which made her smile, until she slipped on the frosty pavement and Alistair grasped her arm, pulling her close to steady her. His body heat seeped into her, relaxing her. It felt so good to have finally confided in someone. And he was a man who might actually be capable of helping her.

At least Alistair had conceived some sort of scheme, which she herself certainly had been unable to do. Leaning on this man could become too easy. But if he ever discovered her remaining secrets, he would likely loathe her. Best not to become too dependent on him.

"Where is this 'charming little establishment,' Lady Helen?" Monty asked.

A sharp crack rang out. Cicely ran into a body and nearly fell backwards from the impact.

"Ow! Bloody, bleeding hell!" Monty cried out. "Damned blackout. I'll have a ruddy black eye out of this."

Reaching forward, Cicely grasped Monty's shoulders, steadying them both. "What was it, Monty?"

"A bloody lamppost! Can you believe the irony?" She kicked the offending pole. "Ouch!" The headlamps of a passing coach momentarily lit Monetary, who was gingerly touching her eye and rubbing one foot against the back of her other calf.

"You need an ice pack or a cold compress," Cicely said, wrapping one arm around her friend and clasping Alistair's arm with the other hand. "Come, soldier on."

"You poor thing," Lady Helen shouted above the rumble of the passing motor coach. "We should be there any moment now. Let's stop, wait for another vehicle to pass and light our way."

There was a shuffle and a stifled giggle in the dark. Monty made a sound very like a growl.

"I say, old girl, you letting this pass is a novelty," Cicely whispered to her friend.

Monty muttered in response: "Wearing one's heart on one's sleeve is so common, *old thing*. Men generally take clinging women for granted—or aren't at all interested in them."

"Lady Helen is definitely not playing hard to get," Cicely remarked dryly.

"Did I hear my name? Don't be so formal, darlings, just call me Helen."

"Don't fash, Monetary," Alistair confided quietly. "Helen never fixes her interest for long."

"I'm not worried in the least, Alistair, it's no *affair* of mine," Monty said crossly. "Bland, where are you? Here, take my hand lest I smash into—"

"Here it is!" A door opened, spilling the smoky glow of a pub interior onto the pavement. "Alistair's favourite haunt, The Scotsman's Umbrella. Come on!"

Inside, a coal fire provided a cheery radiance, flickering from a circular brick fireplace in the centre of the room. A metal chimney hung low to catch the smoke. A piper played a reel in the corner, and several kilted men gathered at the bar. Alistair headed to the fireplace to secure seats. Cicely stopped at the bar to request a cold cloth.

"No!" Monty frowned. "We only need drinks, no cloths." Turning to Cicely, she said, "My eye can wait until we return home. I am *not* about to sit here next to that forward blonde with my cosmetics running down my face."

"You shan't be sitting next to her, dear." Cicely nodded to a shadowy corner where Helen and Hep were seating themselves.

Monty's lips tightened. "And there are those who have the nerve to call *me* a Piccadilly Lilly."

"Pecker up, darling, she's only a spot of bother. It looks like she might just be a bit of crumpet tonight, as it is progressing so quickly. Besides, he's a Yank. I doubt her exalted father would countenance such a thing."

"He might ruddy well, as much good as it will do me. I thought 'sis' mere jive slang. The bugger actually thinks of me as a sister. A *bloody sister!* I think that cheeky blighter is going to break my heart." Monty stared daggers at Cicely. "Don't you *dare* share that with anyone. A broken heart is one thing; everyone knowing it is another."

Cicely clasped her friend's arm, steering her toward the fireplace where Alistair and Bland were waiting. "My mouth is sealed, dear. Now come along. What you need is a very large gin and tonic."

Monty shook her head. "More like four fingers of that delightful dark and potent Caribbean rum a Canadian sailor gifted me with. But I'll make do with gin. I'm *not* going to become rat-arsed in front of Hep and that . . . that *cow*."

Cicely thought it best not to mention that Hep and the cow likely wouldn't notice.

Fortunately, the men had already ordered their drinks. Cicely shrugged out of her coat and held her hands out toward the fire. Leaning forward, she felt the heat soak into her body and the flames numb her mind. Her grandmother had seen pictures of the future in fire. Cicely almost wished she could, too. She shook herself. No, the future made itself, and it was constantly changing according to human action. Or so she preferred to think. Alistair was going to help her. He had formed a plan. It had better be a life-saving one.

"Where's Hep?" Bland craned his neck, looking about the pub. "Not like him to not be at the centre of things."

"Apparently we're gnat's piss tonight," Monty replied, nodding caustically in Hep's direction.

"Ouch." Bland gazed at Monty as if seeing her for the first time. "Didn't know the wind blew in that direction."

Monty narrowed her eyes. "And if you know what's good for you, dear fellow, you will keep that mouth of yours shut tight."

Bland cleared his throat. "Er, yes ma'am. Now, um, what shall we drink to?"

"To the First Queen's Own Camerons," boomed a voice from the bar. "And to Fielding!"

"Aye, cheers," chorused several voices.

Cicely raised her gin and tonic with a sideways glance at Alistair. "You are quite popular here."

"Aye, the Scots in London keep close tabs on one another."

"Were any of these men with you at Dunkirk?"

Alistair nodded. "Aye," he said again. "A few. Most are

friends or family of the soldiers who perished in that campaign."

"But why do they toast you particularly?"

Before he could answer, a tenor at the bar began belting out "Road to the Isles," to which nearly everyone sang along.

When the song ended, the piper tuned up and patrons looked expectantly at Alistair. He complied in a rich baritone:

> *I'll raise my voice and heart once more*
> *and sing another song . . .*

Cicely watched in wonder as Alistair carried the tune perfectly. It was difficult to identify the serious police inspector she'd known thus far with this ebullient Alistair Fielding before her, tapping his foot in time to the music and swinging the lager in his hand. The Scotsmen in the pub, however, took it in stride and sang along.

> *And let it sound and I resound*
> *So brave and free and strong . . .*

Even Hep and Helen sat up to take notice.

> *It's Scotland's dales and Scotland's*
> *Hills for me—*
> *I'll drink a cup to Scotland yet*
> *And to her honours reap!*

The applause deafened Cicely, but the assault on her ears was by no means over. Another Scot, an old one with

a white beard, positioned himself next to Monty and ser-
enaded her with "My Nut-brown Maid":

> *Ho Ro, my Nut-brown Maiden,*
> *She's the maid for me.*
>
> *Her eyes are wildly gleaming*
> *Her looks are frank and free*
> *In waking and in dreaming*
> *Is ever more with me. . . .*

Monty beamed, sat back in her chair and raised her
glass to the Scot.

> *In the land or on the sea*
> *My heart beats true to thee*
>
> *Ho Ro, my Nut-brown Maiden*
> *In Glasgow with maidens fair to see*
> *Couldn't lure my eyes from thee*
> *And when with blossoms laden*
> *Bright summer comes again*
> *I'll fetch my Nut-brown Maiden*
> *Down from the bonny glen*
>
> *Ho Ro, my Nut-brown Maiden*
> *She's the maid for me!*
> *Ho Ro, my Nut-brown Maiden*
> *She's the maid for me!*

The pub patrons roared their approval and clapped with
enthusiasm, and the piercing scream that followed at first

sounded like a continuation of the commendation. Everyone froze as the air raid siren blared again and again, and as the growl of overhead engines grew closer.

Cicely dropped her drink, but she barely heard the crash of the glass by her feet. Her blood turned to ice in her veins, adrenaline rushed to her head, and for a moment the room spun.

"But," she gasped, "it wasn't supposed to be tonight!"

EIGHT

The thousand doors that lead to death . . .
—Thomas Browne

Alistair stared hard at Cicely for a moment, then said, "Come, the proprietor has opened his bomb shelter. We'd best move quickly."

Cicely closed her eyes and took a deep calming breath. Once more in control, she stepped into the forming queue. The barkeep had opened a trapdoor in the floor behind the bar, and patrons were negotiating the steep ladder into the underground shelter as speedily as possible. Already she could hear the German bombs exploding outside. Yet no one pushed or attempted to cut ahead. Londoners were only too used to this nearly nightly exercise. Despite her attempt to steady herself, she felt gooseflesh prickle on her skin. Sometimes whole blocks of building were destroyed, leaving one lone structure standing amidst the wreckage.

Suddenly a blast splintered a blacked-out window, showering shards of glass everywhere. Women gasped and cried, men shouted, and the queue moved faster. Smoke billowed into the pub, but not thick enough to block the sight of several fires burning in adjacent buildings. Sirens howled, anti-aircraft cannons blasted, aeroplane engines roared and some wailed, thank God, as they were shot down. Ambulance alarms shrieked, victims screamed in pain, and the rumble, pop, and crack of crumbling brickwork and masonry were the last sounds Cicely heard as the heavy door to the shelter swung shut behind her.

Candles were lit, sending flickering shadows dancing on the concrete walls. Everyone was silent. Some looked apprehensively at the ceiling as if it might become transparent at any moment and allow them to observe the carnage above. Others huddled on the benches lining the walls. Alistair led her to a bench, but Cicely whipped around, squinting in the near darkness. "Monty? Monty!"

"Here, luv." Monetary leaned against the wall by the door. "Sit. It's all we can do for the next few hours."

Alistair pushed on Cicely's shoulders, forcing her down onto the hard wooden bench. She started to shiver, then to shake in earnest, so she wrapped her arms around her body and bent close enough to her lap so she could bite her dress in order hide the chattering of her teeth.

"Sit up so you can put on your coat, Cicely," Alistair commanded. He draped the garment over her shoulders.

Her coat? She'd forgotten it. But Alistair had brought it. And when he'd managed to get her into it, he enclosed her in his arms so snugly she could barely breathe.

"You see the candle just there?" He pointed to a thick columnar candle about two feet distant on the floor. When she nodded, he continued, "Just gaze into the flame. Watch the flare dance and flicker—that's it. Keep your eyes glued to that bit of fire as if your life depended on it. Now relax. Sit back in my arms because you are sleepy and you'd like nothing better than a little kip. That's right, lass, close your eyes, go to sleep."

Cicely did as she was told. Anything was better than

the hell of the blasting bombs shuddering their underground shelter, and the destruction happening outside.

Alistair leaned back on the cold concrete wall of the shelter, Cicely in his arms. Hypnotism was a trick he'd learned prior to Dunkirk. It helped work up the nerve to charge into battle as cannon fodder. Brave, ordinary, or coward, no one actually *wished* to run headlong into enemy fire. What separated the three were the lads who charged as ordered in spite of their fear. And because of it.

The usual raid shelter sing-along started with the old white-haired Scot bellowing "Scotland the Brave." Alistair added his voice to help ignore the shaking shelter and the crashing sounds overhead in the pub. Also, to take his mind off the statement Cicely had made upstairs. *What* wasn't supposed to happen tonight?

Loud voices woke Cicely. Opening her eyes, she watched as a young burly man in trousers stood in an aggressive stance in front of the pub owner. "I'll be leaving now, sir, and that's that!"

The proprietor, a tall, slender man with a shock of white hair, stood firm at the shelter exit. "I'm no' lettin' anyone oot this door 'til dawn! As soon as the door opens, sure eno' a fire bomb will be a flyin' through the air only to land in here."

"The raid let up two hours ago, man! I must go to my wife and bairns. I must see——"

"He's right." An Englishman came to stand by the young Scot. "Let those who wish to chance it leave. I'd rather be in my own home myself. We all need sleep. It's business as usual tomorrow."

Several people rose from their seats, ready to climb the ladder back into the pub. Cicely wanted to do nothing but stay, to snuggle deeper in Alistair's embrace—until a solution to her problems suggested itself.

"Alistair, I wish to leave, as well. Will you accompany me?"

"The barman is correct, it's lunacy to leave so early. A lull in the bombing has occurred many times, only to begin again shortly before dawn."

"You mentioned you had a scheme. So do I. But it means leaving now—especially if the raid isn't over yet." Cicely squeezed her eyes momentarily to block the abject fear of moving about aboveground during an air raid. She must do this. She *must*.

"I don't know why I'm trusting you on this when you've held back so much, but I don't suppose we have the time for anything else." He paused. "We go, but I swear to God I'm about to lock you up if you don't spill the gaff. All of it."

When they emerged into the pub, they saw the whole south wall crumbled, all the windows blown out, and every liquor bottle broken. Cicely carefully negotiated her way through the fragments of glass, solid wood beams, mortar, bricks, and broken furniture. The pub smelled of smoke, petrol, and the spirits spilled on the floor.

Once outside, it seemed the whole of the London skyline was on fire. There was no trouble finding their way now. The fires and the searchlights made it nearly as bright as day. The air raid sirens still blew, as did the ambulance alarms.

Cicely looked over her shoulder to make sure Monty hadn't followed them. Good, she still must be sleeping on the shelter floor. Many of the structures on the street had collapsed, but a few appeared untouched. Men, women, and children climbed and rooted about in the great mountains of rubble that had once been their homes and businesses. Medics treated the wounded where they had fallen, and carried them on stretchers to the ambulances. So many ambulance drivers and their patients died on their way to the hospitals during the bombings.

Alistair grasped her arm when Cicely nearly lost her balance picking her way through the debris. "Just where is it we're going?" he asked.

"Home. Russell Square. Unless we're able to hitch a ride, we must walk."

A little over two hours later, an exhausted ambulance driver on his way home let them out a few yards from Cicely's flat. Russell Square had sustained little damage. When Alistair and Cicely reached her flat, they found the door ajar. Again. She had locked it herself when she and Monty left earlier in the evening. After listening at the door, Alistair pulled out his pistol, told Cicely to stay put, and walked into the dark flat.

A few moments later he returned. "No one is here, but you'd better check to see if anything is missing."

Cicely first checked the box of Graham's effects. Everything seemed as she left it, so she stoked the Aga and put the kettle on. Then she sat down at her kitchen table and told Alistair about what had happened before she and Monty left for the Jive Palace.

They ate a few biscuits with their tea as Cicely spoke, and now she stood and began clearing the tea things.

Alistair grasped her wrist, stilling her. "No. Before you otherwise occupy yourself, I want to hear your brilliant scheme that had us leaving a perfectly safe air raid shelter."

"Since I have no idea who is behind all this cloak-and-dagger, I can't trust anyone. Not even the seeming authorities. It occurred to me to go to the one person whom I may trust with my life, and who is acquainted with most of the upper-level government." She took a deep breath. "My father. Sir Harold. He performed . . . tasks for MI-5 and MI-6 before he retired. He will know who is dirty and who is not. And his position is exalted enough to call off the government dogs—if it's HMG after me. Don't you see? This is the perfect time to leave: in the confusion of an air raid."

Without comment, Alistair headed to the window. Moving aside the blackout blind, he looked carefully outside. No one was out there, not even his own tails.

"Right, then. Pack a small bag and let's go. Now."

"You are *not* coming with me!"

"Cease arguing and pack. If your scheme is to be successful, we need to leave as quickly as possible." He opened the kitchen door and motioned her through.

Cicely nearly stamped her foot in frustration; this wasn't going the way she'd imagined it. But she made her way to her bedroom and lifted her overnight bag from a shelf in her closet. Slamming it on the bed, she began throwing in toiletries and a few changes of clothes.

"Alistair, you are a young and, at first glance, able-bodied man. You will draw attention because you are not in uniform. As a woman alone, I shan't attract a second glance. You endanger both of us by accompanying me."

Alistair snorted. "You underestimate yourself. You are stunning and will always garner a second glance." He moved closer.

Stunning? He thought her stunning? Looking up into his eyes, she saw they were warm and inviting. He stepped closer again and she could smell his sandalwood cologne mixed with a male muskiness.

She hadn't let herself feel attraction to a man for a very long time. There was a war on and men died. So did women. He lifted her chin and leaned nearer, giving her every chance to back away. But she didn't. Loneliness and the air raid had taken their toll on her. It felt intoxicating to depend on this tall and capable man.

Cicely lifted up on her toes, placed her arms around his neck and touched her mouth to his. She was quite unprepared for the quickening of her senses. Her heart thundered against her ribs and her blood pooled low in her belly. His mouth was molten and his tongue explored, finding an eager partner in hers. Moaning, she arched into him and felt her breasts swell as they crushed against his chest.

He grasped her buttocks, pulling her even closer and soon she was nearly riding his erection through their clothing.

He was about to lower her to the bed when she yelped and sprang out of his arms, startled by the sensation of something soft slithering along her ankle. She cried out and backed away.

It was . . . *Henry!*

The robust ball of long white fur placed his front paws on Cicely's knee and mewed. She picked him up, and he gave her his cold wet nose.

"What in blazes are you doing here, Henry?" she asked.

Alistair forced his breathing to slow and eyed the beast with disfavour. "Doesn't he live across the hall?"

"Vi and Adele belong to him," Cicely affirmed smiling

and scratching Henry behind the ears. He purred like a well-lubricated Hoover.

Alistair's eyebrows shot skyward.

"One sees you are not a cat person," Cicely pronounced around the feline's massive body. She felt a mixture of relief and disappointment at the interruption. Arousal never came to her so quickly as it just now had with Alistair. This portended a cataclysmic union. It was the consequences with which she wasn't ready to deal.

"Oh my God!" Suddenly serious, Cicely hurried to the flat door. "They never let Henry out on his own!"

Reaching her neighbours' door ahead of her, Alistair ordered Cicely to stay outside. "They could still be in there," he warned. Again, he extracted his firearm and turned the doorknob. The door opened with a click. He flipped on lightswitches, making his way through the rooms of the flat.

After several minutes with the struggling beast, Cicely dropped Henry in her own flat. Nervous, as she hadn't heard a sound for some time from her neighbours' rooms, she called out for Alistair.

He joined her in the doorway, his face pale and haggard. Running a hand through his dark hair, he said, "It looks like a murder/suicide. Doubtful, of course, as we have found a few too many convenient suicides recently."

Her hand trembling in shock, Cicely covered her mouth. "No! Oh God, no." Suddenly she felt cold all over, and hugged herself. Alistair wrapped her in his arms, but she pushed him away, shaking. "I must see them. I need to know. No, don't stop me. I did see Graham, for Christ's sake."

They were in Adele's bedroom. In the bed, Adele looked peaceful at last, her eyes closed as if she were only sleeping. The pain Cicely remembered creasing the woman's features was erased in death. But Vi's eyes were open and stared in terror. She slumped across her friend's chest, her arms out-flung. On the nightstand stood two stemmed glasses, remnants of blood red wine still in each. Also there was an open chemist's envelope, with a white powder spilling onto the polished wood.

"I could almost believe it," she murmured. Alistair had followed her, and she looked up at him with wide, moist eyes. "They were quite devoted to one another, and Adele suffered tremendous pain recently from her stomach cancer. Just the other day I picked up another supply of her painkiller."

Alistair nodded to the powder. "What is it, and how much did she normally take?"

"Sodium pentothal. I don't know how much she dosed herself with, but more than the standard lately, I imagine."

"A human must ingest an enormous amount of sodium pentothal to actually expire. Something else was used. I'm thinking Graham and Rupert ingested the same substance."

"I'm listening."

"Notice—Vi, is it? Pinprick pupils. It's a sign of narcotic overdose. Morphine. It's a white powder, very slightly bitter to the taste. With wine, virtually undetectable." He moistened a finger with his tongue and dipped it in the white powder on the nightstand. Touching it to his lips, he nodded. "Except no evidence was left at the murder scenes of Graham or Rupert."

"Does that mean different culprits are responsible, or that they were surprised by someone, something, and forgot to take the evidence with them?"

Alistair grasped Cicely's arm and, pulling her with

him, left the flat to go to hers. "We'll discuss that later. Right now, here's what we are going to do. Finish packing. It's nearly dawn now, so it's no use traveling to Cornwall now."

"But—"

"Hush." He kissed her lightly on the lips. "We are going, just not today. It's a hotel or a hostel for us toni— today that is. Someone I trust will proceed to my flat, bundle up a bag for me. It may take up to two days for delivery to make sure no one is followed."

"I must pen a note to Monty telling her to go north of Watford immediately," Cicely said. Alistair nodded.

After propping her short letter on Monty's bureau, Cicely threw a few last items into her overnight case and led the way out of her flat and down the stairs. Just as Alistair ushered her out the door, she heard a howl.

"Henry! I've forgotten Henry!" she cried, and turning, spotted the cat bounding out from beneath the staircase, his blue eyes as big as fifty-pence pieces. Blood was dripping from his long, white fur.

NINE

Fortunately, the blood wasn't his. Alistair sprinted across
the foyer and under the staircase, while Cicely examined
the howling cat.

Unable to see anything, Alistair pulled the body he
found by the legs into the light. Cicely cried out and
dropped Henry. The knife still lodged in his heart, Flynn
Dooly stared sightlessly at her. The coppery stench of
blood and the pungent odour of urine assailed her nostrils.

Frozen in horror, Cicely developed tunnel vision. All
she could focus on was Dooly's bloody shirt, his gaping
mouth, and the dark patch in the crotch of his trousers.
She watched Alistair pull the knife, a switchblade, out of
the corpse's chest. He wiped it clean on the cuffs of
Dooly's trousers and slipped it into her coat pocket.

She jumped. "I don't want it! Get it away from me. I'm
not touching that."

"Hush," he said. "Do you want everyone in your building down here? Traveling on a train is close quarters. A
knife can be handier than your Enfield. Your life—and
mine now—are at stake. Don't be squeamish about using
any weapon at hand."

Still, Cicely felt dirty carrying a switchblade used to murder someone—someone she had known—on her person.

"I take it you are—*were*—acquainted with this gent. You can fill me in later. For now, come on. You must change your wrap," Alistair said in a low voice.

Looking down, Cicely saw Dooly's blood smeared over her chest. It was from holding Henry. "He was no gentleman," she whispered. "But I certainly didn't wish him dead. Although, Ruby may say otherwise," she added to herself.

They hurried back to her flat where Cicely cleaned herself, prepared a cat box and dinner for Henry, and added a postscript to her note to Monty, asking her friend to care for the cat.

Alistair made a quick phone call, and from there they went to a nondescript flat he seemed to know well, though he said it wasn't his. He left Cicely outside, telling her to wait. He dashed inside.

A moment later he returned with a case, saying, "Only Alex Walker could I trust to get a few things from my apartment. I've known the man forever. Although"—a twinkle caught his eye—"I'm crying off from their engagement party, which his fiancée is throwing tonight. I doubt he'll be able to speak my name to Pearl for years." He shook his head. "But they'll be married soon and on their honeymoon. That might cheer her up."

Cicely simply nodded, overwhelmed.

From there she and Alistair secured shelter at a modest bed and breakfast in Kensington, registering as Mr. and Mrs. Bennington. Smith or Jones, Alistair informed her, only served to raise eyebrows, what with so many servicemen and their girls renting rooms with regularity.

Much to Cicely's relief, they were given a suite with connecting rooms.

Inside, Cicely enlightened Alistair about Flynn Dooly, and Alistair explained that the first rule in espionage was to tie up loose ends. Therefore, it was likely Dooly who had killed the elderly ladies and entered Cicely's flat.

"But why?" Cicely frowned. Tears formed in her eyes and slipped down her cheeks. "Violet and Adele never hurt anyone. They were absolute dears."

"Perhaps they saw him trespassing. No witnesses allowed, I'm afraid. And in the coming and going, the cat wandered into your flat."

"Could it be that Dooly managed to get himself murdered because he witnessed the scene? He might have come calling merely to harass me, and seen something."

Alistair rubbed his eyes. "Anything is possible at this point. Let's get some kip. It seems safe enough to leave now. We'll take a roundabout way to Cornwall just to be safe, starting tomorrow with the night train to Gloucester."

"Where from there?"

"Depends if we see any 'action.' A number of routes are open to us. From Gloucester, we might go to Cardiff, take a fishing boat across the water to Devon, then a train into Cornwall. Or perhaps straight to Cornwall from Gloucester. Go to sleep, you will need your rest."

The next evening Alistair led the way into an empty train compartment and stowed his and Cicely's baggage and outerwear on the overhead storage shelf. Cicely made herself comfortable, but soon found Alistair giving her a narrow-eyed stare from the bench seat opposite. He had taken her advice and worn his old army uniform. Both his official appearance and uncompromising bearing gave her confidence, but at the same time, he frightened her.

He moved to the door, locked it, returned to his seat and continued to regard her. It was time to pay the piper.

She'd known it was coming and still she didn't want to deal with it, so she leaned back and deliberately closed her eyes.

For two days she had avoided his company as much as possible, knowing the question was on the tip of his tongue. But now her time was up.

"Cicely, look at me," he said.

Reluctantly, she opened her eyes.

He removed a flask from his uniform jacket, which he offered to her. She took it, uncaring of the contents—she needed some kind of spirit. It was brandy, and it seared her throat, burning its way into her stomach, where it pooled like liquid fire. But instead of expanding in her veins and making her warmer and braver, the alcohol only served to induce nauseousness. When he pulled out his box of Woodbines, she took one and allowed him to light it, but she avoided his eyes over the flame of the match.

"What did you mean the night of the air raid when you said, 'But it wasn't supposed to be tonight'?"

Cicely pulled long and hard on her cigarette, and exhaled a cloud of smoke.

Alistair canted his head to one side. "You acted as if you'd never experienced a bomb raid. But that can't be. No one can be that lucky—even if they only live in London part-time."

Cicely flicked ash off her Woodbine. The fingernails of her other hand tapped a tattoo on the leather of the seat. "I haven't . . ." She stopped, cleared her throat. "I haven't experienced an air raid. That was my first. Monetary's weathered a couple, but only because she was ordered to cover another duty spot due to illness of a co-worker."

Alistair leaned back in his seat, studying her face. "Now, how could not just one, but two, women be so lucky?" His eyes bored into her.

Cicely shifted, took one last pull on her cigarette before stabbing it out in the astray in the armrest. "Alistair . . . I did inform you that . . . that I file all of Bletchley's secrets."

He sat forward, his eyes even more piercing than before.

Cicely reminded herself of the old adage that the coward dies a thousand deaths, but the hero only one. She was no hero, but she'd be damned if she were a coward. She straightened and told him everything in a level voice, as if she were reciting a shopping list. Everything about Enigma, the war, and the purpose of Bletchley.

For a moment he sat immobile; then he began to laugh. When he sobered, he lit a cigarette and said, "Enough, Cicely. This cloak-and-dagger stuff is getting a bit brown. Tell me the truth."

"But it *is* the truth, Alistair!" She glanced toward the compartment door. No one occupied the corridor. She lowered her voice anyway. "The Enigma machine resembles a typewriter. But this is no ordinary cipher! It is extremely sophisticated. Enigma enciphers a message by performing a number of substitutions instead of just one—as in one letter for another in the alphabet. These substitutions are achieved by electrical connections. To enable all twenty-six possibilities—the number of letters in the alphabet—the wiring embodying the substitutions must be set on a wheel. Shifts in the substitutions are achieved by the rotation of one wheel against another. I shan't go into the minute mechanics. Suffice it to say, two rotors make it complicated, three make it all but impossible unless one wishes to make it a lifetime hobby. Until recently it employed three rotors. Now there's a fourth that the codebreakers cannot solve. We cracked the code before the war started, but the Germans cannot be made aware of this. Because we are able to unscramble their code, the Navy has all but destroyed the German blockade in the North Sea. We're nearly starving now, but if we didn't know the location of their U-boats to sink them, absolutely no supplies would arrive on our shores.

"Have you noticed General Montgomery making progress in North Africa?" she went on. It's because we know Rommel's orders before he himself is given them."

Alistair looked like he'd been hit by an anvil. His eyes seemed suddenly sunken in his head. His face was grey, and the ash on the end of his cigarette grew long and fell off, forgotten.

"Yes, we know exactly where those German bombs will drop," Cicely admitted. She leaned forward, placing a hand on his knee. "But don't you see? If we notified the populace, the Germans would recognize that we possess the key to Enigma. Immediately they'd implement another code that we might spend months—years—attempting to crack!"

Alistair came to life. "You've known? Thousands—*tens of thousands*—have died in three years of bombing raids." His cigarette burned his fingers, and he threw the stub across the train compartment. "I can't believe this is government-sanctioned. I *won't* believe it." He stood up to pace.

He turned and stared at the girl before him, her expression so earnest, so assured. The train compartment actually swam for a moment. He sat, shaking his head in confusion, denial. How could she—a girl he'd been coming to admire as well as desire—and how could the government for which he'd risked life and limb, possibly be behind a scheme so foul, so abhorrent, as to allow their own people go to their deaths like lambs to the slaughter? This he knew only too well, sweating and bleeding on that beach at Dunkirk for four days. He'd witnessed the bombs zooming out of the sky, razing the shore, tearing men apart limb by limb. He saw that beach again in his mind's eye: a montage of blood, body parts, and thick black smoke. It was a nightmare he'd carry with him the rest of his days. And those were soldiers trained for battle! It chilled him to the bone that the government deliberately allowed this torment on innocent women, children, and the elderly.

"My cousin was killed last year by a Jerry bomb," he said. "She burned to death. When her husband realised she hadn't escaped, he dove in after her. The building collapsed, crushing him." He paused, gazing at the blackout blind covering the window. There was nothing to see outside anyway; the night was moonless. The train rocked and swayed on its tracks. He felt empty. As if everything he believed in were a lie.

"My flatmate from Oxford perished a month ago," he went on. "He survived Dunkirk and North Africa, only to die here, home on furlough. German aircraft fire caught him while he was leading a troop of schoolchildren to a shelter." He looked up. "And you condone this. You aren't the woman I thought."

"Don't you understand?" Cicely said. "If word on the bombing raids leaked, Bob's your uncle, the Germans would immediately present us with a new code." She pulled her handbag into her lap and rifled through it. "If we allowed that to happen, the war would be over tomorrow, the Germans the victors. If we'd said anything, they'd have starved us into submission through the U-boat blockade in the North Sea and we'd be decimated in North Africa. All this before the Yanks even entered the fray!"

Alistair resembled a broken man, and Cicely felt a shiver of apprehension. He wouldn't go to the local authorities, would he?

Finally finding her box of DuMauriers, she fished them out, set them aside and dove back into her bag. But when the train gave a sudden violent lurch, sending the contents spilling on the floor, Graham's silver cigarette case, which she was taking to her parents' for safekeeping, crashed and splintered.

"Oh, damn, damn, damn! Nothing is going well," she complained. Alistair ignored her, staring blankly at the blackout blind.

So frustrated she was ready to cry, Cicely reached for the remnants of Graham's case. But when she touched it, she saw it wasn't ruined after all. The lining of the case had merely separated from the shell. Picking up the two pieces, she discovered a very thin slip of paper. On it was a series of numbers and alphabet letters. And when she noticed the heading, her fingers trembled.

"Oh my God," she breathed. "Alistair, this is what Graham was hiding. It's the code to the fourth rotor. This"—she held the paper toward him—"is what he died for!"

TEN

A sudden banging on the compartment door caused them both to jump. Cicely quickly thrust the precious paper between her bodice buttons into her bra, while Alistair unlocked the door and jerked it open.

"What the devil?" he said between clenched teeth, glad to blow off even a bit of his temper. "This is a bloody private compartment."

It was the conductor. The man straightened to his full height, which was medium at best, and squared his shoulders. His face darkening in colour, he spoke through his white muttonchop whiskers.

"No such thing as a 'private' compartment with a war on, sir! We seat people where there is room—and certainly this compartment affords it." He turned; then, leading an elderly lady into the compartment, he said, "Make yourself at home, Madam. I'm sure this kind gentleman"—he shot Alistair a sharp look—"will be very happy to stow your baggage. Goodnight, pleasant journey to all." He tipped his cap to Cicely, ignored Alistair, and slid the door closed behind him.

"Oh, I do hope you two young people don't mind an

old woman playing third wheel." The newcomer peered at Cicely and Alistair with lively blue eyes behind round, wire-rimmed spectacles. Her short grey hair curled energetically around a soft brown tam. She was surely eighty-odd years old, but her cream-and-roses complexion and slender build belied her age. "I just couldn't find a place to sit. No, young man," she said as Alistair hefted her second, smaller bag to the overhead shelf, "not that one. My knitting is inside. Thank you, you are so kind."

Alistair immediately felt petty for his earlier display of temper. He felt colour rising in his cheeks as he handed over the knitting bag. He cleared his throat and sat down.

"It's no trouble at all, madam," he said.

"No, indeed," Cicely agreed. "It's just"—she flicked her eyes to Alistair—"long absences tend to contribute to lovers' spats."

Alistair raised his brows.

"Indeed!" The old woman pulled knitting out of her battered leather satchel. "I hope your next separation isn't a long one. By the way, my name is Kit Skinner. Do call me Kit."

"I'm Cicely Bennington, and this is my husband Alistair," Cicely said.

Kit surveyed Alistair's uniform. "It's such a pleasure to meet a brave soldier and his wife. Where is your regiment just now, Major?" she asked.

Alistair switched his gaze from Cicely to Kit. "Calcutta. First Queen's Own Cameron Highlanders, at your service."

"A valiant regiment, to be sure, Major. The tales regarding your regiment's second battalion at Tobruk are legendary."

"Aye. We're all proud of the poor blighters."

Cicely sat forward, pleased to see Alistair thinking of something other than their earlier conversation. "If there's a story here, I'd like to hear it," she said.

Kit obliged her without slowing her knitting. "Last June those brave lads held out against the Germans a full twenty-four hours after the order to surrender. When captured, they marched three abreast, led by their pipers into the prison camp."

Alistair nodded to Kit with a grim smile, and with admiration ringing in his voice, added, "They marched in tune to the pipes, each company led by its commander. Even the German sentries sprang to attention. When they halted at the prison camp gates, the Colonel reported to the Brigadier, saluted and dismissed the men."

Disappointment welled bitterly in Alistair. If not for his knee he would have marched into Burma to fight the Japanese with his battalion. Instead he battled piles of bumf day after day. Now he actually had a case he could sink his teeth into, and he didn't have the heart to continue. How he wished for a good honest out-in-the-open fight instead of the dirty skullduggery of espionage. His very core radiated an unsophisticated straightforward simplicity. Chicanery and deceit were foreign to him.

His country betrayed its populace every day. HMG allowed its civilians to die each night in agony from burns, explosions, and smoke inhalation—innocents who led the war effort, nearly starved themselves, saving eggs and meat for the fighting men, toiled in Victory gardens, worked day jobs and then trotted off to act as air wardens and ambulance drivers by night. His stomach roiled.

Cicely noted Alistair's darkening expression, and she

floundered to change the subject. She felt horrible enough knowing her country's secrets, but bearing the antipathy of a man she admired for them was even worse.

"Kit, that doesn't look like typical wool," she said. "It's quite gorgeous."

The old woman glanced up from the fuzzy cream-coloured fleece. "Ah, that's because it's not typical wool, my dear. Not wool at all." Seeing Alistair wasn't paying them any heed, she continued. "I think I may tell you my little secret." She winked. "This comes from my giant Angora rabbits. If my neighbours knew I harbored rabbits under my roof, my poor Bertie and Liz would end up in a cooking pot! As it is, my bunnies provide an adequate living for me and good warm socks for our brave soldiers. I'll knit you something warm and cozy, shall I? How about a tam or a pair of bedsocks, my dear?"

"No, Kit, I don't need anything," Cicely argued. "Save it for our fighting lads."

The woman would not be swayed. "Nonsense. You'll not be sleeping with your husband tonight, as the best these train men can do is render these seats into bunk beds. A pair of bedsocks will keep your feet toasty, as the Major shan't be providing that duty tonight." She smiled.

Cicely blushed. She hadn't thought quite so far ahead. Thank goodness for Kit's presence. "It's quite generous of you, Kit, thank you," she said.

The old woman gave her a curious glance. "When does the Major return to duty?"

"That's not clear yet."

"It must be so hard to love a man enough to marry him, then give him to your country to fight and very possibly not return." Kit's needles flashed as she knitted with lightning speed. "I was engaged once. In the Zulu War. We were to marry upon his return. Papa wouldn't hear of me marrying my Quinn with a war on. He thought me of too tender an age for the possibility of widowhood." Her hands stilled momentarily, and she stared at the opposite wall. Then her hands were busy again. "Might it have been better to marry and be widowed, or never to know the culmination of love? At any rate, Quinn didn't return. He fell to a tribal spear weeks before the war's end. At least it was quick. Such horrid stories I heard about the torture those Africans practised. I never married. No one ever measured satisfactorily to Quinn." The old woman smiled at Cicely again. "No long faces now," she admonished. "The past is the past."

"But that is quite my way of thinking—before I met Alistair, of course," Cicely quickly added. "Not to marry before the end of the war, that is. Too many men die— both abroad and on the home front. It must prove easier not to form attachments."

"Quite, my dear. But then, that isn't living. It's existing," Kit argued. "You will have noticed morals of the past few years are lax compared to the last decade. It happens during war. One never knows if one is going to be alive when next the sun rises. One must live life to the fullest."

Cicely lit a cigarette and glanced at Alistair above the curls of smoke. He was leaning back with closed eyes, yet she knew he was merely feigning sleep. Turning back to Kit, she said, "What a formidable task, to love when time and again that person dies."

"You've lost several loved ones in this war then, my dear?" Kit paused in her knitting and touched Cicely's hand.

Cicely dragged deep on her cigarette and wished for a

swallow of Alistair's brandy. "Yes," she answered shortly. "My older brother at Dunkirk. My former fiancé in the North Atlantic, and a man for whom I cared greatly in Africa. And a cousin in London."

Kit sighed. "I afraid it doesn't become any easier. I'm eighty-six. Most of my family is gone, and my contemporaries are all dead." She gave a half-smile. "But if I didn't follow my own advice, I wouldn't make any new friends at all, for fear that as soon as we became close they'd cock up their toes!"

Cicely gazed at her with admiration. "You are so resilient," she said.

Kit laughed. "At eighty-six I must be, or I'd wither away! And I've far too much yet to accomplish. No time to slow down."

The women's conversation became a faint buzz in Alistair's ears. Cicely had been engaged and seriously involved with another man. And she'd lost her brother on the same beach where he himself had nearly died. Where Graham had lost his leg. He had suspected Cicely of being a strong woman, but he felt slighted that she hadn't shared these heartaches with him.

Yet, why would she? She kept secrets all too well. Perhaps it was a necessity. If she admitted pain, maybe she couldn't rise from her bed each morning.

Yet, to allow countrymen to die without a word of warning? Intellectually he knew he couldn't blame Cicely, even if she was part of the appalling debacle; but she sat before him, while Churchill was likely stashed safe in some underground bunker. He thought of the song the Prime Minister had borrowed for a speech, "There'll Always Be An England," and nearly snorted in contempt.

What kind of England would it be? One that let its inno-cent civilians perish in the name of victory? What did that say of honour or pride in one's country?

Alistair's skin crawled. He felt trapped between two concrete blocks. He couldn't not do anything in his power to assure Britain's victory. War was nasty business. Given time to reflect, he knew keeping the populace in igno-rance was the only possible solution to keeping the Enigma code a secret. But he'd take no pride in it. He cer-tainly didn't envy the government toffs making these de-cisions. Just being privy to the ugly secret made him feel dirty.

And what was he to do about Cicely? He'd come to de-sire her, as well as to respect her immensely. Not only was she stunning, she was intelligent and courageous. She didn't come down with the screaming ab-dabs when con-fronted with danger; she took it head-on. She was steady, plucky, and was too strong to wear her life on her sleeve. She made decisions without asking male permission. Per-haps that wasn't every man's dream, but it was rapidly be-coming his.

The conductor rapped on the door, this time announc-ing dinner. Kit packed her knitting into her satchel and stood.

"We'd best hurry before all the seating is taken," she said. "I confess, I am peckish."

Cicely laughed. "And I confess to wishing for a large glass of wine with our meal. Excellent. You're awake, Al-istair. Give us each an arm, darling, we ladies are posi-tively weak with hunger."

Alistair obliged, and the trio made their way along the corridor, now and again pausing to find balance on the swaying train. When they reached the door to the next carriage, Alistair stepped through first to hold it open, and allowed Kit to proceed.

Cicely had only taken one step to follow when a blow from behind catapulted her between the doors. Suddenly gasping for breath, she lay on her stomach, hanging off the platform between the carriages, an icy wind ripping through her hair. The clack of the moving train screamed in her ears. The last thing she saw were the tracks flying past.

ELEVEN

And how can that be true love
which is falsely attempted?
—William Shakespeare

Light burned a red-gold through her eyelids, beckoning them open. Cicely ached all over, and a dull pain throbbed in her head. Waking did not appeal to her at the moment, but the memories leading to Cicely's blackout blitzed her and she reached for her chest. When she heard a crackling of paper she went limp with relief and attempted to turn from the light.

"Dear? Are you awake?" a voice asked. A gentle hand patted her face.

Opening her eyes, Cicely saw Kit bending over her with a concerned look. She struggled to sit up on the chaise, and recognized her surroundings as the ladies' lounge. A candle burned on the vanity a few feet distant. The flame reflected in the mirror, multiplying the dancing shadows.

"Many thanks, Kit, for using the candle and not electricity. My head is booming. Anything brighter and I believe I'd pass out again." Cicely gave her new friend a lopsided smile.

"No choice, my dear. We are suffering from one of

those many and infamous train stops for the night. They've doused the lights on us, too."

"Never thought I'd cheer conservation." Cicely held a hand over her eyes. It felt as if they were in immediate danger of falling out. Now that she sat up, her head felt as if it might just explode where it sat on her shoulders. Her stomach roiled. "Oh my. I'm afraid I'm not quite myself. I'll stay here for a time, I think."

"Your noggin' caught quite a blow, dear," Kit agreed. "If I hadn't been just in front of you, you'd have gone flying clear off the train! As it was, you crashed into me then bounced clear, so to speak. The Major immediately saw to us and shouted for help. However, by that time, that damned rogue had done a scarper."

"Wh-what did he look like?" At last, a chance to discover who might be after Graham's code!

"It was too dark. No light at all between the train carriages, you know. He either retraced his footsteps or jumped off the train. No sane person jumps off a moving train."

Cicely thought no sane person charged into gunfire, either, but one did what one must in wartime. "Saneness is in short supply nowadays, Kit," was all she said.

The old woman sat in an overstuffed chair and swept a grey curl off her forehead. Her tam was gone. "Point taken, dear. I know the dregs of the world don't hibernate while a war is on, but I still find it dastardly to toss defenceless women off a galloping train in a blackout just to nip their handbags! As if any one of us is better off than another just now. Why, even the aristocrats own the very same ration booklets as we do!"

"He took our handbags?"

"Just yours, dear. Mine is safe."

Thank God she'd kept the code on her person. And her heart leaped until she remembered she'd placed her Enfield in her toiletries case at Alistair's suggestion. But now she had no money or her ration book. Not to mention incidentals like lip rouge. Sometime on this trip, lip rouge had risen in importance. Looking her best while travelling with Alistair now seemed critical if she wanted his help, especially as he appeared to think only the worst of her.

"Don't worry, your husband has spoken to the train authorities, so it shan't be difficult at mealtimes. In fact he's arranged for us to be served in here, while our compartment is made up into sleepers. I believe he's eating in the dining carriage while waiting on our meals."

"When did the train stop and the lights go out?" asked Cicely, wondering if the timing had anything to do with her attack.

Kit tipped her wristwatch toward the flickering candle. "About thirty minutes now. It was delayed about twenty minutes while several conductors and male travelers searched for the ne'er-do-well who assaulted you, dear."

"And how are you feeling, Kit?"

The woman laughed. "Tickety-boo, dear! I was quite ready to race after the knave myself and give him the right blazing part of my temper—as well as a good stab with the business end of my brolly." She patted her grey curls. "But I was told to leave it to the men, we women being such frail individuals." She winked and added, "I've heard many a woman say men should try childbearing. However, it is quite handy occasionally to let them think us delicate."

Cicely gave a smile and sat up properly, with her feet on the floor. "I'm ashamed to say I am feeling delicate," she admitted. "But at least my stomach isn't feeling as dicey as a few minutes ago. Perhaps a meal is just what I need."

"Now then," Kit said, as she rifled through her handbag, "I possess a special medicine my doctor gives me for rheumatism. I never take the stuff, or I'd be so potty I'd try knitting with my hairpins, and my bunnies wouldn't care for that one bit. Ah, here it is," she spilled two tablets into the palm of her hand from a medicine bottle, "take these before dining, my dear, and your head—and the rest of you—shan't keep you awake. Mind, it'll make you a bit fuzzy. Likely the Major will need to carry you to your bunk."

Cicely looked dubiously at the pills. "What's in them, Kit?"

The woman frowned. "Why, I'm not absolutely sure. But it can't be bad, can it? My GP gave them to me. Dosed myself with them one damp, cold day when I didn't think my old aching bones would make it out of bed. Well, they made me so cack-handed I nearly left for my daily errands quite starkers."

Cicely clapped a hand over her mouth to keep from laughing. "What stopped you?"

Kit cleared her throat. "Ahem, well . . . when I opened the door, it seemed a bit colder than usual. At least I'd remembered my bonnet and handbag. And my boots."

"Oh, Kit!" Cicely nearly collapsed laughing. "You are kidding, aren't you?"

The woman laughed with her. "No, dear, I'm not. It's precisely why I don't take them. But I can't bring myself to throw them in the dustbin. Just in case, you know. Since you have the Major to protect you from wandering about the train starkers, I'm sure they will do you a world of good."

Anything was better than the busy blacksmith in her head. Cicely swallowed the tablets with the water Kit handed her.

"You must be very proud of your husband, Cicely dear. Oh my, you should have heard him bark out orders after he'd picked both of us up off the platform. One sees why he attained the rank of major so quickly. Why he—" A sharp rap sounded on the door to the ladies lounge, and without waiting, Alistair and a waiter with a loaded tray entered.

Alistair forced himself to hold back asking after Cicely until the waiter left. Satisfied she was well enough to eat a meal, he exited to lay out their nightwear, and to make sure the sleepers were ready for them.

Somehow the chef had found real butter instead of Oleo in which to grill their cod and large potato jackets. Cicely swirled her mashed squash in the last of the butter and drank the rest of a fruity white wine before sitting back with a sigh. The pounding in her head had subsided, and she felt a pleasant laziness. She was almost tiddly, in fact. The medicine Kit had given her must be working.

"An excellent meal," remarked the old woman, dabbing at her mouth with a linen serviette. "I'm quite ready to retire. Alistair shall have to vacate the compartment while I change into my jimjams." And with that, Kit said good night.

When Alistair returned to the ladies' lounge, he found Cicely asleep on the chaise.

"Cicely, wake up," he said. He gently nudged her

shoulder. "I've brought you your night kit, so you can change." She blinked and sat up. Her eyes didn't quite focus on him. "How much wine did you drink with dinner?" he asked.

"Only one glass, but Kit, the dear, gave me a couple of tablets for the pain." Cicely smiled. "They're working, too!"

Ah well, he'd planned on carrying her to the sleeper anyway. "Good. Now change so we may get some rest. Don't worry, I shan't peek. I'll step over there into the toilet room." He did so.

Closing it behind him, Alistair leaned against the door and pinched the bridge of his nose. Good God, his life was becoming surreal. Hell and damnation, he was a copper and a soldier, not a secret agent. He'd always been a straightforward sort of chap, not particularly secretive, and not used to sneaking about. Now he found himself privy to far more filthy secrets than he'd ever wanted to know, helping a female spy—there was no other word for Cicely, he supposed—take a secret code to a supposedly safe location. He knew spying was necessary, of course, but uniformed soldiers usually viewed it as an unsavoury activity. Now Cicely had been attacked, and if she hadn't had the foresight to place the code on her person, they'd be right bollixcd indeed.

He glanced at his wristwatch. Ten minutes had passed. That should be sufficient time for a female to change into nightgear. He opened the door and shook his head.

Cicely sat on the chaise, her nightgown rucked above her knees. One foot was bare, flat on the floor, and the other, still stocking-clad, was placed on the edge of the low table in front of her, which still held the remains of her meal. She stared into the candleflame on the vanity.

"Cicely! Wake up. Let's get you to bed," Alistair said. He began picking up and folding her clothing, which she'd left scattered on the floor.

Cicely canted her head to one side and gazed dreamily at him. "You can't come with me, you know."

Alistair gave her a baffled look.

Cicely began unrolling the stocking she still wore, but didn't take her eyes from Alistair. "Everyone may think we're married, but we're not. So you can't sleep with me." She held her leg out straight, toe pointed, and continued to unroll her stocking.

"We're not sleeping together, you widget! You're taking the bottom sleeper. I'm on top," he explained.

Cicely's stocking stopped at her ankle. "Naughty boy. Men always want to be on top." She gave him a silly grin.

Alistair rolled his eyes. Taking her foot against his thigh, he finished the job. But his fingers lingered both on her ankle and the stocking. Her ankle was fine-boned and pleasingly curved. The stocking was silk and slipped through his fingers; no snagged and baggy rayon stockings for this girl. He held her foot a moment too long.

"Are you trying to seduce me, Alistair?" she asked. She leaned back and gave him a glassy-eyed, albeit beguiling look. "If you are, there are more . . . sensitive places to touch me than my feet."

As if she had to tell him! He could see her heart beating in the base of her throat, and the shadow of her full breasts through the thin lawn of her nightgown. That gown didn't hide the curve of her waist or the swell of her hips, either.

He mentally shook himself with the reminder he possessed scruples. He sighed. It portended to be a bloody long night. Damned scruples.

"Right then, you're in no shape to walk on your own, are you? Let's go, I'll carry you." He left her street clothing on the chaise and picked her up in his arms. She wiggled her bottom and snuggled her face into his neck. He shut his eyes and counted to ten, then bent to reach the door handle. When he did, it seemed the most natural thing for her to slide her mouth across his face until his lips met hers. She slipped her tongue into his mouth and slowly, languorously, swirled it in a dance with his. She explored every corner of his mouth, then gently started to suck his tongue.

Alistair felt his legs turn to water, and his body rose hard and pulsating to the cleft in her bottom. She rubbed against him, moaning and pressing herself closer. Then she was kissing his face, his neck, pushing her breasts against his chest.

Fire blazed in his veins, and without thinking Alistair let Cicely's feet slip to the floor while he crowded her against the wall. One hand ran through her long hair, the other weighed her breasts and plucked at her nipples.

"Please, Alistair, please," she whispered in his ear. He was reaching for the hem of her nightgown, but reality splashed him in the face like a bucket of ice water. Someone was pushing on the door, attempting to enter.

Like lightning, he picked Cicely up and pushed outward, bursting through the door past the two outraged ladies waiting for admittance.

"Pardon us, please, my wife is incapacitated," he murmured. He ignored their huffs of annoyance.

Back in the main compartment, Alistair thrust aside the heavy velvet curtains to the lower bunk. As he set Cicely on the bed, she let out a soft snore. Good God, he'd nearly seduced an unconscious woman! Was there no end to the record lows he was achieving? Oh Lord no, he thought as he climbed up to the higher bunk and his head hit his own pillow. Why am I even tempting fate by asking?

TWELVE

Oh what a tangled web we weave
When first we practise to deceive!
　　　—Sir Walter Scott

Cicely held her head in her hands at the linen-covered breakfast table in the dining car, eyeing her porridge in disfavour. Her head pounded behind her eyes, and she wasn't in the least hungry.

Alistair looked at her, clearly groggy himself. He said, "Eat while you can. Once we're off this train, it will be a spot of trouble replacing your rationbook, lass."

"You don't appear as if you feel very well, dear," Kit suggested. She pushed her clean bowl away and reached for some tea. "Perhaps another two of my special pills?"

"No!" both Cicely and Alistair said at once.

Kit blinked and sipped her tea. "If you say so, dears. Of course not."

Cicely glanced at Alistair and wondered what his objection to the medicine could be. For herself, everything after dinner was quite blank. As much as she'd appreciated the benefit of a restful sleep, she'd woken with what could only be described as a hangover.

Alistair actually sported bags under his eyes, poor chap. Looking at him, she nearly felt guilty for having slept so well, even if she felt terrible now.

Unable to tolerate her breakfast, Cicely gazed out the train windows. Fortunately, it was on the move again. But as farm and grazing country hurtled by with dizzying speed, she turned back to the table to steady herself. Apparently she still suffered the effects from the blow to her head.

"Speaking of ration books, I'm acquainted with a fellow in my village—which is just south of Gloucester—who might expedite that chore," Kit offered.

Cicely knew she'd not go far without a ration book. She couldn't share Alistair's or they'd both starve before arriving in Cornwall. "Why, thank you, Kit—an excellent idea," she said. She wondered what the old woman had in mind.

Kit said, "You must stay with me, of course, at my home, Wisteria Cottage. There's plenty of room. Oh my, I haven't had the pleasure of visitors in donkey's years."

Always cautious, Alistair wanted to know how long obtaining another ration book might take.

Kit avoided his eyes. "Oh, um, I shouldn't think any more than, er, a couple of days."

Alistair gazed at Kit for nearly a full minute. "Must be someone quite high up. Government works at a sloth's pace. Two days is very fast indeed."

Cicely frowned. What made Alistair so suspicious? Two days seemed a very long time to wait for a ration book. At Bletchley they were handed out as needed.

"Well," Kit replied. "There are fewer people to deal with in a small village. Let's return to the compartment, shall we? It's only another hour or two before the stop at Hammersmith."

"Your invitation is so kind, Kit," Cicely remarked. "But you hardly know us. We can find lodging at a B and B."

"I wouldn't hear of it, dear! I'm not fortunate enough to have children and, well, you remind me so much of myself at your age. Already I think of you as a sort of granddaughter." Kit beamed at Alistair. "And my Quinn nearly comes to life in the Major. Please, say you will be my guests. Make an old woman happy and give her the feeling of family again."

Alistair threw down his serviette and said, "Put like that, Kit, how can we refuse?"

It happened to be more like three hours, as they were ordered to stop for a troop train, the side of which was adorned with various posters and slogans? Winston Churchill, the Prime Minister, made the statement—"WE SHALL GO FORWARD TOGETHER." Pictures of troops were next to the slogan: NEVER WAS SO MUCH OWED BY SO MANY TO SO FEW. And on one panel, a gorgeous blonde was surrounded by servicemen. KEEP MUM, SHE'S NOT SO DUMB, it admonished.

A few other signs followed, like: BE LIKE DAD, KEEP MUM. CARELESS TALK COSTS LIVES; DIG ON FOR VICTORY!; "KILL HIM (a Nazi rat) WITH WAR SAVINGS!" And ironically, a poster depicting a well-dressed couple in a train depot staring at the sign, IS YOUR JOURNEY REALLY NECESSARY?

The Allied soldiers in the troop train were sombre, giving none of the hip-hip hurrahs that had marked the beginning of the war. As if nature sympathised, the day was grey and wet with a nasty east wind blowing in.

Stepping off the train in Hammersmith, Cicely shivered. The wind sent needles of ice beneath her heavy coat. Tucking her collar tighter around her throat, she followed Alistair and Kit to baggage distribution.

Luggage in tow, they soon caught a horse-drawn taxi for the short ride to Kit's home. The party smothered themselves in heavy blankets against the stout wind and spitting rain.

Although smaller than London, essentially Hammersmith was no different. Queues of women with sturdy shopping bags stood outside the butcher's and the baker's. The greengrocer had closed shop for the day, though it hadn't struck noon yet. Most people grew as large a Victory garden as was allowed by what land they occupied. If typical, the grocer would buy the extra to sell to those who didn't possess a patch of ground to grow produce themselves. Cicely didn't notice many young people. Likely all the able-bodied men had joined the armed services, and the young women were off to the Land Army and the Women's Voluntary Services.

The taxi stopped at a garden gate which danced on one hinge in the vigorous wind. Beyond they found the path bordered in winter jasmine. The garden itself featured an odd squash and pumpkin or two, as well as what appeared to be carrots, potatoes, and Brussels sprouts ready for the picking. On either side of the door a camellia and quince tree bid welcome. The cottage was built of stone, and the roof was thatched.

Inside, Kit told them they must take the loft guest room upstairs. When Alistair hefted the baggage, Kit said to Cicely, "Why don't you and I fix a simple lunch—not that any meal these days isn't simple, mind you—then we can all retire for an afternoon nap? You two youngsters may not need one, but these old bones have sustained enough excitement, and I need to rest. I don't sleep very well on trains."

Cicely nodded.

After lunch, Alistair set to repairing Kit's garden gate with tools he found in the old shed behind her cottage. Cicely was trying to coax some heat out of a small coal fire in the guest room when Kit entered, an envelope in her hand.

"Cicely, dear, why don't you take this to the butcher in the high street?" she asked. She held out the envelope. "But don't go to the front door. Go around back, there's a good girl."

Cicely looked at the envelope a moment before taking it. It was merely a plain white envelope. She studied her friend's face. Or was the woman her friend?

"Kit, why are you asking me to do this?" she asked.

The woman wrung her wrinkled hands. "I'm sure—no, I know Alistair, a fighting man, wouldn't approve. I'm not at all sure you would either, but you will obtain your ration book a good deal sooner from this man. He's Greek, but his family has lived here since the last war."

"Tell me all you know, Kit. I'm not walking into a . . . foreign sort of situation, so to speak, blind."

The elderly lady sat on the foot of the bed, folding her hands in her lap. "You know about my bunnies. Well, I kept them in the shed with plenty of food while I was away. Right now they're soaking up the warmth of the Aga. Yes, I'm getting on with it," she said, when Cicely gave her a pointed look. "The first Mrs. Kalakos gave birth to five boys. The new missus recently produced a girl. An infant, who is allergic to wool. I knit her clothing from my Angora rabbits. Now the poor little dear is quite comfortable.

"Mr. Kalakos possesses . . . black market ties. Occasionally, as we both, er, work under the table, he performs a favour or two for me. Oh, nothing serious, mind. Maybe a bit of extra coal or a morsel of bacon here and there. If anyone will be able to help you, he will." She cleared her throat. "Alistair is quite right, HMG works at a sloth's pace. Likely it might take up to a fortnight to acquire a replacement ration book through proper channels. Such a fuss to wait so long. Go out the back way so Alistair shan't see you. Telling a man something after the fact, I think, is easier—don't you?"

On her way out, Kit handed Cicely a small package wrapped in brown paper. "Just some jimjams, booties, hat, and scarf for little Anthea," she explained.

Cicely tucked the parcel in her coat and stopped short when she caught sight of Kit's bunnies nested in front of the Aga. "Good God, Kit! Bunnies? They're nearly the size of hunting dogs!" The two white rabbits sported very long ears, and each looked as if he weighed two and half stone.

As soon as Cicely spoke, the beasts' ears wiggled and their eyes darted wildly around, looking for an escape route. Kit hurried forward to open the pantry door for the frightened rabbits.

"Hush, dear," she said. "They frighten easily. Their fur is a good four inches long, so they aren't quite as enormous as they seem." Kit opened the back door for Cicely. "It's not far, dear—this road connects to the high street. Leander Kalakos's shop is just half a dozen doors down from there. Hurry back." Kit studied the sky. "It looks as if it might snow."

Cicely thought a look at the front of the shop would be a good idea before she slipped around back. It was closed for the day. In the alley behind the butcher's, Cicely heard rustling in the dustbins. She shuddered, thinking of the huge rats the alley must harbor.

Opening the screen door, she knocked loudly on the ill-kept door beyond. White paint chips rubbed off on her knuckles. Hearing a spate of Greek that she took to mean "come in," she opened the door and stepped inside. An immense man, obviously of Mediterranean heritage and wearing a bloodstained apron, frowned when he saw her.

"Who are you? Why do you come to the back? The shop is closed. Go away." He made a dismissive gesture with his hand.

"Kit Skinner sent me," Cicely answered, and handed him her envelope and package.

He grunted and took the note. He was tall, well over six feet with a girth to match. Silver laced his black hair. His countenance was swarthy and pock-marked, and his fingers short and blunt. Blood crusted under his nails and around his cuticles.

After reading Kit's letter, he gave Cicely a short stare. "Wait here. Won't be long." With that, he pounded up the staircase.

Cicely cast about, searching what appeared to be the preparation room in hopes of a place to sit down. Whoever worked in this room didn't sit. She didn't know which was worse: making the acquaintance of large and brave rats outside in the alley, or waiting in here.

A pig hung upside down, its blood dripping into the sink beneath from a gash in its jugular vein. A rack of beef ribs were ready for cutting on an island board in the centre of the room, and entrails from goodness knew what were spread out on another cutting board.

It smelled of a butcher's shop, of meat gone bad, the gasses of dead animals' bowels, and blood—both the coppery scent of fresh blood and the nauseating, rank odour of days-old gore. The latter reminded Cicely of finding

Graham in his bathtub. She gagged and dug in her coat pocket for a handkerchief. Not finding one, she opened the back door for a breath of outside air.

A handsome young man walked in from the shop proper, wiping his bloody hands on a cloth. He was a younger version of, and several stone lighter than, his father. He eyed Cicely up and down with an insolent gaze.

"What's a nice bit o' alright like you doing standing in our five star kitchen?" he asked. He eyed the prep room in distaste. "Aye, a right Ritz of a kitchen, i'n' it?" He sauntered closer, his eyes on her breasts. "Givin' up a bit o' crumpet for an extra sausage?" He laughed at his joke. "If you service me instead of m'father, you won't have to work as hard. He's out of breath just climbing those stairs. Come on then, birdie, peel off the coat, let's see the charlies."

Cicely backed up until she hit the screen door. She'd left her Enfield at Kit's. Bloody stupid thing to do. She followed Ruby's advice and yelled, "Clear off!"

The young man raised his eyebrows. "Not very friendly, are you?" he remarked.

"I've no need to be friendly. Keep your distance."

He stepped closer. "What have you come through our back for, if not to be friendly?" He reached out to touch her.

Just then Mr. Kalakos's heavy footsteps sounded on the stairs. The young man glanced up and snatched back his hand. "Well fuckery duckery dock, here comes his nibs to save the day." He smirked. "Or to make you work for that extra bit o' meat. Be careful, birdie, or you'll end up with a Greek bastard in your stomach. He's prolific, he is." He turned to leave, but his father's sharp voice stopped him. The senior Mr. Kalakos pointed to Cicely and turned to his son, yelling at him in Greek. Then he made a sound of disgust and motioned him out of the kitchen. The younger man reddened, and his face settled in sullen lines before he turned on his heel, retreating to the shop front.

The butcher handed Cicely a large brown envelope and nodded to her. "My son, Aristos. He'll not be bothering you again. You will tell me if the treats you with less than respect." He snorted. "Adversity will make him a man, mark my words."

Cicely gave the Greek emigré an uncertain smile and opened the envelope. Inside she found a perfect ration book, quite good enough to be her old one minutes the wear and tear.

Mr. Kalakos took a meat cleaver to the ribs on the centre island, hacked off several, and wrapped them in newspaper.

"Give this to Mrs. Skinner with my thanks."

Alistair leaned on the low stone wall surrounding Kit's garden and rubbed his knee. It ached more than usual when the weather became damp and chilly. It was only a fortnight into December, ordinarily a bit early for snow, but between the leaden sky and his joints, he'd say they were in for a few inches. He'd found an old work coat in the shed with the tools, and was glad for the extra warmth.

He was about to return to the cottage when he heard the back gate creak open. It was Cicely, huddled and shivering in her wool coat, and she went completely still when she saw him.

"I thought you were upstairs napping, Cicely. A bit cold for a walk. Where did you go?" he asked.

She shrugged and looked him in the eyes. "You gave me a start. Kit sent me on an errand. To the butcher's."

She held out a bloodstained package. "We can look forward to a hearty rib dinner."

Beef ribs? That was a cut reserved for the armed forces. He was surrounded by perfidious females, and it saddened him more than he'd expected. He genuinely liked Kit. And Cicely . . . well, he'd liked her before he discovered the worst of her secrets. Now he didn't quite know how he felt about the young woman. He desired her more than any other girl he'd ever known, but she lacked his sense of honour. Or was it possible he was being too picky?

He sighed. "Cicely, I'm heartily sick of subterfuge. For God's sake—and my own—what the devil have you and Kit been up to?"

Cicely opened her mouth to deny everything, but she stopped. Working at Bletchley had trained her in lying too well. Lying had become second nature to her. If she lived through this madness, she'd not go back to Bucks. Not after taking a peek at herself through Alistair's eyes.

Studying him, she found a different man than she'd first seen. Previously she'd seen a tall, proud, strapping Scotsman, far too handsome for his own good, yet who didn't show the characteristics of a man who knew women found him intensely attractive. She'd seen a hard-working and idealistic lawman. He'd held an overpowering appeal to her from the moment they met, even if he'd scared her a little. She'd spent so much of her energy ignoring that magnetic pull and keeping her inner self buried, she wondered now what might happen if she just let go and fell for him. He'd get himself killed, of course. She nearly felt like a black widow.

But his face had changed. Now it was shadowed by fatigue, disillusionment, and could it be hopelessness? Instead of standing straight and tall, he was bent like an old man. His eyes were flat, lifeless.

She stepped forward, taking him by the arm and heading for the cottage. Pausing momentarily to gaze up at the fallow vines tangling and reaching over a latticework shade, the roof of the shed and along the rock wall, she observed, "One can see how Wisteria Cottage came by its name. It must be quite charming come spring and summer."

Alistair was undeterred. "Cut the codswallup, Cicely, and answer my question."

Cicely hovered over the Aga, thawing out her body. The bunnies had decided to trust her and huddled at her feet.

"How did the Major take it, dear?" Kit arranged the ribs in a cooking pan.

Cicely shrugged. "Calmly. He's disappointed, of course. He's too idealistic for the real world, I sometimes think." Above them, the pipes creaked and groaned and they heard a thump. "Alistair needs to soak his knee, so he'll be a while in the bath, I believe."

"It's surprising he's still in the army with that wound," Kit commented, and she pushed the rib pan into the Aga.

Cicely longed to confide the truth to Kit. She wondered if she might end very much like her one day; never marrying because her true love perished, keeping only rabbits for company. Kit held no pretty illusions of the world, yet took life full-on, with a smile on her face. Nothing slowed her down. She made deals with the devil—or at least the local equivalent—something an able-bodied man might hesitate to do. She made the world work for her, and Cicely admired that. A wave of guilt nearly smothered her, but for the sake of national security she couldn't tell Kit the truth. For Kit's own safety as well.

"The army is taking nearly everyone these days," Cicely prevaricated. She glanced down at the rabbits. "Don't rabbits reproduce frequently? Why is it you don't own a menagerie by now?"

Kit scrubbed potatoes at the sink, but turned to wink at her. "Precisely why I traveled to London, dear. They had two sweet little babies. I took them to a breeder. I don't think these two will go at it again very soon." She dried her hands on a tea towel and placed the clean potatoes in with the ribs. "Now then, the turnips are peeled and ready to be boiled when the meat comes out of the Aga. If you aren't indulging in a nap, there are a number of books in the parlour you may choose from, then pull a chair up to Aga and enjoy the warmth." She glanced out the window.

"The snow's started," she said.

THIRTEEN

Had we never loved sae blindly,
Never met—or never parted,
We had ne'er been broken-hearted.
    —Robert Burns

Cicely smoothed her nightgown down her body and moved from behind the dressing screen. Kit had installed her and Alistair in a guest room, and Alistair lay on the bed, his arms behind his head, staring into the glow of the coal fire.

He barely spared Cicely a glance. "I'm not sleeping on the floor or that damned thing that passes for a settee. You will just have to take my word as a gentleman that you have nothing to fear from me tonight."

The coldness in his voice pierced her to her heart. She hadn't forgotten that enthusiastic kiss he had given her back in London in her flat. But what was she thinking? It was just as well if he didn't hold a torch for her. Straightening her spine, she approached the bed.

"I don't expect you to sleep anywhere but the bed, Alistair. I'm a big girl now, and as such, I'm aware two adults may sleep in the same bed without any untoward events."

Cicely climbed onto the mattress and took a deep breath to relax. She must forget they occupied the same bed, inches apart. Already she felt his warmth. They both desperately needed sleep. Neither of them knew when another chance similar to this might arise: a warm, safe place where they could sleep the entire night. She had to concentrate on relaxing to sleep.

"We'll take the train to Cardiff in the morning," Alistair said, turning over.

"Have it all planned, do you?" she asked.

He turned back to face her. "Hell and damnation. No, woman, I don't! I've learned the bloody hard way that planning too far in advance is disastrous. One must keep one's options open and ready for the next attack." He scrubbed his hand down his face, suddenly contrite. "I'm sorry, I shouldn't have raised my voice. It's the milk run, I'm afraid. The bloody slowest train in the country, I think, is between here and Cardiff. I know"—he raised a hand as she opened her mouth to speak—"that taking the slowest transportation to Cornwall isn't in our best interests, but . . . whoever is after that code isn't likely to suspect we'd take the slowest transport. Moreover, he, they, whoever, probably thinks we're on our way back to London or on to a larger industrial city." He paused for a moment, narrowing his gaze on her. "Cicely, you are truly talented at holding back. I want that to stop here and now, do you understand?" At her solemn nod, he continued, "Do these spies—for lack of a better word—could they possibly be aware we're heading to your parents' in Cornwall?"

Cicely closed her eyes, giving in to defeat. "They may," she murmured. "The truth is . . . I just don't know! They may already be approaching my parents' house. This code in invaluable. It could very well mean the end of the war. I shudder to even think Graham acted as a spy, but if he did and it's HMG after us, mum and dad are far more able to take care of themselves than we. No, don't ask," she said when Alistair raised his brows. "If the Jerries know about this code leak, all bets are off. As far as they know, we haven't cracked the code. So the key would be useless to us—until it reaches the right hands. Codebreakers' hands. If they can retrieve it before that happens, they've relieved themselves of the chore of installing a whole new cipher system and training hundreds of personnel. Undoubtedly another code is waiting in the wings, but retrieving this bit of paper is easier all around." She climbed out of bed, heading to a writing desk in the corner of the guestroom. "I should have though of this earlier. I'm making a copy of this code for you to carry, Alistair. One copy just isn't enough."

When she got no answer, Cicely glanced at the bed. Alistair was soundly asleep. She'd make a copy of the code tomorrow. Gently, so as not to disturb his slumber, she climbed back into bed beside him.

Cicely opened her eyes to a shadowed room. The coal fire, banked for the night, glowed in its grate. The blanket slipped from her shoulder and she realized how cold it was outside her cocoon of covers. Intent on adding more coal to the fire, she swing her legs to the floor but froze seeing a movement by the window. Alistair stood like a phantom, staring at her, his dark eyes glittering in the low light. The illumination glazed the stark planes of his face on one side, leaving the other side in complete darkness. His flannel pajamas were rumpled and the shirt only half-buttoned, showing a sculpted chest dusted with curly hair.

"It's cold, Alistair, come back to bed before you catch cold."

Alistair laughed. "An invitation to be devoutly wished for." He didn't move.

His odd tone garnered a glance, but Cicely was too cold and sleepy for games. She headed to the fireplace, scooped more coal on the fire, and stirred it to encourage a few flames. When she straightened and turned around, Alistair still gazed at her intently. He raised a cigarette she had not before noticed to his mouth and drew hard on it; the ash burned orange and raced toward the tip in his mouth.

He exhaled the smoke, strode forward and threw the cigarette into the fire. "I couldn't sleep. Would you like to know why?" He stood no more than two feet from her and she could see his heart beat on the side of his throat. He smelled of sleep, male muskiness, and sandalwood.

Cicely didn't feel cold anymore. The fire warmed her back and look in Alistair's eyes warmed the rest of her. She had a feeling there was no going back if she answered him. Yet she couldn't stop herself.

"Why?"

"I want you." He shook his head. "In spite of all the reasons I shouldn't, I do. I itch to touch you—everywhere. I want to possess you in every way a man can possess a woman."

Cicely tingled all over and felt a warm lassitude descend on her body. "What reasons shouldn't you want me?"

"We couldn't deal together in a relationship." He canted his head to one side. "I need to trust my woman implicitly. Deceit is second nature to you. I want you so much I'm past caring."

A jolt of disappointment hit her. She hated it that she needed to be less than truthful. But she did what she must, regardless if it flew by his requirements. Besides, she had no use for a relationship, not while a war raged. Too many died.

"It needn't go so far as a relationship," she whispered, taking a step closer to him. She craved him. More than anything she needed the comfort he could give with his body. "It's wartime. Things are different. We take comfort when we can. Who knows when another chance will arise. We may come together for a moment in our lives. Let's leave it there."

His eyes softened a moment and then he took a sharp breath. In one movement he swept her up in his arms, strode to the bed, and placed her gently on the mattress.

He said, "The hell with it." And joined her on the bed, kissing her lips, her throat, her face.

Cicely's blood sizzled in her veins. Her fingers roamed over his muscular, hairy chest. His erection wedged itself between her legs, which she lifted for more access. The wiry sensation of whiskers rasped her cheeks, and warm lips finally settled on hers. His tongue swirled in her mouth lazily, enticingly.

One hand cupped the back of her head, then traveled down her body searing her skin, clasping her bottom and pulling her closer, riding her on the hard ridge of his erection. She moaned and hitched her leg higher on his hip. Her heart thundered against her ribs and she heard a roaring in her ears. Moving so both her hands were free, she unbuttoned the rest of his pyjama shirt. She peeled it from his body so she could touch all of his chest, his hard stomach, his back, and wander further down to the cleft of his bottom. Alistair lifted her nightgown, his fingers skimming up her leg just short of touching her centre.

He flipped her on her back and straddled her. After

looking down at her for several moments, he shrugged all the way out of his shirt then clasped her wrists above her head with one hand.

Then he kissed her—hot, wet, and out of control. Such a transformation from the regulated, cool facade he showed the world. He let go of her wrists and fondled her breasts, teased her nipples, stroked her hip, the soles of her feet, discovering the curves of her body, touching her everywhere but where she needed it most. Then he seized the hem of her nightgown and pulled it over her head.

She stretched languidly while he shucked his pyjama bottoms. He straddled her again and gazed at her, brushing the hair off her face. The whiteness of the snow outside reflected into the bedroom. Cicely could see Alistair's trousled hair, a magnificently contoured chest with just the right amount of hair, heavily muscled shoulders and arms. His face, however, remained in shadow.

"So much for my word as a gentleman. I've wanted you since I first saw you. Did you know that? You've been hell to keep out of my blood."

"Alistair . . ." She didn't want to talk, she wanted those magical hands of his all over her body. Reaching up she rubbed his nipples with the tips of her forefingers. He gasped and moved her hands from his chest to his erection.

It was her turn to gasp as she learned the size of him. She couldn't quite fit her hand around him, and as she pulled and squeezed he began to pant. He wrenched himself out of her grasp, spread her wide and plunged in all the way to the hilt. If she'd been virgin he'd have torn her asunder.

Alistair squeezed his eyes shut and savoured the sensation of finally being in her liquid depth. After the night before, he'd nearly been in a constant state of arousal. He was desperate with need and was afraid to move lest he climax immediately.

Her breath came in short gasps and her hands moved frantically over his back and then began to explore the cleft of his buttocks. When he still didn't move she moaned and writhed under him, begging him for more. Her inner muscles milked him with every gasp she took. Finally, gritting his teeth, he grasped her hips and began to move slowly, measuring each thrust. Desperate with need, he touched her everywhere, savouring her perfect curves, kissing until he was lunging mindlessly into her.

Cicely could only feel. She couldn't hear, she couldn't see, she was aware only of Alistair's body. He reached the very core of her time and again until the tension was too much and she broke, gasping and crying.

He covered her mouth with his, and when he could hold off no longer he grasped her knees, splaying them widely, arching his body so he could tease her nubbin with his hardness as he drove into her.

Cicely thought he was done, but he rode her to another climax even more powerful than the first. *That* had never happened to her before. With a cry Alistair climaxed, burying his face in the crook of her neck.

When the echo of his cry had faded, he didn't move. She didn't blame him. She didn't think she could either. Her limbs felt like lead.

He lifted his head from her neck and looked at her in wonder. "I've never, ever lost control like that."

"I've never experienced two climaxes before."

He slid off of her, nestling behind her spoon-fashion and stroked her long tangled hair. They both gazed out the window in silence watching the snow fall. At least two inches had collected on a bare branch of the apple tree outside.

"Do you think the train will leave as scheduled tomorrow if this snow keeps up?" Cicely snuggled further under the duvet and closer to Alistair's hard, warm body.

"It's unlikely to snow that much this early in the season. In all probability it will turn to rain by morning."

Cicely sat up and swung her legs to the floor. "Then let's relish the spectacle while we may." Seizing the duvet, she headed for the window. "Come on!

"Isn't it a magical sight?" she exclaimed, rubbing the thin layer of frost from the window. "I'm so glad we didn't use the blackout cover tonight."

Alistair flung the blanket around them both and pulled her against his chest. "The first snow always is. Gets bloody old seeing white everywhere after a few days."

"No negativity tonight, Alistair. Please?" she asked, looking up at him.

He nodded, and when she gazed out the window again he rested his chin atop her head. After several moments he sighed. "This is not a good example of keeping my word.

"Hush, Alistair. I told you—things are different now."

He tried to dismiss the stab of disappointment he felt. Why should he feel it? He himself had said they wouldn't deal well together. Because he'd never experienced such intense lovemaking. "Two ships passing in the night sort of thing?"

Cicely forced herself to say, "Exactly." She couldn't allow herself to think of the future. Facing him, she said, "If we live through this, we return to our own lives and remember each other with fondness."

Taking him by the hand, she led him back to bed.

The stab twisted deeper in Alistair's chest. What had he expected to hear from her? A pledge of undying love? He knew by now Cicely was far more complicated than he. Stifling a sigh, he pulled her more closely against him in the bed.

True to Alistair's prediction, sometime in the early hours of the morning the snow turned to rain. Moving away from the bedroom window, Cicely eyed her high Victory rolls in the dressing table mirror with a critical eye. They were fine. As were her short rope of pearls and her long-sleeved bright blue, belted dress. And it was surprising her eyes were fresh and bright considering the amount of sleep she hadn't gotten.

Alistair had made love to her three more times. Each time had been more satisfying than the last, but . . . they had taken on a sense of desperation.

She felt a soreness in certain places, but she didn't mind. In fact, the pain sent her daydreaming about Alistair and what he had done to her. Never had anyone made her feel so— She shook herself. None of this nonsense! Alistair must not know how their lovemaking affected her.

She practised a businesslike demeanor in the mirror, and when satisfied with it, descended the stairs to share breakfast with Alistair and Kit.

It was a leisurely meal, but at last it was time to go. After bidding Kit an emotional good-bye, Cicely and Alistair boarded another horse-drawn cab and returned to the station to wait for the train.

Cicely stamped her feet, both to dislodge the freezing slush and to warm them. The fur lining in her pre-war boots had worn thin over the years, but she was better off than many waiting in the queue. Her new angora scarf covered her face, but her nose was still numb. Her fingers were fast following. Alistair stood apart from her, almost as if they weren't traveling companions. He shuffled his feet and rubbed his gloved hands together, and he didn't look her way. In fact, since rising for breakfast he'd been ruddy careful not to touch her, either. It was almost as if he were making up for touching her last night. Cicely couldn't think of a place where he hadn't.

Remembering Alistair's lovemaking caused her blood to again sizzle. She felt desire pooling low in her belly, and flowing through her like potent brandy on an empty stomach. Yet it was obvious he now felt uncomfortable about having made love to her all night. Could it be he was disappointed in her? That he'd previously thought her a "good girl" only to find out she was fast? The thought made her face heat. Too bloody bad! She'd not apologise to anyone for having loved her fiancé, or for . . . the other. She'd be damned if she would have died without having known love.

Or might he simply be truly uncomfortable about having broken his word? Sometimes, Cicely thought, a person could be too honourable. Alistair fit that mold. Only now was he coming to terms with the true dishonourability of war, of which straightforward fighting was only one part.

One aspect of their lovemaking did disturb her, however. Her two previous lovers had always worn prophylactics. Alistair hadn't. Cicely frowned. If she . . . No, it wasn't the right time in her month; she was sure. Still, the thought cast a pall on the day. Perhaps that was the reason for Alistair's discomfort. She must tell him not to concern himself.

A young woman walked up to Alistair's side and gave

him the once-over. She touched his shoulder, gave him a coy smile, and pointed somewhere behind her. Cicely watched as Alistair glanced in the direction the woman indicated, then he nodded and left the queue. The young lady next took her compact out of her handbag and renewed her lip rouge. With a pat to her gleaming chestnut Victory rolls, she turned as Alistair came back, giving him a wide smile. Cicely caught a note of her laughter. Alistair grinned back, and set the woman's portmanteau next to his own. This emboldened the girl, and she slipped her arm through his and started an animated conversation.

A little dagger of jealousy stabbed Cicely, but she quashed it. She had no right, she told herself. Besides, the more she thought about it, the more convenient Alistair's discomposure actually proved. Because, given half a chance, she would lose herself in him; really leap over the moon for him. And that wouldn't do. Not at all. All her men died in the war. It would not happen again. If it did, she would never recover.

"All aboard!" came the conductor's cry.

"Well, finally!" Alistair's new lady friend announced.

Alistair didn't glance at Cicely, but shepherded his companion ahead of him. Cicely fought the hurt rushing through her.

Inside the packed train, she looked in vain for an available compartment hoping Alistair would follow. At last she settled for one with only two other passengers. She nodded at them and lifted her case to the storage shelf above the seats, but met with difficulty in wedging it between a satchel and a trunk.

"Please. Do allow me, lovely lady," intoned a tall, portly, ruddy-faced gentlemen who leapt from his seat.

"Why, thank you. Very kind of you, sir," Cicely replied, relieved. But where was Alistair?

The middle-aged lady sitting next to the gentleman sniffed in disapproval, and turned to gaze out the window.

Once the gentleman resumed his seat, Cicely set her toiletries bag some distance away on the bench, and said, "I'm expecting my hu—"

"Mummy! Daddy! Brilliant!"

The girl who had accosted Alistair stood framed in the compartment doorway. Then she entered, dragging Alistair by the hand.

"Isn't this just the cat's pyjamas! Isn't it just too brilliant for words! I was hoping you'd be on this train! And look who I've brought to meet you—my very good friend, Major Alistair Bennington! Alistair, love, this is Mummy and Daddy," she simpered. "That is the Honourable Mr. and Mrs. Hillier!"

Alistair bowed to the lady and shook the gentleman's hand, sat down and began to rub his knee.

"Alistair?" prompted Cicely.

"Ah, yes." Alistair gave her an uncomfortable look. Turning to the others he said, "Please allow me to introduce you to Cicely Bennington. My sister."

FOURTEEN

Alistair admired Cicely's fortitude. While her eyes shot daggers at him, when she faced the others in the compartment, she was smiling serenely.

He fought back regret.

The only way not be separated while traveling was to pose as brother and sister or husband and wife—and he'd be damned if he ended up in the husband role again. It was too damned tempting. Intimacy with Cicely could not go any further. She appealed to him deeply. Too deeply. As well as owning a lively mind, she had a pin-up's body. She was very much his type of woman. But he didn't feel he could trust her. Hiding the truth appeared her stock in trade. Besides, she'd made it quite plain he was only a comfort in the current storm. It was all or nothing for him. And so, to escape being caught in something he couldn't control, he'd even brave Lydia Hillier's blandishments for the duration of the journey.

"I say, an honour to meet one of our brave soldiers—and his sister, of course." The Honourable Mr. Hillier stood again to shake Alistair's hand, and nodded to Cicely. Sitting back down next to his wife, he fished in his pockets and drew out a package of tobacco and a pipe. He struck a match and nearly lit his tobacco when his wife cleared her throat and gave him a pointed look. "Er, so sorry," he said. "Haven't asked the ladies' permission. I say, girls, may I smoke?"

Lydia giggled. "Of course, Daddy."

"Please do." Cicely nodded.

The Honourable Mrs. Hillier snorted and turned to the window.

Lydia glanced between Alistair and Cicely. "How very curious it is, Major, that you speak with a Scots note in your voice, but you sister seems quite English."

Cicely smiled at Alistair, as if to say, *Yes dear, explain that one.*

He nodded. "Actually, my dear Miss Hillier—"

"Oh, do call me Lydia."

"Lydia, then. My sister and I come from different mothers. Cicely's insisted upon her education in England." He smiled brightly at the young woman, quietly despising himself. Good God, now he was following in Cicely's footsteps, lying to everyone.

"Of course." The girl nodded. "And Mr. Bennington is English—"

Mrs. Hillier turned to rebuke her daughter. "Mind your manners, Lydia! Ladies do not question gentlemen in such a fashion."

"Of course, Mama." Lydia showed a chagrined expression—for all of two seconds. Then she burst out, "I'm so excited! Mummy, Daddy and I are on our way to my sister's wedding in Cardiff. The lucky man is a captain in the army."

"Even if he is Welsh," Mrs. Hillier grumbled.

"How enterprising of your sister." Cicely leaned back and crossed her legs. "Which regiment?"

Lydia frowned. "I don't exactly know. Who can keep regiments straight, anyway? David is a captain, and according to Diana, my sister, he has a brilliant career ahead of him."

If he can manage staying alive, Alistair thought. Cicely met his gaze, and he knew she was thinking the same. Without breaking eye contact, she took her box of DuMauriers out of her coat pocket and leaned forward for a light.

Her touch on his wrist to steady the flame was a caress. She blew out a cloud of smoke, which Mrs. Hillier attempted to dissipate by waving her hand. Cicely ignored the woman and smiled at Lydia. "You must give me all the details of Diana's wedding. You are, of course, a bridesmaid?"

Alistair promptly forgotten, Lydia launched into a purely female conversation of gowns, flowers, favours, and whatever else weddings involved. Mr. Hillier seemed to have dozed off, his pipe still between his lips.

Alistair at last stood. "If you will excuse me, ladies?"

Lydia stopped mid-sentence to smile at him, while Cicely raised her eyebrows in question. He gave her a slight shake of his head and left the compartment.

In the corridor, on his way to the connecting platform between the two carriages to get some air, he passed a young mother with two chattering toddlers. He fought back a sigh. Only eight o'clock in the morning and already he needed two fingers of whisky. Escaping outside, he took a deep breath of frigid air and watched the countryside stream by.

Patches of snow still dotted the landscape. Sheep and a few cows wandered the lowlands, but became fewer as the train headed for hilly country. He shoved his hands deeper in his pockets as the temperature lowered even more. His knee ached like the very devil. Early for snow this year, it was only—good God, where had the time gone? It was less than a week before Christmas, now that he thought of it. Ah well, with war and shortages it would prove a rather deary affair anyway.

He arched his right foot and felt the familiar crackle of the paper in his boot. This morning Cicely had insisted on giving him a copy of the code. So much responsibility. . . .

Oh, the hell with it. He fished his silver flask out of his coat pocket and swallowed two gulps. They left a satisfying burn down his throat, pooled in his stomach, and expanded warmly through his body. And he found himself thinking about the last night. God, if he ever experienced that gratification and pleasure again, he believed he could take all the horrors that life—even *war*—could dish out. But he wouldn't ever experience it again. Not with Cicely. He must forget last night. He hadn't been with a woman in nearly a year; that was the only reason he felt so drawn to this one. Maybe he should find another girl, one who wouldn't be so keen on deception. Maybe . . .

He'd just turned to go back inside when the door opened and another man stepped onto the swaying platform. And another man from the other carriage. Facing them both, Alistair seized the nearest handhold and braced himself.

Cicely stretched her legs but kept her polite smile. Never in her life had she met anyone who talked more than Lydia Hillier.

When the girl had finished with the wedding, she began asking questions about Alistair. Did he go out with a lady friend presently? How was his army career progressing? Where were he and Cicely reared? When Cicely had managed to field those questions with broad answers, Lydia progressed to fashion—or what remained of it during the war. She was warming up to all the makeovers she'd accomplished with her wardrobe when her mother interrupted.

"Enough, Lydia!" she said. "Miss Bennington is likely ready for a bit of rest. I know I am."

Lydia flushed, apologising. "I do go on. So sorry, Miss Bennington." She pouted and gave her mother a sideways glance.

"No apology necessary. And do please call me Cicely. However, it's true—I wouldn't mind a nap. I didn't sleep well last night. I never do before travel."

"Well, we shan't wake you, Miss Bennington," Mrs. Hillier said. The woman didn't bother glancing over, but kept her gaze on the passing landscape.

Mr. Hillier opened his mouth in a distinct snore, which let loose his pipe to fall into his lap. Mrs. Hillier ignored it, but Lydia leapt forward, emptying the pipe and setting it aside.

Cicely closed her eyes, but instead of sleep, images of the night before haunted her: Alistair exploring her body with his tongue, taking her to heights she'd only imagined. After every increase, had let her fall back only a little, creating even more tension and pleasure. She'd never felt anything like it. She didn't consider herself an experienced woman by any means, but she'd never derived such a feeling of contentment from making love to a man.

Unfortunately, she clearly wasn't what Alistair wanted.

She'd come up wanting in his eyes. She kept the government's dirty secrets, which made her just as dirty and dishonourable. Lying had become second-nature working at Bletchley Park. Alistair hated liars. His understanding didn't stretch beyond the straightforward. Oh, he'd enjoyed last night; he loved her body and what it could do for him, but he despised *her*. She supposed it was just as well he'd claimed she was his sister, rather than his wife. It would be far less complicated.

She couldn't wait until she delivered this code to her father, bringing her journey to an end. The relief of giving up the code and of calling it quits with Alistair were running about even, actually. She didn't care for the way he made her feel: vulnerable, sneaky, dirty. But last night: carnal, erotic, and alluring. More than anything, she wished to feel like herself again, wished for the familiar.

Ah well, there were perks to this situation. Watching Alistair perform some fancy dancing to stay out of Lydia's clutches might prove entertaining indeed.

"I say, damned crowded out here," said the first man stepping onto the platform. He was blond, with a neatly trimmed beard and a black patch over his left eye. He was about Alistair's age and quite fit.

The other man possessed a dark, foreign sort of countenance, black oily hair, small dark eyes and was of medium height. He merely nodded and looked out into the passing countryside.

Alistair relaxed his hold on the hand rail.

"Came out for a smoke. Suppose I could've used the smoking lounge," commented the blond man.

The dark gentleman responded. "Too packed. Too damn many women smoking these days. Shouldn't allow

123

them into the smoking lounges." His voice held a trace of an accent Alistair couldn't place. "If you ask me, it's time to take back one of our only asylums."

The blond man grinned. "I say, old chap, you're quite a boffin! Jolly good idea. Tell you what—let's take a seat in the bar carriage. The ladies don't drink this early. . . . Should introduce m'self," he added after a moment, looking at both Alistair and the dark man. "Terrence Wilkins, His Majesty's Postal Service."

Alistair nodded. "Bloody excellent idea. Lead the way. I'm Alistair Bennington, First Queen's Own Cameron Highlanders."

But as Wilkins and Alistair started inside, the foreign gentleman didn't move.

"Coming, old man?" Wilkins asked.

The dark man's eyes darted between him and Alistair, then he glanced back at the carriage he'd stepped out of. He scratched his head, then said abruptly, "Yes."

"Strange fellow," Wilkins murmured in Alistair's ear as they all went inside. "Still, one must be sociable."

In the bar carriage, all three men removed their outerwear, lit cigarettes, and ordered brandies from the steward. The steward raised his brows at requests for spirits at such a young hour of the day, but promptly served them and disappeared behind the bar.

Wilkins raised his bowl glass. "Gentlemen, here's to escaping the Blister and Strife!"

"Hear, hear," agreed Alistair.

The third man simply nodded and sipped his drink.

"I say, old fellow," remarked Wilkins, looking at him, "I didn't catch your name."

"Carl Barnes, veterinary."

"No wonder you're not in uniform. Someone must

keep our livestock healthy! Marvelous new cures these days I hear." He turned to Alistair. "You must be on furlough, Major. Take advantage of it. If I hadn't lost my damned eye in an automobile crash years ago, by God"—he slammed his fist on the shelf just below the window—"I'd be sending those Jerries and Japs back to their maker like billy-oh!"

Alistair nodded. "On holiday yourself?" he enquired.

"One might say so. On my way to m'mother's deathbed. It's the fifth or sixth time, mind, so who knows if the old gal really will kick up her heels." He glanced out the window and shuddered. "Bloody jammy being inside out of that frigid weather. If m'mother hadn't the decency to call me to another of her deathbeds, I'd be out there right now mucking about in that bloody snow, delivering His Majesty's post."

Alistair cleared his throat, not sure what to say. "I, er, do hope she will live to summon you to another deathbed."

Wilkins shrugged. "She's a tough old bird. Probably will outlive me. Where are you off to, Veterinary?" he asked, turning to the dark-haired man.

"I must take tissue samples to a laboratory in Cardiff." The vet dug in the pocket of his threadbare black trousers and brought out a handful of coins, which he began to count.

"Put it away, Mr. Barnes. This round is on me. You two do far more for the war effort than I, delivering letters." Wilkins went in search of the steward.

"You didn't say, sir, where you are bound," Barnes observed after a moment, looking at Alistair.

"I'm visiting family while on furlough."

"Are you Welsh then?"

Alistair frowned. Why was the man so interested? His eyes were sharp. These weren't social questions. "No, I'm not Welsh. But I do have family living in Wales. Where are you from, if I may enquire, sir? I must say, you look neither Welsh nor English."

Barnes flushed and sat back in his seat. "No need to take offense, just making conversation. To answer your other question, I was born in London. That makes me English, no matter where my parents were born."

Alistair nodded. "Just so. Forgive my forwardness. Here is Wilkins with our brandies."

"We're on the honour system, old boys!" the blond man said, returning. "The steward helps set up for lunch in the dining car, so we have this fine bottle of Remy to ourselves." He poured a finger in each their glasses. "Still, we must be careful, what, if we're to make it in to luncheon."

After another round, Alistair noticed his companions were wavering before him. One moment it was as if he viewed them from the far end of the carriage, and the next he was nearly in their laps. Good God, he hadn't that much to drink! Had he? He attempted to discover the level in the cognac bottle but could barely focus on it. Lifting his left hand, he aimed it at the solid shelf under the window. It would give him purchase. But he couldn't control his hand. It lifted a few inches, then fell heavily to his thigh.

The last thing he remembered was staring stupidly at his renegade hand.

"I'm positively peckish!" announced Lydia.

Cicely started awake and peeked at her watch. It approached noon. The second seating for luncheon must be in progress.

Mr. Hillier harrumphed, sat up, and placed a heavy hand on his wife's thigh. "Wake up, m'dear. Time for nourishment. Steward hasn't come, has he, to announce a seating?"

"No, Daddy, and Major Bennington hasn't returned either," his daughter replied.

"Likely the major has pursuits of his own, Lydia." Mrs. Hillier brought out a compact, examined herself, and returned it to her handbag. "Let's be off. We could wait forever for the steward."

They were seated almost immediately in the dining car, and filled themselves with the ever-present cod and root vegetables. One could nearly eat as much cod as one wished, for fish wasn't rationed. Any other kind of meat, however, even served in a soup, was rare. More than anything the populace craved eggs, beef, and fresh fruit. Absent from Bletchley for over a fortnight, Cicely dreamt of juicy roasting joints, cooked eggs, and ripe oranges. Food certainly proved a solid benefit of working in that ultrasecret facility.

For dessert the train passengers were treated to the very blandest of blancmanges. Cicely swallowed the last of her dry white wine, the most palatable nourishment of the meal. At least she was full. Many weren't so lucky.

Cicely and the Hillier family traveled back through eight or ten carriages before arriving at their compartment, but still there was no sign of Alistair. Cicely began to be worried.

Lydia was clearly used to Alistair's absence by now. She embarked on the subject of Christmas:

"It's less than a sennight away. After Diana's wedding, we *must* think what we are to do for the holiday," the girl said.

Christmas, a week hence? Cicely thought, shocked. *Was it true?* The thought of normal festivities seemed bizarre. Usually she adored the Christmas season, and delighted in buying presents all year long. This year her Christmas closet remained nearly empty. Which showed her, she thought, as nothing else might, just how the war, and in particular Bletchley, had changed her. She sat on the bench seat she had all to herself, dumbfounded. Lydia Hillier's voice was a mere buzzing in her ears.

It wasn't just the war. It was Bletchley Park, damn it to hell, that had turned an open, easygoing girl who took joy in the smallest of pleasures into a suspicious, cynical, secretive cow.

Cicely wished more than anything that this was all merely a bad dream, and that she might awake in her old room at her parents' home, smelling the sizzling bacon her mother cooked and the homey scent of bread toasting. She'd go down to breakfast, dressed for school. Her father would be sitting at the breakfast table, his newspaper hiding his face, and her mother would be pouring her a cup of tea. A cup of real, undiluted, second-blush Darjeeling.

She leaned back so that her head rested on the seat cushion, and sighed. When life tended toward the difficult, her parents probably indulged in fantasies, too. But it was time to grow up. To take charge. First chores, first. She had to deliver the code to her father. But first she had to find Alistair.

Glancing at her wristwatch, she saw it was nearly two o'clock. Definitely, something was wrong. No matter how much he wanted to avoid her, Cicely knew Alistair was too responsible to be absent so long with no word.

"Please excuse me," she said to the Hilliers. "Luncheon is sitting in my stomach like an anvil. I'm going for a bit of cold air."

"Do be careful!" Lydia advised. "You don't want pneumonia, especially with most medicine going to the soldiers. And be sure to drag that errant brother of yours back with you if you see him."

Earlier she'd gone forward, to the dining carriage, and had seen no sign of Alistair, so Cicely worked toward the back of the train. Since she didn't hurry and was careful and leisurely in her perusals, many soldiers both Yank and British gave her the slow eye. Some of the Yanks even offered invitations. For most she simply lowered her eyes demurely and shook her head, but she had to grind her heel into the boot of one young Yank who proved overly fresh.

At the end of every carriage, she checked behind her. If anyone appeared too close, she stood aside to let them pass. Progressing from one carriage to the next was a nerve-wracking process—if there came another attempt to throw her from the train, she might not be so lucky as last time.

Finally she came upon what looked to be the third to the last carriage. The sign on its window proclaimed it the drinks car and closed until further notice. She frowned. If it was closed it wasn't locked. Leaning on the door she peered into the thick glass window, but the interior lights were off, and the only illumination was the waning light of the late winter afternoon. She listened, but could hardly hear anything with the roar of the train rushing along to its destination.

The door easily opened. Inside, the room reeked of cigar and cigarette smoke. In the moment it took for her eyes to adjust to the dimness, she caught sight of a figure crouched beside a shoeless foot stretched into the aisle. Cicely had managed to slip her Enfield into her coat pocket before leaving for luncheon, waving the Hilliers ahead of her. Now she reached in and curled her fingers around it. Her heart beat so loudly it seemed impossible only she could hear it. Bracing herself, she fit both hands on her weapon. Her shoes were silent on the thin carpet until a shard of glass crunched under her foot.

A dark head shot up, and the squatting form reached for something in his pocket. The face remained in shadow, but she saw the shape well enough to aim at his forehead.

"Stop!" Cicely cried. She steadied herself despite the sway of the train. "This is a revolver, and I'm an excellent shot. Stand up and bend over the table behind you. Now!"

The man, of medium height, rose slowly. His dark clothing blended with the shadows. She needed some light, damn it! Why were the blinds drawn? Where was the switch? The trespasser didn't utter a word, but did as she ordered.

"Place your arms above your head. That's it, toward the window. Spread your legs wide." Her eyes darted about, frantically searching for the lightswitch . . . and in that split second, her prisoner moved. Like lightning, he threw a glass at her and tore toward the carriage door.

The goblet struck her head and splashed her face. Fire exploded in Cicely's eyes. The Enfield dropped from her grasp like a hot coal, and she screamed. The more she blinked, the more the spirit invaded her eyes. Ripping a handkerchief from her pocket, she dabbed roughly at the liquid. The worst of the pain was past, but tears were still running down her cheeks, and so she made her way back to the bar, found the faucet and saturated her handkerchief. Leaning over the basin, she bathed her face for several minutes. When she grabbed a dry bar towel, she heard a moan. She froze.

Whipping around, she saw nothing she hadn't before. Spotting her Enfield, she took it up and wiped her dripping face on her sleeve.

"Who's there?" she asked. Again, her heart beat like a drum in her chest. Adrenaline raced hot through her veins. She crept up the aisle between the tables and booths. The hair on her neck stood on end, and she could feel perspiration beginning to drip between her shoulder blades. At last she reached the booth from which the strange man had appeared. She darted forward so that the booth was in front of her, so no one could surprise her, and unlocked the safety catch on her revolver.

The crumpled heap in the booth moaned again. Cicely replaced her pistol's safety catch and sighed, set the weapon on the table.

Bending down, she took the form by the lapels of his uniform jacket, attempting to pull the man upright. "Bloody hell, Alistair, at your age you should know better than to drink so much, especially so early in the day."

He was dead weight and gave no response, so she slapped his face several times. It was then that she noticed his uniform jacket was unbuttoned, and one of his trouser pockets was turned inside out. And one of his shoes was half off. Promptly she bent to pull it completely off, and felt inside. Nothing. She seized the other shoe from the floor like a madwoman. Nothing.

Collapsing to her knees, she stared at his feet in shock.

Now she truly knew what it meant to have the wind taken out of one's sails. Oh God, they'd given up the code. The man who'd taken it had likely jumped off the train by now. Bloody dangerous act, jumping off a train, but if he stayed on, he would be running the risk that she and Alistair would eventually track him down. No, the code was long gone.

Numbly she stood, made her way to bar and filled a glass with water. Returning to Alistair she unceremoniously dumped it over his head.

He spluttered and blinked his eyes open. Giving her a silly grin, and slurring his words, he said, "You're bootiful, Shicely. Have I tol' ya tha'?"

Sighing, she flung herself in the seat opposite. "Too little, too late, Alistair," she muttered.

He blinked at her again, and managed to sit up by himself. "Ish never too late, lass." He looked about the bar car as if confused. "How did we come here?" At least his speech was improving. He took another look at his surroundings and rubbed his eyes. "By the way, where is here?"

Cicely leaned back in her seat, totally deflated. "The bar car, darling. Where you've spent the last several hours getting rat-arsed. You're completely pissed. Squiffy. Sloshed. Sozzled."

Alistair squared his shoulders. "I am *not* drunk. Haven't—" He stopped, smacking his lips and studying the table at which he sat. His eyes widened when he spied the empty glasses. "Daresay I might've indulged in a few"—he sniffed one of the dead soldiers—"brandies, but I do not gratify myself with an extravagance of liquor, especially at . . ." He eyed at his wristwatch, blinked, held it at arm's length then brought it back close to his face.

"What the devil time is it, anyway?" he demanded, his voice testy.

"Nearly three o'clock in the afternoon. You left the compartment around eight A.M."

His eyes nearly bugged out. "Seven hours! And you're just now waking me? Why didn't you come sooner?"

"Alistair, look at yourself." Cicely gestured to his uniform jacket. "Now look at your feet. What happened?" she demanded in a sharp tone.

"What the devil?" He quickly surveyed himself, then stood a bit unsteadily and headed for the bar.

"Good God, Alistair! Tell me you're not going for the hair of the dog, please. I need you sober. A good dose of java is what you need."

Alistair threw her an irritated glance over his shoulder. "No, you widget. We were drinking from a bottle of Remy—I do remember that. But it's not on the table." He paused and walked back to her. "And there are only two glasses here."

"So?"

"There were three of us. A chap named . . . Wis . . . Wilson, Wil . . . Wilkins! That's it: Terence Wilkins! He bought a bottle of Remy." He paced between Cicely and the bar. "That's it—Barnes, a dark fellow, veterinary, and Wilkins of the postal service."

Cicely felt an angry throbbing in her temple. Making an effort to keep her voice low, she said, "What on Earth were you doing, drinking with two strangers? We must be suspicious of *everyone*."

Alistair could have hit himself. What *had* he been thinking? He'd been attempting not to think of her.

Cicely continued. "I found a dark-haired chap crouched beside you when I entered. I drew the Enfield, but he threw a glass at me with brandy in it. He's long gone. And Alistair, so is your copy of the code. He searched your person and your feet. He found it, and now both are gone." Cicely buried her head in her hands. All was lost. Emotions swirled in her like a lightning storm. She felt as if she were drowning and couldn't even weep. But that would happen later, when she fully comprehended the disaster. Much later.

She heard Alistair sit down, then heard a crackle of paper. He grasped her chin, raising her head, and waved something in her face.

"It was in my sock, Cicely. Not my shoe. It's safe."

Cicely began to weep. Torrents. She wept for her own lost innocence at Bletchley. She wept for her neighbours, those two dear old ladies, now dead. She wept for those who perished in the nightly bombings she might have saved. She wept because she'd enjoyed the most wonderful night of her life with a man she could never have.

And she also wept—stupidly, she realized—for the code they'd never lost.

FIFTEEN

And drinking largely sobers us again . . .
—Alexander Pope

For a moment, Alistair simply gaped at Cicely. He never would have imagined seeing her thus: helpless, weeping. Together they'd experienced an air raid, murders—she'd nearly been thrown from a train, and still she remained the strongest woman he'd ever met. Generally, he knew how to deal with weeping females: give them a handkerchief and pat them on the back. But witnessing Cicely so vulnerable, so broken, softened his heart.

Perhaps keeping so many secrets did wear on her conscience. Given second consideration, it shouldn't be surprising she'd finally broken.

No, not broken. Not Cicely. This was simply a good cry. If he knew her at all, she would dry her eyes and emerge from this episode stronger, more determined than ever.

Still feeling wobbly, he made his way behind the bar. Filling a glass with water for her and dampening a cloth, he listened to Cicely's sobs weaken, dwindle to gasping breaths. For some reason, hearing her try to regain control of her emotions struck him more profoundly than the sound of her weeping had.

He returned to Cicely's side, set the glass on the table

135

and handed her the cool cloth. Several minutes passed before she sat up and blotted her face. Her nose was red, her eyes swollen, and she looked exhausted.

"My apologies. I can't remember when last I made such a fuss." A hiccup escaped her lips.

"Rubbish. Likely it was far overdue. You keep it all locked inside you, lass. It's bound to break loose sometime."

Cicely gave him a weak smile, and he felt the urge to take her in his arms, to tell her everything would work out tickety-boo. But chances were, this scheme would end in disaster, so he didn't bother lying.

Needing some distance from her, he stood and cleared the table of dirty glasses and full ashtrays. Rooting about behind the bar, he found another towel. Coming back, he wiped down the table and sat opposite her.

"The tension is wound too tight in me as well," he admitted. "That's why I was here drinking with two blokes I didn't know. I should have known better." He shook his head, watched her sip the water. She didn't raise her eyes.

"The Remy that Wilkins chap bought isn't at the bar. I kind of liked the fellow, so I want to believe he took the bottle with him when he left—although it's damned unsporting to leave someone passed out. I suppose whatever drug I ingested could still be in that bottle. I didn't see anyone do anything to my glass.

"Now the foreign sort of chap was right queer." Alistair rubbed his chin and stared off into space over Cicely's shoulder. "You caught him going through my pockets? He didn't seem intoxicated?"

Cicely finally looked at him. She shook her head. "All I saw was that he was crouched in front of you. I didn't actually see him search you."

"What else could he have been doing? Why else would

he throw a full glass at you and tear off like a bat out of hell?"

"Perhaps because I pointed an Enfield at his head."

"Touché." Alistair grinned. He should have known. "I suppose that might do it. Of course, not many men expect a woman knows how to shoot," he joked.

She rubbed her eyes and tried to focus. "I didn't manage a good look at him. From where I stood, he was in shadow. Dark hair and a medium build are all I really could see. And he was quite sober, if his excellent aim and sprint are anything to go by."

"Which leads me to think he doctored the brandy. Old Wilkins likely wandered off with the bottle quite, er . . ." Alistair tossed her an ironic half-smile, "rat-arsed. Poor fellow could have fallen off the train by now. We should take a shuftie."

Cicely stood. "Later. Innocent victim or not, he's not our first responsibility. We both need a good strong coffee. I'll muck about at the bar, see what I can find."

Several minutes later, she returned with two steaming cups, remarking, "The steward left in a hurry. He left on the tap." Sipping her coffee, she grimaced. "A bit rough, I'm afraid. Didn't want to take the time for it to percolate, but it's the strongest either of has enjoyed since before the war." She canted her head to one side. "Do you think Wilkins bribed the steward to leave when he bought that bottle? Nothing is locked up. These days undiluted coffee, tea, and cream are of more value than spirits. And not turning off the hot water is a serious offense on a train."

Alistair rubbed his eyes. His head was beginning to pound. "He told us the steward went to help with luncheon. We made toasts, I watched them drink."

"Were both these chaps well-to-do?" Cicely rummaged

in her pocket for a cigarette. Alistair declined when she offered him one. She drew on her cigarette, then threw him a startled look. "Do you still have your wallet, money, and ration book? We were so concerned about the co—*paper*," she corrected herself, "that we could be making Ben Nevis out of an old Saxon burial mound."

"Bloody hell!" exclaimed Alistair, realizing she was right. Immediately he checked the breast pocket on the inside of his uniform, and found every note of Sterling accounted for and his ration book. He leaned back in relief, commenting, "Actually, only Wilkins appeared well-off. The veterinary chap, Barnes, wore threadbare clothing— like most of the populace nowadays." He gave Cicely descriptions of both men.

Cicely ground out her cigarette and swallowed the last of her coffee. "Isn't it reasonable to believe the steward should have returned by now?"

Alistair shrugged and stood. A wave of dizziness hit him, and his head pounded harder. The carriage swam before him. "Good lord, I haven't felt this dicky since my salad days." He laughed, but it didn't hold much humour.

"There's aspirin in my overnight case. I'll give you a couple when we return to our compartment, but let's begin searching out those chaps in the cars behind this," Cicely suggested.

Alistair shrugged. "To avoid traffic through the drinks carriage, the cars behind are usually extra baggage and supplies to be delivered en route. They should be locked. Still, let's have a go anyway," he agreed.

He was right; the back carriage was locked. Instead, they went toward the head of the train. It proved excruciatingly slow going. The passageways of several cars were crowded with passengers stretching their legs, forthing and backing to the lavatories, and socialising. Blinds were drawn on several compartments. The smoke was thick, and several men sipped from flasks. Spotting two young able-bodied men in civilian clothes shouldn't be hard, but Cicely, suspiciousness ingrained in her, studied each face on the off chance their foes had disguised themselves.

When at last they reached their own compartment, Alistair nearly sprinted past, heading for the next carriage.

Cicely shook her head. "Why, Alistair, don't you want those aspirin? My portmanteau is just inside."

Alistair whipped around, but his eyes were wide and his face flushed. "No! Yes, but not now. We need to cover these last ten carriages or so before supper starts."

"It will only take a moment, Alistair," Cicely suggested, reaching for the compartment door.

"No!" He seized her arm, nearly dragging her out onto the platform between cars. "Are you kidding? The way that scatty bird chatters? We'll be into next week before escaping."

They were outside now, and Cicely had to laugh. "You did set yourself up, dear."

He wheeled around, glaring. She could actually see the pulse beating in his temple. He opened his mouth, appeared to change his mind, and shut it. He opened the door to the next car and gestured her through. When she did so, he growled, "You can damned well give me four of your bloody aspirin. It's the least of what I'll need putting up with you both. Skin and blister, trouble and strife—too right," he complained.

"Now, now, Alistair, calm yourself. This is no place for a wobbler." Cicely bit her lip to keep from laughing more.

139

"Wobbler my arse!" he hissed in her ear.

She ignored him. Walking over to a group of three Yanks in army uniforms, she said, "Good afternoon, gentlemen. I wonder if you could help my brother and me. We're looking for our cousin and his traveling companion."

One sandy-haired soldier studied her from head to toe. "Duchess, we'll do anything for you," he said. He winked at her lasciviously.

One of his mates put an elbow in his ribs. "Cantrell, you gotta knock off that hooch, chum. Her brother is bigger than you."

Alistair loomed behind Cicely, a dark look on his face. He described Wilkins and Barnes, then added, "Men will be men, so I'm not concerned about them. But my sister is anxious."

"Blond with an eyepatch. . . . Believe I did see him," the sandy-haired Cantrell answered. "But can't remember where. Sorry. We'll spread the word, miss. Where can we find you?" He winked at her again.

"You'll likely find us in the dining car. Thanks chaps," Alistair said. Nodding, he urged Cicely forward by exerting pressure on the small of her back. He grumbled in her ear, "Aye, he's seen Wilkins like he's seen a unicorn. He's just interested in you."

Cicely smiled and patted his arm. "You're my brother, Alistair, and with you looking out for me, he shan't get fresh."

Alistair's eyes blazed briefly, then they continued down the passageway.

It was nearly 5:30 when they reached the dining car, but they still hadn't spotted their prey. Seating for the evening meal had just begun, and they were shown to a small table by a window, which of course was covered tightly by a blackout blind.

Instead of wine, they ordered coffee. Both surveyed the dining car while sipping the steaming brew. Abruptly, Cicely pushed her cup and saucer away and leaned closer to Alistair.

"As a Special Branch inspector, do you possess the tools to pick locks?"

He looked at her. "Yes, but not with me. I didn't think to add them to the list I gave my friend of things to collect for me." He lowered his voice and guessed, "You want into those baggage and supply carriages."

She nodded. "I've got hair grips and pins. Will those work?"

"Tweezers?"

Cicely thought for a moment, mouth pursed. "Yes. Can you do it?"

Alistair leaned back in his chair, rubbing his neck. "It's worth a try. No promises. And even if we get in, we may not be able to move about. All those cases and trunks sometimes reach to the ceiling." He lifted his coffee cup and said casually, "Flag down the steward. Your knife is missing."

Looking down at the table, Cicely frowned. "Don't be sill—"

"We may need it for lock breaking—if picking fails."

"Of course." She slipped the knife in her place setting into her pocket and raised her hand for the steward.

Cicely tied the belt to her dressing gown securely around her waist, bent to stuff her jimjams under the settee cushion in the ladies' lounge, then slipped on her winter coat. As soon as she and Alister finished their search of the

141

supply carriages, she would slip back here, out of the street clothes she wore under her dressing gown, and back into her sleeping apparel. Alistair would do the same. This way, if they were seen, they merely resembled insomniacs or sleepwalkers. Of course, depending on how late it was when they returned—or how early—she might only have to remove the dressing gown.

She shivered as she stepped into the passageway to await Alistair. It didn't appear that the train was stopping for the night, and it would be cold as they stood between cars and picked that lock.

When she and Alistair had returned from supper, the Hilliers were just themselves leaving for the dining car. Lydia, the clever creature, bored with Alistair's absence, had made the acquaintance of the two middle-aged gentlemen in the next compartment, and put forth the idea that Alistair and her father should sleep with them in their compartment, and that the ladies of the two compartments should all sleep in the other.

"So much more proper when the gentlemen aren't family," Lydia had urged. Lydia's mother as usual didn't care, and Cicely thought she knew why. She'd come upon Mrs. Hillier in the ladies' lounge tucking a good-sized cobalt bottle into her purse. Mrs. Hillier acted a bit too casual, and for the first time Cicely had noticed the woman's slightly glazed eyes. Mrs. Hillier could be an addict, or perhaps was suffering from a cancerous disease like Adele. It would certainly prove interesting to discover just what the substance was. If the woman was an addict, it was all the more surprising. It was hard to obtain a narcotic, as the bulk of those medicines went to soldiers.

The door to one of the gents' toilets opened, and Cicely glanced over expecting to see Alistair. But it wasn't him.

She froze in terror and turned away, hoping the man had missed seeing her face. Her heart beat so fast it seemed very possible it would leap out of her chest. A moment later she heard the carriage door open and close. She took a deep breath and turned around.

Alistair emerged from another of the gents' toilets. He was attired similarly to her, and she ran to him.

"Th-that man. You must follow him quickly. Bring him back here." She paused to catch her breath. "He's medium height, large belly, nearly bald—resembles a labourer. He left for the next carriage. Or maybe the next one." Her voice rose to an hysterical note. "Go. *Go!*"

Alistair nodded. "Stay here," he ordered, and then he was gone.

It seemed hours that Cicely waited, and more than once she started for the carriage door. Always she stopped herself. She paced, she shivered, and she caressed the Enfield in her pocket.

At last, Alistair returned. He was alone. He shook his head as he approached. "Made a few enemies, I'm afraid," he said quietly. "I'll own the reputation as a masher by morning. Acted the jolly drunk who'd lost his compartment." He half-grinned. "Ladies really should lock their compartment doors. And the men cursed, threw shoes or pillows at me. Searched through two cars. Obviously your friend escaped. He locked his compartment. By the way, just who *was* I chasing?"

"One of the men following me in London. He was very consistent. Easy to recognise, too, because he always dressed in labourer's togs." Cicely leaned bonelessly against the blinded window.

"Did he ever threaten you?" Alistair asked.

"His presence was threatening in itself."

143

"Well, let's hope that's the end to the excitement tonight." Alistair straightened the dressing gown under his coat. "Come on, let's see if we can accomplish any breaking and entering now. Of course, it might be a blessing if we can't pick those locks. I'm still knackered from this afternoon. I'll be dead on my feet tomorrow."

Cicely arched a brow. "Not to worry, darling. Lydia will be only too happy to lead you about."

Ready to open the carriage door, Alistair stilled and regarded her in amusement. A lock of his wavy hair rested on his brow. *"Meee-owww,"* he mocked.

Cicely examined her manicure. "Really, Alistair, a woman isn't fully developed until she's grown claws."

His eyes roved down her well-covered body. "As a man I possess a different idea of a woman's development." He grinned.

"Cheeky blighter. Open the door," Cicely commanded. But she wasn't displeased.

They met few passengers in the fifteen cars they traversed. Once they entered the dark drinks carriage, Alistair removed a torch from his pocket. He pointed it around the car. Finding it empty, they made their way to the end. At the back door, Alistair stopped.

"It's going to be bloody difficult for you to hold the light steady and for me pluck the damned lock out there. Just don't drop the torch," he ordered. She nodded.

Outside, between the cars, the icy wind tore at their clothing and drops of snow and rain beat at their faces. Cicely was glad she'd tied her hair back, and she tucked it into her jumper.

Alistair tried the tweezers first. On his second try, they dropped from his nearly numb fingers.

"Hell and damnation! Shine the torch over here," he

shouted over the noise of the rushing train. He indicated a spot next to his left foot.

Cicely took a step back and braced her feet wide for balance. There, just a few inches from the edge of platform, were the tweezers.

Seizing the door handle with one hand, Alistair bent, his fingers crawling along the platform toward the tool. But as the train moved into a turn, Cicely lost her footing and careened into Alistair. Both of them tumbled, and Cicely landed on Alistair. The torch went rolling, following the tweezers, and Alistair made a mad grab for it, only barely snatching it back.

After a moment Cicely attempted to stand. Panting, she leaned against the drinks-car door. "We needn't chase any of the tools. Even the torch isn't worth falling off the train. Alistair? Can you get up?"

He groaned. "I bashed my bad knee on the way down."

"Here, take my arm, I'm braced against the carriage," Cicely offered.

"Think you can lift me, do you?" Alistair asked. He gave a ghost of a laugh.

Cicely grimaced and placed his arm around her shoulder. "We've no choice, so heave-ho."

Several minutes passed while Alastair attempted to gain his footing. At last, propped against the drinks carriage door with Cicely, he let loose a string of curses and wrapped both hands around his knee. But he was standing.

Taking the torch from Alistair's pocket, Cicely handed it to him and said, "Give me the knife, and point this at the lock."

"It's a waste of time, Cicely," he argued. "Picking that wee besom will take luck and an expert, without the proper tools."

"The knife, Alistair, please," Cicely said, determined.

Alistair handed her the knife. "You'll need two tools, lass. One to open the tumbler pins, the other to manipulate the lock."

Cicely ignored him and slid the thin blade into the padlock. When it hit the mechanism, she gave a good jab and turned the knife. The lock opened.

"I'll be damned," Alistair said in wonderment. Then he limped forward to help with the door.

Lydia Hillier was dreaming, and she smiled in her sleep. *She* was walking down the aisle instead of her sister, and that handsome Major Bennington was waiting for her with the priest by the altar. It was spring and the war was over. The church overflowed with guests and flowers. At home, the manor servants squeezed more and more food onto groaning outdoor tables. There were hams, joints, legs of lamb, beefsteaks, every kind of cheese imaginable, clotted creams, cakes.

Her wedding gown was perfection: yards of the finest white silk, intricate lacework, and real pearls sewn into the bodice. Orange blossoms decorated her veil.

They were exchanging vows, Alistair smiling down at her. The priest said something about anyone objecting to the union, and suddenly the church door reverberated under blow after blow after blow. Everyone stared at the back of the church as the door began to cave in . . .

Lydia started up in bed. Someone was banging on the door! The three other ladies sharing the compartment for the night all peeked out from their bedcurtains. One, wearing a puffy pink nightcap, screamed and disappeared behind her curtain again.

Another, one with hair in curlers, shouted, "Oh my

God! It's the Jerries come to murder us in our beds! Where's my Clive? Clive! Steward! Help!"

The third lady, her short brown hair mussed, simply stared at the door, her eyes wide and her mouth open.

Lydia's mother snored.

"Open up in there! This is the steward, and it's an emergency! Open the door!"

Slowly, Lydia climbed down off her top bunk. Something didn't seem quite right, yet if the train had caught fire she wasn't going to be left behind. None of the other ladies made a move, so she walked to the compartment door, unlocked and opened it.

Sixteen

He who would search for pearls must dive below.
—John Dryden

Pitch blackness and a temperature only slightly warmer than the outside air greeted Alistair and Cicely in the baggage and supply car. Mustiness assailed their nostrils. Closing the door behind them, they stood silently listening and trying to acclimate their eyes to the darkness.

At first Cicely felt relieved to be out of the frigid wind, but now, in this black void, she sensed hysteria rising in her. No beginning, no end, no nothing. She bit off of a scream, sternly telling herself claustrophobia had never killed anyone. Drove them crazy, yes. Reaching out a trembling hand, she grasped Alistair's arm.

"Turn on the torch. Now, Alistair!" she ordered in near desperation.

"Half a minute, lass," he replied, fumbling in his pockets.

At last the light appeared, flitting about the trunks and luggage piled up along the walls, with only a narrow path left down the middle of the car. Dust filled the air, and there were probably rodents inhabiting the place. Cicely's hands fisted. Too damn bad, she told herself; she could ruddy well accomplish anything as long as she had light.

"Damn," Alistair murmured. "I must sit down a moment or you'll be carrying me back. Blasted luck, falling on my bad knee."

Cicely took the torch from Alistair as he sat down on a trunk. Inching forward, she found another trunk standing on its end, cutting off the narrow aisle. Squeezing through the constricted space to the other side, Cicely found herself looking at much the same surroundings, only now she was cut off from Alistair.

The swaying of the train and the bobbing of her torch created strange shadows that ricocheted everywhere. Enough of being spooked, Cicely admonished herself. Down to business! She began studying luggage tags. What she'd really hoped to find were signs of habitation; perhaps whoever had followed them was hiding in one of these back carriages.

Bending close to one case, Cicely heard a surreptitious scratching that made her skin crawl. She closed her eyes, steeling herself. Likely she was about to make the acquaintance of a rat or two. Well, she'd just whack the ruddy thing with her torch. If the torch broke . . . well, she could find her way out with her lighter in a pinch.

Moving a case to one side, she was able to get a better view of a few smaller pieces of luggage. She frowned, examining a rich brown leather portmanteau. It appeared brand-new. It sported bright brass hinges, corner guards, handle, and lock. Who owned a piece like this when leather was rationed and metal was used only for the military? One possibility was a black marketeer. Another, a German spy. The Nazis were known for not skimping, especially not on favoured party members.

"Cicely? Finding anything?" Alistair called from the other end of the car.

"Perhaps. I'm coming back with it," she answered. Giving the rest of the carriage interior a quick survey with the torch, she began making her way back to Alistair.

The shadows still cavorted, making queer shapes on the ceiling and baggage. She shivered. Only a few more feet and she'd be at Alistair's side. Just on the other side of that mammoth trunk blocking the aisle. But . . . was that a shuffle behind her? She whipped about, breathing fast. There were only shadows. No, wait. Something in the back had made a quick movement. Hadn't it?

Quickly Cicely pivoted, and she nearly ran back to Alistair. She felt prone; holding her torch in one hand and the bag in the other, she was in no position to snatch her weapon out of her pocket. But Alistair would protect her.

Cicely dropped the case in front of him, breathless, and pointed the torch at it. "Think you can pick that lock with my hair grips?" she asked.

Alistair straightened from rubbing his leg. Pain shot from his knee to his ankle, and it didn't just ache anymore; he was in bloody agony. He'd been breathing deeply, employing the breathing exercises a nurse in hospital had taught him. Taking one last breath, he clenched his jaw and studied both the case and the lock.

"Fancy case," he managed to grit out. He turned the bag this way and that, leaning into the light. "If all else fails, we can bash the lock with the butt of your Enfield."

"As a *last* resort, Alistair," Cicely remarked. "The owner *might* prove innoce—" She stopped, sensing a movement in her peripheral vision.

A figure loomed up from her side, swinging a Cricket bat.

She screamed and dropped the torch. Everything went dark. She heard the thud of a body slamming into another. Bloody hell! She also heard her Enfield smack onto the floor.

While the two men fought, Cicely knelt on the floor, her fingers scrabbling for anything she could touch, desperately hoping to find the weapon—any weapon.

The men swore, thrashed, and writhed in the darkness. Cicely inched closer to them, reckless in her quest, and received a painful blow to her arm. Her arm seared from her wrist to her shoulder, and she yelped in pain.

"Got him," she heard Alistair grunt, panting. "Turn the bloody torch back on, will you?"

Widening her search, Cicely found the lighter that must have fallen out of her pocket as well, and fumbling with it a moment, finally got it going.

Swinging the light around, she found Alistair on his feet and leaning on a trunk, bent over and breathing heavily. His opponent was curled in the fetal position, groaning and grasping his groin.

Spotting the flashlight, Cicely grabbed it and nearly dropped her lighter, which was now burning her fingers.

Alistair gave a weak smile. "Lucky punch," he said. "Couldn't see a thing. Now let's see who this tosser is."

Apparently recovering, the "tosser" reached for his fallen bat, but Cicely kicked it away. "He looks like a train steward, Alistair."

Alistair frowned. "Doesn't he just. Good God, were you put in here to guard the baggage?"

The man on the floor grunted, then pushed himself to a sitting position. His hair was matted with blood, which had also left dry trails down his face. Alistair hadn't caused that, but he had cut the man's mouth, which was dribbling fresh blood down his chin. The steward squinted up at Alistair and wipcd blood from his chin. "I thought you were him."

"Who?"

"Bludger who crowned me." He gently explored his head with his fingers, and winced. "What time is it? Haven't I been missed?"

Cicely studied her wristwatch. "Nearly half past eleven. At night."

"Um, it is still Saturday?" the steward asked in a small voice.

"Just," Alistair answered.

The steward sighed. "Blighter crowned me just after the last of luncheon. Returned to the lounge carriage, and next thing I know my head explodes and everything goes black. Woke up a few minutes ago. Heard voices and movement. Thought he was returning to finish the job." He studied Cicely and Alistair with new suspicion. "Just who are you two, anyway? What are you mucking about in here for?"

Lydia looked at the conductor and steward on the other side of the door. "Why are you banging on our door in the middle of the night? Is the train on fire?"

"Miss, please excuse our rough entry, but we're searching for two fugitives from the law. May I speak with your husband or father please?"

The lady in the curlers peered out from her bunk curtains. "I was right! We'll be murdered in our beds. Clive! Where are you, Clive?" Her voice was tinged with hysteria.

Lydia pivoted to face her. "Mrs . . . ? I'm sure—"

"Fowler. Mrs. Clive Fowler. Oh, where is Clive? What is the use of a ruddy husband if he isn't there when you need him?"

Lydia turned back to the train officers. "My father is next door, so you will have to tell me."

The conductor and steward looked at each other, hesitating.

"I'm a big girl, so come tell us: Who is so important to find that you terrify a compartment full of women?" Lydia propped her hands on her hips.

"A Mr. Alistair Fielding and Miss Cicely Winterbourne."

Lydia frowned, her hands falling from her waist. "Alistair and Cicely?"

"Yes," the steward spoke up. "They are traveling as Major Alistair Bennington and Cicely Bennington, brother and sister."

SEVENTEEN

False as dicers' oaths . . .
—William Shakespeare

Lydia's mouth fell open, and she backed up until she felt the corner of her mother's bunk. She perched on the edge of it.

"What did they do?" she snapped.

"Nazi spies!" announced the steward.

"Murder, miss. In London. They're on the run," the conductor informed her, jabbing an elbow into the Steward's side.

Spies? Murders? Lydia looked about the compartment in confusion. No, it couldn't be. Not Alistair. It must be some sort of mistake. She didn't believe it. They could not so deceive her. If they had . . . by God, she'd have a thing or two to say to them!

Decisively she turned back to the train officers. "No," she said. "I haven't heard of them. And you needn't bother visiting next door. My father and his, er, friends haven't been anywhere I haven't on this train." With an effort she made her smile flirtatious. "Except, of the course, the ladies lounge. Besides, my father has a bad heart," she lied. "I don't wish for him to be disturbed. He has precious little medicine left."

154

The two men looked doubtful, but they nodded. As soon as the door closed, Lydia parted the drapes to Cicely's bunk. It was empty. She seized her dressing gown from the foot of her own bunk and pulled it on.

Just as she reached the door, Mrs. Fowler startled her. "Why did you tell them not to go next door? My Clive could very well have seen them."

"Don't be ridiculous, Mrs. Fowler." Lydia caught a whiff of a familiar pungent odour. "I don't want my father disturbed, and you certainly don't wish anyone to know you, er, couldn't control your bladder."

Mrs. Fowler gasped in outrage and disappeared behind her curtain. Lydia smirked and left the compartment.

Cicely managed, with a little help from Alistair, to half-carry, half-drag the steward into the drinks carriage. Settling him in a booth, she went to the bar for a glass of water and a wet cloth. Déjà vu, she thought, and rolled her eyes.

She returned to find Alistair sitting against the bulkhead of the train, his bad leg stretched out before him on the bench seat. "I don't suppose, ministrating angel that you are, you could find a hot water bottle for my leg?" he asked. "A generous dose of opium or laudanum would do even better. I'd even settle for sodium pentothal."

Cicely gave him a piercing look and attended to the other man, wiping the blood from his face and hair, taking a closer look at his head wound. She ignored the ache in her own arm.

Apparently, the steward believed their tale of searching out Cicely's suitcase, which contained jewelry that she had mistakenly given to the porter for storage.

Alistair shrugged. "Wishes and dreams." Then he addressed the steward. "I say, what's your name, old chap? Did you happen to see anything before you were bludgeoned?"

"Bill, sir. And yes, as a matter of fact I did catch a glimpse—of you, passed out over there." He pointed to the booth where Alistair awoke. "And that dark-haired fellow as well. Didn't see the chap with the eyepatch who bought the Remy."

"Don't usually sell by the bottle, do you?" Alistair asked. He stopped rubbing his leg and studied Bill.

The man flushed. "Er, no guv, we don't. But he gave me an extra fiver."

Both Cicely and Alistair's brows rose in surprise. Five pounds was a fortune. Bill tenderly felt his injured scalp and winced.

"Is there a medical kit in this car?" Cicely asked. Nursing the two men, she knew their snooping was at an end for the night.

Bill fished in his waistcoat pocket, brought out a small keyring and told Cicely where to find the kit. Going to the cabinet above the bar, Cicely retrieved and opened the box, which was large enough to hold nine or so tins of vegetables. She found gauze, plasters, alcohol, several vials and a hypodermic needle.

"First I'm cleaning this with alcohol, so it will sting a little, Bill," she said, reaching to tend the steward's wound.

The poor man jumped and let out a strangled cry when the alcohol touched him. "Bloody— Excuse me, Miss, but it doesn't sting a little. It smarts like billy-oh!"

"Almost done," murmured Cicely, next applying iodine. She leaned back and eyed his head with an amused expression. "When I am done, your bandage will pass for a turban. Now tell me, Bill, what is in those vials?"

"Morphine," he replied. "But I shan't take any. Not for a head wound. Must stay awake, as I likely have a concussion."

"Are you trained in giving hypodermics, Bill?" Cicely asked. She placed a thick pad of gauze on his injury and began winding a bandage around his head.

"Yes, Miss," the steward said proudly.

"Before we came upon you, my brother suffered a painful fall on the platform. His tussle with you worsened it. Would you be so kind as to give him a needle of that morphine?"

When Bill didn't answer, Cicely pointed out, "He can barely walk, Bill, and he's got German shrapnel lodged in his knee."

The steward reflected for a moment. "Seeing as he is a soldier, I suppose I wouldn't be doing any harm," he finally agreed.

"Hate to admit it, old chap, but I could really use it," Alistair remarked. "It's throbbing like the Devil's pitchfork is at it."

Cicely tied off Bill's bandage and pushed the medical kit toward him. She watched him remove a hypodermic from its sanitary package and upend a vial on the needle. When she glanced at Alistair, she noticed for the first time he'd lost his dressing gown—probably in the scuffle with Bill. If Alistair noticed he said nothing, merely struggled to remove his coat and uniform jacket, and to roll up the sleeve of his shirt.

Bill tied a length of rubber around Alistair's upper arm and tapped the inside of his elbow before inserting the needle into a vein. While the steward was busy, Cicely popped a needle and morphine vial into her pocket.

Finished, Bill rolled the hypodermic in a sheet of paper and placed it and the empty vial into the medicine box, then returned it to the proper cabinet.

Cicely could see the morphine was already taking effect. "Before you become insensible, Alistair, let me help you on with your jack—"

The door to the carriage suddenly flew open, and Lydia burst in. Her wide frightened eyes darted between the steward and Alistair. Cicely watched the girl take a deep breath and smooth her hands down her dressing gown.

Bill looked quizzically at Lydia. "The lounge car is closed, miss," he said.

"Oh," she replied brightly, with a dismissive wave of her hand as she joined Alistair and Cicely. "I was looking for my friends and here they are."

"I'll leave you to them, then." Bill busied himself cleaning up behind the bar.

With a grimace of pain, Alistair moved his leg so Lydia could sit. Cicely frowned and sat opposite. Lydia glanced nervously at Bill, then gazed at them with angry glint in her eye and twin spots of colour on her cheeks.

"I want to know," she announced in imperious whisper, "did you two murder someone in London?"

Cicely gasped. *"What?"*

Alistair paused in his battle with his jacket to stare.

Lydia pursed her lips and nodded; their reactions told her all she needed to know. "Train officials are banging on every compartment door searching for you. They are working their way up to the dinning car."

"Good God, Lydia! Did you approach us believing we may indeed be murderers?" Alistair stared at her.

Lydia tossed her head. "They also claim you are spies—and not brother and sister. Are you spies?"

Alistair buried his head in his hands. Cicely frowned and asked, "My dear, what would you have done had we admitted to being murderers? Weren't you afraid? We might have murdered you to keep you quiet."

"Oh!" Lydia's eyes bugged out. "I really hadn't thought of that. I really didn't believe you to *be* murderers." She lowered her eyes. "I thought . . . well, I thought if you were guilty I might be just the one to apprehend you—or at least inform on you. If not, to warn you." She shrugged. "For once perhaps *I* might garner attention instead of my sister."

Cicely reached for Lydia's hand and rubbed it between her palms. "Lydia, thank you for warning us, but you must never embroil yourself in situations you know nothing about. You might get yourself killed. Go back to your compartment and stay safe."

At first the girl appeared rebellious, then at last seemed to emerge from her fantasy world. She stood, hesitated a moment, and started to walk away.

Alistair immediately turned to Cicely. "They think they can get it by arresting us," he ground out between clenched teeth. "Damn, the morphine is taking effect."

"Except they aren't real coppers," agreed Cicely.

In an instant, Lydia pivoted and stood facing them with her hands on her hips. "What are we going to do?"

We? Cicely gazed at Alistair. His eyes were glassing over. Making a decision, she seized Lydia's hand in both of hers. "Listen carefully. Someone is trying to kill us because we possess an item they need desperately. But we—Britain—need it even more. I can't tell you anything else or you'll be in as acute danger as we are."

159

Lydia's eyes became saucers; then she threw back her shoulders. "I'm a patriot. Tell me what to do. I will do whatever I must for my country."

Cicely squeezed her eyes shut momentarily. The girl was a complete innocent and had no idea of reality. She lived in her own world. Yet perhaps, if Lydia reached deeply enough, she would find steel under the surface. This might prove a chance to find out. Immediately Cicely was sorry for any unkind comments she'd made about this girl. She thought for a moment. "This is what we'll do—return to our compartment to retrieve my portmanteau and Alistair's bag. I hope by then the steward will have left and we can hide in a baggage car until the next stop."

Lydia looked critically at her. "They know what you look like. You'll have to use a disguise. Cover your hair turban-style with a large bar towel, otherwise you'll be a dead giveaway."

Cicely did as the girl suggested and, leaving Alistair dozing and Bill cleaning, the pair began the tedious trip traveling back through the train carriages. They were fortunate; at the late hour they passed very few passengers.

When they reached their compartment, Lydia whispered, "Stay here, or that old cow Fowler will say something."

Cicely waited on tenterhooks in the passageway, ready to sprint into the ladies lounge if anyone came upon her. In a moment Lydia appeared again with her case, then disappeared into the next compartment to fetch Alistair's bag. Once Lydia returned, the two women made the journey back to the lounge carriage.

Both felt brave and a little cocky for successfully retrieving the two traveling bags. Lydia giggled at a joke she'd made and entered the lounge car first. Cicely stepped in behind her, only to stop short when Lydia backed up, treading on her toes.

"Ouch, Lydia—" Cicely froze.

A handsome blond man with a black eye patch held a Luger to Alistair's head.

"Welcome, ladies," the stranger said, smiling.

EIGHTEEN

When sorrows come, they come not single spies,
but in battalions . . .
—William Shakespeare

The blond stranger's left hand was buried in Alistair's hair, holding his head up. Alistair blinked, his eyes glazed from the morphine. Bill the steward sat next to him on the bench seat, his face ashen.

"Come, join the gentlemen in this cozy booth," the blond man politely requested, as if they were all attending a garden party.

When Lydia didn't move, Cicely grasped her shoulders and urged her forward. The poor girl trembled and stared horrified at the man with the gun.

Cicely closed her eyes briefly and took a deep breath, attempting to control her own fear. A prickling sensation crawled down her spine, and her skin blossomed with goose flesh. Even her knees were feeling shaky. This was it then. They were to die like the others. Graham, Rupert, Vi, Adele, and Flynn—how many people had this man murdered? So much for one's whole life playing out before one's eyes; only regrets came to Cicely's mind. What she *should* have done, and the actions for which she was ashamed.

Cicely's eyes were drawn like a magnet to Alistair. *No!*

By God, no. There were things she had yet to accomplish. One of which was getting this code to the right people. Another was showing Alistair she needn't justify herself to him. By no means was she perfect, but she'd done her part to save all they knew and loved—and she would continue to do so.

Throwing off her fear, she buzzed with adrenaline. She forced a cool facade to her features. Wrapping an arm around Lydia, she walked toward the killer.

"Well, aren't you a dasher?" she said, nearly dragging Lydia with her. "No wonder you haven't been caught."

The blond nodded, gave a laugh and snapped his heels together. "You are too kind, my dear."

"You might just as well tell us your name. I take it you *are* planning to kill us?" Cicely pushed Lydia, who still acted like a zombie, into the booth.

The blond man laughed. "Quite right, dear Miss Winterbourne. Manfred Richter at your service."

"Kill us?" Lydia shrilled. She buried her face in hands, sobbing.

Richter sighed. "If you hadn't played Miss Busybody, *you* wouldn't be here." He shrugged. "There's really nothing to be frightened of. If you are still, my aim will bc true and you won't feel a thing. I promise." He smiled, and Lydia sobbed even louder.

Cicely canted her head to one side. Inside, adrenaline licked at her body like a flame. "I believe, Herr Richter, that you are a sadist. You really should control that part of yourself. It might prove your downfall."

Richter frowned. "You pretend to know me, Miss Winterbourne. Don't. I assure you, your attempts at threats are comical."

Cicely forced herself to laugh. "Threats, Herr

Richter? Come, you are aware of just how amateur I am. I'm scared to bloody death. But I don't like dying in ignorance. So tell me—does frightening and murdering innocent women excite you? Do you perform . . . vile acts upon the bodies after death?" She took Alistair's box of Woodbines and his silver lighter off the table. Giving Richter a curious glance over the tip of a cigarette, she braced herself and said, "Or is it men that excite you?"

Spot on! Her question drew blood. Richter leaned forward past Alistair's head, his face red and twisting grotesquely. "Dooly claimed you were a bush bumper. He—"

The door crashed open and a thickset bald man in labourer's togs stood framed in the doorway—the man who'd followed her for the past week, whom Alistair had gone in search of earlier that night. He pointed an old Webley .38 revolver at Richter.

Oh God, a Webley! Cicely thought, staring at the weapon. No other handgun had been proven more capable of bringing a man down—if the operator were practised. Not many were, as it was a Great War–era pistol, and overweight.

Alistair fought his delirium. Taking the opportunity of Richter's surprise, he wrenched his head out of his captor's loosened grip and seized the man's gun hand. The sudden movements made his head spin, but he managed to knock the German off balance—but Richter dragged him down, too. Alistair's instincts to survive overcame his weakness from the morphine, and before his foe could recover, Alistair bashed the man's gun hand on the table, sending the weapon skittering away.

Too late, Bill reached for the gun. Richter dived under

the table to get it, but he collapsed when shot twice—once in the bottom, which was the largest target not under the table, and once behind the knee—by the newcomer's revolver.

"One down," the newcomer commented, making his way to the fallen German and giving him a good kick.

Cicely closed her eyes. Oh lord, did he mean there were still three to go?

Eyes wide and shining with tears, Lydia stared at the man. Bill did the same.

Alistair's voice came out gravelly: "Who are you?" He placed his hand on his knee but didn't rub it; the less this stranger knew, the better.

"Do you have it?" the man asked. His eyes jumped back and forth between Cicely and Alistair.

"W-what?" Cicely managed.

The man curled his lip impatiently and jerked the Webley. "Exactly what this sod was after. *The key*, damn it. The key to the fourth rotor."

Lydia moaned and slumped against the wall. Bill's mouth gaped open. Cicely looked at Alistair, who was now sitting on the floor, but he kept his gaze on the Webley. Who was this man? No discernible foreign accent escaped his lips.

"Key? Rotor? What the hell are you talking about, man?" Alistair demanded.

The stranger grasped his revolver by the barrel and swung the butt at Alistair's jaw. Alistair recoiled, then collapsed with a thud, his head falling against the edge of the table.

Pointing the weapon at Cicely, the stranger said carefully, "Some draw the line at hitting women. I do not. Talk. I want that key."

Cicely felt frozen to her seat, all her adrenaline vanished. She ordered her mind to work, but it remained blank and she felt tears forming in the corners of her eyes.

The man took a menacing step forward, then caressed the curve of her throat with his Webley. "I really don't care if you live or die. I can kill you, search your body and belongings. If I don't find it, I'll visit your compartment and toss it—but not before I kill the inhabitants." He glanced at Lydia. "Your parents are still there, I presume."

Lydia whimpered and turned her face to the wall. "Oh God, Cicely, give him what he wants. *Please.*"

"It-it's in my handbag," Cicely whispered.

"Get it. Now!"

Cautiously, Cicely stood and made her way behind the bar. Frantically scanning the shelves and floor, in the corner she spotted a bulging canvas drawstring sack. As she bent to pick it up, she pulled out a wad of dirty bar towels and slid the Enfield from her pocket into the bag.

When she stood she found the bald stranger behind her, and her heart nearly leapt out her mouth.

"Please back up. You're in my light. Unless you wish me to upend the contents on the bar," she asked. She made a show of rifling through the bag. Only one second to get this right. To aim the Enfield through the bag was the easy part. Pulling back the hammer before he figured out her trick and shot her would prove dicey.

She pretended to drop something. When the man glanced down, she removed the safety and squeezed the trigger. The stranger's eyes went wide with shock, and he looked down at the blossoming red spurting from his stomach. A moment later, he fell.

Lydia screamed, and Bill made gagging sounds. Cicely looked at the gun in her hand in horror, and dropped it like a hot coal. Suddenly everything took on a surreal quality. Her ears buzzed, the room went in and out of focus. She blinked and tried to stay standing, but had to grasp the bar to keep her balance.

Bill tried to revive Alistair by slapping his face, but having no luck, he manoeuvred around him and made his way to the bar, fastidiously avoiding the two bodies on the floor.

After a moment, the room finally righted itself. Cicely knelt to discover if the bald man still lived. He was gasping, and blood poured out of his mouth and down his chin. She gently propped his head in her lap after removing the Webley from his grip. He desperately tried to speak, so Cicely bent over his face. At first he seemed to utter unfamiliar names; then she realised he spoke another language. Russian? But . . . the Russians were their allies. Why would he want to kill them?

"English, please," she urged. "I don't understand Russian."

"Russian?" The steward stood over her with a pitcher of water.

"Please, Bill, help me move him from behind the bar." Cicely grasped the Russian's shirt collar to drag him, but Bill set aside the water pitcher, brushed aside her hands and dragged him toward the table where Lydia sat.

"Y-you have the key?" whispered the wounded man.

"Yes, but why do you want it? You are our allies." Cicely didn't understand.

"Allies?" He managed a weak smile. "We are not *true* allies. The British and American Capitalists only tell us what they want us to know. They leave us in the cold. So we search out the rest." He coughed and attempted to sit up. Bill helped him to lean against the bench seat.

"Water?" Cicely asked.

"No. M-make sure the key is safe. We may not trust you, but . . . we can't fight Hitler by ourselves. Richter cocked up—he let someone steal the code from him before he memorised it. Now he's . . . activating moles . . . to recover it. German High Command . . . is . . . still ignorant . . ." He closed his eyes, and for several moments Cicely thought he might have died. Then his eyes popped open and he seized Cicely's hand with amazing strength. "You mustn't keep a paper copy. Too dangerous. Memorise it!" A gunshot rang out and his eyes widened. A fresh blossom of blood covered his chest.

Cicely turned and saw Richter, half-sitting on his uninjured side holding his Luger. Why hadn't they checked on him? This was all happening too fast. Without thinking, Cicely grabbed the Russian's Webley and shot back. At this range, the pistol couldn't miss. It kicked like a shotgun and sounded like a cannon. Cicely threw it down and scrambled from underneath the Russian.

Two dead men and a lot of blood. She trembled and stared at the gory scene until she heard sputtering. Looking up, she almost laughed hysterically. Bill had poured his water pitcher over Alistair. For the second time that day, Alistair was shaking water off his head.

"What the hell?" he said. Then he groaned and cupped his purpling jaw.

"Alistair, what on earth are we to do now?" Cicely asked. She sighed, feeling totally numb, which she supposed was a blessing. She'd had enough of fear, horror, and tragedy for a lifetime. She leaned on the bar, wishing simply for a large scotch and eight uninterrupted hours of sleep.

"I think that's a good question, guv," Bill said, scratching his head through its bandage.

Alistair fought his dizziness. "Got that Webley, Cicely?" he asked. At her nod, he continued, "Break the lock on the fancy case. I think I know what it contains." Grasping the table, he pulled himself upright.

Cicely nodded. Bill held the well-made leather and brass case steady while she unloaded the hand-cannon of bullets, then bashed away at the lock with the butt. After clearing the remnants of the lock, Cicely opened the case. She gasped and turned it so the others could view the case's contents.

"A bloomin' radio!" Bill's mouth fell open. "German, if you ask me." Studying both Cicely and Alistair for several seconds, he finally said, "This helps prove your case. This is proof these two weren't just anyone. This is proof these berks were spies."

Alistair sighed. "There's no name on the case, Bill. It could belong to anyone. There's no proof, and no question we'll be arrested."

Silence fell momentarily, everyone lost in thought. Cicely went to search the waiter's station and behind the bar for a suitable replacement for the handbag she'd lost a few nights previously; she couldn't very well keep toting her Enfield about in her coat pocket.

Alistair studied the steward. "And what will you say, Bill, when you're questioned about this mess?"

"Well now, guv." The man looked critically at the bodies, then at Alistair. "Seems to me the country's security is at stake."

Face grim, Alistair nodded.

"I see two choices." Bill pulled out a chair and sat. "We

apprise the authorities of these two spies." He frowned. "But then we'll spend our days being grilled by said authorities. They'll want the key that baldy here was going on about." He shrugged. "Of course, they're the right ones to get it."

"But what if they aren't?" Cicely asked.

Bill rubbed his chin. "I'd say you're in a tough situation."

"We could throw them off the train," Lydia piped up in a trembling voice, nodding at the bodies. "Clean up the blood. This could all go away. Like it never happened," she suggested.

Everyone's eyes flew to Lydia. She'd seen far too much already. Cicely didn't know exactly what to say.

"Lydia, go back to your compartment," she said after a moment. She pulled a small bar towel bag, similar to the one that she'd been hiding her Enfield in a few minutes before, from a drawer at the waiter's station, then went to help the girl out of the booth. "Bill, give her a small sherry to calm her and help her sleep."

"I'd rather have rum," Lydia said, showing a bit more life. "It's all the rage you know, and I've never tasted it. Mummy won't let me. All the Yanks drink rum and Coke. You don't happen to stock Coca-Cola do you, Bill?"

Bill gave her the fish eye, then unlocked a cabinet. Pouring a finger of dark liquid, he said, "Just the rum, miss, then off you go to bed. Sleep tight and pleasant dreams."

Lydia nearly choked swallowing the rum, but it was unclear as to whether that was due to Bill's comment or the fiery spirit.

The girl wiped her mouth with the back of her hand and headed for the carriage door. After it shut behind her, Bill set three glasses on the bar, into which he poured generous portions of rum. Then he returned the bottle to its proper place and locked it up.

Alistair limped to the bar and took a rather large sip of rum. Cicely transferred her Enfield, morphine, and the other bits from her deep coat pockets into her new handbag, hooked it around her wrist, and followed Alistair to the bar. She'd never tasted rum, either. Taking a tentative sip, she found it quite delicious, slipping down her throat like sweet lava.

However, just as she set the glass back down, Lydia burst back through the compartment door. "The train officials are coming to arrest you! They're right behind me!"

NINETEEN

I am escaped with the skin of my teeth . . .
—Old Testament

"Right, then. Come on," Bill ordered, making his way around the bar, stopping to pick up Cicely's portmanteau. He paused to grasp Alistair's case and proceeded to the carriage door opposite Lydia. "See if you can delay them a moment, there's a good girl," he called to the girl over his shoulder.

Cicely followed Bill, tightening the drawstrings on her bag as she went. Pivoting to check Alistair's progress, she watched him hobble forward, muttering.

"Hell and damnation, we'll be bloody lucky not to break our legs."

Break a leg hiding in the baggage carriage? She wondered, turning back to follow Bill.

A blast of icy wind blew in when the steward opened the carriage door. Cicely braced herself, then stepped outside. She grasped the handhold, peering into the darkness. From the little she could see, the snow seemed to have disappeared. They must be nearing the Bristol Channel, which meant they weren't that far out of Cardiff.

Then Alistair hobbled up beside her and closed the carriage door behind him. "Thank you, Bill. I think."

"Right, guv. I'll sort it best I can." Then he threw their bags off the train.

"Bill!" Cicely couldn't believe her eyes. "What the bloody hell have you done?" Her mouth dropped open in shock as realisation dawned. Backing up, she thudded into Alistair's chest. "Oh no, I'm not," she said firmly. "No, I am *not* leaping off this train. We can't even see what's out there. Just pop us in the baggage carriage."

"Too late, Cicely. You think they won't look there now, what with two dead bodies back there?" Alistair jerked his head toward the drinks car. "See? The train is slowing. They took one shuftie at the carnage and pulled the emergency brake. They're about to search properly. Now go!"

Cicely scrambled for the handhold on the baggage carriage. She felt it, but when her fingers scudded off she lost her balance and struck Alistair again. Scrabbling forward, desperate for a handhold, she made for the baggage carriage door again.

"We don't have *time,* lass!" he said.

"Noooooo!" Cicely screamed, as she suddenly found herself flying through the air. It was as if her stomach had dropped out of her body. She clamped her eyes shut, even though the blackness outside prevented her from seeing anything.

"Safe journey, guv," Bill said to Alistair, his hand on the door, ready to re-enter the drinks carriage.

"Aye, lad. Same to you," Alistair replied. Then he stepped to the edge of the platform and leaped into nothingness.

Cicely hit the ground hard on her right hip, bounced onto her bottom, and rolled so fast downhill that she lost her breath. Instinctively, she covered her face and head with her hands, until something solid and sharp stopped her dead.

Merciful heavens! She hurt everywhere. Muscles, bones—every square inch of her now ached. Opening her eyes, she saw nothing but shadows. Swinging, dancing shadows. No wonder she was dizzy. She must have rolled a good fifty yards or more. Several more minutes passed before she gingerly sat up. She could see a bit better and realised it was a farmer's rock wall that brought her horrifying journey to an end. Damned jammy her back had hit it; if she'd struck with the front of her body, likely her hands would be broken.

Taking inventory, she discovered a shoe and her new handbag were missing, and that half of her dressing gown was gone. Touching her legs, she knew her stockings were beyond repair, and her tweed skirt sported a rather large rent.

Bracing a hand on the rock wall, she pushed herself to her feet. Clouds covered the sky, so there were no moon or stars to help her see, and the ground proved uneven. It wasn't a plain, but wasn't hilly either.

Crickets buzzed, and hinges on a shed door whined several yards distant. She could hear no train sounds, though. Did that mean it was out of earshot, or had it stopped just after Alistair pushed her off?

"Alistair," she called, just loud enough to travel a few feet. "Alistair?"

She limped forward, and her shoeless foot landed in something thick and squishy. Cicely sniffed. Thank goodness! It was mud, not sheep or cow droppings.

After nearly half an hour of searching, not knowing if she walked in circles or not, she heard a moan.

* * *

Alistair felt hair tickle his face and opened his eyes.

"You are the most difficult man to find, Alistair. How are you feeling? Sorry, forget I mentioned that. Is anything broken?" enquired Cicely.

Above her the wind gusted, propelling clouds across the sky, uncovering the winter stars, giving some meagre light.

"Damn lucky I had that shot of morphine before jumping," he said. He didn't know which throbbed harder, his jaw, knee, or tailbone.

"The morphine softened your landing?" Cicely sounded puzzled.

"The sisters in hospital explained it to me. When one ingests a painkiller or relaxant, one's muscles tend not to tighten and strain when heading for a fall or a smash-up. If the muscles stay relaxed, one isn't as badly hurt." Alistair groaned and attempted to sit upright. "Give me a hand, will you?"

Cicely snorted. "I don't think I shall. You pushed me off that train, Alistair!" she accused.

"Would you have moved if I hadn't?"

"Of course not."

"Aye. And if you *had* jumped on your own, likely you'd be suffering several injuries. The surprise prevented you from tensing. You should be thanking me."

"We'll be ice-skating in the lower regions before I do *that*," Cicely said, helping him to his feet. "That's the barmiest thing I've ever heard. Now . . . I found my missing shoe but not my handbag. Are you all together?"

Alistair winced. He'd gained his feet and everything seemed in place, if he was a bit achy. He tried to make light of their situation. "You'll start a new fashion, wearing only half a dressing gown, my dear. Quite fetching."

Cicely answered dryly, giving him a sideways glance. "You shouldn't speak, *my dear*. Half your face is swollen and purple."

Alistair unbuttoned one of his uniform pockets, extracting a box of matches. "Right, then. I believe we're out of sight and sound of that train. Let's find our baggage before the clouds cover the starlight."

The sky had lightened to grey, but their missing pieces were all found. Alistair and Cicely sat leaning against the rock wall, exhausted.

"What's next, Alistair?" Cicely closed her eyes, resting her head on her folded dressing gown, which was wedged between her and the rocks.

Alistair stretched out and propped his bad leg on top of his case. Sharp pain raced from his hip to his ankle. He wished for more morphine, but he figured he might just as well wish to fly. "I believe we're between Newport and Cardiff. We need to stay clear of public transport, so we must walk or hitchhike south. Once in Cardiff, we can rent—if we have the lolly, and if not . . ." He sighed. "Steal a fishing boat to North Devon."

Cicely yawned. "Can you operate a fishing boat? I have thirty pounds. It's all I have in the world, in fact."

He offered her a half-smile. "I'll operate it. I find I'm performing many feats I never before dared."

Cicely frowned. "We're not crossing Dartmoor, are we?"

Alistair's brown eyes actually twinkled, and she felt her heart skip a beat. "Superstitious?" he asked.

"Not in the least," she snapped, angry with herself for again feeling an attraction to him. "It's notoriously easy to become lost on that bleak landscape. And it's winter—there's no shelter out on that moor. I don't like it, Alistair."

His lips flattened into a thin line. "My sense of direction is excellent, Cicely. We shan't get lost. Besides, I don't see another choice. Once we find the road, we'll simply follow it. We can hitchhike or perhaps board a passing omnibus."

Cicely pushed herself up from the wall. Reaching for her handbag she said, "You need another shot of morphine."

Alistair scowled. "In a perfect world."

Cicely grinned, and held up a hypodermic. "How's this for perfect? Now take off your coat and uniform jacket. This is the last, so I hope it helps."

"How are you?" Alistair asked. Shucking his coat and uniform tunic, he made a fist. He looked her over as she prepared to give him the shot.

Cicely inserted the needle into his arm. "I hurt like the Devil's lorry slammed into me," she grumbled. After giving him the injection, she removed the needle from his flesh and popped the used morphine gear into her handbag. A dry note entered her voice. "Or like I fell off a train. As abused as I feel, I'm right ruddy jammy nothing is sprained or broken."

Alistair dressed himself again. "You're healthy probably because you're an athlete, lass. Quite fit you are, what with all that dancing. I imagine it takes a lot of practise and exercise to perform the feats on the floor I witnessed several nights ago."

Leaning on the rock wall, he groaned and considered their options. "We must get some rest now. In a bit we'll move on, and I must rid myself of this uniform, and you shall cover your hair." Her towel turban had come off in her fall from the train.

"And come up with another name," she replied. "Bennington hasn't proven successful. How about Smith this time?"

"Very well." Alistair sat down, fished his trilby out of his case, and covered his face with it. Leaning back against the wall, he fit his head into an indentation in the rocks. "Mrs. Smith it is."

"Back to being your wife, am I?" Cicely asked. Her voice was dry.

Alistair's only reply was a snore.

Pink lightened the sky in the east. There wasn't much time before a farm worker would stumble upon them; only time for a very short sleep. Cicely drifted off, dreaming of hot baths, soft sheets, and a feather bed.

And of Alistair making love to her.

TWENTY

Lang may yer lum reek.
(May your hearth be forever warm)
—Scottish blessing

Cicely stepped out of the warm bath, thoroughly relaxed. Her cuts and scrapes were now cleansed and her aching muscles had benefited tremendously from the heat of the water.

After a brief nap that morning at sunrise, she and Alistair had trudged for miles along a narrow country road. The driver of a hay cart had offered them a lift into a hamlet on the outskirts of Cardiff, and once they found what seemed a low-profile inn, they'd gladly registered as guests.

Cicely now wrapped her damp hair in a towel, pulled a borrowed flannel dressing gown from the bathroom door hook and, wrapping it around her body, made her way to the room she and Alistair shared.

Their rosy-cheeked, plump hostess straightened from poking the fire when Cicely entered. The room was cozy and welcoming, with a large four-poster bed, complete with old-fashioned bed curtains. An old red Persian rug covered the darkened wood floor; two wing chairs with a small round table between occupied the corner in front of the window, and a walnut armoire with a matching dresser took up the opposite wall.

"There you are, Mrs. Smith," the hostess said, brushing debris off her apron and tucking a stray salt-and-pepper strand of hair back into her chignon. "I've built you a nice wood fire, I have. Mr. Hall and I don't care for coal fires. Unhealthy, we believe. Our property includes a good stand of trees beyond the garden, allowing us a plentiful supply of wood." She replaced the poker in its stand beside the hearth. "I've a nice mutton broth tonight, with thick slices of bread. Will you be dining downstairs or up here, luv?"

Cicely approached the fire eagerly. "Here, I think, Mrs. Hall, thank you. Is Mr. Smith down in the pub?"

"Lingering over his post-bath brandy. Poor fellow. He told us about that horrid fall he suffered," she said, referring to Alistair's explanation regarding his swollen and discoloured face. "I'll bring up your supper presently, shall I?"

"Thank you, Mrs. Hall," Cicely agreed. The hostess left the room, and Cicely seated herself on the cushioned bench before the fire. The leaping orange flames crackled and popped, and she stared into them, letting them mesmerise her senses.

She couldn't remember the last time she had warmed herself before a wood fire. Nearly everyone used the cheaper and more readily available coal. Leaning toward the flames and holding her palms just inches from the heat, she closed her eyes and luxuriated in the warmth. The light glowed orange through her closed lids. She wished she and Alistair could stay here for several days, to recuperate from tumbling off the train and heal the blisters from walking all those miles. A hot bath, a fire, a meal and a feather bed seemed like a dream. A dream she hated to end. Perhaps they might stay until midday tomorrow. After all, they both desperately needed sleep.

The door snapped open and Alistair entered, a newspaper clutched in his fist. His mouth was tight. He was just as handsome in civilian clothing as in his uniform. Now he wore tailored wool trousers, a shirt, tie, jumper, and a tweed jacket. He looked quite the country gentleman.

It was dusk, and the only source of light was the fire. The flames mounted higher, sending shadows cavorting and alternately bathing Alistair in golden light and transforming him into a dark spectre.

He threw the newspaper on the floor in front of the fire and turned, pacing to the window, staring out into the darkening countryside.

Cicely read the bold headline, and gasped. "Oh my God, Alistair, how can this be?"

Pivoting back to look at her, his stance rigid, he replied, "Read the article. I'm on my way back downstairs to buy anything they bloody well sell by the bottle." The door shook when he closed it.

Biting her lip, Cicely re read the headline.

COUPLE WANTED IN MURDER!
Masquerading as Major Bennington and Sister,
Alistair Fielding and Cicely Winterbourne are
sought for questioning in the murder of two elderly
London women and an unknown man . . .

The newspaper went on to say Cicely lived across the hall from Adele and Vi, and that her place of work and her volunteer status were unknown. Also, Alistair's supervisor at Scotland Yard was unable to comment, as his residence had sustained a direct hit by a German bomb several nights before. A description of Cicely and Alistair concluded the piece.

Stunned, Cicely leant back on the bench and closed her eyes. It *was* real, and not a rumour instigated by the men seeking the key to the code! How had this happened?

Her hands flew to the towel covering her hair. Thank goodness she'd washed it, or it might not have been covered. When would she learn? *Safe* didn't belong in her vocabulary anymore.

As she tossed the newspaper in the flames, Alistair returned, a bottle in one hand and several other newspapers under his arm. Chucking them down before the fire, he retrieved drinking glasses from the dresser.

"Had I not been thrown into such a shock, I'd have taken all these copies the first time. As we're the only guests here, and Mr. and Mrs. Hall are not in evidence, I assume we're safe for the night." He seated himself next to Cicely and began feeding the newspapers into the blaze. "Pour us a couple of fingers, Cicely. It's gnat's piss, but I'm not choosy at the moment."

"Alistair, who else besides you and your supervisor knew what you were up to, investigating me?" Cicely asked.

The fire backlit his profile and made his eyes glitter. "There's the rub, I'm afraid. No one else knew anything. The doctor who performed Graham's post mortem was aware something terribly secret was up, but that's it." He rubbed his eyes. "Gordon, my superior, was a good chap. I'll miss him."

"It seems a fantastic coincidence, Gordon being bombed. In addition to the loss of his life, it quite cocks up everything for us." Cicely stared into the flames, while

GET UP TO 4 FREE BOOKS!

You can have the best romance delivered to your door for less than what you'd pay in a bookstore or online. Sign up for one of our book clubs today, and we'll send you **FREE* BOOKS** just for trying it out...with no obligation to buy, ever!

HISTORICAL ROMANCE BOOK CLUB

Travel from the Scottish Highlands to the American West, the decadent ballrooms of Regency England to Viking ships. Your shipments will include authors such as CONNIE MASON, SANDRA HILL, CASSIE EDWARDS, JENNIFER ASHLEY, LEIGH GREENWOOD, and many, many more.

LOVE SPELL BOOK CLUB

Bring a little magic into your life with the romances of Love Spell—fun contemporaries, paranormals, time-travels, futuristics, and more. Your shipments will include authors such as LYNSAY SANDS, CJ BARRY, COLLEEN THOMPSON, NINA BANGS, MARJORIE LIU and more.

As a book club member you also receive the following special benefits:

- **30% OFF all orders through our website & telecenter!**
- **Exclusive access to special discounts!**
- **Convenient home delivery and 10 day examination period to return any books you don't want to keep.**

There is **no minimum number of books to buy**, and you may cancel membership at any time. See back to sign up!

*Please include $2.00 for shipping and handling.

YES! ☐

Sign me up for the **Historical Romance Book Club** and send my TWO FREE BOOKS! If I choose to stay in the club, I will pay only $8.50* each month, a savings of $5.48!

YES! ☐

Sign me up for the **Love Spell Book Club** and send my TWO FREE BOOKS! If I choose to stay in the club, I will pay only $8.50* each month, a savings of $5.48!

NAME: _____

ADDRESS: _____

_____

TELEPHONE: _____

E-MAIL: _____

☐ **I WANT TO PAY BY CREDIT CARD.**

☐ VISA   ☐ MasterCard   ☐ DISCOVER

ACCOUNT #: _____

EXPIRATION DATE: _____

SIGNATURE: _____

Send this card along with $2.00 shipping & handling for each club you wish to join, to:

Romance Book Clubs
20 Academy Street
Norwalk, CT 06850-4032

Or fax (must include credit card information!) to: 610.995.9274. You can also sign up online at www.dorchesterpub.com.

*Plus $2.00 for shipping. Offer open to residents of the U.S. and Canada only. Canadian residents please call 1.800.481.9191 for pricing information. If under 18, a parent or guardian must sign. Terms, prices and conditions subject to change. Subscription subject to acceptance. Dorchester Publishing reserves the right to reject any order or cancel any subscription.

JOIN NOW!

Alistair continued burning newspapers. "Might you call that doctor? Ask him if he's been questioned, get his view of what's happening?"

Alistair stilled. "You know, that's not a bad idea." He ripped more paper and threw it on the fire. "When our hosts have retired, I'll use the telephone at the registration desk—leaving money for the charges, of course. Yes, perhaps Percy may shed some light."

"But why do you suppose the authorities think we killed Adele and Vi? I loved them like aunties." Cicely felt tears welling in her eyes. She really hadn't a chance until now to mourn her neighbours.

"Likely because we were missing when they were found. Do you suppose Monetary came upon their bodies and called the coppers?" Alistair tossed the last of the offending newspapers into the fireplace.

"Probably. Of course, she'd have informed them they were on the wrong track. But then . . . if she followed my instructions, she took Henry and hied herself north of Watford." Cicely gasped. "Oh lord—I hope the coppers don't think Monty's involved, too, if she did disappear." She gazed into the fire again. "She'd met Dooly, unfortunately—at the Jive Palace one Saturday night. She may have inadvertently informed the authorities I didn't care for him, supplying a motive. But what motive could they possibly think I had to murder my neighbours?"

"Did the ladies have any relatives?" Alistair asked.

Cicely pursed her lips. "None were mentioned, and none came calling."

Alistair shrugged. "It might be a smokescreen, after all," he decided. Tired of waiting for Cicely to do as he'd asked, he uncorked the bottle of scotch, pouring a good measure in both glasses. "Hope you're not used to the finest single malt." He sipped the liquor, then grimaced. "Nearly no smoke and it's blended. Better than dishwater, however."

Cicely tasted hers and gasped. "Good lord, it's raw. But still, it's heaven after a day of tramping on the hard tarmac and through various livestock fields, tripping on uneven ground, avoiding piles of cow, er, excrement, and mole hills. Not to mention that brutal wind and the occasional snow mixed with rain." She shuddered and moved closer to the fire. "Too bad this solace won't last."

Alistair nodded. He placed two Woodbines in his mouth, lit them and handed one over. "Yes, we're lucky to have this for the night. Tomorrow I intend to visit Cardiff's docks. No, you shan't accompany me. It's safer that way. If questioned, witnesses will say they saw a lone chap and not a couple toddling about asking questions about renting a boat."

"Quite right," Cicely agreed. She inhaled and sipped her scotch. "I'll spend that time shopping for food and perhaps a vacuum flask of tea." Kneeling by the fire, she added another log from the woodbox. The fire popped, sending sparks onto her lap, but she coolly brushed them off.

Taking a seat beside Alistair, she said meditatively, "Smokescreen, hmmm? The paper didn't mention a motive behind the murders. Suppose it's Bletchley attempting to reel us in? The coppers will salute and say 'yes, sir' to any request from the government. If so, not only are there Germans after us, but coppers *and* government agents. At first I didn't know who could be after me, but suspected everyone. Now, knowing a little bit . . ." She shivered, despite the growing warmth of the fire. "I'm really frightened, Alistair. A mole makes so much sense. How far up is he? Or she?

"Consider," Cicely continued. "Why, having the key,

didn't Graham reveal it at Bletchley? Perhaps they planned to draw out the mole? Make him come and retrieve it from them."

A knock on the door made her jump, but it was only Mrs. Hall with a supper tray. The woman smiled.

"All cozy I see. This is just what you need after the hard day you two experienced. You're sure to find a mechanic for your motor in the morning. They do become scarce come mid-afternoon—but not scarce in the pubs, mind." She winked at them. "How far down the road did it stop? The leeches will want extra lolly for leaving town to fix it," she warned, placing the tray on a table by the window. "Don't forget the blackout blind," she added, looking pointedly outside.

The rich aroma of mutton soup and fresh bread had both Alistair and Cicely racing for the table.

"We expected it might cost more to drag a mechanic out of town," said Alistair. To cover their bedraggled condition, the story of a broken-down motor car had been the first thing to occur to him. Soon he might surpass Cicely in the art of deceiving.

Seeing her guests dig into their supper, Mrs. Hall adjusted the blackout blind herself.

"Mr. Hall and I are listening to the BBC on the wireless tonight. If you care to join us, please come to the parlour," she said over her shoulder. Then she left, closing the door behind her.

Cicely couldn't decide whether to savour each bite of the thick soup or guzzle it as fast as she could. Usually a pot of soup only contained a bite or two of meat, but this mouth-watering stew held at least a bite of mutton per spoonful. When her bowl was nearly scraped dry, Cicely sighed and leaned back in her chair.

"I wouldn't be surprised if the Halls had an understanding with the local butcher" she guessed. "Firewood for meat."

"And bless them for it," Alistair mumbled around a mouthful of bread and butter.

Cicely laughed. "I'm ready to *worship* them for it!" she said. She stood, unwound her hair from the towel, and made her way back to the fire while running her fingers through it. "All this comfort has me drowsy. Or perhaps I haven't allowed myself the luxury of admitting my exhaustion before. I believe I shall enjoy another bit of scotch and a fag—then I'm passing out on the bed." She raised her brows as Alistair stood and donned his tweed jacket. "Going down to listen to the BBC? You need sleep, too. A phone call in the middle of the night and a dawn start, remember."

"As a soldier, one learns to do without sleep—for days if need be," he said. "I slept only in snatches for four days on that bloody beach at Dunkirk. One of us needs to know what's going on in the world. I've only read one paper in days, and neither of us has listened to the wireless since we boarded the London train. Besides, I'm interested to discover if we're mentioned."

Cicely felt a sudden stab of guilt. All she could think of now was sleep, and Alistair had bled and suffered for a country he now felt betrayed him. A country whose agents even now might be hunting him down.

"Of course, Alistair," she said. "I hope you needn't listen for long. If you need any more aspirin for your knee, I put the bottle on the dresser," she called out as he left.

But listening to the BBC wasn't the only reason Alistair left; occupying the same room with Cicely clouded his thoughts. Her skin was rosy and dewy from her bath, and knowing she was naked beneath her threadbare dressing gown tormented him. Her freshly washed hair was tousled and gleamed in the firelight. It reminded him of when he'd awoke next to her in Kit's cottage. When she'd stood in front of the fire he'd seen the outline of her nipples, her round behind, the sleek line of her thighs.

Taking a deep breath, he forced her from his thoughts. At the bottom of the staircase he noticed the wall phone behind the registration desk. At least they didn't keep their blower in a locked office.

Turning the corner, he knocked once on the double doors leading to the parlour. Inside, a warm domestic scene greeted him. Mr. Hall sported a white buzz cut and a stocky form. He was leaning back in an old velvet-covered wing chair, his feet propped on a footstool, a cigar in one hand and a bowl glass of brandy in the other.

Mrs. Hall glanced up from her mending. "Good of you to keep us company tonight, Mr. Smith. Is your wife too sleepy to join us?"

When Alistair nodded, Mr. Hall roused himself to offer brandy and a cigar. Alistair accepted the brandy but refused the smoke.

Mr. Hall puffed on his. "Acquired taste, cigars. Help yourself, the brandy is on the sideboard."

Glass in hand, a moment later Alistair seated himself on the leather settee with Mrs. Hall by the cheerfully roaring fire. A Tchaikovsky symphony murmured from the wireless. A moment later, BBC news took over.

First came reports of German bombings in London and other large cities, along with casualties and damage. Then, other news: Montgomery had managed to outwit Rommel again. The Royal Navy had sunk two German U-boats in the north Atlantic. Alistair's attention faded when he thought of Bletchley's codebreakers as being responsible for these victories. But when news of local crimes began, his ears sharpened again.

Break-ins were reported at various butcher shops, and trampled Victory gardens. The newsman announced a crackdown on Spiv operators and the black market. Undercover investigators were to pose as would-be customers to bring an end the outrage of black marketeering.

The beginnings of relief relaxed Alistair until he heard the reporter mention a triple murder in London. Trying to draw the Halls' attention, he knocked his nearly full brandy glass on the carpet.

"Ruddy clumsy of me! I'm so sorry, Mrs. Hall. Have you a cloth with which I may blot this?" he asked.

"Calm yourself, Mr. Smith." Mrs. Hall rifled through her mending basket and handed him a flannel. "At least the glass is whole. I don't believe it will stain."

"Stain!" Mr. Hall sat forward. "Who minds if it stains, by God. You, my boy, need to appreciate good brandy! A waste." He shook his head. "Bloody waste."

His wife shook her head. "Pay no attention to him, Mr. Smith. Likely he'll spend the night in here just for the smell."

"Hell and damnation, woman! The damned carpet isn't thirsty, is it? No business spilling good brandy." Mr. Hall drank off the last of his liquor and slammed his glass on a side table.

"He didn't spill it on purpose, Reggie. He dropped it accidentally," Mrs. Hall said sternly. "Why don't you toddle off to bed now?"

"I am most sincerely sorry, Mr. Hall, and will gladly pay for it." Done blotting the brandy spot, Alistair stood.

"See that you do pay for it, young man," Mr. Hall snapped. His gait was unsteady as he made his exit.

"You will do no such thing," Mrs. Hall said. She switched off the wireless and picked up her mending basket. Looking at Alistair she added, "Reggie will have forgotten everything by morning. Now I'm off as well. Would you mind banking the fire? So good of you. Sleep well," she said, closing the parlour door behind her.

Alistair did as requested, then poured himself another brandy and positioned himself before the fire to wait a reasonable interval before attempting to ring Percy.

The floor above creaked as the Halls prepared for bed. He heard Mr. Hall fussing and Mrs. Hall's soothing voice. Alistair turned off the lamp and found staring into the leaping golden flames finally relaxed him.

He woke with a start, his eyes flying to the clock over the mantel. Eleven o'clock. He'd slept more than two hours by the fire, which was now smouldering embers. He rubbed his eyes and shook his head to clear the sleep from his brain. Carrying his shoes, he walked softly to the registration desk and picked up the phone. Several minutes passed before the call went through and Percival answered.

"Who the hell is there, and why the hell are you calling in the bloody middle of the night?" the doctor growled.

Alistair explained, and Percival sighed. "The bobbies are after you right and tight." He snorted. "Stupid notion, you killing those old ladies and the what's-his-name. Ridiculous! Don't know what they will come up with next. Who's this bird you supposedly ran off with, though?"

Alistair sighed. "Remember the secret post mortem I had you perform? She's the cousin. But I can't tell you much more or your life will be in danger as well."

Percival grunted. "Like to see the buggers try! I'm not one of those 'lay me down and kill me' chaps. Too old and too tough to kill," he bragged.

"Too gnarled and gristled," Alistair agreed. He allowed himself a low chuckle. "Rumours abound, I'm sure. Now, who advanced the belief Cicely and I were involved in all this? High or low level? Local coppers or the Met?"

Percival didn't speak for some time. At last he admitted, "I don't know, old son. Police didn't release details. It all seemed to happen in a great hurry. Investigating officers haven't acknowledged *why* they're sure you and your bird committed the murders, just that the both of you were the last persons to be seen exiting the building before the unfortunates were found." He paused. "Are you about to tell me what goes? I might be useful to you, you know."

"I'm sorry, Percival," Alistair said, quietly glancing toward the shadowy staircase and thinking of Cicely in bed by herself. "It becomes more complicated and more dangerous by the minute. Likely you'd presume I was pulling your leg, anyway. Truth is stranger than fiction."

"Rubbish!" Percival said, out of patience.

Alistair fought his desire to have help. "Good night, old friend. You never heard from me." He replaced the telephone handset.

An electric nightlight glowed behind the registration desk, allowing him to find a candle and light it. The flame dipped and wavered in the draughts as he crossed the lobby and climbed the steps. The stairs groaned under his stockinged feet. The banister and the floor overhead creaked, too.

Except for the small illumination the candle permitted, the darkness was all-encompassing. Suddenly Alistair felt jittery. He shook his head. For God's sake, one might think he was acting out a gothic movie.

Reaching the bedroom door, he snicked it open. The fire burned low in the grate. He set the candleholder on the nightstand and thrust back the dark blue velvet bed curtains. Cicely lay on her side, facing him, the blankets at her waist. The long row of buttons from neck to chest on her old-fashioned nightgown were undone, and one breast with a pale pink nipple had escaped, rising and falling with her breathing.

Alistair closed his eyes and gritted his teeth, but desire rose like a tidal wave within him.

Cicely opened her eyes. Alistair stood silhouetted between the bed curtains, his stance rigid and his eyes sparkling with heat in the candlelight. His eyes were fastened on her chest, and looking down she discovered why. She swallowed. Her first instinct should have been to cover herself, but the way Alistair regarded her gave her the inclination to offer her breast up instead.

"You're letting the cold in," she said. Her voice sounded husky, sensual, even to her own ears.

"Of course, sorry."

He dragged his gaze from her body and turned to the side to empty his pockets on the nightstand. When he did, Cicely caught site of the long hard ridge outlined by his trousers. His hands went to his belt, paused as if noticing that hard length for the first time, and bent to pull off his pants. Cicely propped herself on an elbow, letting the breast that had been poking out from her nightgown swing free.

His fingers at his shirt buttons stilled momentarily. "Cicely . . ." His voice was gravelly and held a hint of menace.

Cicely frowned and leaned back on the pillows. Why weren't they supposed to make love again? Ah, because she'd fallen for him and had sworn not to do that again. Because he would never consider her an equal. In love-making, yes, but not as a life partner. She didn't meet his high moral standards: she lied, she deceived, and she lacked honour. But he'd loved it when they'd come together. And so had she. When had she ever enjoyed his calibre of lover? Never.

She rose to her knees and pulled her nightgown over her head, moving toward Alistair just as he pushed his trousers down over his hips. Sensing her movement, he turned . . . and took in a sharp breath.

Placing her hands on either side of his head, she pulled him down so that their lips met. For an instant Alistair froze, then he seized her, urging her closer and thrusting his tongue nearly down her throat.

Gently she eased herself from his embrace, leaving him panting, to kiss and caress his chiselled chest. She tipped her head back to study his face, while her hands explored him. His eyes were nearly black and his jaw was tight, as if he were holding himself in check. Continuing her ministrations, she nibbled at his nipples and sucked them into her mouth.

Oh, how Alistair's torso reminded her of the Greek statues she'd seen in the British Museum! His chest and shoulders were so broad, with a light coating of curling hair. Following with her tongue the arrowlike trail leading into his underclothes, she finally pushed his trousers all the way down.

He threw his head back and groaned when she fit his erection between her breasts and rubbed up and down the length of him. "Cicely . . . Jesus, stop," he gasped.

She replied by taking him in her mouth, all the way down to the hilt, swirling her tongue around, nipping, sucking, licking.

For a moment Alistair quit breathing altogether. Then he fisted his hands in her hair, pulling her back, then forward, groaning, telling her never to stop.

"Christ," he panted, abruptly pulling back. "I want to be inside you. Now."

Guiding her down on the bed and grasping the headboard for purchase, he thrust himself into her. She was ready, and she gasped as he entered her, filling her to capacity. He stopped, gazing down at her in wonder.

"Where did you learn to do that?" he asked.

She writhed under him, urging him to move. She needed his body, his rhythm, his firm flesh making her wild. A cocky smile touched her lips. "Actually, I didn't 'learn,' " she murmured. "I'd only heard of it. You're the first. Now, please Alistair, make love to me."

He studied her for a long moment, then grinned and complied. Cicely was caught in a vortex of pleasure. Nearly at the pinnacle, she gasped. He'd pulled out.

"Patience," he whispered, a wicked gleam in his eye.

Not leaving her totally bereft, he bent to kiss her throat, her breasts, and took several minutes on her nipples. Then he worked his way down. Finally he positioned himself between her thighs, combing his fingers through her curls and folds, then lowering his mouth so his tongue could follow suit.

Cicely whipped her head to and fro on the pillow, delirious in pleasure. She couldn't think, could only feel. Alistair's whiskers scraped the sensitive skin between her thighs, but she was beyond caring. No one had ever done this to her before. No one had ever made her feel this way.

Alistair lifted his mouth for the merest moment. "Let go, love," he demanded, his voice raw.

Cicely needed no second urging, for his tongue brushed her secret spot and she felt her world explode in a shower of silver stars. Her inner muscles were still vibrating as he entered her again. He placed one hand on her bottom, bringing her closer to him, while his other hand fisted in her hair and forced her to watch their bodies meet again and again, overwhelming her with the carnality of the moment.

"That's it, Cicely lass, look your fill," he urged. "Watch me make love to you."

She heard the restraint in his voice and saw him gritting his teeth, so she grasped his buttocks with both hands, pulling him nearer. He leaned down further to kiss her, hot and wet, his tongue plunging into her mouth like his lower body plunged into her. Feeling another climax coming, she dug her nails into buttocks.

Alistair had never had to use such control with a woman before. Such selfless giving and uninhibited sensuality were new to him, and when Cicely's nails dug into him, he lost all concentration. Jack-knifing into her, his whole body trembled as he reached his culmination.

His shout of pleasure faded, and he slid off of her. They lay next to one another, panting and slick with perspiration.

"I'll be right back," Alistair murmured, parting the heavy bed curtain to stand. He strode to the jug and bowl of water left for them on the dresser, dipped a flannel in

194

the water and wiped off his face and chest. Then he dropped the flannel into the bowl and braced his hands on the edge of the bureau, head bowed.

So . . . the first time with her hadn't been an anomaly. But he wished it had been. Perhaps that was the reason he'd resisted making love to her again—he'd feared this same exaltation. Alistair hadn't been with a lot of women, but they all paled in comparison to Cicely. They were dishwater, and she was . . . the finest eighteen-year-old single malt scotch.

What was he to do? Permanence was anathema to her, she'd said. But he just wasn't the type of chap to—what was it the Yanks said: "Love 'em and leave 'em"? He poured water from the pitcher into a glass, and gulped some. The hell with it. He'd take all he could get of her while they performed this thrice-damned mission. For all he knew she'd tire of him before they even reached Cornwall.

If they lived that long.

He shook his head, attempting to rid himself of both heretical ideas, but realised the only way to do so was to make love to Cicely again. And again. And again.

Cicely's eyes flew open as she felt the nudge on her shoulder. Alistair stood over her, buttoning his shirt. It was light outside. He nodded to her bedstand, where he'd placed a glass of water from the jug on the dresser. "Only water for now, I'm afraid. We'll purchase tea and breakfast after I've made enquiries about a boat. Hurry, the sky is turning grey."

"How can you wake just when you need to?" Cicely asked. She sat up against the pillows and began combing her fingers through her hair.

"Soldiers develop automatic alarms." He finished tucking his shirt into his wool trousers and sat on the bed to don his shoes.

"Automatic alarms?"

"Before I go to sleep I tell myself I must wake at a certain time." He stood. "Now come on, slug-a-bed, arise. Your day awaits."

Cicely swung her legs off the bed to the floor. "Oh, do shut up, Alistair. I can't think why you're so cheerful after only a few hours of sleep."

He grinned. "More like only two hours of sleep. But the, er, other time was very well spent."

Cicely rolled her eyes. Seizing her dressing gown from the foot of the bed, she said, "Men! You don't understand we women need a decent amount of sleep merely to tolerate you. I'm off to the loo for ablutions."

When she returned from the loo, intending to dress, Cicely saw that Alistair was absent. His case rested beside the door. Walking over to one of the wing chairs where she'd draped yesterday's clothing, she frowned at her tweed skirt. It was quite ruined, as were her only pair of stockings. She rummaged through her portmanteau for a warm pair of socks, then pulled on a bright blue dress and wound a kerchief, turban-style, over her hair. Alistair came to collect her just as she fastened her coat.

On the high street they parted, Alistair on his way to the wharf, Cicely to shop for the day's meals. As she took her place in the queue outside the greengrocer, Cicely marveled at how replete and content she felt. Her whole body ached from tumbling off the train, and several blisters on her feet had needed attention when she bathed the night before. And with almost no sleep . . . she should

196

feel cross and exhausted, but instead there was a definite spring in her step.

She found herself smiling broadly to the other women waiting in the queue. No one had ever made her feel like Alistair did: sensuous, beautiful, cherished, treasured, as if she were the only woman on Earth. She felt her face heat with a blush when memories played like a film reel in her mind. The things they had done! But she felt no shame.

Neil, her fiancé, had tried to hide his embarrassment at her eager responses to him, but he had never quite seemed to let loose of the notion only kerb crawlers enjoyed sexual relations. Her second lover had proved clumsy, but she'd adored him for the amusing and entertaining campion he was. Now both men were dead.

Cicely lost her smile. Everything, even life itself, was fleeting. She'd take what joy she might. Yes—she nodded to herself—she'd take her own advice. She'd take what precious time she had with Alistair, and not worry about the future. If they lived through this venture, she knew he'd tell her good-bye.

But that was the future, and she had now.

TWENTY-ONE

Speed bonny boat, like a bird on the wing . . .
　　　　—Skye Boat Song

All day Cicely and Alistair huddled under a bare horse chestnut tree on a hill overlooking the wharf at Old Quay, southwest of Cardiff, waiting for darkness to fall before heading to the dock where waited the twenty-five foot commercial fishing boat Alistair had hired. It had cost them a small fortune for the transportation, and for the captain to keep his mouth shut about his passengers. Even with the incredible sum of money, the man wanted to keep it to himself, so he gave his assistant the night off and informed them Alistair must help with the night's haul. The gnarled branches of the horse chestnut provided scant protection from the rain and brutal wind; by the time they reached the boat both were nearly wet to the skin.

Now in the draughty fishing boat's wheelhouse, Cicely shivered and hunched deeper into her damp coat. The boat did anything but bob gently on the sea. It crashed and dived in the deep waves of the Bristol Channel. She clutched the instrument board to keep her balance.

Cicely could barely see through the misty and wave-lashed windows. For hours Alistair had acted as the fishing captain's assistant, hauling on the nets and operating the winches outside. If she felt frosty, he must be frozen.

Finally, the door to the wheelhouse flew open with a violent slam. A dark silhouette loomed in the doorway. "I hope you are not seasick, pet," Alistair said. The illumination filtering from the large torch on deck was anaemic, and she'd not have recognized him but for his voice.

"I grew up sailing. No troubles here," she said. Her numb fingers trembled as she reached for her thermos flask. "Tea?" she offered.

"God, yes!" Alistair coughed. It came deep from his chest, as if his lungs were thick with phlegm.

"You shouldn't be outside assisting anymore," she admonished, handing him a cup. "That cough is sounding dangerous. I'm unable to carry you, you know, if you give way to pneumonia."

He gulped down the hot tea and threw himself in the collapsable chair beside her. "Aye, lass, but it's part of the deal. The fewer that know about this the better; therefore I'm taking his partner's place one-way. And it was sea lane robbery, let me tell you. Twenty pounds? A bloody fortune."

Cicely gave him the last of what passed for their meat pies. They had to save the rest of the food for the next day. "Eat, you need your strength," she said.

The torch flashed on the deck outside, and she gasped, catching her first clear look at Alistair since they'd boarded. Water ran down his face. His lips were bluish and his face resembled parchment. Thank goodness he wore the waterproof mac provided by the fishing captain!

A strange tingling crept down her spine. The feeling that Alistair would fail to complete this trip overwhelmed her. But then the boat lurched, distracting her as she latched onto the instrument board to steady herself. Alistair careened forward, nearly squashing her. The scent of wet wool, seawater, and old fish assailed her nostrils. His skin felt hot against hers.

They steadied themselves, and she placed her palm on his forehead. He swept it away immediately. "Don't mother me," he muttered, irritated.

Cicely grasped his arm. "Mother you? You're burning up, Alistair. You mustn't go back out there! You are weakened by spending all day outside in the wet and brutal cold—not to mention lack of sleep and all your recent bang-ups. Going back outside is suicide!"

He stared out the window. The rain fell sideways in the vicious wind. Even with the anchor deployed, the boat climbed the steep waves, hovering at each peak before diving straight down. It always seemed the boat might collapse in on itself on the upward turn, and bury itself in the sea's depths on the way down.

At last, he looked at her. "One of us must do it. You're not capable of handling that heavy equipment. We're nearly done out there. See?" He pointed to the fishing captain, Tregarth, reeling in a net. "That's the last. He'll take over the wheel and we'll make straight for Minehead in north Devon." He shook his head and added, "It's beyond me how these lads make a living in this weather."

Cicely nodded. "They fish all year round, now that fish is nearly the only food not rationed."

Alistair stuffed the meat pie in his mouth and left the wheelhouse to help with the net. The door stayed open, and it took all Cicely's strength and weight to shut it.

She returned to the window and hung on to the instrument board, peering out at the black sea. The wind howled and rattled the cabin. Alistair had pushed himself unsteadily to his feet and she'd sensed it had taken all his strength to walk out that door. No, unless some miracle occurred, he wouldn't make it to Cornwall.

Cicely opened her eyes to a granite-coloured sky and drizzling rain, wondering how on Earth she had managed to sleep on what practically amounted to one of those new electric carnival rides, and in a tiny collapsible chair no less. First things first: she needed the loo. She lifted her shoulder to ease a cramp when she heard a deep bubbly rumble next to her.

Alistair had returned to the wheelhouse while she dozed. He was sitting in the other collapsible chair, his head leaning against the bulwark. She could see that his chest rose and fell with difficulty. Air wheezed between his blue, cracked lips. Droplets of water sluiced down his face from his hairline. Touching him, Cicely knew it wasn't seawater, but sweat.

Delaying her trip to the loo, she poured tea from their flask, barely warm now, and woke him, coaxing him to drink. She supported the back of Alistair's head with one hand, while holding the cup to his mouth with the other. He managed only two sips before grumbling and turning away to sleep again.

He needed medical help, and fast. Perhaps there was a doctor in the village. The idea of traveling to Cornwall on her own over the moors set Cicely's fingers trembling. She'd been depending on Alistair's sense of direction, as she had absolutely none.

She was pouring the remaining tea back into the flask when Captain Tregarth entered.

"Might be a bit o' trouble here. Best get yer man

about," he said, nodding toward the wharf. "Believe we can both do wi' out the coppers." He gave her a hard look. "Get a move on then. I don't want trouble."

Cicely's head whipped around. She stared in disbelief through the window, then watched as Tregarth left the boat and headed toward four men standing on the wharf. Two wore police macs, and the other two were dressed in long wool coats and trilbies.

The "game," it appeared, was up. Whirling around to Alistair, she shook his shoulder firmly. "Alistair! Emergency! Do wake up. Coppers! Outside now."

He groaned, shook his head, and at last focused glassy eyes on her. "B-bloody hell. Help me up," he said.

Cicely bent down for him to throw his arm around her shoulders, but the burn in her lower abdomen worsened. God, she needed to use the loo!

As Alistair gained his feet, she glanced out the window again. The policemen had made their way to the end of the pier. Fifty more yards and they'd be aboard the boat.

"Oh God. Hurry, Alistair! We can hide in the loo closet," she suggested.

Alistair fought to speak. She nearly had to press her ear to his mouth to hear his words.

"No. Leave me, Cicely. I'm ill. Shan't make it," Alistair whispered. "Hell, no voice. Cease your hovering. Just *go*."

"*No!* Come on, walk!" Cicely tried to drag him.

Alistair dug in his heels. "Listen!" He paused in the effort to breathe. "Not going anywhere. They take . . . me, they must provide medical care which I need like billy-oh." A ghost of a smile passed over his face, then he removed his arm from around her shoulders and held on to the boat's wheel to keep himself upright. "Go, hide in the closet. Perfect solution: I go to hospital, you go to Cornwall." He pushed her hard and coughed violently before speaking again:

"I've never known anyone who can use subterfuge better than you. Smile and deceive them. You're a looker. You can do it if anyone can." He tried to laugh but it ended in another cough.

Cicely stood stock still, shocked by his dog-in-the-manger attitude. "You beast! How dare you, Alistair!"

He stared at her with dead, emotionless eyes. "The truth hurts? You are so perfect for the spy trade. You lie, deceive, and when all else fails, seduce. You are quite experienced—and satisfying. The only accessory you need now is a tougher skin."

Cicely's mouth fell open and she forgot to breathe. For a moment is seemed as if the wheelhouse tilted. But it didn't. She shook herself and backed up a step. "You're doing this because you wish me to go on without you."

"Don't flatter youself. The sooner you know, the better. The truth is you're too much work, Cicely. Fast women are only temporary. You should know. If you offer it, a man will take it."

Outside, the coppers were mere feet from the boat. If they even glanced at the vessel instead of keeping their eyes glued to the slick ground they traversed, they'd have seen Alistair in the window. Cicely gasped, then whispered, "I thought—I actually thought I loved you." She backed up until she bumped into the bulwark, then whirled and ducked into the loo closet.

Panic, hurt, and disillusionment warred inside her. She couldn't imagine doing this alone. Even worse, Alistair's abandonment crushed her.

She heard him coughing long and savagely. She ached

to leave her hiding place to comfort him, to hear him say he didn't mean those awful things he'd said. Her trembling hand touched the door but she snatched it back. If she were caught now by the wrong people, who knew when the fourth rotor might again be solved. If ever. God only knew how many more people might die. And it would give the Nazis all the more advantage. It was unthinkable that Hitler might actually win this war.

Heavy feet descended on the fishing vessel and fear shot through her. No, they wouldn't find her. Indeed, if she didn't know the loo was there, she wouldn't have found it; the door melted into the bulwark and was so tiny, she could only very carefully take care of her "business," or it might end up on her person.

"As you can see, the lad is ill," came Tregarth's voice. "He needed to attend his mother's funeral." The captain grunted. "If you ask me, it might just be a double funeral. Much worse, he is, than just two hours ago."

Even from inside the closet, Cicely could hear the wheeze in Alistair's chest each time he breathed. She closed her eyes and pressed her knees together.

"Aye, he's burnin' up," an unfamiliar voice declared.

Alistair coughed again and said, "Mo-mother?"

One of the policemen laughed. "Out of his mind. Delirious, he is."

"There, you see?" Tregarth said. "Can't be your man. You said he was dangerous, and that he traveled with a woman." He paused. "As you can see, ain't no woman here."

Cicely heard murmurs, then Tregarth spoke up again. "Do ye mind, sirs, stepping off m'boat now? Bloody long night, and this fellow wasn't much help. I need a bit of kip and a good hot breakfast before I share this fellow's malady."

She heard footsteps, and then Tregarth again: "What's this now? Yer not taking him with you? Damned if you aren't! I can't lift him, and it was you lot who came looking. Take the poor fellow to hospital!"

"Big man that. We'd require a stretcher," came a reply.

"Ochkk, he's not *that* big. Just flip 'im over my shoulder, shall I?" a third voice said.

Still another man exclaimed, "Only you, Ralph, would say he's not that big!"

Cicely heard a thump, and she thought perhaps it was the sound of a man staggering.

"You see? Not a man alive I couldn't lift," Ralph bragged.

His friend was unimpressed. "A regular Sampson of the north, you are. But can you hold him there til we arrive on dry land?"

Cicely heard a grunt, and felt the boat rock in the water as Ralph made his way off. It proved difficult counting footsteps. Waiting a full two minutes, she at last unlatched the door hook and peeked outside, then out the front window. The policemen were nearly halfway down the pier. Closing the closet door once again, she eyed with disfavour the tin provided, and obeyed the needs of her body.

It occurred to Cicely that the policemen might spend the better part of the dark, wind-lashed afternoon in a waterside pub before setting out for their next destination, so she stayed on the fishing boat all day. When dusk fell she left, before Tregarth returned, carrying her suitcase, her thermos flask and the few leftover bites of food.

Fortunately she no longer felt damp, thanks to spreading her outer clothing in the wheelhouse to dry as best it could in the damp sea air. Outside the wind had died a bit, but the sky still drizzled. She dreaded the night to come, which would surely be spent in the elements. She couldn't risk registering at the local inn in a such a small hamlet. Tregarth had informed her that the train skipped this village in favour of another five miles south, and only horses and carts appeared to traverse the town with no motor cars at all. It would be much too difficult to explain how one had arrived.

She pulled the hood of her coat up to keep from being seen or recognized. After climbing the steep stair from the sea to the village street level, her eyes darted about, searching for a discreet way out of town. A pub door opened, spilling light and noise onto the street, but Cicely walked briskly on without pausing, as if she knew exactly where she was headed. She'd studied the rough map provided by Tregarth, and knew she must walk past the pub, turn down an alley, then another, then a third to make her way out of town without accessing the main road.

Somehow she got lost. Frustration mounted with every wrong turn she took after that, and twice she took shelter behind piles of garbage when someone came out a back door to smoke or to take out rubbish. Some of that refuse moved. Where was Henry when one needed him? She found herself beginning to laugh, and with effort tamped down the hysteria. Besides, Henry wouldn't have known what to do with the rats mucking about in the rubbish; he would have gazed up and expected a human to skin and roast the thing before presenting it to him on a platter.

Which brought Cicely to another thought: God, she

hoped Monetary had managed to escape London without leaving a trail.

No! She told herself. She wouldn't think of either Monty or Alistair. She couldn't do anything about them, and she needed all her mental and physical energy to take care of herself. Nonetheless, she felt relieved that she and Alistair had spent the previous chilly afternoon memorising the code key.

Closing her eyes momentarily, she shuddered as bits and pieces of memory, of Alistair making love to her, came to mind. No! she admonished herself. Keeping a clear head was essential.

Full dark had fallen by the time Cicely found her way out of the warren of back alleys of Minehead. On the moor, clouds scudded over a sliver of moon, allowing her peeks at the landscape. Desolate and ruddy cold, it was. She knew from traveling both Dartmoor and Bodmin Moor by motor car that various streams and creeks could be found, bogs, and that the landscape was hilly and rocky with many tors. It was quite beautiful in spring, with blooming heather, but now was dark winter, and it was brutally cold.

The wind blew up her legs, and shivering she tightened the belt on her coat. One foot in front of the other; she must keep walking. The frost crunched under her sturdy boots. She switched her travel bag between her hands with rapid regularity. Starting out it had felt light, but now it might as well be filled with rocks. Her feet were lumps of coal, and her fingers were fast going numb.

Pausing to take stock of her surroundings, she took a deep breath, rubbing her gloved hands together and stomping her feet. No trees were visible, but she espied several outcroppings of rock. Perhaps she'd huddle under one of them for shelter until daybreak.

Incapable of stopping herself from doing so, she stared into the shadows. It appeared one in the distance to her right was moving. Wolves had been wiped out centuries ago in Britain, hadn't they? Was it another person? She felt the hair on the back of her neck stand up. Of course, humans were rarely stupid enough to risk exposure out on the moor at night. Probably it was only a fox or perhaps a stray dog. She hoped to God that none of the nocturnal animals here proved rabid.

Another shadow flitted and stopped. Cicely closed her eyes, hard, and opened them. Nothing moved. Then something black swooped at her from the side, and she let out a scream. Hearing a breath of a sound, she swung her portmanteau and ducked. A bloody bat! She hated bats.

She bolted left, toward a tor she'd spotted. It seemed perfect. The rock shelf actually leaned over, covering her like a brolly. Taking her precious matches from her coat pocket, she lit one to survey her shelter. The rock blocked out the wind, and smaller rocks on either side jutted out like armrests. The ground in between was smooth and offered plenty of room to stretch out if need be.

Approving, Cicely placed her case against an "armrest," opened it and pulled out the heavy blanket she'd bought at Old Quay. Sitting atop her case, she snuggled into the wrap and mentally reviewed the road map of north Devon and Cornwall. Once the sun rose, she'd walk parallel to the coast road until she guessed she was even with Porlock. Then she'd hitchhike to Barnstaple. That was a large enough town to melt into the throng, and to find a small bed and breakfast.

At last, Cicely allowed herself to think of Alistair. She missed him mightily. From the night they'd found Vi and Adele, Alistair had proven himself a rock. Never had she

208

so come to depend on a man—even her fiancé. No man had ever been so indispensable to her. Because she didn't allow it.

But it was more than that. Not only had she fallen for Alistair, she was in love with him. The realisation made her want to laugh and cry at the same time.

He should be in hospital now, receiving the best of care. He was too ruddy difficult and stubborn to die! Bloody hell, if she proved a black widow a third time . . . ! This one must live. He *must*.

A sob escaped her, but no one heard. She was alone on a deserted, dark moor. And for the first time, being alone troubled her.

TWENTY-TWO

Life's uncertain voyage . . .
—William Shakespeare

Cicely awoke stiff but surprisingly warm. The tor blocked both the wind and the rain. Crows cawed overhead in the grey sky. The sun must be newly risen, but was hiding behind the threatening clouds. Peat and dampness assailed her nostrils. Feeling reluctant to move, she closed her eyes and made the monumental effort of reaching outside her cocoon for the vacuum flask.

The tea was cold, of course. Placing the flask on a patch of flat ground, she stood, replaced the blanket in her portmanteau, and reached into her handbag for the last of the bread and cheese from the day before. Savouring the tang of the thick slice of cheddar and ignoring the staleness of the brown bread, she paced the small enclosure the tor provided, working the kinks out of her limbs.

Indulging in one more gulp of tea—leaving one last swallow for later—she emerged from her shelter, took her bearing, and headed west. It couldn't be more than, what, six or eight miles to Porlock? Ha! Easier said than done. She winced as she began hiking and almost wished for numb feet again. Her feet burned from assorted blisters and raw spots. As she already wore three pairs of wool socks, there was nothing to do but ignore the hurts and continue.

Adding up all her fatigued muscles, bruises, and scrapes, she was still better off than Alistair. Able-bodied men died from lung diseases every day. Cicely stopped in her tracks, stamping her foot and dabbing at her tearing eyes with her coat sleeves. This worry solved *nothing*. Taking several deep breaths, she continued walking. She'd best concentrate on watching her feet rather than worrying about Alistair and his last words to her, or she'd end with a broken ankle.

Indeed, this part of the moor proved to be extraordinarily rocky. Moor grass grew fitfully around the rocks and boulders littering the bleak landscape. She saw peregrine falcons and crows, but no ground creatures aside from a beetle or two.

When she'd traversed perhaps half the distance to Porlock, she found herself in a valley of sorts. There were hills to the south and north, so she chose the highest pointing south and started trudging upward.

Cicely was panting and actually warm when she reached the crest. A spectacular view stretched as far as she could see. There were far fewer rocks and tors. Grassland unfolded before her; leafless trees and sheep dotted the vista. Relief flowed through her like a warm breeze, for below a road glistened wetly and curved like a snake across the moor.

A raven cried and swept by just above her head, giving her a start. Gazing to her right, she saw that she had almost passed Porlock. At least she guessed the hamlet was Porlock. It appeared tiny from her lofty perch, like a miniature display in a museum. So far, luck had smiled on her. This was the perfect spot to come upon the road.

The hill proved far more difficult to descend than to ascend. Twice she tripped and ended up sliding down several feet on her backside. During one of those ignominious falls, her portmanteau burst open and littered the hillside with her knickers and extra clothing. It took the better part of an hour to collect her belongings.

Reaching the road at last, she paused to rest. The sky had cleared, allowing a weak show of winter sun, but the blustery wind probably meant rain by nightfall.

Cicely had trudged no more than twenty steps when she heard a rumbling in the distance behind her. It turned into a whine, and then what she thought sounded like gears stripping.

She stood waiting at the side of the road, anticipation and excitement welling within her. She nearly jumped for joy when the omnibus rounded a corner, choking and spurting clouds of exhaust out its end. Like an elderly man finding it difficult to walk, the vehicle sputtered and lurched up the road toward her. Stepping into the middle of the road, she waved her hands at the driver and waited for him to stop.

The coach stopped and the door swung open, and Cicely hesitated, wondering for the first time if she resembled the veriest rag-picker after spending the night out on the moor.

"Boarding are ye, Miss? Best hurry before this pile of old bones fails altogether." The bus driver's voice was weary.

"How far do you go?"

"Barnstaple. Coming?"

"Yes."

Cicely boarded and handed the driver the fifty pence he required. When a quick glance showed that only a few people occupied the bus, she quickly slipped into the right front seat, leaned her head on the window, and fell asleep.

At dusk, after the bus had reached its destination, Cicely stopped in front of a sprawling Edwardian house on the outskirts of Barnstaple. The coach driver had recommended this bed and breakfast as likely the most economical in town. She was about to open the gate when she caught a movement out of the corner of her eye. Whipping her head around, she spied a man in an overcoat and a newsboy's tweed hat, with a jaunty perk to his step as he strolled in her direction.

She mentally shook herself. Good lord, she was becoming paranoid. Not *everyone* was trailing her, after all. But when she turned to latch the gate behind her, something in his profile as he passed or the way he carried himself seemed familiar.

Cicely frowned, watching him turn at the next corner. From where did she know him? It was extremely annoying not to put her finger on it, and worry ate at her as she entered the bed and breakfast.

"Hello, luv," greeted the sturdy hostess. Although the woman must be into her sixties, her hair gleamed bright red and was carefully arranged in the perfect finger waves of the last decade, reaching just to the nape of her neck. "Goodness, you do look a fright, don't you! What have you done, luv, spent the night with the chickens?"

Cicely smiled and approached the registry desk. "Just a spot of bother on my journey. Have you a private room and bathing facilities?"

"That sorry I am, luv. The two rooms I keep for couples are taken. All that's left is the communal ladies." The woman grinned. "But that bath is available, and if you fancy supper added to your tab, we have fresh cod with roast potatoes and peas."

"Wonderful," Cicely said, signing the registry. It was Cicely Tolhurst this time, her mother's maiden name.

After luxuriating in a hot bath, Cicely made her way down to the small guest dining room, wearing a wrap on her hair, a navy wool skirt and a pale yellow cardigan with pearl buttons. Two of the six dining chairs were occupied.

"Good evening." Cicely nodded to the two gentlemen who were dining, and proceeded to the sideboard to pour herself a cup of tea from the teapot.

"I say, 'gel, quite a looker you are," commented one, a heavyset man. His sagging jowls swung to and fro when he spoke. He raised his hand to smooth sparse white hair over his largely bald scalp.

His companion licked fleshy lips before speaking. "Where did our Doreen find you, eh?" He adjusted his monocle and eyed her from head to toe. His beard and hair were dyed a singular shade of ginger. Both men were coatless, and sat at the table with unbuttoned waistcoats.

Cicely stopped in her tracks and raised her eyebrows, taken aback. "I beg yo—"

The first man nudged his friend in the ribs with his elbow. "Shut up, Algie! Now you've frightened our little dove." He openly studied her breasts, outlined by her cardigan, with dark eyes. "Doreen!" he called. "Get that sweet bum of yours in here. A guest is waiting on you."

Still standing halfway between the dining table and the sideboard, Cicely's eyes rounded and her mouth fell open. Good God! Could this be a bordello?

The swinging door to the kitchen opened, and a dishevelled Doreen emerged smoothing her apron. "Hold yer damn horses, Bean. I'm cooking." She rubbed a floury hand over her sweaty face. "If I don't keep a close eye, I'll burn the bloody house down. Oh, there you are, Miss Tolhurst. Didn't think you'd be down so soon. Supper is nearly ready. As for you two," she said, pointing at Algie and Bean, "behave yourselves. Lady in the house."

Algie snickered. "Not often a real lady blesses us with her presence. Not the sort of custom our Doreen encourages."

"Don't listen to the berk, Miss Tolhurst," Bean said, slurring his words. "Always ready to do a lady justice." He waggled his eyebrows and Algie burst into laughter.

Cicely nearly sprinted to the kitchen, but not before she heard Bean's answering remark.

"Weren't exactly 'justice' you did to your last 'lady,' buckaroo!"

The kitchen was warm and private, although it did smell like fish. Cicely sipped her tea and replaced her cup in its saucer with a rattle. Doreen looked up from her old Aga. "Chaps loud and boisterous? Don't you worry. You may eat here." She nodded to the small kitchen table under the blacked-out window.

Cicely cleared her throat. "Where are the . . . other guests, Mrs. Singleton?"

"Call me Doreen, love, everyone does." The woman pulled cod and potatoes out of the oven and took peas off the burner. "A mother and daughter are in the hostel room. They ate out at a pub earlier. My two couples enjoyed supper about an hour ago. One is on their honeymoon." She winked at Cicely. "And those two blighters"—she jerked her head in the direction of the dining room—"prefer to drink their suppers. They're traveling medical equipment salesmen, if you can believe it. Don't know how they do it. Never had the pleasure of making their acquaintances when they were sober. I do believe they share a bottle upon arising, for courage in facing every new day, because their heads are trapped in the devil's own vise."

Doreen plated two suppers and disappeared through the door to the dining room. While the door was open Cicely heard what she thought was a particularly loud burp. Apparently the two men thought this was the funniest thing since Charlie Chaplin, because they laughed uproariously, and one managed to say between bursts of laughter, "Ha, ha! You get the prize, Chester McTraffwind! Ha, ha!"

When Doreen came back, she shook her head and tried not to laugh. "For goodness sake! They're performing a traffing contest, of all things."

Thankful for the privacy of the kitchen, Cicely sat down at the small table, and her hostess set supper in front of her. "Er, Mrs.—Doreen? Might there be a key to the women's hostel room? To lock it?"

Doreen frowned. "Can't say as there is." She shrugged. "The boys pose no harm, luv. They get rat-arsed and pass out in the mens' hostel room. Never bothered anyone before. If it makes you feel safer, prop a chair under the doorknob. Now then, I have a basket of laundry needs folding—though I should return by the time you finish."

Just before she exited, the woman retraced her footsteps to open a cupboard above the sink. She pulled out a dark blue bottle, picked up a stemmed glass from the counter and deposited both next to Cicely. "Harvey's Bristol Cream, luv," she said. "I save it for special occasions. Enjoy a glass or two on me." She grinned. "Make up for those two buggers badgering you. Be back in a minute or two."

Cicely poured herself a glass of the sherry and sliced into the cod. It was delicious! She must remember to convince Doreen to part with the secret ingredient that made the fish so tasty.

Forty minutes and two glasses of sherry later, Doreen hadn't returned. As the "boys" had fallen silent some time before, Cicely felt brave enough to peer out the door. She grimaced in distaste. It appeared both men had passed out.

She decided it was safe to steal past them. Bean was bent over the table, his face in his plate, muttering incoherently into what was left of his peas. Algie leaned back in his chair, chin sunk into his chest, making his jowls resemble long rabbit ears. Food littered both the table and the mens' chests.

She sighed in relief as she made it to the staircase undetected. Her foot hit the first step when suddenly she felt the hem of her skirt pulled from behind. Whirling about she found Bean, his stance wobbly, directly behind her.

"Pretty. Show ye goo' time." His eyes were bloodshot, grease dribbled down his chin, and he reeked of gin.

She whipped her skirt out of his grasp and backed up the steps. "Clear off, y-you ponce!"

He tried to grin but belched instead. She turned and ran up the stairs, her heart pounding madly in her ears. To think, she'd escaped Nazi and Russian spies, only to be put in more immediate danger by a drunken and disgusting British would-be Casanova!

When she arrived in the hostel room, out of breath, she found the other female guests reading books by candlelight. She nodded to them as she half-carried, half-dragged a ladder-back chair to the door and fixed it firmly under the doorknob.

The room, just large enough for the six cots it contained, proved to be well kept. The paint didn't peel; the curtains although old, looked clean and pressed, and a braided rug covered most of the dark wood floor. A jug and bowl rested on a dresser at the back.

Sitting on her bed to catch her breath, she introduced herself and explained the chair.

For a moment, the mother and daughter guests only stared at her. Then the lady gasped, holding a hand to her curler-covered head. "Oh dear! I did wonder if this was, er, well, quite the place. The price, you know, was quite low. One gets what one pays for, apparently." She sat up straight in her narrow bed. "It was so remiss of me, I'm afraid. I'm Mrs. Erskine, and this is my twelve year old daughter Tess. Tess, blow out your candle and go to sleep, there's a good girl."

Tess's cot remained in deep shadow, but Cicely caught a glimpse of a swinging veil of hair before the blankets were drawn up to the girl's chin.

Mrs. Erskine discarded her spectacles and book, and wrung her slender hands. She looked toward the chair bracing the door. "Is that quite enough protection, do you think?"

If it isn't, Cicely thought, then the Enfield under my mattress is. "Just a precaution, Mrs. Erskine. They are quite squiffy. In fact, they may have even passed out already."

The woman shuddered. "If you say so, Miss Tolhurst. If only Mr. Erskine were here. The world can be a truly frightening place without a man's protection."

"Is Mr. Erskine serving?" Cicely inquired.

The woman's eyes welled with tears. "He was. Now he's a prisoner of war in Tobruk."

Remembering the conversation on the train with Kit and Alistair, Cicely caught her breath. "He was one of the Queen's Own Cameron Highlanders?"

"Why, yes." The woman's face cleared.

"Second battalion?"

Mrs. Erskine nodded. "You've heard of their formidable march? Forcing the Nazis off the road? I'm *so* proud of him! But I'm worried. So many prisoners of war never return. They're given so little food, and no medicine. They're confronted with drinking tainted water or no water all. One way they die of thirst. The other, they die of cholera."

"I sympathise most awfully with you, Mrs. Erskine. I suppose all there is to do is keep a stiff upper lip and pray." Cicely bent down to remove her shoes. "I heard bombs fell on London again last night. Any word on the casualties?" She opened her portmanteau to remove her nightgown.

Mrs. Erskine hesitated. "I'm ashamed to admit, I don't listen to the casualty reports. The situation is too depressing. Besides, Tess is traumatised enough with her father a prisoner of war and a schoolfriend getting killed in one of the first Hull bombings."

Cicely turned her back to remove her blouse and cardigan. "Understandable, Mrs. Erskine." She decided to make conversation. "Where are you bound, if I may ask?"

"Launceston. Tess and I are moving in with my widowed sister. I just can't stick out London anymore at all."

Cicely pulled her nightgown over head and stood to shimmy out of her wool skirt petticoat. Facing Mrs. Erskine, she admitted, "I'm heading that direction myself. Are you taking the train or omnibus?"

"The omnibus is far less expensive. Tess and I must watch our pennies." Mrs. Erskine shrugged. "That is precisely why we are staying here—where pissed men stalk the corridors!"

Nodding sadly, Cicely threw back the duvet on her cot and climbed in. And when Mrs. Erskine blew out the candle, she reached under the mattress to touch her Enfield.

Near dawn, Cicely awoke with a need for the loo. Listening to Mrs. Erskine's and Tess's soft snores, she removed the chair from the doorknob, lit a candle, and retrieved her Enfield.

The door creaked as she eased it open. Closing it quietly behind her, she tip-toed two doors down to the facilities. Loud snores issued from a room upstairs. Doubting any bride could sleep through that cacophony, she assumed it must be the gents' communal room.

Her flickering candle sent silhouettes dancing on the walls, glancing off the massive wooden beams in the ceiling, and leaping from the darkness in the far corners of the corridor. The floor groaned under her stockinged feet. Was that a movement out the corner of her eye, beyond the loo door? She stopped, holding her light high. Her skin started to crawl. She could have sworn she'd seen a movement.

Standing for a full minute, she studied every shadowed doorway. Nothing. An overactive imagination. Still, her heart continued to flutter in her chest. Just to be safe, she let loose the Enfield's safety switch before proceeding.

Inside the loo, she locked the door and held her candle high. The room was quite large enough for a single bedroom, but it contained nothing but what she'd sought out.

When her necessity was finished, she pulled the door

open and stepped back into the corridor. Only two steps out, an arm wrapped around her waist from behind, snatching her off the floor. A large hot hand covered her mouth, smothering her scream. Her Enfield and candle clattered to the floor.

TWENTY-THREE

Final ruin fiercely drives . . .
—Edward Young

"Sister, when was this patient admitted?" The young doctor snapped open the patient's record clipboard, which was attached to the foot of the hospital bed.

An equally youthful nun rushed down the aisle to his side. "Two days past, Dr. Rhys-Jones. No improvement."

The physician swept an errant dark blond lock off his forehead, and studied the male patient through the oxygen tent covering his head and shoulders. "Take his vitals now, and bring the results to me," he ordered.

Rhys-Jones made his way back to his gnat-sized office, just off the ward at Saints Hospital in Cardiff. He sat at his pockmarked Boer War–era desk, switched on the lamp, and pulled a recent letter toward him. Picking up a pencil, he turned it upside down to bounce the rubber end on the desk while he considered. It just might work, he thought.

The young brunette sister knocked on his open door a few moments later. "The results, Doctor," she said. She studied him boldly, then dropped her eyes and stepped forward to hand him her notes. "Will there be anything else?"

"No thank-you, Sister . . . ?"

"Penwith, Doctor." She curtsied.

"This is a hospital, Sister Penwith, save your curtsies for parties. That's all."

Sister Penwith left with an air of disappointment, but Rhys-Jones ignored her to study the information in his hand. The patient's blood pressure was decent, but his pulse was not good at all, and he had a temperature of 106 degrees. Rhys-Jones rubbed his eyes. Likely the man would expire within the next few days if something wasn't done. Unfortunately nothing *could* be done, except to keep him under the oxygen tent and give him fluids.

If he could only save one life in this miserable war. This winter influenza and pneumonia season had been ravaging the countryside, and here he was, powerless to stop it. His fist hit the desk. He was so bloody sick of watching his patients die. And this patient, this one was a war hero—even if the coppers wanted him sorted for some reason. If he could only do *something,* stuck as he was here, unable to fight or help his comrades in North Africa.

He bounced his pencil's rubber several more times, then threw it down and picked up the phone.

"Yes, operator, give me Oxford University," he said. "Dr. Howard Florey, please."

Ellie Winterbourne scattered dried breadcrumbs on her back garden's rock wall for the robins and sparrows, but it was the crows who circled and cawed, and the seagulls who screeched.

"Oh, do clear off," she snapped. "You lot spend the summer destroying my fruit orchard, I'll certainly leave no snacks for you." She waved her arms to shoo them away. The large birds ignored her, but she decided it was unlikely they'd steal the bread from its intended recipients. The crumbs were probably too tiny to interest them.

The oyster-shell path to the cottage crunched under her feet as she walked back. A crust of frost coated the ground of her large garden. The small, slender woman shivered and hurried to her back door, giving her root vegetable patch a cursory glance on the way. Not much left, she observed; a good thing the bins in the cellar were nearly full. She had to cover the raspberry canes with burlap after luncheon, and her roses with the last of the chestnut leaves. The apple and pear trees needed pruning this year, but that was Harold's job, thank goodness.

A gust of wind blew, bringing the tang of the sea with it. And the smell of a storm. Only a stone's throw from the ocean, storms here at Cape Cornwall could be brutal. She had to remember to walk into the village for supplies. Likely they could expect a power outage.

Ellie brushed off her apron, entered her warm kitchen and filled the kettle to put on for tea. It had been a stroke of genius to reconstruct this place just before the war, to downsize the kitchen from the sort of cooking space used to employ several servants. With no children around anymore, she and Harold lived in the kitchen and lounge, and only climbed the stairs to retire to bed. They certainly didn't use the library, dining room, drawing room, or the two top floors of this sprawling Edwardian manse.

Before she could throw a pinch of what these days passed for tea in the teapot on the stove, she heard a loud knock at her front door. Harold always buried himself in his study until luncheon at one, and as it had only hit eleven, it was up to her to answer it. She walked toward the entry hall, wondering if it might be her friend Daisy with the promised raisin scones. What a delightful afternoon snack that would be to look forward to.

"Coming," she called, hearing a second knock, but stopped at the mirror by the door to smooth any stray auburn tresses that had fallen loose from her French twist.

As soon as she turned the knob, the door crashed open, striking her in the forehead. She screamed and was smashed into the wall. Two men in trilbies and trench coats strode in immediately, slamming the door behind them.

Leaning against the wall, her heart in her throat and shaking, Ellie stared at the intruders, then she pressed her eyes shut. When she opened them again, everything appeared blurry, and it wasn't just the blood running into her left eye. Pain radiated out in waves from the cut on her forehead.

"Come, Lady Winterbourne, show me your drawing room," one of the men ordered, while the other pulled a Walther P38 out of his pocket and disappeared down the corridor.

"W-what do you want?" Ellie's voice sounded hoarse even to her own ears.

The man nearly dragged her into the lounge, and tossed her on the settee. Her gaze snapped beyond him as she heard a palava coming from Harold's study.

"By God, sir! How dare—" She heard her husband's outraged voice cut off by a distinct crash.

Ellie's hands flew to her mouth. "Oh my God! What have you done?"

Her captor grunted. "He's not dead." He gave her a piercing look with colourless eyes. She'd never seen eyes like that, and they terrified her. "Yet," he amended. "We still need the two of you for leverage." He gave a nasty smile.

Her captor's partner entered just then, pulling Ellie's husband. He dwarfed Harold, who at just under six feet could normally more than defend himself. Ellie gasped when she spied her husband's swollen bottom lip and the blood dripping from his mouth.

"Harold!" She made to stand, but was pushed back onto the settee. She looked up at her captor, who was himself more Harold's size, with wide pleading eyes. "Please, let me see to him?"

"It's just a scratch, Ellie dear," mumbled Harold, who was pushed into one of the wingback chairs by the fireplace.

Ellie snorted. "Just a scratch. That's what men always claim." She studied her spouse with a critical eye. "Do you still possess all your teeth, darling?" she asked.

"Shut up!" The man standing over her removed his trilby and his coat, switching his pistol to his other hand while doing so. He threw his coat on the floor. He was an odd-looking man with white-blonde hair and black eyebrows. His torso muscles strained the seams of his long-sleeved shirt.

Although furnished with two wing chairs and lamp tables, a settee, and a low table, the lounge proved crowded with four people.

Harold's captor also removed his outer clothing, revealing a square jaw and dark blond waves. He was quite handsome, in fact, Ellie found herself thinking. Just the sort of man one might seek out at a party or a social gathering.

Her husband was tall and wiry, and quite strong despite the fact that he was over sixty. But if it came to overpowering them, Ellie wouldn't be much help—not at five feet two inches tall and just as slender as the day they married.

226

Brute strength was not her forté. But she did own one particular accomplishment. If only she could get to it.

Harold spoke up in a gruff voice. "What are we supposed to call you? Number one and number two?"

The white-blond man scowled and looked at the dark blond giant, who shrugged. "Suit yourself," he said. "Call us what you like." He jerked a thumb at the giant, who left the room.

"Perhaps you might inform us of the reason for this, er, emergency meeting?" Sir Harold continued.

White-hair made himself comfortable in a wingback chair, still aiming his firearm at the Winterbournes. He smiled without humour. "Your errant daughter, Sir Harold. We believe she has stolen, or at least is aware of, the location of a very important piece of intelligence."

Ellie felt the wind knocked out of her. Harold's eyebrows disappeared into his salt-and-pepper hair.

"Cicely?" Harold said, incredulous.

"She is your only child, correct?"

Sadness passed through both Ellie and Harold's eyes.

Ellie folded trembling hands in her lap. "Now she is, yes."

"Ah, yes. You lost a son at Dunkirk. Well, you'll want to keep your remaining progeny alive, won't you?"

Harold narrowed his gaze on the stranger. "You will keep all three of us alive if Cicely gives what you want?"

White-hair laughed. "I shan't spoil the outcome of a good mystery. But if Cicely fails to appear with what we want, your deaths are guaranteed."

Harold looked grim, blotting both his bloody lip and perspiring temple with a handkerchief.

"Cicely may not arrive for a day or two, so we might as well get comfortable," White-hair announced. "So

227

you"—he pointed his Walther at Harold—"better get over here to build a fire."

"A fire would be quite welcome," Harold agreed in a mutter. He limped to the fireplace and knelt, reaching for the coal scuttle. When he was finished, he placed a hand on the mantel to assist himself in rising. "I say, my wife's head needs tending to, and I know she is disturbed. Surely you will permit her to make a bit of tea?"

Just then the giant returned, nodding to his companion, and seated himself in the other chair. At the mention of tea, he shrugged and rose. "Wouldn't mind a cuppa myself. I'll go with her," he said.

Ellie went into the kitchen, seized a tea towel and pulled the whistling and now nearly dry kettle off the burner. The giant seated himself at the table. After placing the kettle in the sink to soak, Ellie took another from the cupboard and went about preparing tea.

A loud crash and a curse sounded from the lounge, and the giant shot up and ran into the next room. Ellie opened the silverware drawer, picked up the Browning Hi-Power 9 mm nestled there, tucked it into her skirtband along with an extra clip, and arranged her bib apron to hide the bulge.

Alistair opened his eyes and gazed out past his oxygen tent. So weak he could barely turn his head, all he could see was the end of his bed. He attempted to swallow, but nearly gave up as the job required to much effort. At the same time he struggled for every breath. His head throbbed as if it served as a blacksmith's anvil. He must be about to buy it, for he'd never before seen so many medical professionals gathered at his bedside: three doctors, one young, two old; five nuns, one young, the rest middle-aged.

He licked his dry, chapped lips, and knew at the moment he would willingly sell his soul to the Devil for a glass of water. And for a cool breeze. Yes, he'd give everything in the world for water and a breeze. Was he too big to fit in an ice box? Hell, the ice could be dragged out and he'd curl himself around it. He'd embrace it, as if it were Cicely.

The young doctor came toward him, holding a hypodermic needle containing a transparent liquid. A pretty brunette nun followed, rolling up Alistair's sleeve to expose the tender skin of his inner elbow.

Alistair felt a prick, and he watched the doctor push the mysterious liquid into his body through the needle. When finished, the doctor took Alistair's hand, squeezing it and giving him a nod before leading his entourage out of sight.

Alistair felt beyond caring what was done to him. He didn't much care even if they were using him for a guinea pig. Then he recalled Cicely with her hurt and frightened eyes as she finally gave up and ran for the loo closet on the fishing boat.

She'd told him she loved him. Had it been a fantasy? Or had she really uttered those words?

Cicely. Beautiful, passionate Cicely. Courageous, spit-in-your-eye Cicely. Warm, intelligent Cicely. Deceiving Cicely. He frowned. Could he be seeking perfection? It was stupid of him to waste himself on such an unproductive task. Bloody, bloody stupid. Who the hell was he to judge her? Likely he'd raised that unconscious wall to protect himself. What girl as beautiful, confident, and brave would look twice at what amounted to a crippled man? If the chance existed to win her, he'd damned well work to his dying breath to do so!

He imagined Cicely greeting him when he returned from a day at the Met. Cicely in his kitchen, cooking for him—sitting in a rocking chair darning his socks. Cicely in bed with him, vulnerable and untamed. He couldn't picture his life without her anymore.

It was bloody well time he pulled up his socks and started caring what these hacks did to him. He must concentrate on recovering, and quickly. Because if he didn't, he'd never see Cicely again and ask her to marry him. If she'd ever forgive him.

Cicely's captor allowed her to slide slowly to her feet. As she slipped down his body, she could tell he was too slender to be either Algie or Bean. He kept her mouth covered.

"That's a lot of firepower for a bird," he laughed. His voice! She knew that voice! But from where?

She twisted in his hold and he tightened his grip.

"Not yet, Miss *Bennington*. First you must promise to stay silent. If you do, we'll talk. If you don't, I'll smash your face to kingdom come. Understood?"

Cicely nodded.

"Right then, walk with me. We're going to enjoy a nice sit on this window seat." He led her to the window seat on the other side of the hall, which was situated in a private alcove.

Her attacker pushed her down, but remained standing in front of her as he removed his hand from her mouth. "Stay here," he ordered. It was too dark for her to see, but she heard his footsteps walk away. An instant later, he returned.

"Take these and light this candle," he instructed, pressing matches into her hand.

Cicely fumbled with the box, nearly dropping it. Finally a match flared and she guided it to the candle clutched in her captor's hand. When the flame caught, he raised the candle so she could see his face.

Cicely gasped, and for a moment stared speechless at the man in front her.

"But wh-what are *you* doing here?" she demanded.

TWENTY-FOUR

Time shall unfold what plaited cunning hides . . .
  —William Shakespeare

The candlelight gave the appearance of a halo circling his dark head, but this man was no angel. He was the man she'd seen passing just as she entered this house last night.

"How did you find me?" she demanded.

Aristo Kalakos, the son of the butcher Kit had sent her to, removed a cigarette from the breast pocket of his wool overcoat, held it to the candle and lit it. Then he leaned against the wall and studied her over the curling smoke.

"It wasn't easy. I followed you."

Brow creased, Cicely shook her head, still staring at him in incomprehension. "But . . . why?"

Kalakos rolled his eyes. "Because you're the most beautiful, beguiling bird I've ever seen, so needs must I risk life and limb to find you and pledge my undying love." He shook his head and laughed. "I rue the day my stepmama gave birth to that mewling little rotter."

Cicely had the feeling she'd fallen down the rabbit hole. "What are you talking about?" she asked.

Kalakos's mouth twisted. "My baby sister—the one

who gets special clothes from that old slag Skinner. Since that damn brat was born, m'brothers and I are naught but chopped cabbage."

Cicely buried her head in her hands, rubbing her forehead and eyes. Looking back up at him, she said, "Are you being deliberately obscure? Tell me why you're here."

He took a last draw on his cigarette, threw it on the floor and tapped it out with his boot, then raised that boot to rest on the opposite wall of the alcove, effectively blocking her escape. "I'm bloody well here, Miss High and Mighty, because there's nothing that Skinner woman won't do for my little sister and stepmama. My father feels he owes her." He gave a quiet, humourless laugh. "If a Greek owes you, he'll die making good, you know. That note you carried to my father? It didn't merely request a new ration book—Kit wanted you followed."

Cicely's jaw dropped. "W-why?"

Kalakos dropped his boot to the floor and faced her. "Because she thought you and your 'husband' were up to something."

"She thought we were hiding something, and she wanted to know what it was?" How strange, Cicely thought. Kit hadn't struck her as a busybody.

"She thought you might be in over your head with something dangerous. She said you seemed jumpy. The old slag wanted you protected." He bowed in a courtly seventeenth-century manner, waving his hand several times in front of his body before actually bowing. "I am meant to be your protection, my lady."

Cicely's jaw dropped again, and she suppressed the urge to laugh uncontrollably. She covered her mouth and shook her head. Now, *that* she could believe of Kit. How sweet of her! But, oh God, poor Kit didn't realise how dangerous the game was.

Kalakos scowled at her. "Can you comprehend how arse-over-tit you've made my life? I lost you days ago—just got lucky when I followed the right coppers."

"That *was* you! You searched Alistair's pockets on the train, when he was out cold."

"Not I. That was some chap with an eyepatch who was hot for his nibbs's pockets. Thought at first he was bent and knotted on insensible men. But he was hunting for something, and it t'weren't dosh."

"Didn't you drink with them?"

"A single sip." He shrugged. "Don't mind saying I thought you might throw a spanner in the works by following your chappy into that lounge. I saw your chappy glaze over and I felt the drug, too—pretended to join him. A few minutes later I actually did pass out."

"How did you get away? The baggage car was locked."

Kalakos grunted. "You'll be owing me a set of togs. I bloody climbed onto the roof of that damned bar car. Managed the length of it, God only knows how. I climbed down at the other end and I was on my way." He leered down at her. "Strange stuff. But know a few things about you, I do now. Old Skinner shan't be happy when she discovers you and his nibbs murdered those old ladies in London. Didn't know she was buying protection for a murderess, I'd bet."

Cicely shot to her feet. "*I'm not* a murderess! Neither is Alistair." She stood eye to eye with Kalakos.

"Doesn't matter to me if you are." The man shrugged. "Not as if I haven't done my share. M'father, as well."

Cicely felt a stab of fear and sat down. "Is there anything you haven't done, Mr. Kalakos?"

234

He grinned. "I've certainly broken all the commandments." He shrugged again. "And then some." He took a step closer. "That frighten you?"

Beasts of prey smell fear, her father had taught her. *Don't show it to them.* Crossing her legs and looking him in the eye, she countered in a soft voice, "So . . . what do you know of me, Mr. Kalakos? I'm very good with that Enfield you took. What do you think I might have done in my life?"

He shook his head. "Besides murder two defenceless old women?"

"Don't forget that unidentified man who was stabbed to death," she added with a sneer.

Kalakos stroked his stubbled chin in consideration. "Right, then. I believe what you said earlier. You haven't killed anyone. Why are you running, and where to? I've got to return to the butcher shop soon before m'father disinherits me."

Cicely's eyes clouded. "You're wrong, Mr. Kalakos. I have killed. But not the three people the coppers say I did."

Giving her a good look, he said, "Why, I believe you have, pretty bird."

"Mr. Kalakos, why don't you return to your father's butcher shop now? Say you saw me safely delivered to wherever I was going. Your father won't know any different."

"You don't know my father." He snorted. "It'd be just like him to send m'brother Christos to watch my back and to see the job's done right."

"Have you seen him? Christos, I mean."

"Doesn't mean anything."

Cicely sighed. She could use help, but this man wasn't trustworthy. For all she knew, he'd throw her to the wolves first chance he got. And she didn't want his death on her conscience, either.

"Determined to protect me, are you? If I shake you, you'll only attempt to find me again?" Cicely asked carefully.

Kalakos leered at her. "You're stuck with me, pretty bird."

"Oh, for goodness sake—do call me Cicely," she snapped.

"Okay, pr—Cicely. Your turn to answer questions. What's going on?"

Cicely considered. Because of official police involvement, likely anyone after her now knew she was headed to find her parents in Cornwall. The trick was to not get caught on the way.

"Indeed, Kit was quite right. I am in over my head. I've, er, left Alistair for a bit," she prevaricated. Let Kalakos think he was due to join her any time. "But he'll catch up soon. Make no mistake"—she looked him in the eye—"that what I'm attempting is highly dangerous. Life and death." At his unbelieving look, she added, "At least seven people have been killed already, maybe more. Those two elderly ladies and the stabbed man—it was believed they might know too much."

"Now you have me interested," Kalakos said. "Sounds as if this intrigue would do m'father proud. Now, don't tell me," he chuckled softly, "this is for King and country?"

"Would it make a difference?"

He shrugged. "Of course not. A job is a job."

"Then let's just leave it as an intrigue."

She froze when she heard the floor creak, and footsteps followed. Kalakos glued himself to the wall and whipped out a switchblade. Cicely grasped his wrist and shook her head. The look he gave her was poisonous as hemlock.

The loo door opened then closed. A moment later, they heard a flush and the door opened again. Soft shuffling steps went in the opposite direction. The floor creaked again, and the footsteps disappeared.

But a moment later, they heard a young girl's trembling voice. "Is a-anyone there?"

Cicely held her finger to her lips and stood up. Kalakos seized her forearm, but she shook her head. Emerging from the alcove, Cicely said, "It's just me, Tess. I couldn't sleep. Go back to the room, I'll be along in a moment—after I've used the facilities myself."

"You did give me a start, Miss Tolhurst," the girl said. "You have a candle back there?" She, leaned around Cicely to get a better look.

"Don't tell anyone, but I don't like the dark," Cicely said, stepping in front of her.

Tess smiled. "I don't either. Good-night then," she said, and disappeared back into the room they shared.

When Cicely returned to Kalakos, the man's switchblade was nowhere in sight and he was grinning. "Nice-looking young bird," he said.

"She's twelve, for God's sake!" Cicely whispered.

"Jealous?"

Cicely rolled her eyes. "Pay attention. That girl's off limits. I'm taking an omnibus to Bideford. I may travel with her and her mother. Then I'll go to Okehampton by any transport available. We are not acquainted. Do not approach me."

"I bloody well hate taking orders from a woman," Kalakos groused.

Cicely growled, "Pecker up, Kalakos—you're taking orders from your father."

The man sighed. "Don't know which is worse."

Cicely stepped out from the alcove, intending to go back to bed. Then she turned around. "By the way, how did you get in?"

"Locks don't stop me." Kalakos laughed.

"You may indeed come in handy." As soon as the word escaped her mouth, she winced. "Convenient, I mean."

He grinned. "Oh, you chose correctly the first time, Cicely. I'm *very* handy."

"Good-night, Mr. Kalakos," she said sternly, then headed for her room.

"Don't you want this?" He held out her Enfield.

Cicely retraced her steps, snatched the pistol from his hand and went to her room.

For the first time in days, Alistair woke with no oxygen tent. And he could swallow. And breathe. In fact, he felt jolly good. When he coughed, he realized he wasn't quite jolly yet, but he was a good deal better. What he wanted was a tall cool glass of water and a medium-rare beefsteak. Sighing, he realized he'd be lucky to get beef broth.

Leaning forward in an attempt to study his surroundings, he found he couldn't see past the hospital curtain on his right. To the left was the wall. Across from him, another chap languished in his cot with a leg in traction, and because of the curtain beside him, he could only see the outline of legs and feet in the next bed.

He eyed his bedstand, and at last spotted the pullcord to bring the sister. He had only to wait a moment or two for a very attractive brunette to appear.

"Awake at last, are you? You'll be wanting water, and

we've a nice chicken broth for you. I'll give that to you straightaway. Then Dr. Rhys-Jones wishes a most particular word with you."

"Doctor . . . ?"

"Rhys-Jones, your physician. He saved your life. Rest, I'll return directly," she said, and sailed down the hospital ward.

When Alistair finished the meal that was brought, his stomach growled, wanting more nourishment. Maybe they could spare a slice of bread or two? He was about to use the pull again when a young doctor appeared at the foot of his bed.

The man frowned. "Good afternoon. I'm Dr. Rhys-Jones, your attending physician," he said.

Alistair held out his right hand in an enthusiastic manner. "I'm informed, Doctor, that I have you to thank for single-handedly saving my life."

The doctor glanced at Alistair's outstretched hand but ignored it. Alistair slowly lowered his arm, studying the physician closely.

"Yes," Rhys-Jones confirmed, "I used a rare, expensive, and experimental drug on you. It's called penicillin. It kills bacterial infections. It's the new wonder drug."

Alistair nodded, waiting for him to continue.

"Unfortunately, we are unable to give it to our fighting boys. There's not enough of it, for one thing. For another, more tests are required. A school of thought exists that when it works it's only by chance. Some of the old boys aren't ready to give up the garlic yet. More quantities exist in America, so that is where most of the testing is done." He bowed his head and grasped the footrail of Alistair's bed. When he looked up, his eyes were burning. "I pulled strings to acquire the penicillin. My superiors informed me it was a waste of time and much-needed funds. It was better left to experimenting, they said.

"I didn't listen. More than anything I wished to save a life that I could save. Especially that of a war hero. The penicillin only took a day by special courier to arrive from Oxford. I injected you with a number of syringes. You recovered—but not before I discovered you're wanted for a triple murder!" He looked furious.

Alistair's stomach fell. "It's a mistake, Doctor." His voice came out flat, emotionless. "We found those bodies, yes. But we did *not* murder them."

Rhys-Jones straightened. "At any rate, the local constable is just outside. He's waiting for a word with you."

TWENTY-FIVE

. . . We shall fight on the beaches, we shall fight on the landing grounds, we shall fight in the fields and in the streets, we shall fight in the hills; we shall never surrender. . . .
—Winston Churchill

Fortunately, no snafus followed Cicely to Bideford. Aristo took a whole seat to himself in the rear of the bus, apparently using the chance for a bit of kip. He did as he'd been told and stayed well clear of her. Once the omnibus let them off, Cicely and the Erskines planned to board another coach headed to Okehampton almost immediately. It was nearly too good to be true, having had no problems, but she refused to dwell on it.

Cicely experienced one tense moment, as Mrs. Erskine surveyed several headlines in the Bideford terminal, commenting, "What a shame you share a name with a murderess, Miss Tolhurst." The woman shuddered delicately and moved on to the coach yard to be sure she and her daughter boarded the next coach.

"Imagine that," she continued, taking her daughter by the hand. "A murder spree in London! Isn't it enough that thousands die in all these bombing raids and in the war? No, these maniacs must kill two defenceless old ladies and the man guarding them."

Cicely's heart stopped, but she managed to reply, "Heavens, they had a *guard?*"

"Granted, I really don't know much about the episode, but it stands to reason. Ladies need a man about, and he was found dead in the same building. One merely puts two and two together." She shrugged.

Cicely stopped herself from rolling her eyes. She said, "Of course you must be correct, Mrs. Erskine. If you will excuse me a moment or two, I'll pop into the food stand to purchase supplies for the journey."

The woman nodded. "By all means, dear. Tess and I made purchases for the journey in Barstaple. If needs be, we'll hold the coach for you."

Cicely nodded and left for the food stand. While she waited for the attendant to fill her vacuum flask with tea, she studied the busy terminal. Other than Aristo, who was heading toward her, she didn't note anyone looking remotely interested in her presence. Two grim-looking coppers made the rounds, serious-faced and occasionally stopping to check travelers' papers. Cicely's palms moistened as they came closer. She fought the urge to hurry the attendant. Finally he handed over the vacuum flask and a bag of fresh scones, a wedge of Cotswold cheese, and a sorry yellow apple, and just as she left, Aristo appeared and ordered a *Times,* tea and scones. Ignoring him, Cicely headed for the coach to Okehampton.

Taking a seat behind the Erskines in the middle of the bus, she made herself comfortable for a little kip. During the ride here, she'd still been too keyed up from the dawn meeting with Aristo. Used to Kalakos's presence now, and ready for the milkrun to Okehampton, she was more relaxed.

Leaning her head against the cold window and watching the light flurry of tiny snowflakes outside, she hoped more than anything Alistair remained in the world of the living. Even if it had been the truth he'd spewed at her on the boat, her love for him refused to die. She itched to speak with him, to hear him deny it. Hope for the delivery of the code, for Britain, existed as long as she and Alistair lived. But most of all—hope for the love she bore Alistair.

No, on this journey, the Enigma code wasn't the only important matter. If she managed to deliver the key but Alistair died, life would become stale and tasteless.

Alistair felt cold steel clamp around his wrist. His spirits sinking, he watched the grey-haired constable cuff him, and wrap the other cuff around the bed rail.

"Constable"—he noted the man's identification plate pinned to the his uniform tunic—"Hunter, neither Miss Winterbourne nor I committed those murders. You must—"

"It's not up to me to decide your guilt or innocense, young man. That's for the courts. My job is to arrest you and keep an eye on you until Scotland Yard arrives. Shouldn't take more than a few days, and you need more bed rest anyway." The constable pulled up a visitors chair, sat down and crossed his arms over his chest. He studied Alistair with watery blue eyes.

Alistair compressed his lips in irritation. "Can you at least discover the names of the inspectors who are coming for me?"

"Doubt I'd be informed, even if I were to ask." The constable scowled. "Believe me, this isn't my chosen duty. Fancy a smoke I do, and that bit of alright sister informs me I'm not to do so because of your damaged lungs." He snorted. "As if a little pipe smoke ever hurt anyone."

Alistair leaned back on his pillows, and as he did so the

handcuffs rattled. The aged constable just sat in his chair, staring down the length of the ward and glowering.

In Alistair's line of work, he'd been taught to get what he wanted from people, both as a soldier and as a Special Branch inspector. Psyching up infantrymen to charge into battle, into a wall of bullets, was no easy task. Neither was pulling information from reluctant suspects and witnesses.

"Served in the first War, did you?" Alistair prompted the bobby.

Emotion charged the constable's eyes. "Bloody right I did. Fought in those filthy, disease-ridden trenches. Survived a Hun bullet, shrapnel, mustard gas, and that Spanish influenza." He uncrossed his legs. "Many a mate of mine took their last breaths on those French battlefields. Still barren wastelands they are, too—except for a poppy patch here and there."

"Do you serve in the Dads Army when off duty?" Alistair prodded.

"Indeed I do. We guard the beaches. Keep all that barbed wire in place. No Hun'll get past us." Constable Hunter uncrossed his arms and narrowed his eyes. "Seems to me a strapping lad like you ought to be fighting the Jerries and Japs instead of creeping around London on a night of a bombing raid, stealing from and murdering two helpless women."

"I did serve," Alistair said quietly. "At Dunkirk. Nearly lost my leg. Thank God gangrene didn't set in. Still, a bundle of shrapnel is all warm and cozy in my knee. I received my walking papers, and the rest of my battalion is now in Calcutta—when the chaps aren't marching into Burma to wreak havoc with the Japs."

Constable Hunter's jaw dropped. "That's a lie! Riff-raff like you are cowards."

Alistair's eyebrows rose. "I suppose you think it's all nonsense that I'm in the Met's Special Branch."

Hunter nodded. "Of course. I heard you possessed false Scotland Yard credentials."

"Well, why not take shuftie in this cabinet?" Alistair suggested, indicating the locker-like cabinet between the bed and the wall. "My personal effects will be there—including my Army discharge booklet and Scotland Yard identification."

"Why not, indeed? I'd fancy a peep at a good forgery." The constable stood and opened the cabinet door. Pulling out a large brown envelope, he emptied the contents on Alistair's cot.

Sorting through the papers in a leisurely manner, Hunter examined Alistair's Met identification and glanced briefly up him as he opened the discharge booklet. A moment later, Hunter's eyebrow rose. "Major? Top-lofty, aren't you?" He perused further and snapped his head up in shock.

"Recipient of the George Cross?"

Following the large man who'd come to watch her make tea, Ellie Winterbourne ran to her husband in the lounge, who was on his knees by his wing chair. "Heavens, Harold, what is it? What happened?" she asked.

The giant snorted and settled himself in a chair.

Harold raised his gaze to his wife, and slowly closed and reopened one eye. "Nothing really, my dear. Tried to stand and a wave of dizziness descended. I assure you, I'm quite alright." He grasped Ellie's waist in an apparent attempt to steady himself, then seized the arms of the chair to pull himself up. Once seated, he said, "You see? All right and tight. Is the kettle on the boil yet?"

"I'm sure it is. I'll return in a moment with a nice cup of hot tea for you," Ellie informed him, then sailed back into the kitchen. The giant rose and followed.

Ellie proceeded to prepare a late luncheon, and cleaned up afterwards over the course of the afternoon, all under the watchful eyes of her guard, the giant. After the small repast of toast and cheese, the giant retired to Cicely's old room on the second floor for a few hours sleep. White-hair stood guard. He would take his turn sleeping in the bed later, but Ellie and Harold were not to be allowed such luxury. They had to make do in the lounge, curled up in a settee, a chair, or on the floor.

An hour after the giant retired, Ellie suggested they turn on the wireless. Their guard agreed. "Let's see what propaganda the BBC spew tonight," he said. "That always makes for good entertainment."

They listened to several minutes of *Top of the Pops* before the news broadcast. Near the end, the newscaster announced that half the notorious couple wanted in a triple London murder had been captured and lay near death in a Cardiff hospital.

". . . Meanwhile the search continues for his accomplice, Miss Cicely Winterbourne. The manhunt is concentrated between London and St. Just, Cornwall, where it is believed she is headed."

Ellie gasped. "Oh, dear heavens! Our girl is on her own."

"What do you chaps intend if our daughter is arrested?" her husband asked their captor.

White-hair's voice was cold. "You'd better hope she's smart enough to arrive here on her own. If she isn't so lucky, we shan't need you."

Sir Harold swallowed, but he managed to keep his countenance casual. "I could use a smoke. May I retrieve my pipe and tobacco from my study?"

"No," White-hair answered flatly. "You're going nowhere by yourself, not even the WC. Not while my, er, friend is sleeping. So I hope you don't mind both your wife and I watching." He tossed Harold his box of Players. "Smoke one of these if you need it so badly.

Harold caught the box instinctively, studied the fags for a moment, then shrugged and pulled one out. He went to the fireplace for a box of matches, returned to his chair, and slipped the matches in his cardigan pocket after he was done lighting the cigarette.

Watching her husband smoke, Ellie mentally tallied the firearms stowed in various locations through the house. There was a shotgun in the coal shed, though little good that might do; Harold could go out for coal, but he could hardly come back shooting when they could still use her as a hostage. Her favourite gun, a one-shot derringer, lay under her folded stockings in her vanity. Harold had a Browning locked in a compartment in his study desk.

Ellie's fingers itched to use the Browning tucked in her skirt band, but dared not. Nearly a lifetime's experience told her never to take a chance unless the situation was desperate. It was grave, yes, but not yet desperate. Harold must arm himself first, then they must wait for the just the right time. If they made a move before they were sure to succeed, and failed, it would prove all but impossible to take charge of the situation again. At worst they'd be killed outright. No, Harold must be armed before she used her weapon.

Once in British secret services, always in the secret services. One's naivety quickly dissolved there, never to return. It made for a life of paranoia. Bringing up children and not passing it on had required a great deal of skill, but Ellie thought they'd succeeded admirably with both Cicely and Harold, Jr. Now she wished they hadn't, because Cicely would need all the paranoia she could get. Skill, too.

She studied her husband critically. As he didn't wear an apron to disguise the bulge of a gun, it seemed the only good hiding place might be his sock. How she could retrieve her derringer and pass it to Harold would require some thought.

The overnight trip to Okehampton proved deadly slow and tedious. The Erskines had brought a large supply of books with them, and offered Cicely her choice, but she refused; she couldn't afford to lose herself in a story. Fortunately, a fellow passenger passed on an old *Times*. She read the far-fetched account of herself and Alistair committing the heinous triple murder. Dooly had finally been identified. When interviewed, his wife claimed she had every confidence in the police finding those responsible, and had kept a strangely calm demeanor, wrote the reporter. If anything, Cicely thought, poor Mrs. Dooly was probably relieved the bounder was dead.

In a smaller article on the next page, Cicely learned Alistair lay near death in Cardiff with pneumonia. Her stomach convulsed and she caught her breath. It was true! He did suffer from pneumonia. She collapsed against the back of her seat and stared out the window. Ironically, the sun showed itself for the first time in days.

Tears began to roll down her face, but although she hiccupped now and again, she managed to remain silent. Leaning her head against the window and closing her eyes, Cicely let misery flood her. It didn't seem likely Alistair would recover. Large, strong men expired from pneumonia all the time. She tried to imagine a life without Alistair, but came up with nothing but a blank slate. She couldn't go back to Bletchley, and now what was left to her?

"Miss Tolhurst? Are you weeping?" Cicely opened her eyes to find Tess looming over the back of the seat she shared with her mother. The girl frowned.

"I had a bad dream, dear," Cicely explained. She removed her handkerchief from her pocket and wiped her face.

"I have bad dreams, too," the little girl murmured. Then she turned to face forward again.

Time for the old stiff upper lip, Cicely thought, remembering her words to Mrs. Erskine. Alistair wasn't dead yet. At least, not at the time of that article. She wasn't going to think of him as dying. Not until she dragged the truth out him. She'd concentrate on him fighting for his life because she knew he would do so until the last. She nodded to herself. As far as she was concerned, he lived and would be waiting for her in London or Cardiff when she completed her journey. She looked to that beacon of hope.

If she concentrated hard enough, she might actually believe it.

* * *

"The George Cross is second only to the Victoria Cross," Constable Hunter said in awed tones.

"Yes. I earned the GC, among other medals," Alistair murmured. "They are quite real, I assure you. And they didn't come cheap."

Constable Hunter fell into more than sat in his chair, still holding Alistair's army discharge book. "I don't believe it," he said in a faint voice. He studied the booklet once again. "It *is* difficult to believe a falsified document would make such a fantastic claim. Tell me, how did you earn it?"

"If I tell you, will you believe me that I didn't kill those ladies?"

Hunter tapped his chin with his forefinger. "Perhaps . . . but I shan't let you go. My duty is to keep you until the toffs arrive. I tell you what, though. After I confirm your service record with a mate of mine in military records—I'll even spend my own blunt on the phone call to London—I'll take the blower in hand again and make that call you wanted a while back. How's that for a bargain?"

Alistair nodded. "Very reasonable. But you must talk to Walker, my superior—none other. I'll provide his residence calling number as well."

"All right. Tell me a war story." Hunter leaned back in his chair.

"It happened at Dunkirk. Afraid that's all I saw of the war up close—other than bombing raids, of course. We horribly underestimated the Jerries' numbers, firepower and equipment. Not just us, but the French and the Belgians. The odds were overwhelming, and we soon found all avenues of escape to the Channel cut off. We could only retreat to the harbour and the beaches of Dunkirk.

"The German dive bombers had us pinned down. A great many of the ships sent for our rescue were sunk, effectively blocking the harbour. We all thought we were done for. And then the civilian navy came to the rescue— in trawlers, motor yachts, fishing smacks, paddle-steamers, and lifeboats. Nearly anything that floated, appeared. They started picking us up off the beaches, manoeuvring through the flaming and sunken graveyard of British destroyers, and transporting us to whole destroyers laying offshore. The dive bombers went after them, as well, and many of them didn't make it out of the harbour, but the better portion did, delivering load after load of soldiers until every last one of the B.E.F.—all three hundred thousand of us—were off that bullet- and bomb-ravaged beach."

Hunter nodded impatiently. "Yes, I'm aware of the basics. I'm interested in *your* doings, young sir."

Alistair took a deep breath. His memories were hell, and he hated looking back on them.

"Thousands of us were sitting ducks on that beach. All we could do during the day was dig into the dunes or make trenches to hide in. The Jerries shot at us and bombed us, all day every day. They used sirens, too, to further unnerve us. There was no cover, except at night. No food and no water for four days. Very little before that. We'd all marched up to forty miles to get there, with no sleep.

"I was trained in neutralising bombs." Alistair gestured to his knee. "I neutralised one too many. Although the chaps it spared wouldn't say so." He shrugged. "That's how I earned the George Cross. I took care of three unexploded bombs. Made a target of myself doing so, and afterwards helped drag the injured into the dunes and trenches. Conspicuous gallantry, I guess.

"When the boats came"—Alistair shook his head in wonder as he continued—"there was no panic. We all took our turns at night, wading out to help the wounded onto the boats, and finally the able-bodied took their own places. It was called the 'Dunkirk Spirit.' The comradery, at times, was even quite jolly. Likely we acted so to hide our horror at all the dead bodies, blood, choking smoke, fire . . ." Alistair stared into space, witnessing again the gruesome sights and sounds of the beach. He said, "Your mate is standing right beside you one moment, and the next his head explodes, hanging by a thread to his body. Another one crawls toward you, saying everything is tickety-boo because, 'The little ships are here for our rescue. Give me a hand, old boy,' he says. 'We'll limp out, help each other to the boats.'" Alistair looked at Hunter. "But he's hemorrhaging, crawling away from his severed leg and doesn't yet realise it."

"Aye." Constable Hunter nodded, his eyes more than just watery now. "Like the trenches. And no matter how much one tells people about one's war experiences, there are always some you keep to yourself." He stood and cleared his throat. "I'll be using the hospital blower. Back in a trice."

Alistair watched the aged constable make his way down the ward. It was with his old military bearing, head up and back straight—proud.

252

TWENTY-SIX

These troublesome disguises which we Wear . . .
—John Milton

Cicely paused on the top step of the coach. Excitement sizzled in her veins. After three days on various omnibuses, she'd finally arrived in Bodmin.

"Planning to stand here all day, Miss?" asked the irritated coach driver.

"Sorry!" Cicely tossed a smile over her shoulder and descended to the pavement.

Bodmin always served as the mark that meant she was nearly home; it had been only four hours away by motor car before petrol rationing. Now it might take three to four days by omnibus, and who knew how long it would take by train, what with the unscheduled stops for the night. Cicely shook her head. It would be a cold day in Hell before she boarded another train.

It felt strange to be traveling alone again. The Erskines had made good travelling companions as well as efficient cover, but now they were gone.

Grasping her portmanteau and makeshift handbag, she slowly made her way through the throng in the coach yard heading toward the terminal. Why was the crowd so thick today?

It was ruddy cold, and the heavy, stone-grey sky threatened snow. Many people stamped their feet and swung their arms in an effort to warm themselves. She did likewise as her progress slowed. Then she heard it: singing and bells ringing. Of course! Christmas must be only a few days away now. A good portion of the populace was on Christmas furlough.

At last, progress. The throng made great strides forward, and Cicely found herself in the terminal. Standing on her toes, she attempted to peer through the mass of people in search of the food stand, which was usually located outside, on the opposite side from departures.

She froze and felt panic take hold. Several police constables were checking papers and identification. It appeared random, but she couldn't take the chance.

"Taking root, Miss?" a voice said behind her.

"Sorry, please go ahead." Cicely nodded to the elderly gentleman who'd spoken, and he passed and disappeared into the throng. She sidestepped toward the side of the building where the loos were generally located. Perhaps she might wait in there while the mass of coach passengers thinned out, checking occasionally to see if the coppers still did their duty. If they did, she would retrace her steps and board the first coach leaving.

Outside, beyond the coppers, a variety of taxis, a motor car, and a horsecart waited. A woman with four small children waved a handkerchief to someone in the terminal building, and three women of dubious virtue postured, smiling at the gentlemen.

As Cicely watched, one of the "ladies" bent down to smooth a non-existent stocking. The line drawn up the back of her leg was a bit crooked, and she hadn't bothered to use leg maquillage. She slid her hands just above her knees, while her eyes darted here and there searching out any men who might be interested. An RAF man approached her. She grinned, took his arm and walked off with him.

Prostitution, of course, remained illegal, but these days the authorities generally gave it Nelson's eye. It kept the chaps in uniform happy, and sometimes even kept them from bothering decent women.

Another of the working girls entered the terminal, pausing to unbutton her coat and to show off her very low-cut red dress. She sashayed past the coppers, winking at them. One called after her, and she smiled over her shoulder, then tossed her head and headed for the loo. Cicely followed her in.

After taking care of business, the girl sat at the vanity and applied another layer of her already heavy cosmetics. Her Jean Harlow hair appeared to be molting.

Cicely smiled and approached. The girl shot her a defiant look and smeared on more bright red lip rouge.

"I say," Cicely began. "Your wig is spectacular."

The girl snorted. "Bugger off. I don't do women."

Cicely's eyes widened with shock. "Er, you mistake my meaning. It's something else I want."

The girl eyed her suspiciously. "What could posh *you* possibly want wi' me?"

Another woman walked in, and disappeared into a toilet stall. Cicely lowered her voice. "Will you take five pounds for your wig?"

The girl raised her eyebrows, then narrowed her gaze on Cicely. "Make it ten pounds and it's yours," she countered.

Cicely winced and did a few quick financial calculations. Likely it was more than the tart made in a fortnight.

It meant hitchhiking and perhaps skipping a meal or two. "Alright, but I want your handbag, too," she demanded.

The girl regarded the worn and cracking black leather handbag, then nodded. "But I want that thing in return," she bartered. She pointed to Cicely's drawstring bag.

"Done," Cicely announced, reaching for her wallet.

Twenty minutes later, Cicely emerged from the ladies loo another woman entirely. She'd borrowed the tart's lip rouge, applied maquillage and rouge with a heavy hand. Kohl lined her eyes, and she'd even lit a few matches, blown them out, and applied them to her eyebrows. Gone was any hint of a redheaded complexion. She'd taken off her blouse and wore only her yellow cardigan, unbuttoned nearly to her navel, and her navy wool skirt. Her coat rested over her arm.

Pausing a moment in the loo doorway to settle into her role, she immediately noticed condemning glances from women and mixed reactions from men. Some surveyed her head to toe in a openly suggestive manner; others gave her pitying looks. Inside she felt a twinge of shame, but she was determined to ignore it and the reactions of those around her. She walked slowly through the thinned crowd, swaying her hips and trying for a sloe-eyed and seductive air.

Outside Cicely joined the queue at the food stand, and noticed the lone remaining kerb crawler disappearing around a corner, clinging to a customer.

"I say, sweetheart, got time to show an overpaid, over-sexed, and over-here Yank a good time?" Came a voice.

Cicely brushed the soldier's hand off her arm. "Er, no, I'm afraid not," she said.

The Yank's uniform cap was perched back on his fair head at a rakish angle. His pale blue eyes narrowed on her face, and when he grasped her wrist he squeezed it tight.

"Look, *doll,* ain't got much time before my bus comes. Let's get to it. I'll even toss in an extra pound note. You can buy something nice for yourself from one of the spivs." He tugged on her wrist.

"*No!* You've mistak—" Cicely pulled back and nearly lost her balance. "This is a mistake. I'm not what you thi—"

"Bullshit, you whore! You're coming with me, hear?" His face twisted and grew a mottled red.

"Bloody well go with him," groused a man behind her in the queue. "Since when are you bints particular?"

Cicely felt heat rise in her face and saw red out the corner of her eyes. Jerking free, she stamped her foot and rounded on both men with a withering glare.

"How dare you!" She couldn't remember being so infuriated, and admonished herself to take a deep breath before she truly became spitting mad.

First she addressed the Yank, who stepped back and eyed her as if she'd just sprouted two heads. "If I say I don't ruddy well have time for you, *I don't.* So bugger off and find your entertainment elsewhere.

"And as for *you.*" Her eyes narrowed in contempt on the Englishman behind her. "Mind your own ruddy business, and be careful when it comes to calling names." She made a point of studying his face, which was pale and resembled the underbelly of a fish.

"The cheek! Wot's the world coming to when a bin—"

"There you are, luv, the Devil's own business finding you." Suddenly Aristo was strolling at a leisurely pace toward her, his hands in his pockets and a toothpick protruding from his mouth. "I'm thinking your humour might improve, luv," he said, glancing at the Yank and Fish-face. "Frightful temper she has when she's hungry. There's no goin' near her," he confided to the men.

"Too right," Fish-face agreed, standing very straight and nodding. "Bin—she owes us an apology."

"Now, I wouldn't go that far, gents." Aristo gave both men a level stare. "See, she's my favourite bird, she is." He removed the toothpick from his mouth. "So I pamper her a bit more than me other birds. One of the others will be free soon. Surely you can wait ten minutes?" He snapped his fingers at Cicely and, without waiting for her, crossed the street and entered a tea shop.

Without glancing again at either of her tormenters, Cicely sprinted after him, joining Aristo at a table well away from the front. The other customers were mostly matrons with children.

"That was bloody stupid of you." Aristo leaned back in his chair, observing her. "Bloody good togs, though. Had I not heard that familiar squawky voice, I'd never have known it was you."

Cicely fished her DuMauriers out of her newly acquired handbag and lit one with shaking fingers. "I'm supposed to 'entertain' that ruddy Yank? Not on your life!"

Aristo sighed and shook his head. "Kerb crawlers don't make public scenes. They melt into the pavement. In private they may act as nasty as London's sewer system." He waved his arm in a dismissive gesture. "They *do not* make a fuss in public."

Cicely blew out a cloud of smoke. "I didn't think they were so nice in their manners."

Aristo laughed and flagged down a waitress. "Manners have nothing to do with it."

The server stopped at their table, giving Cicely a look to freeze lava. The one she gave Aristo wasn't much better. He ignored her distaste and said, "Bring us a pot

of tea and a plate of cheese-and-chutney sandwiches."
The waitress took the order and walked stiffly to the
kitchen.

"Kerb crawlers keep a low profile so they don't end up
in the nick." Aristo lit one of his fags. "Also, feistiness
would likely earn them a cuff or worse from their ponce.
Selling damaged merchandise may encourage more . . .
er, damage. Vicious circle it is." He leered at her. "Ready
to change professions, luv?" he joked.

Cicely glared at him, but he laughed.

They devoured the meal that arrived, then tore out
coupons from their ration books as well as money when the
bill was presented. Cicely noticed blood under Aristo's fingernails. She wondered if it ever wasn't there.

Outside the tea shop, Aristo fitted his trilby back on his
head and said, "Now go to the loo and wash your face
while I discover when the next transport to—damned if I
know Cornwall. Which route do we need?"

"Just tell the ticket master we wish the fastest route to
Penzance. It's the only way into St. Just from here. Take a
glance at the map on the wall." Cicely headed to the terminal loo, her eyes demurely downcast.

She felt so much better after cleaning her face, but after a critical look in the mirror decided to keep the wig.
She also used burnt matches on her eyebrows again. Rifling through her portmanteau for her kerchief, she tied it
under her chin and congratulated herself on a respectable
disguise. She shuddered at the thought of being approached again by a man who wanted to buy her services.

Confidence added a bounce to her step, but that left
abruptly as she rounded the corner to the omnibus pickup.
Fear clenched her stomach and she backed up so hastily
she nearly tripped.

"What is this?" Aristo was shouting. "You have no call to arrest me. What have I done? You tell me that—what've I done, you bastards!"

"Shut up, you ponce. We'll find your bint, too," one of two constables announced.

Cicely pressed herself to the wall. Her heart beat so fast it was a miracle if the coppers didn't hear it.

"We 'aven't seen you before. The ponces who operate here keep their slags in order. No messy scenes in the street for decent citizens to watch," the other constable said, his voice deep and gravelly.

"I ain't no ponce! Just a bit of play-acting—," Aristo said.

"Shut up!" Cicely heard a rattle and a thud.

"Yow! Hey, that bloody well hurts!"

"Supposed to, ya bloody feriner."

"I'm English! Take a shuftie at me passport! Says I'm a British subject!"

"Stone the crows! Falsified passports are cheaply come by. Come on, you wanker—stand up."

"If that passport is genuine, why aren't you in uniform? Big strong man like you?" The first constable spoke up.

"Cowardice," the gravelly-voiced constable answered. "These dark feriners are all alike, the lot of 'em. Too many of—*Ouch!* You bugger, you come back here!"

Cicely peeked around the corner of the building. Aristo was running and dodging through the omnibuses while one of the heavy policemen pursued him. The other remained stationary, bent over with his hands on his knees and taking deep breaths. At last he stood and lumbered after them.

The yard began filling as one of the omnibuses let off passengers. Four coaches stood empty, and two others were too far away to see anything. Jogging past the passengers heading for the terminal, Cicely spotted a driver in one of the coaches. Reaching it, she banged on the side.

The door opened and the driver looked down, annoyed, from a book. "What can't wait for my tea break?" he asked.

"A-are you for Penzance?" Cicely held the door, panting.

"No. Heading back to London in an hour." He perused the collection of coaches and pointed to one a good seventy-five yards distant. "Number seventeen, that one over there, is leaving on the St. Austell route—may go on to Penzance." He shrugged. "Never driven that route before. You'd best hurry." He nodded in the direction of the coach. "It seems to be leaving."

Cicely yelled a thank-you over her shoulder and sprinted. Mid-stride, she waved her free hand madly. Her first instinct was to shout, but she knew no one on the bus would hear, and she couldn't risk bringing more attention to herself.

Instead of slowing, the vehicle gained speed, exiting the terminal, groaning and spitting a charcoal exhaust into the frosty air as it headed down the two-lane road and out of sight. Cicely ran after it, out of the terminal yard and a good quarter mile down the road before she gave up, panting and flushed.

Alistair shivered and took another laboured breath, drawing a sharp glance from Walker, his new superior. The two men waited with two Cardiff constables and two Met constables in a cold outbuilding on a military airfield east of Cardiff.

"Christ, Fielding, don't die on me," Walker said. "After this monumental cock-up it's all I need."

Alistair shot him a dry look. "A bit inconvenient for me too, sir. And it's bloody awkward calling you 'sir.' "

"Then don't." Walker swept aside his coat sleeve with an impatient hand to glance at his wristwatch. "Where the hell's that plane?" he asked. He paced the confines of the concrete building, which measured all of ten feet by ten feet. He shot Alistair a gimlet look. "How the damnation did you do it? How did you manage to become the most wanted man in Britain?" He shook his head. "Poor old Kingly can't cock up his toes in peace in an air raid, and I bloody well have to give up my honeymoon. Pearl is *never* going to forgive you. Don't know if I shall either."

Alistair rocked back on his heels and chuckled, but it turned into a cough. When he recovered, he said, "Hmm, I seem to recall a certain evening spent in the company of a very bonny vaudevillian actress—er, I believe it was the night right after your proposed to Pearl. . . ."

"All-bloody-right. You win." Walker paced again. "You know, if you hadn't asked me to gather a few belongings for you before you left London, even I wouldn't know what you were up to. You'd think Gordon Kingly might leave a note in a safebox or something."

Alistair tapped the side of his nose, in the now universal gesture meaning: Be careful what you say. Walker joined him at the window. In the west the clouds were grey and billowy; to the east they were an angry charcoal. The chill wind whistled through the casement. Alistair pulled up his collar and pushed his hands deeper into his pockets.

"It's all secret enough to justify my ending in the nick and even perhaps hanged for murder," Alistair whispered. "Only your promotion to Head of Special Branch in the wake of Kingly's death is saving my neck—and saving something even more important. National security. No, don't ask." Alistair shook his head. "Look where it's got me. The less you know the better."

Walker removed his trilby, rubbed a hand over his thinning light brown hair, and jammed the hat back on his head. "I'm going out on a limb for you, old boy. We need to wind this up fast." He shook his head in disgust. "Kingly didn't bother with a filing system, and he damned well didn't confide in anyone either. Making heads or tails of his desk is the Devil's own business. Christ, I don't know which end is up or sideways."

Alistair coughed and drew another ragged breath. His head throbbed, his chest felt like an elephant was using it for a private lounger, and he felt shaky and alternately chilled and hot. "Likely we'll need more firepower than those four," he suggested, gesturing to the constables.

"We'll make do." Walker's gaze searched the sky again. "More eyes are riveted to us than is wise just now. First job as new Chief Inspector, I rescue you from the hounds, then we go haring off to a secret destination. We take any more men with us and both the press and Whitehall will take notice and stick in their noses. If they haven't already." He grimaced and gazed at the sky. "Never flown before. Not natural, I tell you."

Alistair grinned. "So long as there's no turbulence, we're tickety-boo."

Walker shot him a sharp look. "And what happens if there's turbulence?"

"The beast shudders a bit." Alistair shrugged. "But don't worry, old boy, we'll be strapped into our parachutes."

Walker stared at him, turning a peculiar shade of green. "The damn thing is flying us over water. I don't fancy falling out of the sky and into the Bristol Channel in December, mate. Pearl will have both our heads on a holiday platter if we have the nerve to cock up our toes a day or two before Christmas!"

Alistair felt laughter bubble up inside him, but went into a paroxysm of coughing instead, earning him a good slap on the back. Leaning on the wall and gasping for breath, he waved Walker off. "Cack-handed joke, old man." He took a successful deep breath. "No worries about the flight. We'll deliver you safe to the new plates and dishes in a trice."

"Don't let Pearl hear you call her that or I'll be sleeping with the dog." Walker gave a grunt of laughter. "Ha, more likely she'll allow the dog inside while I'm kicking my heels in the garden. No, it doesn't pay to rile Pearl."

Alistair peered into the clouds. Absently he remarked, "I haven't met a couple who deserved each other more than you two."

Walker shot him a suspicious glance, but a low drone from above stole his attention. "Well, fuck-a-doodle-do. About damned time. Come on, Fielding, we're on our way to Cornwall."

The produce lorry hit another rut, jarring both Cicely and the root vegetables with which she shared the lorry bed. Despite the many bumps, she was trying to stay balanced on top of her portmanteau and to keep her coat respectably clean. She was losing that battle. The icy rain drizzled down her collar and turned the earth covering the potatoes, carrots, and rutabagas into a thin film of mud. Her favourite skirt was ruined. Her best boots now sported a hole in the bottom nearing the size of a twenty-pence piece, and her feet were wet and numb. Rain dripped into her eyes from her soaked kerchief, and the wet brought out several unpleasant odours from her ten-pound wig: something fusty, and a strange sort of muskiness that she'd rather not dwell upon. Thank goodness she had no plans to wear it to any upcoming functions.

The three girls in the lorry cabin, now singing Christmas carols, had picked her up just outside of Bodmin. They were members of the Women's Land Army, and very happy to leave the farm on their own for a market day. Traditionally the girls who populated the WLA were kept on a short leash by their hosts. They were required to rise before dawn, retire at dusk, or as soon as their work was completed, and were not allowed to go out walking— or anything else—with men. However, the WLA and the farmers were the best-fed people in the nation. Although the girls were headed for Fowey, they'd promised to let her out on the main road to St. Austell before taking the turnoff.

Cicely hoped Aristo had escaped, suspected he had as he seemed quite a resourceful rapscallion. He didn't pretend to even a drop of honourable blood. But he had helped her because his father ordered him. Of course, it couldn't be all fear of disobeying his father on Aristo's part; if he truly didn't hold any respect for his father, he was perfectly capable of leaving and setting up his own life. She shook her head at Aristo's brand of honour, and mulled over the similarity between Alistair and Aristos. She wondered if either of them might recognise it.

Alistair, she absolutely refused to think about any more. Instead she made plans for her arrival in St. Just— in case her parents were entertaining "company."

Abruptly the old lorry slowed and ground to a halt. One of the fresh-faced country girls leaped out. "We're turning off here for Fowey," she said. She glanced at the darkening sky. "Might be a better idea to accompany us to the farm. We're not keen on leaving you out here by yourself with night coming on."

Cicely stood, brushing dirt and old vegetable stems from her clothing, and jumped down. "Thanks awfully, but I'll take my chances," she said.

The girl shrugged and hopped back into the lorry. Before shutting the door, she called, "Happy Christmas to you!"

Cicely kept to the road as she walked. Dusk became night. Clouds scudded fitfully overhead, obscuring the nearly full moon. Steam escaped from her mouth. She stopped to tighten the belt on her coat, then picked up her bags and trudged for a good two more hours before she heard a motor in the distance behind her.

It was seldom these days that people in the country operated their automobiles after dark, so when the vehicle's shaded lamps shot through the darkness straight for her, Cicely felt jolly jammy and waved her arms.

The old roadster stopped, and the passenger door popped open. The driver, a gaunt, grey-haired man, peered at her through bloodshot, glassy eyes.

"Offer a pretty girl"—he hiccupped—"a lift? Hop in, Miss."

Cicely's hand froze on the door. The man slurred his words, his clothes were disordered, and his hair resembled a haystack. Yet, beggars couldn't be choosers. She tossed her case and handbag into the vehicle and smiled brightly.

"How kind of you, sir. You look exhausted. Why don't I drive while you rest?"

He snorted. "Get in if you want a ride, missy. I don't believe in women drivers!"

Cicely's heart sank, but she dreaded another night

spent outside more than anything else. The moment she hit the seat, he put the motor in gear and squealed off down the road.

Ellie Winterbourne opened her eyes and yawned, studying the two strangers again from the floor by the fireplace. The white-haired man balanced his Walther on his lap, staring out the lounge window at the misty dawn. The giant frowned and muttered something in German.

"English," White-hair hissed. Noticing Ellie was awake, he said, "Get up and make us breakfast, Lady Winterbourne."

"If you don't mind, I must visit the loo," She said. "Oh dear, you're not going t-to watch m-me, are you?" She allowed a note of hysteria into her voice.

White-hair sighed. "Not a job I fancy. However," he warned, "I'll be just outside, listening."

Ellie stood, throwing back her shoulders. "Indeed, this will be a relief," she said.

When she passed the ground-floor loo, White-hair seized her arm. "Forgetting where your toilet is located," he asked, his voice sharp.

"Oh!" Ellie covered her mouth for a moment; then, lowering her hand, she stared at her feet. "Er, you see I, er, need to use my boudoir toilet. I keep, er, certain supplies there that . . . I occasionally need."

He looked uncomfortable. "Go then! I'm right behind you." He pushed her toward the staircase and then, at the top, shoved her toward the bedroom she shared with Harold. The loo door opened off the corridor and, opposite it, a pocket door led into their bedroom.

Ellie entered the loo. Closing the door behind her, she

took the two glasses she kept on the counter for rinsing after she and Harold brushed their teeth, and she dipped them in the toilet to fill them. Then she used the facilities but didn't flush. Instead, she crept to the pocket door and eased it open just enough to squeeze through, retraced her steps and poured half a glass of water back into the toilet, making it sound like she was still doing her business.

Silently she slipped again into the bedroom, opened her stocking drawer and removed her derringer, then rushed back into the bathroom and poured more water into the toilet.

"Are you finished yet, Lady Winterbourne?" White-hair's voice held an impatient edge.

"In a moment," Ellie called, and eased the pocket door closed. Dropping the firearm in the pocket of her voluminous apron, she streamed the rest of the water into the toilet, flushed, and wiped both glasses dry.

Back in the kitchen she prepared porridge, toast, and tea while the giant watched her. Occasionally she stuffed a pot holder or a linen serviette into her apron pocket to hide any telltale bulges.

When the meal had been devoured, Ellie stood to collect the dishes, but leant heavily on the table and swayed.

"Harold! One of my spells is coming on," she said.

Harold caught her before she hit the ground. Holding her high against his chest, he pushed his way through the swinging doors to the lounge and gently placed her on the settee.

"What the hell is going on? What's the matter with her?" White-hair demanded.

Harold rubbed his forehead. "A migraine. I don't wonder at it, what with all the tension you two have caused barging into our home."

The giant fisted his hand in Harold's collar and pulled him to his toes. "Watch that mouth. Don't forget you're expendable," he threatened, then let him go.

Ellie groaned and faced the back of the settee in a fetal position.

"She makes this much fuss over a damned headache?" the giant asked incredulously.

"Not an ordinary headache. A migraine. She says it feels likes a blacksmith is pounding his anvil inside her head. It lasts for hours or days, but she's good for nothing but sleep once one hits. I'd better fetch a bowl—she might be sick."

Both captors scowled and stepped back.

Harold returned with a large ceramic bowl and a glass of water, which he urged his wife to drink. Having no luck, he set it on a side table and reached to untie her apron, making sure her front faced toward the settee. Then he donned her apron, patted her hand, and headed for the kitchen.

"What's this?" the giant asked. "Where are you off to in that costume?"

Without looking back, Harold answered, "Someone has to clean up after breakfast, or the remnants will attract rodents. My wife has a particular loathing of rodents."

To Cicely's surprise, her companion drove straight through the night, narrowly missing ditches, trees, and boulders on the side of the road. For the most part she clung to the dash, and glued her eyes to the dimly lit road. Every time he missed crashing into an object, Cicely let out a high-pitched cry, to which he invariably told her to shut up and relax.

"Birds these days," he muttered, reaching for a pewter

flask. "No confidence in men. And they think they can drive an automobile." He snorted. "Bloody well can't pilot a damned bicycle! Here." He shoved his flask in her face. "Take a finger or two, missy, you can use loosening up." He ended with a juicy belch.

"Er, thank you, but no."

He stared at her, taking his gaze off the road for several moments. Suddenly a tree loomed before them, and Cicely screamed. He cranked the steering wheel, jerking back to the middle of the road.

"Calm down, missy—I saw the damned tree, didn't I? We're not buried in it nose first, are we?" He shook his head. "There's something wrong with a person who doesn't drink a good whisky."

Cicely had never felt more tempted to indulge, but she feared she'd pour the whole thing down her throat.

They reached the city of Truro just as dawn broke, but he didn't bother slowing down as he entered. More than once the old roadster turned a corner on two wheels. Cicely thought her hands might be permanently deformed by grasping the dash in a clawlike grip. Her shoulder muscles burned from keeping the same position for hours.

"I live just outside of town," he informed her. By daylight his face was sunken, pale, and papery. He squinted into the dawn. "Normally my wife would invite you in for breakfast before continuing on your way. Not the thing to do now, however. I'll let you off in the high street."

"I'll be glad of it, thank you, sir," murmured Cicely, her eyes still on the road.

He drove several streets in silence. Then he said quietly, "Lost my son, you know."

"In the war? I'm so sorry."

"They came to tell me yesterday." He finally slowed the car. "Said he showed great bravery and is up for some medals. Much good that does him. Died in the Burmese jungle he did. In a snake- and mosquito-infested foreign jungle, fighting those damned Japs. Died with his kukri gripped in his hand." He gave a ghost of a laugh. "He'd been beheading the little bastards with it. Then one of them sliced *his* head off." Tears streamed down the man's face. "Can't even bury the poor bugger whole."

He stopped the motor car at the beginning of the high street, and sat staring sightlessly through the windshield, his hand gripping the steering wheel. "My wife is inconsolable. Told one another a few nasty things we did, so I took off with six months of saved petrol coupons to inform my daughter in Fowey she's now an only child."

Cicely placed her hand on his shoulder in sympathy. "Why don't we find an open tea shop and have a bite to eat? A good meal and a cup of tea can do wonders."

He looked at her at last, covered her hand with his for a moment, then said, "I'd best be gone. Suppose by now my wife might need me. But . . . thank you, missy."

He let her out and drove away.

TWENTY-SEVEN

Lay the proud usurpers low!
—Robert Burns

Cicely walked a good half mile on the cobbled high street before she found an open shop to ask the direction of the omnibus terminal. The ancient Truro cathedral rang its bells for morning services as she boarded the coach to Penzance. She couldn't remember if it was the twenty-third or twenty-fourth of December today. How relaxing it would be to sit in that stone building, listening to prayers and hymns. And to celebrate her favourite holiday. Instead, she could anticipate a day of traveling with Christmas merrymakers, but a night of danger. It was quite possible now that her parents, indeed, hosted company.

Eating a breakfast of plain scones and drinking from her flask of tea immediately before boarding the coach, she fell asleep slumped at the window at the rear of the bus.

Yet as exhausted as she felt, her slumber was light and restless. Her insides hummed with tension and excitement. She neared the end of her journey, when she could give up the key to her father. But stress nudged any exhilaration aside. What if her parents were dead? Held hostage? What if Alistair was dead? What would she do then?

The code key remained vital to Allied supremacy. To

victory. To fewer casualties of war. Cicely still found it difficult to believe that this tremendous weight lay on her shoulders alone. She'd believed filing the secrets of Bletchley a heavy responsibility, as well as all the lies. Whoever claimed war was hell was only too right. It made beasts of humans, or it killed them. Yet, what else was there to do? Let Hitler and a far-off emperor take over the world?

For the most part, the other passengers remained in jolly moods. If they weren't busy chatting, they read, slept, or sang Christmas carols, war songs, and recent hits. Cicely even took part in a wobbly version of "Waltzing Mathilda," which Australians had brought to England and made a great hit.

The bumpy road cut through the frosty moors, and the occasional palm tree appeared in promise of the end of the journey. Cicely reached with a trembling hand to touch her Enfield to reassure herself. Again, the possibilities of what lay before her flooded her mind. Perspiration prickled under her underarms and between her shoulder blades. She held the cold metal weapon for several moments then drew her hand out, and as she did a few bits from the bottom of the worn handbag came out as well: a few sweets wrappers from the previous owner, and a tablet—no, two tablets. Now what on Earth . . . ?

One of Kit's pills! It seemed a decade ago Kit had given her pills for her aching elbow. How she could have used them when she'd been thrown from the train! Cicely dropped them back into her handbag. She supposed, with a shrug, she might use them later if she again had to jump from a rumbling coach. Shivering at the thought, she peered out her window to discover why the bus suddenly slowed.

A lone man stood at the side of the road. He wore a tweed cap pulled low over his head and a dark trench coat. He limped when he boarded the bus, and he didn't carry a travelling bag.

Walker leaned back in his seat, eyes screwed shut and white-knuckled hands clutching both arm rests.

"Relax, old man." Alistair's voice came out raspy. "We're just flying, not jumping with parachutes into enemy fire."

Walker gave him a sour look out of the one eye he opened. "At least I'd know where I was going. How the hell does the pilot know where to steer this thing? It's dark, and we're in a damn cloud."

Alistair managed a weak chuckle. "Relax, the crew know what to do. This is one of the newer transport aircraft, you see."

"It's a bloody Yank contraption."

"Well, they seem to know what they're doing." Alistair cleared his throat. "At least, some of the time anyway."

Walker snorted. He didn't care for Yanks. Pearl's first beau had been a Yank.

"Really, not to worry, old boy. This is a brand-new Beech C-45. Notice the luxurious appointments." Alistair swept his hand in a wide arc. "We all have seats. We're not sitting on a bloody cold metal floor."

"Minimally civilised," Walker conceded. He finally opened both eyes and peered out his window. "How fast are we going and how high are we? No, don't answer that!"

Alistair patted his shoulder. "If I recall correctly, the maximum speed on this aircraft is two-hundred-fifteen miles per hour."

Walker's eyes popped. "That fast?"

"Aye." Alistair's lips spread in a wicked smile. "The ceiling is twenty-thousand feet—"

"What?"

"As this is such a short hop, I doubt we'll fly higher than ten thousand."

Walker's face paled. Then he sat back and screwed his eyes shut again. "You, m'lad, are skating on damned thin ice. I'm thinking right at this moment I should have let you bloody hang!"

Alistair's laugh segued into a wracking cough. His head began to throb again. "Come now," he said, when the fit passed. "You've never experienced so much adventure in your life, Alex!"

"Never bloody cared for adventure, and you know it," Walker ground out. "How soon until we land?"

"Can't be long now." Alistair sobered. "We're damn lucky the nearest military airfield is at Lands' End, only a few miles from St. Just."

"Do you know our destination in St. Just?"

Alistair shrugged. "We'll find it the old-fashioned way. We'll ask at the local." He wondered not for the first time how Cicely had fared on the moors after Minehead, and hoped like the very devil he and his friends made to the Winterbournes' before she did.

When Ellie heard the popping in the kitchen, she whirled to her feet, seized and cocked her Browning all in one movement. "Drop you Walther *now!*" she ordered, pointing it at the white-blond stranger.

He stared at her a moment, then did as she asked.

"Kick it gently toward me." When he did so, Ellie bent to retrieve the gun, never taking her eyes off him.

The swinging door to the kitchen opened, and the giant staggered through holding his shoulder. "Ah, there you are, old girl," her husband said, appearing. He gave his former captor a good hard push into the room.

The giant sat on the hearth, blood oozing between his fingers, looking to his sullen companion for guidance, but White-hair only shrugged.

Harold pulled a key out of his waistcoat and traded it with Ellie for her Browning. Leaving him with their captives, she headed down the dark corridor to his study to retrieve his Browning and extra magazines. Then, after dropping off her acquisitions with her husband, she went out into the garden shed in search of rope.

"Why don't you just kill us?" demanded White-hair, after he and his partner were firmly trussed and Ellie had taken a seat.

"It's not out of the question, by any means," Harold replied. "But only as a last resort, as you may have some interesting information for intelligence."

The white-haired man snorted. "We'd die first. And if not, immediately after." He shook his head. "You have no idea, do you? We have moles everywhere. In your government, in your military, in intelligence, civilians, and your SOE. The Fuhrer is very careful. Only he knows who and where they all are. If we spilled our guts, we shouldn't live long."

Unimpressed, Harold crossed his legs and leaned back in his wing chair.

"I need medical attention," complained the giant.

Sir Harold glanced at him. "No."

"You've shot me, damn it! You can't leave me here bleeding."

"Shut up or I'll you shoot again. With a real gun this time."

"So, what do we do now then?" White-hair tugged at the ropes binding him and gave his onetime prisoners, now his captors, a dark look.

Harold smiled. "My wife will watch you while I make a telephone call."

White-hair's mouth twisted. "It hasn't rung, has it?" He grunted and rocked back against the hearth. "We cut your line."

"Ah well, I suppose that means a trot to the neighbours'." Harold stood and went to collect his trench coat and hat. Before he departed, he narrowed his gaze on the two Germans. "My wife is a lovely woman, gentlemen. Don't make the mistake of supposing she's weak. She's a crack shot, and 'hesitate' isn't in her vocabulary. Do attempt to restrain instead of kill, darling, hmm?" he said to her.

"Really, Harold! You know I'm not afraid of a little blood. The rug is replaceable."

Harold tossed a grin over his shoulder and murmured, "Bloodthirsty wench." He closed the front door behind him as he left.

"So, you *did* work with your husband in the last war," White-hair muttered. "We couldn't pin you down, but we guessed it was so. Your government didn't appreciate you. Your husband received numerous medals and recognition. No medals for you. Not a damned thing." When Ellie didn't react he continued, "Doesn't it make you feel used, thrown in the dustbin?"

"Tsk, tsk, White-hair, or whatever your name is. Do you really think I expect the lot of women to improve because I risked my life for my country? Since the beginning of time we women have worked behind the scenes, underground, as spies. We are rarely recognized for it. And when we are, it's generally because we're killed for our efforts. Mata Hari and Edith Cavell are two perfect examples."

White-hair's eyebrows shot up. "Don't you feel any resentment? Your husband received all the glory. You were in as much danger as he."

Ellie shook her head. "If my acts on behalf of my country were made public, my good name would be lost like *that*." She snapped her fingers. "Espionage is such a dirty word. Few men even wear it well."

"You are a very odd women." The German canted his head to one side and studied her.

Ellie laughed. "Shame on you, Mr. White-hair. Surely you can find another way to goad me." Her lips curved in a wicked smile. "I'm quite unnatural, I admit it."

The giant groaned. "At least let me bandage my arm, Lady Winterbourne," he begged. "I could contract gangrene before I answer any questions."

His partner glanced at him briefly in contempt, then turned back to Ellie. "A female spy." His expression was smug. "I can see why you don't want anyone knowing. It follows you must have indulged in sexual relations with men other than your husband. And likewise, your husband must have done the same."

"Why, stone the crows!" Ellie exclaimed. "I did mention the loss of my reputation."

"Jesus, she's hard," remarked the giant, scowling.

Ellie laughed. "I still live because of it, gentlemen. Now then, why don't you tell me why you want my daughter so badly."

White-hair leered at her and explained in the vilest

terms possible what he'd like to do with Cicely. Ellie's mouth thinned into a flat line. Then she reversed the gun in her hand so that she held the barrel, and approached her captive with the butt held high.

"If we live through this, I'll bloody well kill you my—" Walker's mouth clamped shut as the aircraft abruptly jerked and fell a considerable distance, then shot back up, rattling like dice in a cup.

"Hang on!" shouted the co-pilot from the cockpit.

"Bleeding, bloody hell. What does the blighter think we're doing—enjoying a toss?"

"Just a bit of turbulence, old chap," Alistair said.

As the Beech fell again and continued to shake, Walker gritted his teeth. Even Alistair felt his heart pound with the beginnings of fear. He lost his stomach every time the Beech fell. Lightning flashed outside, allowing both men to see the lashing rain and the aircraft's trembling wings. Alistair heard one of the constables behind him praying. An engine whined, then returned to its usual roar.

"Did you mention parachutes, Fielding?"

"Sorry, Alex, I was joking. Only the pilot and the co-pilot are equipped with them." Alistair shrugged. "Perhaps not even them, as this is just a hop. But it's only a storm, old chap. Aircraft fly through storms regularly."

As if to prove his words, the co-pilot shouted over the din of the engines and a clap of thunder, "We're heading in, chaps! The wind is blowing us off course a bit, so it may take a couple of tries. But just hold on!"

The Beech vibrated and took a nose-dive. Adrenaline raced like fire through Alistair's veins. He gritted his teeth and tightened his grip on his chair's armrests. Lightning flashed again, and he saw the violent waves of the Atlantic crashing onto the cliffs below. Walker moaned and one of the constables screamed.

"We're going down! God save us, we're all going to die!"

Alistair turned around. "Shut up!" He tried to yell but his voice broke. One Met constable's lips moved, and tears ran down his face. The other stared outside, mesmerised. The Cardiff constable who hadn't screamed buried his head in his lap.

The aeroplane leveled off again, but still quivered. Suddenly it shot upward again, caught in a draft of hostile wind. Below, lights twinkled.

Walker continued swearing and grumbling. Alistair leaned back, closed his eyes and clamped his jaw. More nauseating spurts of adrenaline spurted through his veins, and his heart rose into his throat.

"Trying again!" the co-pilot yelled.

The aircraft slammed to the right and fell. When next lightning flared, the jagged cliffs of Lands' End appeared in Alistair's window—mere feet away.

Cicely pulled her kerchief down until it nearly covered her eyes, and leaned toward the window, watching surreptitiously as the new passenger made his way to the back of the bus to sit two seats directly in front of her. The lumbering vehicle rumbled back up to speed, but as it turned a corner, a black wall of clouds appeared on the horizon and the riders released a collective gasp.

"Aye," announced the man who had just boarded. "Saw that comin', I did. Bones knew it afore my eyes! Achin' fiercely they have been all day." He turned around, giving Cicely a wide, toothless grin. "Lucky I am this omni came along!" Facing a middle-aged woman across the aisle, he said, "Be thinking, I am, this storm be worse than that whirlwind back in twenty-six. Oh, that was a bad 'un all right! Did some damage, it did."

"Ladies and gents." The coach operator raised his voice over the clamour of shifting gears. "This gentleman is correct. Those clouds promise a violent storm. It's not safe to keep this dinosaur going if a flood is coming. I'm stopping for the night at Marazion."

Cicely sat forward like a jackknife. "No!" She wanted to delay no longer.

The second before the butt of Ellie's gun smashed into White-hair's skull, a strobe of lightning filled the cottage. Surprised, she looked outside, only to be blinded by another flash. As she staggered back, she felt rough hands dig into her waist and throw her to the floor. A fist tangled in her hair and slammed her head into the hearth.

When she regained consciousness, she had no idea how much time had passed. Searing pain throbbed in the back of her head, and as she tried to lift a hand, she found her wrists were bound at the small of her back. Her eyes flicked open. She was positioned on her side on the floor. Spots danced in her vision.

"Bad luck, old thing," her husband murmured. "No, don't move, love. Your head must be screaming like a banshee. I'm trussed up behind you, leaning on the fireplace wall. I shouldn't have left you. I'm sorry."

Ellie felt like an ax was buried in her head. "No, you had to. . . . I was . . . stupid." She paused to take a deep breath. "Let the bugger needle me. Acted like a useless, green . . . Did your telephone call go through?"

"Reinforcements are on the way, old girl. No news on Cicely, however. Clever child."

Ellie swallowed. "If she's still alive," she whispered.

"Of course she's alive." Sir Harold seemed very sure.

"Of course." Ellie closed her eyes. "Where are they?" she asked, wondering of the Germans had simply fallen back on their old plan.

Harold grimaced. "In the kitchen. The wankers are wolfing down a week's rations."

Lightning flashed, and Ellie clamped her eyes shut and groaned. She could hear rain pelting the windows and wind rattling the shutters.

"How . . . did they . . . ?"

Harold grunted. "I'm becoming feebleminded in my retirement. Damned berk managed to cut through his bonds with a sharpened wire tucked up his sleeve. Searched him for firearms and knives. I bloody know better. Life's become too cushy."

Thunder exploded in the distance and the house shook. The lamp flickered and went out. It was night. At last, thought Ellie. Even that low light had stung her eyes. Loud cursing came from the kitchen, re-summoning the ache in her head.

The swinging door slammed open. "Where are your candles? We'll need a torch, as well," the giant demanded.

"The pantry," said Harold shortly. The giant grunted and disappeared again.

The wind was whistling in under the front door, and Ellie shivered uncontrollably. The fire had long dwindled to nothing. Surely these awful men would grow cold and re-light it.

"Cold?" Harold whispered.

"V-very."

"Good. That will keep you awake. You mustn't sleep if you are concussed," he said.

"So I sh-should contract pneumonia or influenza instead?" Her stomach lurched and the ax wedged deeper in her skull.

"It shan't come to that," Harold reassured her. "Think of summer and sailing out to St. Mary. The hot sun beating down on your head, the sails snapping in the wind, and the salt water spraying your face. We've brought a picnic of champers, paté, fresh oysters, meat pies, strawberries, clotted cream—"

Light spilled into the room. "What are you whispering about? Shut up," ordered the giant.

"I'm merely whispering sweet nothings in my wife's ear," Harold said.

"Not anymore," their captor replied, taking him by the shoulders and dragging him away from the fireplace. "You're in the way. We're building another fire."

Lightning flashed again, but Ellie felt warmth at her back and heard the hiss of kindling flames. In the dimness cast by the fire, she saw the white-blond man peer out the wet, black windows. "Appears the whole village is out of electricity," he said.

"Think this storm will slow down our bird?" the giant asked, coming to stand by his partner.

White-hair shrugged. "Doesn't matter. We stay until she shows."

TWENTY-EIGHT

Tyrants fall in every foe!
—Robert Burns

Alistair stared at the saw-toothed cliffs and the roiling ocean below. Suddenly the aeroplane jumped and struck the runway with a jolt. The wheels lifted off the tarmac and the aircraft bucked to the right, shuddering in a gust of wind. Then he felt the aircraft bash back onto the runway. The wheels floated off the ground twice more before they remained for good. Both he and Walker hit their heads on the forward bulkhead. Lightning flashed a number of times as the aircraft taxied, or rather raced, bumping over the tarmac into a dark hangar at the far side.

"Expedite evacuation!" ordered the co-pilot, ripping off his harness even before the aeroplane came to a complete stop.

"Yeah, get the hell outta Dodge, chums, and get those hangar doors closed before we get hit by that lightning!" the Yank pilot ordered as he opened the door.

"Bloody Yanks," Walker grumbled. "Well, you heard him," he shouted to the constables. "Run!"

Everyone except Alistair sped down the aircraft steps and ran out of the hangar. Once on the tarmac, they headed toward an arcing torch that appeared. Alistair followed more slowly. The wind tore at his trench coat, and rain peppered his face. The chill felt good after his nervous sweating on the Beech.

The sky flashed again, illuminating the low squat building before them and the chap with the torch. Alistair gazed in every direction. No other light at all—there was an electricity outage. A large rolling dustbin was pushed by the wind across the tarmac.

Unable to run, Alistair was the last to reach the building. Walker stood in the doorway, holding out a cup of tea.

"Worse luck, old man. A bloody huge tree is blocking the road to St. Just."

Alistair closed his eyes, savouring the hot beverage he'd been given. "We'll need an area map."

"Already on the table, old man." Walker gestured to a long table in the centre of the room. Desks facing each other lined the walls. Shadows shifted in what appeared to be a makeshift kitchen off the main room.

A tall flight officer joined them, setting a kerosene lamp on the table. "Understand I'm to cooperate fully and not ask too many questions," he said shortly. "Right, then." He placed his forefinger on the map. "We're here—as the crow flies just two miles south of St. Just. Probably the most challenging length of jagged coastline separates us from your goal. Not to mention this bloody storm. As you are aware, a massive tree is blocking the road. A crew is out there as we speak with chain saws, but completion of the job will take hours. However, you don't have hours." He gave Alistair and Walker a pointed look.

Stepping back from the table, the flight officer placed his hands on his narrow hips and continued: "It goes against the grain, but my orders are to facilitate in any way. The only other course open is to motor over pastures and crops in our all-terrain vehicle. It isn't as easy as it sounds, and it's even more dangerous on a dark night using hooded lamps. If you run into a cow who didn't make it to the barn, you're likely to sustain significant damage. And there are rock walls. . . . Fortunately for you, most of them are in ill-repair. Still, good luck getting past then. One last thing: This area used to be the tin mine capital of Europe. A few of the mine towers are crumbling, and this storm may render them unstable. Stay clear."

Walker frowned, studying the map. "Isn't it possible for a car to meet us on the other side of the roadblock?"

"Nearest military is Portrcath airfield on the north coast, and Predannack field on the south coast. Both are too far to get a vehicle here quickly."

"The local coppers won't do?" Walker asked.

The airman sighed. "I was ordered to keep civilians out of this."

Alistair swallowed the last of his tea, muffling a cough. "I suppose we should be off then," he said.

"You don't sound well enough to leave your flat," commented the flight officer.

"Right-O. Bloody lucky if he doesn't cock up his toes on this one," Walker grumbled.

The airman shrugged. "Best of luck. McLellan will take you to our all-terrain vehicle." He turned his back to roll up the map.

Outside, the rain bombarded all of them like ice pellets, and the wind tore at their clothing. Alistair's trilby flew off when he adjusted his collar closer to his neck. It was lost before he could reach for it. Now rain streamed through his hair and down his face. The urge to cough rose again but he pushed it savagely down. If he started, he'd never stop.

Abruptly the short and stocky McLellan stopped just outside the hangar, gesturing with his torch toward what seemed to be a cross between a miniature omnibus and a small tank. It differed from both in that it had no roof. It sported tracks instead of wheels, doors so low they weren't meant to be opened, and bench seating for at least six. Well, thank God they needn't sit on one another's lap. And for the windscreen.

"Good God! What is it, and how does it run?" Walker shouted above the wind. He boarded the vehicle.

McLellan hopped into the driver's seat and waited for everyone else. "Not to worry, chaps, I'll drive. As to what it is"—he turned the on motor—"it's an, er, modified post-Great War charabanc." The machine vibrated and moved forward.

Good God, Alistair thought, shivering and pulling his overcoat more tightly around himself; they could walk faster than this monstrosity.

"You've converted a small coach into a *tank?*" Walker asked, his voice incredulous.

"It's eminently suitable for bogs and rocky terrain." McLellan shouted over the weather and growling motor.

Once the beast found top speed, Alistair began to see how useful it could be. It sped through endless small lakes the deluge had made in the pastures, mud and frigid water splashing on the passengers. It effortlessly climbed crumbled and fallen rock walls. He was damned glad he wasn't behind the wheel—or whatever this vehicle used for steering—because he couldn't make out anything in the darkness.

"Gawd! I'm going to be sick," one of constables complained.

"Lean over the side!" Alistair shouted. He didn't feel

much better, himself. His head pounded, his throat was raw, his ears throbbed, his chest burned, and the swaying of the vehicle didn't do his stomach any good, either. He hoped he remained conscious until after they'd finished their business. This escapade seemed certain to land him under another oxygen tent.

"Spot of trouble here, gents," McLellan called over his shoulder. "We must follow this wall until we find a low spot."

"How close are we?" Walker shouted.

McLellan leaned forward, peering into the night. "About halfway. If you think to walk, don't. Some of these puddles are hip deep. Not to mention you might trip over rocks and ruts."

Lightning illuminated their surroundings momentarily. There was no other living being in sight, not as far as Alistair could see. The farm dwellings appeared deserted. Thunder followed, deafening everyone.

"At least we're safe from bashing into a cow," one of the Met constables remarked from the back of the vehicle.

McLellan let out a dry chuckle. "Don't count on it because you didn't see any. They're tricky buggers. Blasted steers don't always come in for their supper, and the land army has more important chores than spending all night searching for them."

"Good God, it isn't fit for man nor beast outside," Walker groused, huddling deeper into his coat.

McLellan laughed louder. "Cattle are perverse creatures. Now . . . aha! Found a spot. Hold on!" He steered sharply to the right.

Alistair held on to his low door as the vehicle sped up to climb the rock wall. But then it stopped, pointing straight up. The engine gurgled and cut out.

Cicely reached for the brandy the barman placed before her. The dim pub light caught in the dark liquid, making it glow and giving an illusion of warmth and safety. She shivered and took a sip. It burned going down and she welcomed the bite.

Several of the other bus passengers huddled around the coal fire on the far side of the pub. A few had arranged to stay in the rooms above; the rest had taken the coach driver's offer to spend the night in the vehicle, which was now sheltered in a local barn.

Cicely hadn't made provisions for either. She watched as a local entered, removing his tweed cap and shaking off the water. He glanced around the pub, taking in the strangers, and pulled out a chair at one of the small tables. The barman, a bald and beefy fellow with a florid complexion, immediately pulled a draught and took it to him, greeting him effusively. The newcomer waved him away and hunched down into his chair to enjoy his lager.

Cicely watched the man surreptitiously for several minutes. Now who in their right mind, would walk to the local pub on such a horrid night?

A plan had formed in her mind by the time her meal of fish and chips arrived. She settled the bill before tucking in. The food was marvellously filling, and she felt like a nap upon finishing. Instead, she asked directions to the loo. Perfect: she had to walk past the newcomer's table.

On the way back, she pretended to trip and fell nearly in her target's lap.

"Miss? I say, are you hurt?" The man jumped to his feet and bent to help her up.

Cicely shakily regained her feet and took the chair the gentleman offered. "Oh dear! How embarrassing," she murmured, patting her blonde wig and finding her trilby missing.

Her rescuer found it, dusted it off and handed it over.

"Oh, yes. thank you, Mr. . . ."

"Herrick. Jack Herrick, at your service, miss." He nodded, peering at her with kind hazel eyes.

"Miss White." Her hand fluttered to her brow. "Just a bit dizzy, but yes, I believe I'm quite unhurt, thank you.

"Sid! Bring brandy and double-step over here," the man called to the bartender. He turned to her and said, "I should have asked first, but I think a brandy will do you a world of good." He patted her hand.

"How thoughtful of you, Mr. Herrick. You are probably correct."

He took the brandy from Sid the bartender. "Take a healthy sip, Miss White," he encouraged.

"You're not joining me? Oh no, I couldn't possibly drink spirits alone. It's not quite proper—is it?" Cicely performed her best simpering act.

Herrick smiled and acquiesced. "Bring another brandy, Sid." He pulled a silver cigarette holder out of his breast pocket, offered her one, and lit both their cigarettes. "Such sensibilities are noticeably absent these days."

Cicely pursed her lips. "The war is used so much as an excuse to drop proprieties, but I say it's no excuse at all. One must maintain decorum."

Herrick took his brandy from the barman and raised it. "Cheers to the status quo," he said. When he sipped his drink, Cicely noticed he was missing his left ring and pinky fingers.

"Such a nasty evening. Did you walk tonight?" she asked.

Herrick leaned back in his chair. "Goodness, no! Drove

my old Vauxhall Cadet." He nodded to the ring of keys on the table. "Petrol rationing isn't a concern, as I never motor anywhere but here. Say, do you need a ride to the local bed and breakfast? I notice this ol' place is filled with strangers tonight."

"Oh no, thank you. We're all coach passengers on the way to Penzance, but the storm stopped us for the night," Cicely explained, glancing up at the group still huddled at the fireplace. The few women narrowed their eyes at her, deliberately turning their backs; it wouldn't do to contaminate themselves with the sight of a fast woman in action. The men studied her speculatively.

"Damn good thing, too," agreed Herrick. "Damned dangerous driving a coach on a night like this." He stood. "Excuse me for a moment, will you?" he said, before heading toward the gents loo.

Cicely felt like bellowing in relief. She'd been beginning to wonder if she was going to have to trip again. She scanned the room before casually reaching forward a few inches, emptying the contents of a tiny piece of folded paper into her companion's glass. Pretending the brandy belonged to her, Cicely dipped her finger into the liquid to gently stir it. Then she licked her finger. If anyone still watched her, she supposed the speculation of her being fast was now confirmed.

When Herrick returned, Cicely smiled and made smalltalk while he sipped his liquor. Soon he was nodding over his glass. When she was sure he slept, she lit one of her own DuMaurier's and slipped it between his fingers. The passengers broke up, some heading outside for their cold night spent in the bus. The barman showed the others upstairs to their rooms.

With the pub emptied, Cicely pocketed Herrick's keys

and waited under the shelter of the pub's eaves until the last of the passengers was out of sight, then she made her way to tiny Cadet across the street. Any second the barman would return and try to wake Herrick.

The motor car was cold and smelled musty, but the engine sparked immediately. But just as Cicely was ready to make tracks, the passenger door crashed open and a man loomed in the opening.

McLellan attempted ignition again. And again.

"Should we vacate to lighten the load, McLellan?" Alistair offered.

"Another time or two and that might be just the thing," the man shouted back. He let loose several indecent and original swear words, and tried a fourth time to start the vehicle. It growled to life. The coach-tank rolled backward a good two hundred yards, then McLellan gunned the beast and sped forward.

Again when it hit the wall the vehicle pointed straight up, but this time it merely hesitated. Speeding back down, it hit the ground with a bone-jarring thump and raced through the pasture.

"Blast it to hell! I'd kill for a desk job," Walker groused.

"You'll have to roust me from it first, old man," replied Alistair. He was feeling the chill bone-deep, and now his teeth had begun to rattle.

"Too easy. Don't try me." Walker's voice was dry.

The all-terrain vehicle stalled on two more rock walls and splashed through several more puddles before finally rolling to a stop in a village square, adjacent to a common.

"Right, chaps," called McLellan. "Here you are. And my orders are to wait until your return." He leaped out of his seat and leaned on the small tank, cupping his hands to light a fag. "Oh! Nearly forgot, chaps. Cape Lane is just . . . *here*." He pointed to the nearest road leading out of the square bordering the common. "It's a white turn-of-the-century, three-story cottage. On the left, well back from the road. Last structure on the lane. Best of British to you!"

"Larcenous wench, pilfering an innocent gent's Vauxhall two days before Christmas." Aristo Kalakos threw himself into the passenger seat and slammed his door. "Well, don't just sit there wagging your jaw, floor the go pedal or we'll both be spending the night in the nick!"

Cicely did as ordered, her heart still beating double-time from the shock of his appearance. Once the fishing village was behind them, she glanced at her companion and shook her head. "H-how did y—"

"Escaping the coppers was easy. Finding you required a spot of Greek reasoning. Sure you're not part Greek, birdie?"

"Cicely! Call me *Cicely,*" she said in a tight voice.

Kalakos grinned and stretched out his legs. "More's the pity. Perverse wench that you are, I knew you were incapable of taking the easy route. Admittedly, I followed a few false starts."

Although the thunder and lightning had let up, the rain hadn't. Neither had the wind. It buffeted the car about the road like a ping-pong ball. Cicely fought the steering wheel to keep the Vauxhall from smashing into the low rock walls on either side of the lane. Fortunately she knew the area well.

"Keep it short, Kalakos," she requested, sitting forward, straining to see through the windbreak in the near pitch blackness. She wanted dearly to stop to remove the hoods from the car lamps, but didn't dare. If area telephones worked, the coppers could be on them in a trice. She hoped they weren't already after her for stealing this car. Poor Mr. Herrick. The innkeeper might give him a bed for the night, and she would see to it he was properly recompensed for the use of his vehicle and the petrol used.

"I hitchhiked from village to village along the road to Penzance," Aristos explained. "I'd left the pub and was enjoying a smoke when I saw your coach lumber past. I watched until I saw you climb off. I was contemplating nicking this motor car myself." He chuckled. "Bird after my own heart you are."

"Please." Cicely's voice was arid. "Avoid flattering me so."

Aristo Kalakos merely gave another grunt of laughter. Slumped down in his seat, he covered his face with his hat. Within moments she heard his soft snores. He was clearly exhausted, to sleep on this bumpy ride.

Two hours of struggling against the elements to stay on the road brought the dim lights of Penzance into view. Cicely's shoulders ached with the strain of gripping the steering wheel, and her fingers were numb with cold. The old bucket might just as well been a ragtop for the shelter it offered. Perhaps only another hour and she'd be home. Finally!

Then the vehicle coughed. Pressing the pedal accomplished nothing; the car merely coasted. Then the motor coughed again, jerked, and cut out. Cicely's eyes flew to the petrol gage.

Ruddy empty!

Frustration and despair surged through her. She hit the steering wheel then collapsed against it, tears prickling in her eyes.

No! She was too close to abandon hope. There was no time to indulge in despondency. She shook Kalakos awake and gave hime the ill news.

"Blazing hell." Muttering something about the filthy Nazis and petrol rationing, he stretched and climbed out of the Vauxhall. "Leave your portmanteau and come on," he grumbled. "At least you're not a weak and weepy b— er, lady," he finished, seeing her furious expression.

Seizing her handbag, Cicely yanked open the car door and set out to march into Penzance—only to realize she couldn't see bugger-all. Hefting her handbag on her shoulder she started legging it anyway.

"Here, you can hold my hand. That way we shan't stumble into each other," Kalakos offered. She heard the humour in his voice.

"One might actually mistake you for a gentleman, Aristos," she snapped. "You are too kind, but I'm doing rather well on my own." The wind tore at her coat, allowing it to billow out behind her. The torrential showers made a bog out of the roadside. Clammy, chilled to the bone, and damp, all Cicely could think of was a hot bath, a roasted bit of joint, and a cognac. All of which she could experience if she kept walking. That or a dank grave.

Bent nearly double by the force of the wind, both Cicely and Kalakos entered the outskirts of town. It was dark. Not even the muted lights shone. The pavement bordered the water now. Gazing out at Mount's Bay, she saw nothing but a black canvas. She could hear, though. The waves pounded the breakwater, and further out the water crashed.

For the merest second, everything glowed a bright white; Penzance had the semblance of a ghost town. Cicely counted, waiting for the thunder. It didn't sound for several minutes.

"Well, thank the Higher Power for small miracles. The storm is miles off," Kalakos commented.

"Then it's bound to get worse. Come on, let's investigate that lorry." Cicely pointed to a vehicle parked a few yards distant.

Feeling excitement bubble in her, she ran ahead of Kalakos and peered in the driver side window, looking for the keys. A blast of warm air hit her from behind. Footsteps snapped on the pavement.

"Seeking a wee bit of shelter, lass?"

Cicely swung around at the gravelly voice. Lightning glinted again. A small man in an old-fashioned great coat stood behind her, rubbing his hands. Kalakos stood behind him, switchblade drawn.

"The storm is not over, it seems," she answered. "And yes, shelter sounds cracking. Is that a pub you've just come from?"

"Aye, but he's closing up. The electricity is out. I'm going to St. Just, where the electricity may be on. If not, the church is just off the square. Never closes. It's not very comfortable, mind. . . ." He pushed his cap down on his head and pulled a key from his pocket. "But it's better than being out in this dicky weather. Here you are, lass." He opened the passenger door for her. "Hop in, then."

"I'm traveling with a . . . a friend." She gestured to Kalakos, who quickly hid his blade and held out his hand.

"Rotten evening, isn't it, sir?" Aristos neglected to give his name. He held out his arm for Cicely to precede him into the lorry and jumped in after her, settling himself beside her on the bench seat.

"Thanks awfully," Cicely said, blowing on her hands as

their benefactor pulled the lorry into the road. "My car ran out of petrol down the way. I'm on my way to visit my parents in St. Just. Ari . . . is my neighbour in London." She indicated Kalakos. "He is needing work. I thought my mother might need help in the garden." Thunder growled, but it was distant.

"That so?" the lorry's owner said, looking at her from the corner of his eye and frowning at Kalakos. He too had to struggle to keep to the road. "Lived in St. Just my whole life. Don't believe I know you. M'name's Wilfred, of the Wilfred farm. Where's your baggage?"

Cicely gave a small laugh. "In my motor car. Sir Harold and Ellie Winterbourne are my parents, Mr. Wilfred. My father bought my first pony from you."

He shot her a surprised look. "Stone the crows! It's really you, Miss Winterbourne? We heard about your brother. Very sorry we all are."

"Thank you, Mr. Wilfred. I believe everyone in St. Just has lost a loved one. At the end of this we must build a monument to outdo the one dedicated to the souls lost in the Great War."

Wilfred sighed. "Aye, lass, when it's over. Who knows when that shall be, eh? Now that the Yanks are helping we have a better chance. But why isn't your friend in uniform?"

Cicely touched her temple and shook her head ever so slightly.

"Ah." Wilfred nodded and whispered, "Is he safe? No fits?"

Cicely guessed Mr. Wilfred preferred to think if he couldn't hear a whisper, certainly no barmy person might. "The fits are not dangerous to anyone but him," Cicely whispered back. "He's quite safe. By the way, Mr. Wilfred, are the telephones out in Penzance as well as the electricity?"

"They are, miss. You needing to make a call?"

"This was supposed to be a surprise visit, but I didn't expect to arrive so late. I thought to give a call, in order to not alarm my parents. I can see my father aiming his shotgun at me, thinking the Nazis have invaded."

Mr. Wilfred laughed. "You are quite welcome to use the farmhouse blower if you like, miss, but it's a bit out of your way—the other side of town, like."

"Very generous of you, Mr. Wilfred, but maybe the St. Just local's—if it's open, of course."

"It's only just on nine, so it'll be open if the electricity is on. Blood—er, it's a shame the pubs must close at ten now because of the war. Just when a man needs a good pint, HMG must make special hours. Why, the pubs are the heart of this land!"

Cicely shrugged. "We're all making sacrifices, Mr. Wilfred. Even the royal family is staying in London. Buckingham Palace has been bombed twice! Yet they stay when the King is urged to sail for Canada."

"Aye, 'tis true. I hear not even the King has indulged in a joint since the beginning of the war. Right good 'un he is. Queen Elizabeth, too. In touch with the common folk she is. Even Princess Elizabeth is taking mechanics lessons."

Cicely laughed. "The princess certainly wouldn't have let herself run out of petrol as I did," she commented.

As they entered the St. Just town square, she said, "Please, just let us off at the pub, Mr. Wilfred. We'll discover if the phones are working. If not, we'll walk from there."

"You don't want to leg it a quarter mile in this weather, do you, miss? It's no trouble at all."

"No, but thank you anyway, Mr. Wilfred. The site of an unfamiliar motor may alarm my parents."

The man shook his head but downshifted and stopped his motor at the pub. "It appears the electricity is out here, as well, Miss Winterbourne. Blowers likely, too."

"We'll just check for certain, Mr. Wilfred," Cicely informed him.

Kalakos clicked open his door, exited, and held it open for Cicely. The sky lit with lightning again.

"Thank you again, Mr. Wilfred. I'll remember you to mummy and daddy."

Mr. Wilfred grumbled, but he nodded and drove off in the opposite direction, passing both the local and the church.

"Damned pub is locked tight," Kalakos informed Cicely after tugging at the door to no avail.

She really hadn't expected it to be that easy. "Come, my parents are situated just outside of town," she told him.

She strode across the village square, Kalakos behind her, passed the common, which had been used for football or similar sports for nearly seven hundred years; then, tightening the belt on her coat and pushing her cold fingers deep into her pockets, she set out down the lane to her parents' house. The bare tree branches rattled in the wind above her head. Old leaves blew past, and a dog barked in the distance.

The walk took less that ten minutes in daylight, but she resisted the urge to run. The rain became a drizzle and, looking up, she saw stars between the clouds. At last, a little light! But the light brought shadows that flitted behind the trees ahead, darting into the road before skittering off into the private gardens that bordered the lane. A flash of white caught her eye, making her heart leap into her throat, but it was merely laundry waving on a clothesline someone had forgotten to take in. Suddenly she felt glad for Kalakos's company.

Lightning flared again. Cicely shivered. This reminded her of a Dickensian scene: trees reaching toward the sky like old gnarled fingers, a dark, deserted landscape. Even the dog stopped barking. Thunder exploded. The storm was moving closer.

At last they arrived at her parents' drive. When Kalakos started to follow it, Cicely grasped his sleeve and shook her head. Motioning for him to follow, she skirted the drive to walk in the squishy, sucking grass rather than crunching toward the cottage on the crushed oyster shells.

A soft glow radiated from behind the curtains in the lounge window. Creeping around the corner, Cicely sidled up to the window over the kitchen sink. The curtain hadn't been drawn and she could see a flicker of lambent light. She closed her eyes, took a deep breath, wiped her moist hands on her coat, and, inching toward the window, looked in.

Just beyond the common, Alistair took a deep breath and bent double, coughing. Walker clapped him hard on the back. "Hold on. Nearly done. Good God!" He caught a glimpse of his friend's features in the flash of lightning. Alistair's brown eyes glowed feverishly, and were blood-shot and red-rimmed. The black circles under his eyes reached his cheekbones, which were ashen. "Stay with McLellan, old man. You're burning up, I can feel it from here."

"No! I'm bloody well not ready for a body sack yet. It's vital I get there! Come on, let's go." He headed down the lane at a brisk pace, hesitated, then slowed but kept moving.

Walker caught up with him, the constables on his heels. "Yes, I understand this mission is vital. But tell us what all this secret business is about, and you needn't come. You could prove more a liability than a help at this point."

Alistair kept pace with his friend and superior. His hands fisted at his sides, and adrenaline rushed through his veins. At least he possessed plenty of that, for that alone urged him on. His body felt like caving in.

He clenched his jaw. "I must be there," he replied. "I must know—"

"Know what?" Walker snapped.

Alistair breathed deep and admitted it: "I must know whether the woman I love is still alive," he snarled.

Walker's mouth fell open. "Well, bugger all!"

Alistair kept walking. It took everything he had. His legs felt like rubber. "Don't look so gobsmacked, laddie. It happens. You found Pearl, didn't you?"

"Aye, well . . . I was never the man about town you are. Didn't make a promise not to marry until the end of the war. Didn't look as high, either. Sir Harold's daughter?" Walker gave a soft whistle.

A particularly vicious gust of wind stopped them all momentarily. A half moon shone through the parting clouds. The policemen hastened their pace while they had some light.

"If she'll have me. If she's still alive."

"Hold up," Walker ordered, stopping. "This is it." The crushed-shell drive reflected white in the moonlight. "Having a layout of the place in advance would be too easy," he complained dryly. He pointed to one of the constables. "You. Come here. Reconnoitre and report back."

The constable disappeared into the shadows. The rest

of the party backed into the darkness behind the hedge bordering the lane.

"This is where you take over, Fielding," Walker told him. "Since we don't know what's going on."

Alistair nodded. "Take out your weapons, chaps. Ready them for use," he ordered in a hushed voice. "But do not fire until I tell you. I don't care what you see or hear, *don't fire until I say.*"

He was slipping a fresh magazine into his Browning when he heard a shot ring out through the night.

TWENTY-NINE

Liberty's in every blow!
—Robert Burns

Although the kitchen was vacant, through the swinging door someone had just walked through. Cicely caught sight of a horizontal pair of feet by the lounge fireplace. Those feet were encased in her father's old brown Moroccan leather slippers. She also spied a trail of rope. Panic struck her very core. Where was her mother?

Kalakos pushed her out of his way so he could take his turn peering in through the window. "Can't see a damn thing," he muttered. He pulled her past the window, so they leaned on the house. "It's time to tell me what's going on," he said.

Cicely swallowed. "I believe my parents are tied up and held captive by Nazi spies. The Germans need something I've got."

He stared at her, his eyes wide with shock. He rubbed his face with his fingertips, then fixed his gaze on her again. "I have never in my life met a woman who is as much trouble as you. Not even my stepmama. But . . . alright," he said, digesting her news. "How many spies?"

"I don't know."

"Of course not. Why make the job any easier? I want a view from the other windows. Lead the way."

They waited, Cicely's heart beating doubletime, for the clouds to shift so the moon could light their way. Skirting the shrubs bordering the cottage, they wended their way around the back of the house, peeking into dark windows as they went. Her knees sank into the muddy ground as she knelt at the lower lounge window. Here, too, the curtains were drawn, but a narrow slit allowed her to see into the room. A light flickered inside.

Cicely's pounding heart slowed to a dull thud when a shadow passed by the window several times. Pacing? Was someone glancing out the window because they expected a visitor? Cicely wiped her hands on her coat again. The curtain shook, then was still again and the shadow moved away.

"Get it, then! Bring a cup for me, too. It's damned cold." It was a deep male voice, not her father's. Not a hint of accent either. She heard the swinging kitchen door and dared a closer look.

A tall man in dark clothing stood over her parents, who were both lying on the floor tied like livestock. Blood dripped down her mother's face. Cicely's fingers clenched into fists. The bastards!

Another man—shorter, with white-blond hair—entered from the kitchen with two mugs, and he handed one to his partner. Cicely ducked back, her jaw clenched and blood throbbing in her temple. She wanted to stand up and empty her Enfield into those two monsters!

"Let me look!" Kalakos hissed, and pushed her out of his way.

After his turn at the window, he crouched beside her again. "These wankers mean business. One of us must di-

vert them while the other rescues your mum and dad."
Kalakos stared at her, his dark eyes glinting with anger.
"But I bloody well don't mean to get killed over this. If
this goes balls-up, I'm gone on a Burton, understand?
Even the old man won't find me."

Once Alistair had fallen ill, Cicely fully expected to accomplish this task on her own. Nevertheless, she felt a
stab of disappointment at Kalakos's lack of loyalty.

"Come," she told him. "I have a plan."

As quick as a cat, she crept to the back of the house
where the only windows were to the basement, set just
above the ground. The gap in one of them could be jimmied,
and she could fit through if she removed her heavy coat.

Finding the window, she felt along the top of it. Yes,
the gap was still there.

"What are you doing?" Kalakos demanded.

Cicely ignored him while she searched her handbag for
her fingernail file. Grasping it, she slid it through the gap
and levered the file against the inside knob with both
hands, pushing to the left until it moved.

"Now then," she whispered. "I doubt you will fit
through this window, so I'm going to climb into the cellar
and creep up the staircase. I've noticed your switchblade,
but do you carry a handgun?"

He grimaced and nodded. "Don't care for using it.
Makes too much noise. Gets blokes nicked by the coppers."

Cicely nodded, her mind racing. "Go around to the
front door—it's nearest the lounge and adjacent to the
cellar door inside. When you hear me discharge my Enfield, blast the lock on the front door with your weapon."

He grunted. "And come galloping in on my white steed,
sword swinging, to the damsel's rescue. What would you
have said if I didn't own my own pilfered Luger?"

"I'd have set you to picking the lock—no doubt a hobby you could perform in your sleep," she replied, opening the cellar window.

It creaked, making her jump. She froze, heart pounding, waiting for any indication she had been heard. When nothing happened and Kalakos skulked around the corner of the building, she removed her coat and stuffed it through the window. Then, gripping her handbag with her precious Enfield, she put her feet through the opening and slid into the basement.

It was dark and smelled damp as always. She knew her way to the stairs, but lit a match in case her father might have re-arranged anything. Her foot nearly hit a step when she realized she should remove her shoes. The cellar door was adjacent to the front door, and at the opposite end of the lounge from the fireplace. She'd be entering directly behind her parents' captors; they'd hear any movement on the stair. Just as well, she knew where most spots creaked. She took the Enfield from her bag and, her hand on the rail, she began her climb.

The third step from the top groaned. Cicely stood rooted to the spot, waiting.

"What was that?" snapped one of the strangers.

The hair on Cicely's neck stood up, and she felt a prickling sensation travel down her back.

"What?" the second stranger questioned.

"I heard something behind that door. Where does it go, Winterbourne?"

"The cellar."

"Calm down, you're jumping at shadows," said the second man. "Keep looking out the window, you'll hear fewer ghosts," he teased.

"Ghosts, my arse."

Cicely closed her eyes briefly in relief, and continued her climb. At the top she peered through the door's keyhole. She could see part of one man by the window; a large dark-blond one sat in her father's wing chair, pointing a gun at her parents on the floor.

She straightened, leaned against the wall clutching her Enfield and saying a small prayer. Then she seized the door knob, yanked open the door, and in a two-handed stance shot the man in her father's chair.

Cicely didn't wait to see if she hit him; she dodged the two steps across the corridor and just missed being shot by Kalakos, who had blasted in her parents' front door. The bullet whirred past her hip. Not allowing herself a reaction, she pressed herself into the wall inside the house entrance, panting, as Kalakos entered.

Return gunfire peppered the cellar door and the wall around it.

"Only two of them. You can do it, love!" called her father.

"Shut your bleeding trap, you plonker!" Cicely heard, then a thud and a groan from her father.

Another voice cried, "For Christ's sake, she hit me!"

Kalakos glued himself to the wall beside Cicely. "You do know how to keep a bloke on his toes, luv," he muttered.

Cicely nodded. Holding her breath, she peeked around the corner and stopped cold. The white-blond man had dragged her mother to her feet, and he held her in front of him as a shield. Cicely kept hold of her gun but dropped it to her side. The weight of it seemed to drag her hand down.

Blood seeped between the fingers of the dark blond giant where he held them to his leg. Blood marked his shoulder as well. "Bitch," he spat at her. "You shot me."

"It appears we've trapped our little bird," the white-blond man who held Cicely's mother said, smirking. "Come in, join us. I know you can't wait to give us what we want. By the time I'm done with you, you'll beg to tell me."

Kalakos chose that moment to step from cover, firing at the wounded man. The giant reeled backward, but the man who held Cicely's mother dropped her and shot Kalakos. The Greek dropped like a stone.

For a moment Cicely stared in horror. Already blood formed a pool spreading out from Aristo's body. She glanced at her mother. Ellie Winterbourne lay on her side, facing her. As if in a dream, Cicely noted the blood on her mother's face was dried and her features were sunken and waxen.

She raised her Enfield for a clear shot at the man who had dropped her, but too late—in one lightning-fast movement he seized her mother up from the floor, holding her as a shield once more.

Ellie's eyes blazed at Cicely, and she nodded ever so slightly. Slamming her bound feet into her captor's toes, "Run, Cicely!" she yelled. "The Cape, now!"

Without a backward glance Cicely turned, running out the ruined door and into the night.

A volley of gunfire followed the first shot. Alistair could see sparks of light through the curtains. Using the last of his strength, he ran for the house.

Halfway there, he saw a form tear out the front door. Something glinted in the weak moonlight and fell to the ground. Then a second figure sped after the first, and another shot rang out from the house.

"Here," Alistair shouted to the constables behind him, indicating the entry way.

Inside, he found a bound and bleeding woman and two men struggling with each other on the floor. One was tied hand and foot, but amazingly kept his opponent busy by using his head and knees as weapons. Alistair aimed his Browning but couldn't fire until he got a clear shot.

"If you're British shoot, for God's sake," shouted the bound man.

Alistair did so, and the man on the bottom went limp.

"See to my wife," Sir Harold said, panting.

Walker and the other coppers filled the lounge now. While one untied Sir Harold, two bent over Lady Winterbourne.

"Guv." A Met constable stood in the doorway. "Two of them took off toward the cliffs. You don't suppose there's a U-boat out there waiting to pick them up?"

"One is my daughter," Sir Harold cried, sitting up and shaking his hands. "She's leading *this one*'s partner out to Cape Cornwall." He pointed to the large man Alistair had finished off. "Now, one of you constables stay with me—the rest of you get my daughter back."

Alistair couldn't believe his ears. Fury at himself for being ill and not in peak condition washed over him. The woman he loved was running from a killer along those razor-sharp cliffs. He whipped about and headed for the door.

"Don't leave without a torch, young man," Harold called. "My daughter grew up prowling every path out there. Made a few of her own, as well. She may not need a torch, but you do." He walked toward Alistair and peered into his face. "Do I know you, sir?"

Alistair's feet tingled with the urge to run after Cicely and to kill the German after her with his bare hands. He had no patience for niceties. "We've never met, Sir Harold," he said shortly. "Alistair Fielding."

Sir Harold rubbed his chin. "Your name sounds familiar. Now, then . . . torches are situated in the kitchen cupboard. There's a shotgun in the coal shed and plenty of firearms and ammunition here. Load up and get out there. My wife suffered a severe blow to her head. The damned bastard who's after my daughter threw her down hard."

"I've got the torches." Walker came through from the kitchen. Alistair seized one from his friend and ran. Walker and three coppers followed.

Alistair was breathing heavily and his chest rattled, but he'd be damned if he'd let this dicky body stop him from going after Cicely. Ignoring his wheezing, he allowed adrenaline to control his body and press him on.

At the end of the drive they all turned left and ran about three hundred yards before the road ended. In the torchlight Alistair saw pasture on the left and right, and high grass in front of him. The cliffs weren't yet in sight.

The heavy rain and wind had beaten down the long grass, making it difficult to see the path. Walker and his constables caught up, and they all walked shoulder to shoulder to find the trail. When they found it, they could also see the cliffs. The same steep, jagged cliffs with the violent waves crashing at the bottom that Alistair had stared at through the aeroplane window.

THIRTY

Let us do or die!
—Robert Burns

Cicely hit the long grass at the end of the lane running. She ignored her wet and nearly numb stockinged feet, and was thankful the narrow skirts of the last decade had given way to the more A-lined skirt she now wore. Otherwise, she'd be dead.

The footsteps behind her were faint but catching up. She'd taken a shortcut through the hidden back garden arbor and lost her pursuer for a few precious moments. Her throat ached from panting in the cold, damp air. Fortunately, she had plenty of reserve energy. Her jiving had kept her in peak physical condition.

Once she reached the edge of the cliff, she paused to catch her breath and glance to the right. The path twined around the headland in a warren of trails, all leading to a dead end. Turning left, she headed for the Cape.

The narrow path hugged the edge of the cliff, but in ideal conditions it wasn't at all dangerous, as the vertical fall wasn't nearly as steep as it looked. Cicely hoped it intimidated the German behind her.

The clouds parted overhead, allowing the moon to light her way. This beginning of the path was wide enough for anyone, but a bit further on, as it descended it narrowed. She could hear the waves crashing on the rocks below. The salt of the sea assailed her nostrils as well as the smell of wet earth. Her heart pounded in her chest. She was running out of breath.

Cicely paused, trying like hell not to pant, and trying also to take stock of her situation. Behind her, on the switchback above, boots scuffed on the path; pebbles pinged off the rock-studded cliffs and fell past her. She strained her eyes in the dark but could see nothing. But he could likely see her. She still wore her pale yellow cardigan, and a platinum blonde wig—a beacon in the night. She tore off the wig and sent it sailing down the cliffs toward the sea. But now the wind blew her real hair into her face. Grasping her locks, she tucked them into her cardigan collar and ran.

At the bottom of the path, a third of a mile on, she had to make a choice which path to follow. She could turn right to take the flooded path to the Cape just offshore, or continue on the dirt track, doubling back to the village square. Her life might depend on how much the Cape path had been flooded by the storm.

"I'll find you, you bloody slag, you see if I don't!"

Oh God! Her pursuer was entering the switchback. She bent down to tear her off her soaking socks, as bare feet allowed more purchase on the slippery grass.

Suddenly a thick cover moved over the moon and the rain started again: tiny drops at first, then fat splatters. It went utterly dark. She picked her way carefully, seizing fistfuls of tall grass to steady herself. She could hear the German panting and swearing behind her. He was catching up. Her heart pounded so hard she was certain he

312

could hear it. More than anything she wished to run head-long down the track, but forced herself not to.

Then Cicely stubbed her bare toe on a rock. She bit her tongue to stifle her scream. The wind came up again in a great gust, pushing her forward and causing her hair to rip out of her cardigan, lashing around her head and blinding her. Before she could push it out of her face, she slipped in a patch of mud. Her bum hit the ground and she slid down the cliff path as if she were a toboggan on fresh powder in the Alps. She screamed as rocks and twigs scraped her palms and the soles of her feet. Frantically her hands flailed out, and she seized a thick root.

Her fall broken, Cicely swallowed dryly and gained her feet. An icy chill raced down her spine. She was totally disoriented now. Taking a couple of steps, she knew at least that she remained on the path.

"Still alive? I do hope I won't be deprived of my kill."

Oh God. He was so close. But was he as blind as she? Why hadn't he already shot her?

Her pursuer chuckled. "I can hear you breathing," he said.

Cicely reached for her Enfield. It was gone!

Terrified, she ran, forgetting stealth, holding her right hand out for the one tree that bordered the path on the water side, growing out of the cliff. She hoped to heaven she hadn't passed it. She was dimly aware of shouting, and of what sounded like an army galloping down the track. Flashes of light arced through the darkness.

As one found her, Cicely felt her tummy lurch. She made a perfect target. The German took full advantage, getting off two shots. She actually felt one skim by her. Adrenaline filled her veins. It felt like the world was closing in on her. She couldn't outrun her pursuer. She couldn't hear, couldn't see—but her hand hit the tree! Her hand probably should have hurt wickedly, but it didn't. It was numb. Taking hold of the trunk with both hands, she swung around so she hugged it, hiding on the water side.

Cicely clung to her lifeline, suspended directly over the crashing waves and the deadly rocks below. If she let go, if she lost her grip, she'd drop and break like glass on those saber-toothed boulders.

Above, through her tree's naked branches, she saw the torches swing to and fro, and lanterns bobbing. Shadows crawled over the cliffs and men shouted. Her long hair blew loose and slashed her face, and rain streamed into her eyes.

Tree bark dug into her palms and pushed up like knives into her fingernail beds as she gripped the trunk. Her feet scrabbled for the thick branch she knew was there, trying to find better purchase. Pain shot up her arms and into her back as she strained to hold on. Her feet touched something but immediately lost it. Her grip on the tree slipped, and she fell several inches. Whimpering with fright, she kicked out her feet in a desperate attempt to locate the branch again. The kicking action loosened her grasp even more, and she slid even further down the tree trunk—and kept sliding.

"Cicely!" It was hoarse, but she heard Alistair's voice. "I'm coming for you. Hold on!" he cried.

At that second Cicely's feet found the thick branch. It held and supported her weight. In relief, she nearly unleashed gales of hysterical laughter. Alistair couldn't possibly be aware she was holding on to a tree for dear life.

A gunshot sounded from his direction, and he yelled, "I ordered you not to shoot! Not until I say, damn it!"

The German's voice rumbled not two feet distant. "So . . . we finally meet, Miss Winterbourne."

Cicely's eyes flew to the shadow in front and above her. Abruptly she lost her fear; she was beyond it. A dead calm descended on her. She tossed her head to clear her face of hair. "Your manners are lacking, Kraut. You didn't click your heels."

"You British. So cool and collected—even just before your death." His voice had lost its touch of amusement. "At this point it doesn't matter what you know. You shan't be able to tell anyone."

"What makes you think I haven't already? And it looks as if you've rousted the whole town with all your racket. They're not about to let you escape, you know." Slivers of bark cut into Cicely's feet, which began to lose their grip. Her now bloody hands tightened on the tree.

The German checked his firearm and shook his head. "It's a bonus if I escape. We moles carry cyanide. Very quick. I knew that was a possibility all along—a glorious death for the Fatherland."

He lifted his pistol. Cicely ducked and hid herself behind the tree. Likely he'd not miss at this range, but he would have to step closer. And in so doing, maybe he would slip and crash to his death on the rocks below. It was a wild chance, but just now that was all she had.

The German laughed. "You think to hide?" He did step closer. But he didn't slip. His gun's barrel dug into her temple. Her heart stopped. "And now you're going to—"

A gunshot rang out, but Cicely didn't feel anything. She didn't see anything either. Her eyes were screwed shut. *Was she dead?*

"Cicely!"

She didn't move. She couldn't.

It was Alistair. He was calling her. Slowly, she opened her eyes. A tall shadow loomed before her, and then a flood of lights illuminated him. He was reaching for her and she fell into his arms.

A hot bath and several hours later, Cicely made her way down the staircase of her parents' house. Pausing in the doorway to the lounge, she stared at Alistair's back where he leaned toward the glowing fire. He'd risked his life for hers. Not only by rescuing her from the Nazi, but by gallivanting about the country when he should be in hospital. The thought made her feel . . . loved. Then wary. Their journey had ended. Would he renew his repudiation now? Even if not, they'd agreed only to take comfort from each other during their journey to Cornwall.

She tightened the belt on her dark blue velvet dressing gown and headed to the drinks cart.

"You really should have accompanied my parents and Ari to the hospital in Penzance, Alistair. You quite look like death walking." He'd bathed as well, and wore her father's dark green cashmere dressing gown. His hair was still damp, and several locks waved onto his forehead.

She poured them each two fingers of her father's best eighteen-year-old Scotch. As she handed him the glass, his brown eyes blazed at her. He accepted the drink from her bandaged hand.

"I don't know what I would have done if I'd lost you, Cicely." His gaze stayed locked with hers as he drank.

"Last time I saw you, you wanted nothing to do with me. You were quite disgusted with me, in fact."

Alistair rubbed his face with his free hand. "Ah God, Cicely. The coppers were seconds away. You had to be made to go on without me."

"If you remember, I did voice that concern. Your words were extremely hurtful, Alistair. And what is worse, I actually did feel dirty. It seemed an ongoing complaint of yours."

"Cicely, it was self-defence on my part." He sighed. "I thought it was best at the time. A clean break. You take the code and we're out of each other's lives in one fell swoop."

She sipped from her glass. Paused, took a gulp and set her scotch back on the drinks trolley. "Did you mean it? About my less-than-honest personality and . . . and my being fast?" Her hands fisted at her sides as she awaited his answer.

Alistair slammed his scotch on the trolley and seized her hands in a tight grip. "I thought I did, but I spoke to shove you away. I fell for you. Hard. But you can have any man you desire. Why choose a middle-class copper with a crippled knee? No, I was scared and wanted you out of my life before you said, 'Ta ta, Alistair, it's been brilliant, but it's time to move on.'" He released one of her hands and smoothed her bright hair off her forehead. "Did I hear you correctly on the fishing boat? I thought you told me you loved me. Was it true? *Is* it true?"

Cicely bowed her head, then turned to the window to watch as pink, lavender, and gold gauze stretched across the new morning sky. A new day. A new beginning? So much had happened since their parting in Minehead. She wanted Alistair more than anything. She was sure. First, however, a loose end.

She turned her gaze from the window to scan the lounge. Although a damp spot remained in the rug by door, Kalakos's blood had been cleaned. Someone had forgotten the patches of blood by one of the wing chairs.

"Alistair . . . Aristo Kalakos is undoubtedly wanted for a crime. He's part of an, er, underworld, but he helped me, albeit because of Kit." She informed him of Kit's request of Kalakos senior. "See to it, please, that he is not jailed? He won't talk. He has nothing to tell. All he knew was that I had an item the Nazis wanted."

Alistair nodded. "I'll have a word with Alex." He reached for his whisky, downed it, and returned it to the drinks trolley. "You didn't answer me," he said, pinning her with his sharp gaze.

"What do you want from me, Alistair? You are a straightforward honest man. A hero, I learned a few hours ago. A recipient of the George Cross!" She took a large sip of the precious Oban. It rushed to her head. It gave her courage. A fool's courage. She smiled to herself, remembering that very thought the first time she'd met him. "I'm quite the opposite. Technically I'm not a spy, but I might as well be." She spread her hands. "I'm a veritable well of dirty government war secrets. My job requires lying."

"I want you, Cicely, whether or not you return to that job." Alistair studied her closely.

Cicely took another drink. "I shan't. Not after this. Now that my father has passed on the key, I'm not sure Bletchley would even take me back. One doesn't kick up a palava, you know. Too much attention."

He stepped forward and gripped her shoulders. For a moment he merely studied her. "I find the thought of spending the rest of my life with you exhilarating. I want you. *I love you*. No matter what you do, have done, or know. It's that simple."

Oh God. He *did* love her. And she loved him more than she thought she could love anyone. But she was a black widow. "Alistair—"

318

"Listen to me, lass. You have taught me a life lesson. One may be less than aboveboard and still be honourable." He laughed softly. "You've brought me down a peg or two. Thought myself quite a high and clever clogs." Taking her glass from her, he set it on a side table, then cupped the back of her head and kissed her throughly. "Tell me you want nothing more than to spend your life with a stubborn Scot with a gimp leg?"

When she lowered her eyes, he tipped up her chin with his forefinger. "You shan't kill me by marrying me, you know."

When her eyes widened, he chuckled. "I know you, lass. Either one of us might be killed in the bombing attacks. If it happens, at least we will have lived life to the fullest and known a joy not many are fortunate enough to experience."

Cicely lifted her hand, smoothed back a lock of his wavy black hair and smiled tenderly at him. "You're right, my love. Life is uncertain—but we'll have each other. That's the very best we can do!"

EPILOGUE

The true beginning of our end . . .
—William Shakespeare

6 June 1944

Cicely opened her front door, descended the stairs, and made her way briskly down the walk to meet the postman. A letter from Kit might come today. Her friend had become more of an adopted grandmother and amused her with regular and newsy letters. The old dear never slowed in her knitting and still kept Kalakos's eldest girl in plenty of clothing. The two newer female additions to that family fortunately didn't harbor the skin sensitivity of their sister. Cicely grinned. Just as well that Aristo had recently opened his own butcher shop in Penzance. He busied himself building a family of his own with a local nurse he'd met while in hospital.

It was early on a gloriously sunny Spring day. Her favourite time. The birds performed their morning symphony. Lilacs, petunias, pansies, and azaleas bloomed, scenting the air and filling her garden with colour. The morning traffic had started.

She stood by her gate, breathing in the crisp air of Chelsea, waiting for the morning paper delivery and the post. Soon she would return indoors to prepare Alistair's breakfast, then see him off to work. She would busy herself with housewifely chores for the rest of the morning before standing Air Raid Precautions duty until early evening. It was a plum shift. Her father had likely pulled a string or two as Lydia shared her duty period. Lydia threw herself headlong into whatever passion occupied her at the moment. Two years ago it was husband-hunting. Now it was doing her bit for her country.

"Mrs. Fielding! Have you heard?" The postman, Mr. Shaw, ran as fast as his elderly legs could carry him down the pavement, his letter bag bobbing against his hip. "Today was D-Day! Can you believe it? In the dark of the morning, Allied forces landed at Normandy!" He stopped at her gate, panting, his faded eyes alight with excitement and his cheeks flushed. "Ships they say, so numerous as to completely cover the Channel. So many aeroplanes they clogged the sky—all full of parachute jumpers! They're fighting the Hun as we speak!"

Cicely nearly jumped up and down in excitement. This meant the beginning of the end of the war! It must!

"What brilliant news, Mr. Shaw! I can't wait to tell my husband. Is there any word how it's going for us?"

He shook his head. "But you must tune in to the BBC, Mrs. Fielding. They are sure to announce the latest. I must get on then. A very good morning to you!" He stepped away, then turned back to Cicely. "I almost forgot. A letter for you, Mrs. Fielding—all the way from Canada!"

Cicely absently took the envelope the postman handed her and turned to hurry into the house. Alistair was descending the staircase. He grinned at her.

"Aren't *you* animated this morning! Dare I think it's

my charming company?" He reached the bottom of the stairs and kissed her cheek.

"Oh, Alistair! The most wonderful news." She shut the door behind her. "Come into the kitchen so I may tell you. Oh! We must turn on the wireless immediately."

"Bravo!" Alistair shouted when she informed him of the news. They swung each other around the kitchen and sat listening to the BBC for several minutes until Cicely realized the time and turned to the cooker to prepare Alistair's breakfast.

"What's this?" Alistair murmured, picking up an envelope from the floor.

Cicely glanced over her shoulder. "Oh! A letter. From Canada. Probably Graham's parents. I'll read it later."

Alistair squinted at the small print on the envelope. "It's postmarked British Columbia."

"That's odd. Graham's parents live in Ontario." Cicely poured porridge into two bowls, placed them on the table, and reached into the ice box for the cream. Sitting down, she examined the envelope.

"Heavens, Alistair! It's from Monty!" She ripped into the paper and tugged out the letter, reading intently for several moments.

When she finished, she leaned back in her chair. Her lips curved in a smile as she remembered the early war years and the people so dear to her who had passed. Would she ever see Monetary again?

"Well? What does she say?" Alistair prodded.

Cicely grinned. "When I told her to hie herself north of Watford in '42, I thought in terms of Ireland, Wales, or the north of Scotland. I never did discover her destination— although her parents assured me of her well-being in their annual letters."

She lowered her eyes to her friend's missive once again. "She and Henry—that feline rascal—have made themselves to home on the west coast of Canada. She attempted a go in Montreal, but as her French is abysmal at best, she hopped a train to Vancouver."

"How is she occupying herself?" Alistair touched his serviette to his lips.

"Listen to this: 'Faced with a choice of becoming a shop girl—really, so common—or joining the Canadian version of the Women's Land Army—you know how I abhor fresh air—I opted to join the Canadian Navy. As they say here: "You're in the Navy now, girl." Discipline is lax, or you know I'd never last.

'Thought I could teach these *rubes* a thing or two about Swing! Ha, Sister! They are teaching me!

'By the way, you wouldn't believe who I ran into here at the end of the civilised world. Hep! Seems he barely remembers Helen. Likely because she dropped him like a hot coal when he introduced to her to his commanding officer. He's still a scoundrel, of course, and I'm not at all attracted to him anymore. Still . . . I think he deserves a good show of what he missed, don't you?' "

Cicely turned to Alistair. "Can you even imagine the trouble those two will get into? I wonder if they're listening to the news about D-Day now, too."

Alistair laughed. "Likely, love. Likely people across the world are tuned in. This is the beginning of the end for Hitler. Now come here and give me a kiss."

Cicely did. For her, this wasn't the beginning of the end, but the end of the beginning.

GLOSSARY

B.E.F.: British Expeditionary Force
berk: annoying person
billy-oh: very much, strongly
bint: whore
bish: cock-up
bit of alright: nice-looking person
blister and strife: women or wife
blow the gaff: spill the beans
blower: telephone
bludger: scrounger
boffin: genius
bombes: some of the first computers
bosh: nonsense
brolly: umbrella
bumf: paperwork
cack handed: clumsy
carny: maliciously cunning
charlies: breasts
clever clogs: smarty pants
codswallup: hogwash
cow: woman, bitch
dicky: unsound
donkey's years: a long time
dosh: money
double Dutch: gobbledygook
Flash Henry: a well-dressed man
give us bell: telephone call
gone for a Burton: absent for some time
hair grip: bobby pin

HMG: His Majesty's Government
jammy: lucky
kerb crawler: prostitute
local: local pub
lolly: money
north of Watford: beyond civilization
palava: commotion
pecker up: chin up
peckish: hungry
ponce: pimp
queue: line
scarper: run away
screaming abdabs: the terrors
shuftie: take a look
slag: whore
spanner: wrench
starkers: naked
stone the crows: statement of surprise
suss: guess, discover
squiffy: drunk
toffy-nosed: uppity
togs: clothes
*Top of the Pops***:** British hit parade
tosser: derogatory term
traff: break wind
wanker: derogatory term
wobbler: tantrum